These Silent Stars

Chani Lynn Feener

ALSO BY CHANI LYNN FEENER

*For a list of YA books by this author, please check her website. All of the books listed below are Adult.

Bad Things Play Here

Gods of Mist and Mayhem

A Bright Celestial Sea

A Sea of Endless Light

A Whisper in the Dark Trilogy
You Will Never Know
Don't Breathe a Word
Don't Let Me Go

Abandoned Things

Between the Devil and the Sea

Echo

His Dark Paradox
Under the name Avery Tu

These Silent Stars

Chani Lynn Feener

This is a work of fiction. Names, characters, places, and incidents are the product of the author's imagination, and any resemblance to actual events or persons, living or dead, is entirely coincidental.

These Silent Stars

Copyright @ 2023 by Chani Lynn Feener.

All rights reserved. No part of this book may be reproduced, distributed, or transmitted in any form without written permission from the author.

Front Cover design by Creative Paramita .

Printed in the United States of America.

First Edition — 2023

Author's Note

Dear Reader,

Even if you've read one of my books before please do not skip this note. As some of the triggers couldn't be included on the books main listing, I wanted to take the time to include them here.

This book is a Dark MM Romance, and as such it contains certain situations and themes not suitable for all readers. Kelevra Diar isn't a good person, and he doesn't pretend to be. He's arrogant, impulsive, violent, and spoiled. He's basically one giant walking red flag. If you're looking for a fairytale romance or a redemption story, this isn't it. Kel is a sociopath who doesn't understand boundaries. Rin Varun has a mood disorder that he hides from the world, and this also causes him to be just as explosive and reactive as Kelevra. Basically, they're like pouring gasoline on the fire. This book does have a HEA, but please mind your triggers!

I want to be clear that I in no way condone anything that takes place in this book in real life. This book is purely fiction. These characters are not real and this takes place on a made-up planet in a made-up galaxy. None of my characters are human, though I sometimes use the word humanoid, and this galaxy is nowhere near ours. If you or someone you know is ever in a toxic relationship, please seek help. You deserve better. And if you ever meet a Kelevra Diar in real life, don't let his flashy outer appearance fool you. Run.

There is mention of mood disorders throughout this book. Kelevra is a sociopath and Sila is a psychopath. The other main character, Rin, suffers from an unnamed mood disorder. Please note I try my best to ensure Rin isn't vilified, and I in no way believe or want to express to anyone that real people with mood disorders of any kind are all like this character. He isn't real, and even if he was, his actions and reactions are specifically his own. Again, this is a made-up universe, and he has a made-up disorder that makes him act certain ways based off his species beliefs and biology (which again, is made-up).

This book also has a much longer list of kinks that are explored throughout the story. Please keep that in mind.

Now onto the triggers. **If you aren't easily triggered or you want to avoid potential spoilers, feel free to skip the rest of this note.**

I tried to list all of the triggers I could think of, but please be aware I might have missed one or two. Your mental health is important, if any of these don't sound appealing or may put you at risk, please skip this book. I have other MM books that don't fall under the dark category and may be better suited for you.

Most, but possibly not all, notable triggers include: Non con, dub con, bondage, mild bloodletting, sound play, drugging, blackmail/manipulation, forced betrothal, codependence, mood disorder, sociopath, psychopath, violence, murder, abuse of power, and graphic sex scenes. Finally, lube is only sometimes used. I know that's a big one for some people. Please practice safe sex in real life, and remember this is completely fiction and these characters are not human.

Again, **this book does have a HEA.** That being said, this relationship is messy, twisted, and in many ways, wrong. Kelevra displays serious abuse of power. I in no way, shape, or form condone anything mentioned above in real life. This is purely fiction.

This book is intended for a mature adult audience only.

Remember, your mental health and well-being is more important than reading this book. Always put yourself first and be responsible for your triggers. You're worth it and you matter.

Prologue:
One Hour Ago

If he blew up the pool on the upper level would this one flood?

What kind of moron built a pool on the top floor anyway?

Was that cadet bleeding?

Kelevra cocked his head, allowing his gaze to rest on the blonde female for a second longer before he scowled and glanced away.

Nope. Not bleeding.

Boring.

Boring.

Boring.

"Pretend to find this interesting," a gruff voice to his left leaned in and suggested. The highest member in his Retinue and closest confidant was standing at his side, eyes glued to the scene before them. Madden Odell was the same age, and yet far better at acting the part of dignified royalty.

At least when the lights were on.

Kelevra shifted his weight and sighed dramatically. "Why are we even here again?"

"Because it's part of the program," Madden replied, voice low so their Active, the trainer in charge of the sophomore class who was nearby, wouldn't overhear. "We need to mentor in order to graduate in the fall."

"Boring." All of this was tedious and uneventful. Kelevra honestly wondered why either of them even bothered. It wasn't like their futures were on the line like the rest of the idiots surrounding them.

Kelevra Diar was an Imperial Prince, he bowed to no one—not even his two older siblings—and as such, his trajectory was set. He might not make it to the throne, which was perfectly fine by him anyway, but he'd get close. Close enough that not a damn soul in this entire building or on the whole campus would dare flunk him for refusing to participate in anything.

As a part of his Retinue, Madden could make the same claim. His life had been tied to Kel's since they'd been children, and nothing short of a serious betrayal or death would sever that bond, which meant where the Imperial Prince went, he went too.

"It's almost over," Madden reassured, motioning with his chin toward the two-way glass everyone was staring out of.

Below them, an obstacle course had been set up, a complex maze of sorts created to appear like the innards of a cluttered warehouse. Holographic "bad guys" appeared at random, sometimes flickering around corners of stacked boxes, other times simply flashing into existence in what had been empty space prior.

The sophomore class consisted of thirty students, all carefully selected from others of their age group to partake in this advanced grouping. They were known as A-4 or A-8 or some other bullshit Kel hadn't bothered remembering. None of them mattered enough for him to bother.

None of them were even remotely interesting.

"Just more sheep," he mumbled to himself, crossing his arms as he pretended to scan the bland faces as the cadets rushed about the room, fake blasters held aloft.

They'd been instructed to make their way through the previous room first, which had focused on physical strength and prowess. Kelevra hadn't bothered watching that part, waiting in this room for the final results so he could be on his merry way as soon as possible.

Seven cadets had entered this area already, their fake weapons programmed to act like the real deal, only with censors instead of bullets. They'd be scored on who passed the finish line first and who hit the most targets. Everyone, no matter their placement, would be assigned a mentor from Kel's class, the senior group F-12, but the top three would be given those of the highest ranking.

Unfortunately, Kelevra was one of them. He'd kept his top score because it'd helped pass the time. Not so he could one day be subjected to this nonsense and forced to become a glorified babysitter to some brown-nosing wannabe.

And whoever won this completion would be just that, he could already tell by how intensely they all swarmed about, so focused on the closed door at the other end, below the floor where Kel and the others stood watching. That was the big finish line.

A fucking door.

How blasé.

"They're soldiers," Madden said.

"They're—" He'd been about to say obsolete, but then something interesting happened, and he was so caught off guard, he actually forgot all about the conversation. Certain that he was mistaken, like with the blood earlier, he let his gaze settle on one of the cadets, watching more closely as the man darted around a plastic table and dove beneath a wooden beam.

The man was well-formed, fit, with broad shoulders and corded muscle that was obvious even from where Kel stood at a vantage point twenty feet away. The sophomore Academy uniform—storm gray tactical pants tucked into ankle-high boots and a black t-shirt—strangely didn't appear as bland on him as it did the rest of the flock. The muscles in the man's back rippled as he crouched and took aim at a target.

Only to hesitate when he saw another cadet sneaking up on it.

The man let the other student take the target, then glanced back over his shoulder, taking in the rest of the room.

He was counting how many other cadets were in there with him.

The man tipped his gaze the other way, noted that there were four people ahead of him—now that he'd let that other one take the lead over him—and seemingly satisfied with those numbers, shot back into action.

"Do you—"

"Quiet," Kel ordered Madden, not even noticing the glare he got in return.

The man turned a corner and was almost crashed into by the same cadet he'd allowed to get ahead of him.

Instead of apologizing, that cadet clearly said something rude to Kel's man, before moving on.

A glimmer of something crossed over the man's features, brief, a serious blink and he would have missed it type thing. Then he tilted his head, cracking his neck, and with his eyes set on the back of the rude cadet, he started forward.

Kelevra watched as his man sped through the rest of the course, leaving the two in first place alone. He kept hot on third place's heels, however, sneakily steeling his shots before he could claim them, taking them down one by one.

Every time a hologram was hit by one of the blasters it faded, and Kel's man was a phenomenal shot. Good enough he could have been in first place.

If he'd wanted.

Which clearly he didn't.

"Interesting," the word passed his lips unintentionally, his eyes still locked on his man. He grinned when his cadet sent a wink over his shoulder as he cut the rude guy off, wanting to make it obvious he was doing it on purpose.

Petty.

Kel liked that.

A lot.

"Oh no," Madden groaned and ran a hand down his face in frustration. "Come on, man. Not here."

"Whatever do you mean?" He straightened once his cadet made it to the door beneath his feet and vanished from sight.

"They're younger than us," Madden said, recognizing the gleam in Kelevra's gaze for what it was. "We're supposed to be looking out for them and passing on knowledge as their seniors."

"Of course." He turned his back on the scene below and slipped his hands into the pockets of his silk pants.

"You can't harm any more students," Madden's voice dropped lower, "remember? Your sister's order. If you break it, there really will be consequences this time, Kel."

"Who said anything about harming him?"

Madden pinched the bridge of his nose. "At least it's a him this time. Maybe he'll fare better than that girl you messed with last Monday."

"Who?" Kelevra was only partially listening, too invested in replaying the image of his new interest winking at that rude bastard. It'd been tantalizing. Sexy.

"The last sheep who had the serious misfortune of momentarily amusing you," Madden reminded. "Short, brunette, currently expelled?"

Some of Kelevra's good mood soured. "Her."

He hadn't been amused by her in the least. Quite the opposite, in fact. If she'd been smarter, she would have known better than to follow him to a party she hadn't been invited to. It wasn't his fault she'd been arrogant enough to think her tits were Light's gift to Vitality. In reality, she was the same as everyone else. All of them always after the same thing, slipping him the same coy look, and the same tired pickup lines.

"She was a sheep," he stated.

"And this one?" From Madden's tone, it was clear he figured Kel thought the very same about whatever cadet had just caught his eye.

Kelevra grinned, not bothering to hold back that flicker of anticipation he felt coursing through his veins.

"Good Light. Who are you even talking about?" Madden gave in, knowing there was no way he was going to be able to convince Kel to give up on his pursuit. "And what exactly do you want him for? At least let me be prepared this time. Your sister was clear. If any more of her flock, as you so kindly put it, get injured off Academy grounds at your hand, there will be consequences."

"The one with the sand-colored hair," Kelevra answered absently. "And he isn't a sheep."

"No?" Madden quirked a dark brow. "Well then, enlighten me, your majesty. What is he then?"

The word mine blared through Kel's mind in technicolor, and he took a moment to mull it over. There were very few things in this world that could be considered as not his. The Diar name ensured most everything was accessible to him. His looks ensured most everyone was as well. But that didn't mean he went around making claims. What would be the point? He grew tired of it all eventually anyway, and marking his territory had never been of interest to him.

Taming something meant taking responsibility for it, and Kel?

He hated responsibility.

Too much red tape and rules for his liking. That's why he was content being third in line. Happy even. It meant he got all the perks but none of the demands. Even his sister's threat, the one Madden was so concerned about, didn't hold any true weight.

Kelevra charmed his siblings the same way he did everyone else.

Still, no matter how interested he was in this cadet, voicing the word mine was too strong. Without a doubt, things would end up exactly how Madden feared anyway. With Kel growing tired of his newfound plaything and tossing him to the side.

"Hey," Madden bumped into his shoulder, "What is he?"

Kel considered it, grin returning, vicious and bright. "A flower."

One Kelevra intended to pluck.

Chapter 1:

Cold water sluiced down Rin's back and he clenched his teeth, bearing through it. The locker room was filled with chatter from the other cadets and he stuck his head under the heavy spray, trying to block them all out.

He was pissed at Ives for cutting him off like that, but he was frustrated with himself for allowing it to get to him. He'd had a plan. A good one. An important one. And he'd tossed it aside at the first sign of disrespect from a nobody who didn't even matter.

Ives was a prick, everyone knew it, so really, there was no reason his actions today on the obstacle course should have set Rin off, and yet…

He swore and pulled back, shutting off the shower with more force than necessary before spinning on his heels and grabbing his towel. He dried off and stepped from the stall, one of two dozen cubicles set in this section of the locker room, and then made his way to the main area where others were already in the process of getting changed.

They'd been given fifteen minutes to rinse off and put on a new set of clothes before they were due to meet in the gym, and Rin had wasted more than half of that time just trying to cool himself down. He was moody as fuck. Only, he couldn't be.

Rin Varun wasn't the moody sort. He was charismatic and friendly, always down for a good time.

It took literally everything in him not to punch Ives in the face as he passed the other cadet on the way to his locker.

Friendly.

Yeah right.

"Way to go, Varun," Pen, another cadet who was already dressed, slapped him on the back of the shoulder. "Third place."

"How'd you swing that?" Mile, who was standing nearby joked with a friendly smirk.

Rin got along with just about everyone in their class and on campus, but that didn't mean this wasn't still a competition of sorts. Everyone wanted to be noticed, wanted to climb the ranks.

Everyone except for him, that was.

"By stealing it, that's how," Ives stated bitterly. He was sitting on one of the benches that lined the room, in front of the orange locker with his cadet number on it. As soon as he finished tying his bootlace he sent a glare over at Rin.

A million and one insults danced on the edge of Rin's tongue.

He smiled and ran his fingers through his sandy hair boyishly instead of dealing any of them. "Sorry, man."

"Should have been quicker," Mile scolded Ives.

"Yeah," Brennon, one of Rin's closer friends, stepped in from the showers and added, "Don't blame someone else for your own shortcomings."

Calder, another friend, followed after him, towel cinched at his narrow waist. "For real, Ives. Nothing more unattractive than someone who doesn't have enough confidence to look in a mirror."

Pen grimaced and joined in. "I mean if I had a face like his…Yikes."

"Hitting him where it hurts, boys," Mile laughed.

With a huff, Ives bolted from the bench and exited the locker room, slamming the door behind him for good measure.

Which only made the rest of them laugh even harder.

"You are way too nice." Calder clapped Rin on the back as he opened his locker.

"Right?" Brennon agreed, coming up on his left. "Don't let dicks like that talk shit."

If Rin wasn't nice, he'd currently be holding Ives under the shower spray. Or bashing his skull into the tile. Or—

He chuckled and waved a hand at them. "Come on, guys. We're all just trying to make it through training."

"Don't bother with that one," Pen chucked his chin toward Rin as he spoke to the others. "Dude doesn't have a mean bone in his body."

"Seriously," Mile clucked his tongue. "How do you plan on making it as a Detective with a personality like yours?"

Rin pretended to think it over and then shrugged, the smile never once slipping from his lips. "Make all the bad guys like me so they spill?"

More laughter.

Brennon was close to the same height as him, and a native to the planet Vitality, unlike Rin. When they weren't in physical training classes, he typically had two lip piercings and an eye brow piercing in. His hair was a light chestnut color with red highlights in direct sun, a sharp contrast to their blond friend.

Calder's hair was the shade of wheat, and thanks to their friendly natures, their friends had taken to referring to him and Rin as "the golden boys" whenever they did something that was deemed overly thoughtful or kind.

If only they knew how carefully concocted Rin's personality was, they probably wouldn't call him that ever again. There was little to no fear of that ever happening, however, not when he was so carefully in control of every aspect of his life, right down to the minute details.

Like when to make an exit without drawing too much notice.

Rin headed for the door. "See you guys out there."

At least his mood was improving, that was something, Rin thought as he made his way down the wide hall toward the entrance to the main gym where they'd been instructed to meet. The challenge today had gone mostly all right if he didn't count his blunder at the end there. Third place wasn't that big of a deal. It wouldn't draw too much attention his way, and he could easily slip back into mediocrity once the assignment was completed.

They were being paired with a senior trainer from the F-12 class based on their positioning in the challenge. Rin had been going for somewhere around fourth or fifth place, enough to keep his grades up, but not too high up the ladder for anyone to pay him much mind. F-12 was the highest placed class at the Academy, which meant whoever he was paired with, he could end up drawing a lot more attention from the rest of the school than he wanted.

The program would only last the semester though, so there was that, and Rin wasn't too concerned about getting along with whatever senior he was attached to. He was known on campus as the guy who got along with everyone, even Ms. Sprig, the rude lunch lady who always burned the main dish when she was in charge of it.

He'd just keep up the friendly appearance, get whichever senior he was assigned to pass him, and that would be that.

Most of the class was already there when Rin arrived, his friends and the others who'd been changing still quickly catching up. Each class was given its own Active, a trainer in charge who acted a lot like a counselor and drill sergeant all in one. Theirs, Active Banks, wasn't in the gym yet, so the class was at ease, goofing off, praising or teasing one another for their good or poor performance during the challenge.

Brennon tossed an arm around Rin's shoulders and rolled his eyes at something Calder said.

The three of them had been friends since last year when they'd met during orientation. They had a fourth, Daylon, but he'd been placed in A-7, whereas the rest of them were in A-5. They still saw him frequently enough since he was Rin's roommate though.

They were friends, because having friends was the best way to blend in, and Rin was fond of the lot of them, but he wouldn't say any of them actually knew him. At least, not really.

To be fair though, more times than not, he wasn't sure he even knew himself.

The door to the office opened and Active Banks finally appeared, a trail of senior students dressed in their all-black uniforms coming in behind him.

Except for one, who wasn't dressed in any sort of uniform at all. The guy stood out like a sore thumb in his silk suit—though at least it was the same inky shade of black—his corset vest decorated in some floral pattern Rin couldn't make out. His hair was dark brown and curly, with lighter highlights throughout, and he walked with an air of superiority that not even the Active supposedly in charge was capable of producing.

Brennon tightened the arm he still had slung over Rin's shoulders and whispered, "F-12 is the Imperial Prince's class. Suddenly first place isn't looking so hot."

"Good thing you placed tenth then, idiot," Calder said, grabbing onto Brennon's wrist and flinging his arm off of Rin as they lined up.

Rin chuckled and shook his head, glancing back up just as the approaching group of seniors finally came to a stop ten or so feet away. His breath caught in his throat when he was instantly met with an intense hazel gaze.

The Imperial Prince was staring at him, and he didn't appear to be pleased.

What the hell?

Rin almost scowled, catching himself and forcing his lips to even out and his facial features to remain relaxed.

The corner of the prince's mouth tipped up.

No, but seriously…what the hell?

"Good work out there, A-5!" Active Banks called, and they all spread their legs and folded their wrists at their backs.

"Thank you, Active," they replied in unison, voices ringing throughout the large gymnasium.

Banks had a holo-tablet in his hand and he flicked through digital notes on it, nodding his head as he did. "You know how this goes. I'll assign each of you a senior cadet who will act as a mentor for the rest of the semester. These seniors will be treated as your superior officers from here on out, is that understood?"

"Yes, Active!" they all said.

Rin tried to keep his attention on Banks as he spoke, but he couldn't help but glance a time or two over toward the prince who was still staring at him with that confusing look on his face.

As far as he knew, the two of them had never interacted with one another before. As a senior, Imperial Prince Kelevra Diar, third in line for the throne, wouldn't have been in any of the same classes or training sessions as Rin was. Rin lived on campus, but everyone knew Kel and his Retinue, the entourage who followed around an Imperial Prince, lived in a swanky sky rise closer to the center of the city.

Rin didn't visit that area much, so it wasn't like he could have accidentally run into him there either. Besides, if he had, he certainly would have remembered.

Kelevra wasn't exactly a forgettable person.

Title aside, the guy also had the added benefit of being drop-dead gorgeous. Even the scar trailing down his right eyebrow, stopping just at the rise of his cheekbone, couldn't detract from his stunning exterior.

But Rin knew better than most that a pretty outer shell meant nothing in the grand scheme of things, and it was also a well-known fact that Kelevra Diar had an explosive, and often impulsive, personality. The guy had no buffer, no little voice in his head warning him that maybe he shouldn't say or do something. His reputation preceded him, and for that reason alone, Rin had actually gone out of his way to avoid not only the prince himself, but any known member of his Retinue.

He took in the rest of the seniors, trying to figure out their placements and who he might end up with as a mentor. At least he wouldn't have to worry about being assigned the prince.

One member of the Retinue was there as well, Royal Madden Odell, his purplish-crimson hair left longer than they were technically allowed, so it trailed over the tops of his ears. As Kel's top, he would have had to stay close in ranking, so he would most likely be mentoring Tria who'd gotten second place.

There weren't any others, at least that Rin was aware of, and he let out a small sigh of relief. Being involved with that group, even for a semester, would mean surveillance on him, and that was something Rin could not afford.

His whole M.O. relied on keeping out of the spotlight, and dressed the way he was—on campus, no less—it was glaringly obvious subtle wasn't a word in the Imperial Prince's vocabulary.

"All right, since we've gone over the rules and you all seem to understand, I'll start pairing you off. Starting with Tine, who got first place," Banks began, only to have Kelevra lean in suddenly and tell him something against the curve of his ear.

The entire gymnasium went silent, ears straining to make out what the prince could be saying.

Banks frowned and turned to him, but before he could even open his mouth, Kelevra rested a dangerous smile on him. The type of smile that lacked any and all friendliness and cut straight to the chase.

Whatever he'd just suggested to their Active, it hadn't actually been a suggestion at all.

The Academy was a training branch of the Intergalactic Police Force, owned and run by the Intergalactic Conference. Every galaxy had its own, but theirs was the only one that didn't have an entire planet dedicated to running one. Instead, their Academy had been built on an already operational planet, Vitality, and they shared space with an elite university called Vail.

Though things were a little different, the core curriculum was still the same, and while there were many positions, for the most part, the people in this room were here studying to become a detective, an inspector, or a coast. They had military training in order to ensure they were physically prepared for fieldwork, as well as classes that taught them everything from Intergalactic law to basic ship controls. No matter the class or grade level, however, there was a basic chain of command that was expected to be respected and followed at all costs.

Except, apparently, by the Imperial Prince.

Banks cleared his throat, obviously unsure about whatever order he'd just received—from someone who was technically meant to be his subordinate while on school grounds—and then tapped the holo-screen in his hands.

"Tine, you'll be assigned to Royal Madden Odell," Banks said, continuing down the list even when the entire class frowned. "Tria, you'll be assigned to Silva Ro."

Wait…

Rin's spine straightened, a bad feeling settling over him.

"Rin," Banks glanced up from the tablet and looked at him, "you'll be assigned to Imperial Prince Kelevra Diar."

His eyes widened slightly before he could help it, and when the man standing next to banks chuckled at that, his head whipped in his direction.

Kelevra was smirking at him.

Had he…Had he ordered Banks to switch their placements? Why?

Whatever the reason, it couldn't be good.

The rest of the pairings happened in a blur, with him unable to hear a single one of them. The entire time, that weighted gaze remained on him, like a magnet he couldn't shake no matter how hard he tried to ignore it.

And Rin tried. For the rest of Bank's speech, he chose to look anywhere but at Kelevra, and yet he could feel the prince staring at him all the while, almost as though the guy didn't even have to blink.

Maybe he'd commanded his eyes not to as well.

Rin almost snorted at his idiotic joke, catching himself and forcing himself to focus back on their Active.

Bank's had just finished pairing everyone and now the seniors were walking up to their assigned cadet for introductions. Brennon and Calder had already moved away to meet with theirs, leaving Rin the only one standing there like a statue.

Whatever the reason, Rin couldn't allow this to mess him up. He needed to remain cool on his feet, as usual. Unshakable.

Kelevra came to a stop a few feet away, hands slipped into his front pockets. He tipped his head slightly to the left, as though tilting the eye with the scar at a better angle on him, and then grinned, waiting.

Rules dictated Rin was meant to address him first as the youngest, and sweeping that bad feeling aside, he forced himself to smile broadly and bow before the prince. "Hello, Imperial Prince."

"Rin," Kelevra said his name like he was testing the sound of it, rolling the single syllable off his tongue. "Cute."

Rin's brow furrowed, but he'd smoothed it out again by the time he straightened, that easy smile still in place. "That's the first time I've heard that, but I'll take it as a compliment."

"Will you?" Kelevra seemed to find that vastly entertaining, and for the life of him, Rin couldn't understand why.

Seemed like he was simply doomed to be out of sorts in front of the prince. Which was bad, because the best way to fool someone was by getting a read on them, and Kelevra Diar was almost impossible to read.

But no matter.

It changed nothing.

"It'll be a pleasure learning from you," Rin said.

"Following," Kelevra corrected, watching him closely while he did.

He swallowed. "Sure."

The prince took a single, almost lazy step closer, that one eye still tilted his way. "You're not a fan of that wording, are you, cadet."

It wasn't a question, but Rin found himself responding anyway.

"It doesn't bother me," he reassured. "You're the senior in command here. Technically following is exactly what I'll be doing."

"That so?" Kelevra curled two fingers at him. "Wrist."

This, at least, Rin could understand. He lifted his left arm, presenting the prince with the thick leather band attached to his wrist. The bracelet had the Academy emblem at its center, a large circle with half of a golden sun on the right, and a backing of mother of pearl on the left. There was a silver A in the center of the sun, and the Elusive Star over the mother of pearl, the brightest star in the Dual galaxy.

Using his thumb, Rin slid the emblem over, revealing the screen protected beneath it. They weren't allowed to use their personal multi-slates while on Academy grounds, and had each been given a wristband with a smaller one during their freshmen year. Considering the fact they operated the same as a regular multi-slate, just with a tiny, circular screen instead of the long rectangular one, it seemed like a waste of effort and money, but whatever.

Kelevra took his time rolling up the right sleeve of his black suit jacket, exposing the golden band that held his emblem device. He activated it and held it over Rin's, that smile returning to his full lips.

"Special treatment," Kelevra confirmed, catching Rin staring at the gold. "Not a fan of that either, I see."

"You're an Imperial," Rin said, "and the prince. Of course you deserve special treatment, sir. Who am I to think otherwise?"

"That didn't sound nearly as much like a joke as you meant it to."

Impossible. Rin had perfect control over his tone.

He had perfect control over everything.

It was fucking exhausting.

"I get a lot of special treatment," Kelevra told him, not giving him the chance to respond to being called out. "As my cadet, some of that will transfer over to you."

"No, thank you," he found himself replying, even as internally he recognized he should just roll with it so this conversation could end and he could leave. "I'm not here for that, sir, though I appreciate the offer. I just want to learn as best I can and not be treated any differently than any of my classmates."

"Because it isn't fair to them?" he guessed.

"Because I didn't earn it," Rin corrected.

Kelevra paused and then hummed. "You were telling the truth that time. Interesting."

Rin frowned. "Sir?"

For the first time, he lost that glimmer, full lips turning down as his hazel eyes took on a hard edge. "Cut the crap. Sir? You'll call me by name, starting right now."

"That's against regulations," Rin pointed out. "I could refer to you by title, however, Imperial Prince, if you would prefer—"

"Don't." He took another step, the move putting him directly in Rin's face less than two inches away. They were roughly the same height, with Kelevra only a bit taller. "Just because I'm interested doesn't mean I'll let you get away with things others can't. I give you an order? Take it. Is that understood, Varun?"

A flash of indignation washed through him, but Rin swallowed it down, nodding his head in the affirmative. "Understood."

The Imperial Prince quirked a dark brow.

"Kelevra," he added, hating the way his guts seemed to tighten afterward. Why did it matter so much to the guy what Rin called him anyway?

Kel leaned forward on his toes, shifting so he could bring his mouth to the side of Rin's head. "Good boy."

Rin's spine snapped into place and he stepped back.

Kelevra laughed. "Interesting indeed."

"Yo," Madden called suddenly and waved at him, "Zane is outside."

It was odd hearing someone say "yo" to an Imperial, especially one as flashy and clearly into regality as Kelevra was. Instead of seeming put off though, he merely tipped his chin, indicating he'd gotten the message.

Maybe wanting to be called by name wasn't that unusual coming from him. Was Rin reading too far into it? Seeing things that weren't there simply because the prince made him uncomfortable?

Kelevra turned back to Rin. "You recall the rules of this arrangement?"

"You're my mentor," he said, not really getting where he was going with this either, and opted to use his own wording in an attempt to ease some of the tension, "I've been instructed to follow your command."

"Follow," Kel agreed, "but don't be a sheep, Rin."

...Right.

"I'll summon you when I've got the time," he told him, moving away, finally returning Rin's personal space. "Make sure you come when you're called."

"Of course." Rin was pretty certain he hated this guy. Didn't matter that he was suave and sexy *appearing*. Inside the dude was rotten and he could already tell. He smiled brightly and bowed. "Have a nice day, Kelevra."

The prince laughed and swiveled on his heels, walking away without so much as a second glance.

Around Rin, everyone else was still talking to their senior. It was just him and Tine left standing there like fools twiddling their thumbs. He met the other cadet's gaze.

"Lunch early?" Tine asked.

"Hell yeah." Maybe some food and a massive cup of coffee would help rid him of the bad feeling still coiled in his gut.

Chapter 2:

Rin felt the energy literally draining from his body as he stepped out of the fancy golden elevator and onto the rooftop of Lady Rose, the largest hotel in the city.

And also the home to the Imperial Prince.

Kelevra owned the penthouse suit as well as the rooftop and even had his own private elevators.

The one giving access to the roof had been where Rin had been directed by the burly security guy downstairs when he'd said he was here visiting the prince. He'd thought it was a bit strange that Kelevra had wanted to meet at his place, but he'd assumed they would be dining at the expensive restaurant on the hotel's main level, like normal people trying to get to know one another.

Wrong.

The rooftop was in full swing, music with a heavy staccato rhythm blaring, neon lights flashing from bot-orbs that circled the air over the party. Tables packed with food lined the back patio, pressed against glass walls that gave a view inside to a massive living room. A few people mingled in there, crowded on the black and white couches, lifting bottles of beer and other alcoholic beverages to their lips as they laughed and joked around.

The smell of grilled meat and chlorine tickled Rin's nose as he passed a set of barbeque grills big enough to feed a small army. Chefs who kept their eyes down worked like machines, flipping meat and adding it to golden serving trays that were carried off and added to the table.

Everything was done in excess. Lavish and filthy and over the top in your face wealthy. More his brother's scene than Rin's. If his brother were here instead, he'd be getting a kick out of it, already three steps ahead of everyone else, target selected, plan in place. He'd probably love messing with the half-drunk people and the idiots over in the corner playing a drinking game.

His brother enjoyed when people were sloppy. Got off on the *opportunity*, as he would put it.

Rin, on the other hand, was just tired. And he'd only been there for two minutes. To be sure he hadn't misread the message earlier, he checked his emblem multi-slate, rereading to be sure.

Kelevra: Come to this address. It's time to get to know your mentor.

Seeing the commanding words only had him rolling his eyes all over again like he'd done when he'd initially read it. It'd only been a day since they'd been assigned to each other, and already he was getting on Rin's last nerve.

He was beginning to see just how foolish this pairing was for him. There had to be a way he could get out of it. Tomorrow, he'd go in early to talk to Banks, beg if he had to. Rin had built up enough of a reputation as a nice guy that he was fifty percent sure he could convince the Active to do him a favor and help him come up with some way to slip free from the Imperial Prince.

"Hey, Varun!" a female voice pulled him out of his inner thoughts and he had a friendly smile firmly settled on his face before he glanced up to find her waving at him. Arlet Zamir was the daughter of a famous composer, cute and sociable. Her wavy lilac hair was pulled into a short ponytail, her golden eyes lighting up at the sight of him.

She was in the pool, a huge rectangle that took up almost half of the rooftop, set toward the edge with a glass barrier to keep anyone from accidentally falling off the side of the roof and tumbling to their death.

Which honestly did not sound half as bad as it should to Rin right about now. He hated parties. Hated having to mingle. The noise was grating, the raucous laughter half-faked, and the fact it was a pool party to boot—don't even get him started. This was just an excuse for people to walk around shirtless or with their tits out.

His brother would tell him not to be such a stick in the mud—in less censored terms—but it wasn't that simple. It was a lot harder for Rin to fake it.

"Aren't you looking lovely this evening?" Rin walked over to the pool and crouched down, smile widening when Arlet giggled at his compliment.

It wasn't a complete lie; the girl was beautiful, dressed in a vibrant yellow bikini, the water lapping just beneath her full breasts. And if the flirty way she batted her long lashes at him was any indicator, she'd be more than willing to take their acquaintance even further.

She wasn't his type though. Too many friends, too big into networking and the party scene. All things Rin was set on avoiding.

"What are you doing all the way out here?" Arlet asked, moving closer to the edge so she could rest her arms on the ledge, water coming close to the tips of his boot-covered feet. She didn't seem to notice, still focused on his face. "It's rare seeing you out at night since the semester started."

"Is that your nice way of calling me a boring loser?" he joked.

She snorted. "I doubt anyone has ever referred to you as either of those things."

"No?" Despite his earlier assessment that he wasn't interested, Rin tipped his head, voice lowering suggestively when he asked, "What do people say about me then?"

Arlet answered, probably in a similar, sultry, flirtatious tone as the one he'd just used on her, but Rin didn't hear it. The distinct sensation of being watched had drawn his gaze up and over her head, toward the back of the pool.

Where Kelevra was staring back at him.

The Imperial Prince had his arms stretched over the stone ledge, his bare chest pulled taught, crystal clear water doing nothing to hide the long length of his torso. There was a lollipop in his mouth. Now that he wasn't wearing a suit jacket, the dark ink of tattoos over the tops of both shoulders, leading down to his elbows was visible. He was with a small group, but the second Rin caught his eye, he smirked and pulled away from them wordlessly. There was no rush in his movements as he waded through the water, coming toward where Rin and Arlet were.

The pool was packed, but everyone slipped out of his way without needing to be told, and before long Kel was sliding up next to Arlet, eyes still locked onto Rin's like some damn missile bullseye.

"...could go grab a bite? I know this cute place not far from here," Arlet finished saying, clearly unaware that Rin hadn't caught any of that.

"He's got other plans," Kelevra said for him.

She startled and then noticeably paled, glancing between the two before backing away. "I apologize. I didn't realize."

Kelevra didn't spare her a glance, planting his palms on the ledge and lifting himself with one strong push. He stood before Rin a second later, water dripping from his body, the red swim trunks clinging to his muscular thighs and the jutted bones of his hips. A finely groomed happy trail led up from beneath the tight waistband, dark hairs stopping at his navel. The gold body chain harness he had on draped over both shoulders, layers of chains cascading down his chest, the center of each swoop seemingly carefully sized so they highlighted the dips of his abs. The bottom one touched just over his navel, making it easy for Rin's gaze to travel.

He blinked when he looked back up to find that smirk Kelevra had been wearing had reached his eyes.

Along with a hint of unmistakable heat that had alarm bells clanging in Rin's brain.

The stare-off was thankfully broken when someone ran over and offered a fluffy black towel to Kel.

He took it and dried himself off, taking special care of his curly hair before tossing it back at the servant who was still waiting. Then he motioned with a finger at Rin, the silent order to follow him apparent when he started walking across the concrete rooftop toward a side entrance Rin hadn't noticed.

Rin debated making an excuse and cutting out, but he'd come all the way here, and if he left now, that only meant he'd be making himself available to be summoned like this again for the same purpose. Better just to get it over with.

He'd asked around yesterday to try and get a better feel for what he was up against, and everyone had pretty much the same things to say about the Imperial Prince.

He was quick to react and didn't bother considering the consequences. Volatile, sporadic, and impulsive. Basically, he was a ticking time bomb who didn't even have the decency to come with tell-tale signs to warn when he was about to explode. The upside to people like that was they tended to bore rather quickly.

Rin just had to make it through this meet and greet of sorts, show Kelevra he was just a regular, average guy; ideally, that would be enough for the man to lose interest all on his own. They were both only going through with this because it was an assignment, in any case. He doubted the Imperial Prince wanted to be wasting his time talking with Rin when he could still be lounging in the pool playing court with his guests.

Kelevra led them inside and the door automatically shut behind Rin, though he didn't turn to check if he was being followed like he'd asked. Instead, he headed straight for a narrow set of stairs that led through gray walls and up to a second floor. There, he turned left and entered the first room down the hall.

Rin stepped in after him, pausing just within the doorway when he realized they were in a bedroom.

A bed was pressed up against the right wall, the golden sheets glittering in the dim lighting and the colorful bursts of neon that flashed in through the floor-to-ceiling wall of window directly across from the door. The curtains, also gold, had been pulled back so the full swing of the party outside could be seen. They were above it by a good ten feet, the angle perfect for seeing the expanse of the rooftop and the pool.

A long, low-set white dresser took up the left wall, a holo-strip that would project videos over the blank space above it one of the few things that were there. A stack of old-looking books bound in leather, a golden apple statue, and a couple of other glass sculpture knickknacks were carefully displayed, but that was about it.

"Here." Kelevra offered him a can of beer from a small mini fridge set by another door that led into a bathroom.

"Thanks." Rin accepted but didn't pop the top open, eyes catching onto the tattoos now that the Imperial Prince was close enough he could make them out.

Roses. A mixture of thick and thin delicate lines. The hint of thorns hidden beneath jagged leaves.

"That's quite the collection," he stated dumbly when he realized he'd been staring. Maybe he should drink after all.

"Thanks," Kelevra said. "I'll be adding to it shortly."

"I didn't know Imperials were allowed to get ink." This was dumb. What was he even doing here?

"We're allowed to do whatever we want."

"Right." He fiddled with the can and then moved toward the dresser to set it down. "This doesn't seem like the best time to do this. Why don't we schedule something tomorrow, on campus?"

"On the contrary," Kelevra disagreed. "This is the perfect place. There's no better way to get to know someone than by seeing how they'll react to a party filled with deviants."

Rin had assumed based on the rumors that Kelevra had just been trying to shove this stupid assignment into his busy schedule. Someone like him wouldn't waste his time on a school mentor program.

It seemed he'd underestimated the Imperial Prince.

His eyes narrowed ever so slightly.

"Go ahead," Kelevra said. "Ask me."

"Ask you what?"

"Why I did it. Why I told Banks to reorganize things so you ended up with me."

"So you admit it?" Rin hadn't been expecting that, but Kelevra grinned.

"I never bothered trying to deny it."

When he didn't elaborate, clearly waiting for Rin to ask like he'd suggested, Rin blew out a breath. "Fine. Why'd you do it?"

"Why did you?"

Rin frowned, not sure what he meant.

"You could have been in first place," Kelevra stated, seemingly catching when that had Rin's shoulders tensing. "You gave it up on purpose. I was merely ordering Banks to assign me to the cadet I should have been gifted all along."

Gifted. What a fucking creep.

Kel tipped his head. "You're offended."

"I'm not an object," Rin confirmed.

"Where are you from?" Kelevra changed the topic. "There are people with golden hair here, but yours sparkles like warm sand."

Rin barely resisted the urge to run a hand through the longer strands at the top self-consciously. What was it about this guy's attention in particular that seemed to leave him flustered?

"Tibera," he said. "It's a warm planet."

"So not wet like this one." Kel meant the fact that it rained more than half the year.

"Actually it's mostly ocean, so…It's pretty wet." Rin still retreated to the pool at the Academy whenever he felt stressed. Absently, his gaze wandered toward the window and to the massive pool filled with half-wasted men and women around his age.

"I've never heard of it," Kelevra admitted.

"It's in another galaxy."

Kelevra quirked a brow and took a drag from the can of beer he was holding. "You came all the way from another galaxy? What for?"

He shrugged, making it seem like it was no big deal. Trying to draw his attention away from the fact that it was. "Change of scenery."

The corner of his mouth lifted but the smirk was gone a second later. Kelevra hummed. "I see."

Why did Rin get the feeling they weren't talking about the same thing anymore?

"The man you were standing with in the gym," he switched topics seamlessly yet again. "Friend of yours?"

Rin tried to recall who he meant. "Brennon?"

"He had his arm around your shoulders."

"Brennon," he confirmed. "Yeah, we're friends."

"Just friends?"

"I'm not currently with anyone if that's what you're getting at." Rin refused to volley the question back, getting the feeling Kelevra would enjoy being asked about his romantic life too much.

Sure enough, Kel paused as though waiting, and then sighed in mild disappointment when Rin noticeably remained quiet. "Definitely the hard way," he murmured to himself before moving to one of the end tables by the bed. He tugged open the top drawer and pulled something out.

"So you like water," he asked over his shoulder, his body blocking whatever he was doing.

"Yeah." Rin ran a hand through his hair. "Look, if this is it—"

"Forgetting I'm your commanding officer already?"

He clamped his mouth shut.

Kel chuckled and turned back. "Have you ever fucked another man before?"

Rin's mouth dropped open at the blunt question. "Excuse me?"

"I have," Kel replied smoothly.

"I didn't ask."

"You wanted to know."

"I didn't." He was only a little bit curious, but there was no way he was going to be admitting to that out loud.

"You find me attractive."

"Everyone finds you attractive," Rin stated, lifting a single shoulder. "I'm not understanding the point of these personal questions, Imperial Prince. You were assigned to me to teach me—"

"You were assigned to me," Kelevra corrected, moving over toward the windows. Below the sound of music and laughter could be heard trickling through the glass, and he paused, watching his friends for a moment before he called Rin over to join him.

He didn't want to, but his feet got moving, the reminder that this prick was in fact his commanding officer ringing in his head. He couldn't afford to mess this up, couldn't do something or say something so out of line it would lead to the Imperial Prince failing him. There was still too much he needed to learn in the Academy. Failure wasn't an option.

Rin had barely stepped up to his side, however, when suddenly a strong hand was grabbing him by the back of his neck and slamming him face-first against the glass. It reverberated but held, his palms slapping against the solid surface in a poor attempt to keep himself from being completely pressed to it.

He wasn't weak by any sense of the word.

But Kelevra was stronger.

"Pretty sure I told you to call me by my name," Kel's mouth was close, barely an inch from the curve of Rin's ear as he practically purred the words. There was an edge to it, his displeasure clear. "Look down."

Rin did, sucking in a breath when he realized they'd drawn attention. The partiers on the rooftop level had taken notice, some hooting and hollering up at Kelevra, raising their beers to him.

"They think we're playing a game," Kelevra filled him in, stepping in close so his front was sealed over Rin's back. "They aren't wrong."

"Back off." He ground his teeth and tried to push away from the windows, only to be smashed back against them hard enough that his cheekbone hurt.

"Why'd you blow the competition?" Kelevra asked again.

"I didn't."

"Liar."

"Got any proof?" Of course he wouldn't. Rin had been careful. He'd checked beforehand to make sure the challenges weren't filmed. Some classes and events were, and in those he had to be extra sneaky, but this had been a piece of cake. Or so he'd thought. Apparently he hadn't fallen back as subtly as he'd believed.

Although, even if he had, it wasn't like he'd get into that much trouble. Banks would most likely give him a slap on the wrist and order him on cleaning duty for a week or so. Big deal.

If that was his only worry, Rin would admit it easily and put an end to whatever uncalled-for power trip Kelevra thought he was due. But it wasn't, and he couldn't. If he agreed he'd blown it, he'd be asked the reason, and that he could not give. No matter the consequences.

"I'm an impatient person," Kel told him.

Rin kept his mouth shut. In his head, he cursed the guy a million times, using all the languages he knew. He wished he could take a swing at that pretty face. Doubted anyone had ever had the gall to punch the Imperial Prince.

"Are you embarrassed that people are looking at you?" Kelevra asked then, sidling in closer so that something hard bumped against Rin's lower back.

He gasped, completely shocked into silence this time.

Kelevra was turned on.

"Clearly you aren't," Rin said once he was able to regain his composure.

"Not at all," he agreed, grinding into him for good measure, ignoring the way Rin actually tried leaning into the wall now instead of away. "I've never minded an audience, being watched sort of came with the territory. You however…you seem to want to keep under the radar. Why is that, I wonder?"

"Keep wondering." So much for not flunking. Rin was about to lose it, and once that happened, there was no way Kelevra was going to pass him.

"Are you angry that I'm rubbing my erection over you," he hummed, doing just that, rocking his hips a little more, "or that I'm doing it in front of others? I could stop."

"Do."

"I wasn't finished," Kel chuckled.

"If you called me here to fuck around, I'm not interested," Rin said. "I'm sure you can find someone more than willing downstairs."

"I'm not interested in them."

"I'm not interested in you."

"Are you interested in men?" Kelevra asked, smirking when Rin didn't reply, clearly getting his answer anyway. "Do you find me attractive?"

Yes. "No."

"Liar." He grunted. "I can always sense a lie, call it the diplomat in me."

"Diplomats are meant to be peacemakers."

"And to do that, you need to be able to read someone. Uncover all their…proclivities." It'd seemed like he'd wanted to use a different word but had changed tactics at the last second.

Rin's hackles rose.

"You sure you don't want to go the easy route?" Kelevra sounded like it didn't matter to him one way or the other.

Rin should. He was good at making shit up, could just play the Imperial Prince the same way he played everyone else and be done with it. Though, he had this sinking feeling that Kelevra would somehow see through his lies, like that comment he'd just made hadn't been in jest at all.

"I don't suffer being lied to," Kelevra said then, as if able to read his thoughts.

If he lied and pissed Kelevra off, he'd be flunked.

If he took a swing at him, he'd be flunked.

This was hardly the first time he'd found himself backed into a corner, so what was it about this particular situation that was making him feel well and truly trapped? It must be Kelevra's status. Rin had never trusted anyone with power, had firsthand experience with how people like that typically wielded it.

"Tell you what," Kelevra surprised him yet again by releasing him suddenly, stepping back to give Rin room to spin around and face him, "I'll let you set the tone. How about that? Since it's clear I'm five steps ahead of you, I'll give you a chance."

"A chance for what?" He rubbed the back of his neck, eyeing him suspiciously.

"To choose the game," Kel replied.

"What if I don't want to play?"

"That's not an option."

"Why not?" The guy had tons of friends, hell, an entire party was being held right now at his home.

"Because I decided we were going to the moment I saw you," Kelevra confessed. "If you didn't want my attention, you shouldn't have been so damn interesting while I was watching."

"I had no idea you were watching." Sure, they'd been told the senior class would be reviewing them with Banks, but that didn't mean Rin had known Kelevra specifically would be among them.

"Semantics. Boring. This, however," he held up his hand, showing him what he'd gotten from the top drawer. Two small oval-shaped pills rested in his palm, one white, the other black. "This will be loads of fun."

Yeah, the real question was for who. Rin somehow doubted it was going to be for him.

"Pick one," Kelevra instructed, holding them out. "I don't like wasting time, and I get the feeling you're all about stringing people along, so this will help us cut to the chase."

"What's that supposed to mean?" He wasn't wrong, but Rin was still mildly affronted.

"It means," Kel's gaze lost some of its luster, hardening as his patience really did start to wind down, "I'm being kind. It doesn't happen that often. Accept graciously and maybe I'll decide to go easy on you, no matter which way the night ends up going."

Rin had thought speaking in cryptic bullshit was his brother's personal language, but apparently, Kelevra was fluent in it as well. He hesitated, eyeing the pills, trying to decide what to do. No matter which way he looked at it, he was stuck. If he stormed out—

"You take one step toward the door and I'll take this and any other choices from you in a heartbeat," Kelevra warned. "I'll shove both of these down your throat, cadet. Maybe I should have done that from the start." He pursed his lips, actually considering. "Actually, it's not too late…"

Rin's hand shot out and he snatched the white pill, popping it into his mouth and swallowing it dry. "Happy now?"

"Give it a minute," Kelevra said, but he'd lost some of his edge, his eyes softening at the corners.

"What kind of drug was that anyway?" Rin didn't do drugs. He barely drank either. Control was the most important thing in his world, and even though he'd sometimes like to, it was something he couldn't afford to give up. He rubbed at his mouth with the back of his hand. "Seriously? What did you give me? Can it be traced?"

"There's no drug test scheduled for another three weeks," Kelevra said.

"Of course you know that." Wouldn't want the Imperial Prince to get in trouble and make the planet look bad or anything.

"I don't do drugs," Kelevra told him.

"Then why did you just make me?" Rin sneered. "I—" A pang in his lower region cut him short.

A warmth was starting to spread throughout him, and with a frown, he paused to try and get a feel for it. His skin was starting to feel flushed and…

With horror, his gaze dropped down to between his thighs.

Where his cock was starting to swell in his uniform pants.

He blinked and then looked back up to Kelevra, who was grinning ear to ear.

"You bastard." A wave of lust rippled through him suddenly and without warning, and with a moan, Rin dropped down to his knees.

Chapter 3:

Kel watched his cadet grind the heel of his right hand between his thighs as he dropped to the floor. His skin was brightening, turning hot pink at the tips of his ears and over the sharp rise of his cheeks. There'd been a spark of interest behind his eyes when he'd first spotted Kelevra in the pool, Kel had seen it, and that'd been more than enough invitation in his book to proceed.

"Bastard," Rin growled between clenched teeth as he rocked against his palm, seeming to catch himself at the last minute. He wrenched his hand away and glared up at Kelevra, hatred, lust, and a hint of something else swirling in his mismatched eyes.

Something a lot like fear.

Kelevra inhaled, breathing it in, letting the scent of sea salt, Rin's particular smell, invade his nostrils and fill him up the way he was looking forward to filling the other man.

"Heterochromia," he said, mostly to himself, tipping his head so he could glance between each of Rin's eyes. "They're beautiful." The one on the right was a pale pastel blue, and the one on the left was pastel green. "I've never seen these shades before though."

"What did you give me?" Rin squeezed his eyes shut and then gasped and clutched at his lower abs.

"You picked the poison," Kelevra reminded, a rush of adrenaline coursing through him as he watched his cadet internally fight against the effects. He'd never used this particular drug on anyone before—it wasn't his style—but when he'd asked Madden to get him something that could put someone in the mood, his insane best friend had gone the extreme route.

He held up the black pill, rolling it between two fingers. "This one would have made you tell the truth. We could have had a really in-depth conversation. Could have stayed up all night getting acquainted."

The spot between Rin's brow furrowed. "Why do I get the feeling you don't mean that in the nice way it's meant to sound?"

"Probably because you're smarter than you let on," Kelevra drawled, crouching before him. "I could tell from the first time our eyes met you sensed it."

"Somethings *off* about you," Rin didn't hold back, maybe because of the waves of intense need that were taking control of him, or maybe because he actually didn't care about angering Kelevra anymore.

Everyone had a limit. Maybe getting drugged was his. If so, that would be a major pity.

Kel was just getting started.

"It's in the eye," Rin added when Kel didn't say anything.

"Singular?" Interesting.

Rin nodded. "The one on the right is a fake, isn't it. Can you even see out of it?"

Very few people knew about that, and even fewer ever got close enough to notice the slight difference. Kel was impressed.

"It's an implant," he explained. "Insight Eye. Computer. Connects to my brain and my multi-slate. Yes, I can see, but it's different from a normal eye. For one, I can see a lot more than the average person, like, as an example, the rate of your heart beat—which has steadily been on the rise since you stepped off the elevator. I can also see your body temperature—that's also gone up."

"Yeah," Rin snapped, "because you gave me a drug that's making me feel like my dick is about to be twisted off!"

Kel laughed. "Everyone at the Academy says you're a fun-loving, calm individual. But you aren't are you? You've got a dirty mouth and a filthy mind. You were practically eye fucking me back at the pool."

"You're delusional!" Rin slapped his hand away when Kel reached out to touch him.

He had every right to be angry, and yet Kelevra felt a spark of fury within himself at the rejection. If he were a better person, he'd storm out of here and leave the cadet to handle his needs on his own. Actually, if he'd been better, he probably wouldn't have given him the pill in the first place. But he'd been curious, eager to see which way the night might end up going if the choice were left to Rin instead.

"I'm not just interested in your body if that helps," he explained, noting the way Rin inhaled sharply at that. "I really would have settled for talking if you'd picked the black pill. Alas, you didn't." He rose to his feet, staring down at Rin, not bothering to mask the hunger he was feeling. His cock was already swollen and achy, the tip poking out of the top of his swim trunks.

The second Rin noticed he scrambled backward, hitting the window with a hard thud.

"Have you forgotten about the audience?" Kel asked, motioning with his chin over Rin's shoulder. "Is that your thing?"

"What?" Rin glanced over then turned back, his eyes wide. "No."

"You sure?"

"Stop this," he ordered. "You're supposed to be mentoring me, not," he waved his hand down at his dick, "feeding me sex pills!"

Kel snorted. "Sex pills." That was hilarious. "You were already hot for me, Rin, I merely sped you along."

"I was not, and this isn't going to happen."

Kelevra watched the tiny symbol hovering in the right corner of his vision jump up, indicating Rin's heartrate had increased yet again. The cadet's throat bobbed as he swallowed, and the censor in Kel's eye followed that as well, the word *anxious* popping up on the screen. The eye could detect certain reactions and estimate what those reactions could be toward.

According to the readings, Rin was anxious as all hell.

And horny.

Very, very, horny.

Kel figured Rin wanted to keep believing he hadn't been prior to taking the pill, but he knew better. He'd seen how Rin had held his breath when he'd first spotted him in the pool. The way his eyes had scanned down the length of him, taking in the sweeps of golden chains across his chest.

Rin wanted him, at least physically.

Getting into people's heads was a big turn-on for Kelevra. He liked calling people's bluffs and figuring out why they bothered lying in the first place. No one was honest, not a single person, but there were levels of dishonesty, gray areas that could be excused away. He wondered what kinds of secrets Rin had, and if they'd be worth all this effort in the end or if it'd turn out to be something mundane and stupid.

Like, what if the guy simply didn't want all the extra attention and work being in first place meant he'd receive?

Boring.

"Have you been fucked by a man before?" Kelevra asked, watching Rin flinch. "It's in your best interest to answer this time."

Rin clearly wanted to argue or curse at him, but he swallowed again and then in a tight voice replied, "Yes."

"Recently?"

He hesitated. "No."

Kel viewed the readings to see if that was a lie, but according to his eye Rin was telling the truth. "How long since the last time?"

"Seriously?" Rin growled.

"I'm being—"

"If you say the word kind I swear to Light I'm going to stab you in the other eye," Rin snapped, then all at once seemed to recall who he was speaking to. He didn't cower, but a flicker of worry settled over him as he waited for Kelevra's reaction.

Kelevra was waiting too. Typically, something like that would have set him off and he'd have broken a few bones by now. Not because he minded empty threats, but because when it came to his eyes he was understandably a bit sensitive. There was no rush of anger, however. No annoyance or need to break anything. Instead, his dick twitched.

"Do you want to fight for it?" he asked, honestly surprising himself with the offer. Kelevra was used to taking what he wanted without asking. He'd wanted Rin since the moment he'd first spotted him, wanted to feel that silky sand-colored hair, wanted to taste those lush lips. Wanted to know what he'd sound like screaming his name as he orgasmed around his cock.

What he'd told Rin earlier hadn't been completely untruthful. He was interested in more than just bedding the cadet. But finding out why he'd blown the competition was pretty low on his list when the other thing on it was sex.

Kel was smart enough to know he could only really ever think with one head at a time and wasn't even bothered by it. Why should he be? He was the Imperial Prince coddled by his eldest sisters, one the current Emperor of Vitality, the other next in line for the throne. The only time he'd ever be at risk of any actual consequences was if he did something to upset the delicate balance between his family and the Brumal, a criminal organization that ruled the planet right alongside the Diar's.

Baikal Void, the heir to the Brumal throne, was a friend though. Kel respected him and was respected back, and for that reason, he'd always taken the extra minute to think things through when it came to Void. But anything other than that...

"I'm not having sex with you," Rin said, but the way he was back to rocking his hips took away most of the finality those words would have carried otherwise.

Kelevra had never forced someone before, not because he found the thought distasteful—even knowing that he should—but because he'd never had to. People threw themselves at him all the time. No one had ever come close to telling him no when he'd come onto them.

Rin had said no.

It was just Kel didn't care.

"I could put a bullet up that ass of yours right now and no one would bat an eye," Kelevra told him. He wasn't trying to be crass, merely matter of fact. People like Rin, the friendly ones who felt things, they needed stuff to be spelled out so they'd stop struggling so damn much. "Instead, I intend to feed you my cock."

"I'm not—"

"I'm the Imperial Prince, cadet," he reminded darkly, allowing some of his charming mask to slip, for the real him to shine through. "I fuck who I want when I want. Nothing and no one will tell me I can't have something, and that includes you." It was the kind of thing that typically had people scurrying in sheer terror, but Rin merely focused on him, almost as if seeing him for the first time.

"Oh." The word left his lips and an understanding seemed to come over him. Rin was even nodding to himself now, as though having solved some great mystery.

"Oh?" Kelevra quirked a brow, the first inkling of anger finally making its appearance. He didn't like the fact Rin still didn't seem all that afraid of him. Didn't like that he didn't seem to be taking this as seriously as he should.

Considering he was a big guy, probably around six foot one, about an inch shorter than Kel, with broad shoulders and a toned body, Rin most likely wasn't used to being pushed around by anyone. Maybe that was why, even drugged and horny, he was resisting the pull Kel so clearly had on him.

"My turn," Rin said, not waiting for him to agree before asking, "Do you think drugging me is right, or wrong?"

Kel frowned. "I don't think it matters one way or the other."

Rin nodded to himself again. "And rape? You'll force me if I say no, won't you."

"I want you," he shrugged. "And the drug will help you feel good, if nothing else."

"So you're glad I took the drug?"

What was going on? Why did Kelevra suddenly feel like the shoe was on the other foot and he was the one left in the dark. "I couldn't care less which pill you ended up taking. If I did, I wouldn't have given you the choice at all."

"And if I tell you I think you probably have a tiny pencil dick and couldn't get it up without having to hurt someone in the first place, and that your body chain is stupid and tacky, how—"

Kel shot forward, yanking Rin onto his feet, pinning him roughly against the window by his throat. The only thing that kept him from full-on squeezing was the knowing glimmer in Rin's gaze and the way his cock was still throbbing.

"What the hell are you playing at, cadet?" he growled, low and dangerous, making sure all the malice that was twisting up inside of him, threatening to strip away any of the good feelings and replace them with the urge to kill could be heard loud and clear.

But even after hearing it—and it was so obvious that he understood the threat—Rin didn't flinch.

"Sociopath, right?" he asked.

Kel's grip faltered.

The corner of Rin's perfectly formed full lips turned up smugly. "I like digging around for people's secrets, too, Kelevra."

He'd been diagnosed as a child after the fifth explosive tantrum had ended with his nanny tossed over a balcony. After, he'd been sad she was gone only because no one else read him stories the same way she did, but aside from that, he hadn't regretted it. If she'd wanted to keep her brains in her skull, she shouldn't have told him green wasn't really his color.

Kel looked fucking good in *every* color. That bitch.

"This was impulsive," Rin continued when Kel remained quiet. "You saw me and wanted me because I'm shiny and new. You'll fuck me, get bored, and move on, right? That's typically how this goes for people like you."

"Careful, cadet." He didn't like the way the other guy was analyzing him right now. Like Kel was some lab rat to be poked at and prodded.

"I'm doing the same thing you tried to do with me," Rin pointed out. "Though, I guess hypocrisy probably isn't something you can relate to, can you? That means acknowledging you aren't always right, and that's no doubt something you struggle with."

"You are starting to make the bullet possibility sound a lot more appealing," Kelevra warned. "Or maybe I should stuff your mouth with something to prevent you from speaking."

"I can't tell you why I threw the competition if I'm gagged," Rin said.

Annoyed, Kel slapped a hand against Rin's junk, squeezing him through his pants hard enough to wipe that look off his face. As soon as the cadet gasped, he eased up a bit, slipping lower to cup his balls, testing their weight in his hand.

Rin moaned and arched into the touch, clearly furious with himself afterward. That glare had returned full force, but his pink tongue slid between his lips to wet them, and the sheen of sweat on his brow, as the drug continued to keep him locked in that state of arousal, dimmed the accompanying hatred.

Not that Kelevra cared if Rin ended up hating him. He didn't. Mostly because the guy was right. More likely than not, Kel was going to bed him, get him out of his system, and then wake up bored and over it in the morning. He'd never slept with the same person twice, and he doubted that was going to change just because he was a little curious about Rin's motive at the competition.

"You asked if I wanted to fight for it," Rin reminded. "That still an option?"

"Changing your tune?" Kel narrowed his eyes.

"Well yeah. I know what you are now. That changes everything. Brings it into perspective, you might say."

What he didn't voice was that Rin really meant it provided him with a better angle, a better way to handle Kelevra. He was still trying to get out of this, to escape, he was merely adjusting to the circumstances, adapting for self-preservation. That was clever.

Clever was sexy.

Kelevra pushed a thigh between Rin's rubbing his knee against the bulge in his pants experimentally.

Rin's eyes slipped shut and he tipped his head back, moaning at the contact. He started rubbing himself against Kel, shamelessly reaching out to grab onto his hips to keep him close as he started full-on humping.

"The drug is taking effect," Kelevra said, and Rin made a sound of agreement in the back of his throat but didn't open his eyes. "Still want to fight?"

Rin considered it. "If I go out there like this right now, I'll jump the first person who comes onto me, I just know it."

"I'm coming onto you right now."

"You're the reason I'm in this state to begin with."

"Exactly," Kelevra undid the button on Rin's pants and slid his palm beneath the waistband of his underwear, all the way down until he was grabbing onto Rin's dick. He was hot and heavy, and wet, covered in precome already. "You're leaking for me."

"Not for you," he shook his head, crying out when Kel gave a punishing pump of his fist all the way down his hard length.

"I was going to suggest you try for the door, and if I caught you before you made it, you give in," Kel told him, chuckling. "But that isn't going to work."

"No," Rin agreed. "It's not. I feel like I'm on fire. Running is completely out of the question." He moaned again. "Good Light, I fucking hate you."

"Rin Varun, nicest guy at the Academy my ass. You cuss more than the Brumal, and that's saying something." Kel found that he sort of liked it too. Sort of liked the fight, the spark. His cock grew just thinking about having to pin Rin down and force him to take his load. Listening to all those swear words firing off as he pounded into him.

"I'm nice to people who are nice to me back," Rin argued.

"I'm being nice," Kel corrected.

Rin grunted. "Your version of it, I suppose."

"What? No more threats about my eye?"

"Don't sound so disappointed," Rin said. He was still rocking into Kelevra's fist, but the thrusts were shallow, his movements stilted as though he were fighting against his physical reaction. "I'll come up with a proper insult in a minute."

"Can't seem to control yourself, can you?"

Rin paused, eyes popping back open to latch onto his. "All I ever do is control myself."

"That so?" Kel glanced pointedly down at his open pants. "I have to admit, you're doing a phenomenal job. I was told the drug took exactly five minutes to start working and that anyone who consumed it would absolutely lose their mind after. You want it, but you don't seem on the verge of going crazy. Yet. It'll come. I can spare another moment for you to get there."

The song changed on the roof, the beat louder, and Rin somehow managed to fight against the pull of the drug even more. He planted both palms against Kelevra's chest and shoved with all his strength.

Kel stumbled back, growling as his hand was torn off that hard heat. His anger instantly died when Rin spoke next.

"Shut the blinds," he demanded. "And I'll do it."

"Really?"

"It's just sex," Rin snapped, hunching over slightly, his own hand making to grab himself.

Kelevra shot forward and latched onto his wrist, holding his arm up. "I don't think so."

Rin made a sound of frustration.

"Want help with that, cadet?" Kel teased, inching closer. "Bet I know just what you need to stop that ache in your groin." He turned so his hard-on would bump suggestively against Rin's hip.

"Shut. The. Blinds," he insisted, then he caught Kel's gaze, the determination and promise there almost enough to knock the Imperial Prince off his feet a second time. "And then fix this by fucking me."

From zero to one hundred.

Seemed like Kel wasn't the only one who acted on instinct.

"I knew you were going to be a good time." He reached for the remote and hit the button that would instantly fling the blinds closed, then without giving Rin a chance to change his mind, he shoved him down onto the bed.

Right where he wanted him.

Chapter 4:

Rin was on fire. Not literally, but man he may as well have been. His skin felt too tight, his throat scratchy and raw, and his dick... Good Light, his dick was so hard he thought it might break at a single touch. Just snap off like plaster, turning him into one of those dickless statues at the museums his brother always wanted to visit.

Rin hated museums.

And he didn't want to be a dickless statue.

Kelevra hauled him off the floor, all that taunt, tanned muscle displayed beneath the golden chains flexing as he did, and shoved him onto his back on the king-sized bed. A satisfied rumble traveled up the back of his throat as he peered down at Rin as if waiting to see how Rin would react to having just been tossed like a sack of flour.

Truthfully, for a split second, he wasn't even sure. He wasn't exactly a small guy. He'd bulked up to protect himself back in high school, the training sessions both he and his brother had gotten into loaded and time-consuming. It'd given them focus and purpose. Still, it'd been high school, so of course he'd found opportunities to sneak off and explore his sexuality.

Rin was pansexual, he liked what he liked.

And damn, did he like what he saw when he looked at the Imperial Prince.

The guy having tricked him here, into his bedroom? Not so much.

Fortunately for Kelevra, Rin was too busy feeling like he was about to spontaneously combust to pay too much heed to the screaming war drums in his brain. Instead, he focused on his other needs, the lower ones, hips flicking absently up when he did, another reedy moan rushing out of him.

When was the last time he'd felt anything even close to this? He tried to remember, but if there'd ever been a time, it eluded him. Ever since they'd been kids, life had been about survival, pure and simple. Get through the next hour. The next day. The next year. All to graduate high school and get to leave for college. They'd picked the furthest place they could convince their father to allow them to go and yet it still hadn't been far enough.

They were still fending off their demons, in a warped and constant battle to beat them back into their little boxes, to compartmentalize and drive the door closed for just a little while longer.

"I'm fucking exhausted," he said, the words slipping past his lips without him meaning them to, and even that had him chuckling, because when was the last time he'd done something like that? Speaking his mind? His real mind? In front of anyone other than his brother?

Kelevra, who was kneeling on the bed next to him frowned. "That's odd. I'm not aware of that being a side effect."

Considering he'd slipped him a sex drug, Rin understood the confusion.

He snorted. "That's not what I meant."

As far as he could tell, he had three options. The first was to give into the fury, potentially murder the Imperial Prince or get murdered by him. The second was to fight his way out of this room with a boner and the beginnings of some cramps throughout his entire body. Maybe make it to the party and then end up jumping someone anyway.

The third was to give in.

Yeah, he thought Kelevra was sexy, and sleeping with him wouldn't be all that big of a sacrifice if he was being honest. But it was risky. Maybe too risky. Drawing the attention of someone that high up the hierarchy? Dangerous. Pretty much everything he and his brother always worked toward avoiding.

But…He pressed the heel of his hand down onto his trapped dick and whined like a bitch in heat. That anger slashed through the lust once more and he tried to suppress it, afraid of what it might lead him to do if he didn't.

Kelevra reached for him and Rin gnashed his teeth, giving the other man pause and…fuck. This wasn't going to work.

"Tie me down," he ordered, not bothering to consider how foolish he was being by demanding things from someone who was acting as a commanding officer.

An abuser of power was more like but whatever.

He'd rage about that later when he was safe and alone.

"Demanding thing, aren't you." There was something on Kel's face that gave him away despite the comment. He was intrigued, and if the straining cock still struggling to push its way past the thin barrier of those swim trunks was any indication, he was just as aroused as Rin was.

"Did you take one of those pills too?" Rin asked.

"No, Flower, this is just what you do to me."

He scowled. "Don't call me that."

"Why not? Look at you, all ready to unfurl for me." Kelevra reached for his throat but Rin slapped him away. "Guess you were serious about those restraints."

"Don't act like you're not giddy at the notion," Rin spat.

Kel was in the process of reaching for the top drawer of the end table on this side of the bed but he paused and tipped his head, eyes narrowing slightly. "My, my. You are good at reading people. Interesting that you followed me up here so willingly."

"I was following orders," he bit out. Rin had been trying to manage things. "I vastly underestimated how many laws you'd be willing to break during our first meeting."

Kel clucked his tongue. "This is our second, but otherwise, fair."

They were doing far too much talking. The blood was rushing to Rin's head and he'd started to tingle all over. He'd heard of species on other planets who went into things like heats and ruts, their bodies forcing them into intense arousal to ensure mating. Tibera, the planet he was from, was nothing like that, but sex wasn't shamed or looked down upon either.

He'd meant it before when he'd told Kel it was just sex. He was furious that he was being forced into it, sure, but the actual having of it? He licked his lips.

Kelevra pulled a silver set of handcuffs from the drawer and then made quick work of securing one around Rin's right wrist. He attached it to one of the metal rods in the headboard—clueing Rin into what their purpose was probably for in the first place—and then he shifted so he was kneeling between Rins' legs, forcing his thighs apart with strong arms.

He undid Rin's zipper and tugged the pants off, freeing Rin's weeping cock. At the cool air across his wet tip, Rin gasped and rolled his head on the pillow, biting down into his bottom lip hard enough to draw blood.

"Bondage your thing?" Kelevra asked as he shucked the pants and boxer briefs over his shoulders.

"Never tried it," he admitted.

"Then why'd you ask me to do it now?"

"Because if you didn't, there was a very real chance I would attempt to claw your eye out," Rin grunted. "Still is actually."

"The only thing holding you back is the need to come?" Kelevra let out a low whistle. "Are you usually top or bottom?"

"You asked if I'd ever been fucked by a man," Rin reminded. "You set this stage before I even got here, don't act like there's a chance of flipping the script now."

Kelevra grinned wolfishly down at him, moving forward to rest a hand on either side of his head on the pillow. "Feisty. I like that about you." His gaze wandered down the length of him, settling on the hard length of Rin's cock currently jutting up toward his stomach. "I like a lot about you, actually."

"You sound surprised." Which was strange, considering the Imperial Prince had come onto him, not the other way around.

"The thrill has diminished by now, typically," Kel said, still staring at him. Almost exploratory, he lowered, bumping his stomach against the tip of Rin's dick. At Rin's sharp intake of breath, his grin widened. "I haven't been able to get you off my mind since yesterday. All this sleek muscle, that calculative spark in your mismatched eyes…Wondering the way you taste and what expression you'll make when I'm thrust in so deep you'll be practically choking on me."

"You're aware this counts as sexual assault right?" Rin's indignation flared back to life, slipping past some of the lust. "And that we're both currently cadets at the Academy, a school training us to catch assholes who do things like slip people date rape drugs?"

"Yes."

"Just checking." Prick.

Kelevra laughed. "Your cheeks flush when you're angry, did you know that?"

"They do not." No one knew Rin's body better than he did. He'd had to in order to survive. His poker face was perfect. Flawless.

"Not noticeably for other people," he corrected, tapping just beneath his right eye. "But I see everything. All those emotions you're hiding? Not from me. You get ticked off so easily, and yet not a single cadet I spoke to had anything other than praise for you and your upbeat disposition. You're a very good liar, Rin Varun."

"Is everyone else aware of the extent you violate them with that eye of yours, or are you just letting me in on a secret?" Rin drawled, mostly because he wanted the other guy to shut up. It was disconcerting though, knowing how much that tech in Kelevra's face was able to tell him.

There were plenty of reasons for someone's body temperature to rise, for their heartbeats to fluctuate. Kelevra's eye gave him insight into things Rin would easily be able to hide from others.

"I'm not as interesting as you think," Rin found himself saying, even as his dick screamed at him to shut the fuck up, hips lifted off the mattress to run himself against the short trail of hairs leading down from Kelevra's navel. It wasn't enough friction and he lost more of the hold he had on his own strings. "Tiberans are all like me. We're trained from a young age to regulate our emotions. If you type us into a search online, the first thing that pops up is a sentence about how we're all cold and aloof."

"Except," Kelevra said, "you're neither of those things. Proof that you're trying to throw me off now on purpose. What? Changing your mind already? You're the one who asked me to tie you down. Was it so you couldn't leave when you came to your senses?"

"I haven't, actually," he admitted. "I'm barely holding it together."

Kel brushed the back of his finger against the curve of Rin's jaw, chuckling when Rin turned his head away. "You don't like to be touched."

"The only reason I'm lying here and letting you do any of this is because of the drug," Rin growled. "If you hadn't tricked me into taking it—"

The Imperial Prince pulled himself off, kneeling between Rin's spread thighs, careful not to allow any parts of them to make contact. Even the challenging glint in his eyes wasn't enough to keep Rin from whining.

"What the hell do you think you're doing now?" Rin hated this. Hated how on fire he felt. It was almost like he was burning alive and the only cool balm in sight was the massive member straining behind Kelevra's swim trunks. Inadvertently, his gaze dropped down to it again, and he licked his lips, thrusting into the air shamelessly. "Screw this."

Rin grabbed at himself, giving one tight stroke of his dick, the feeling so good he moaned and repeated the motion. More of the fear and the anger settled as sparks of electricity brought on by the friction skittered throughout him. He fucked into his fist harder, the springs of the bed creaking, his breaths coming out sharp. Because of how long he'd been waiting, it wasn't long before he felt his balls tighten and draw up, and he was so close to—

He swore when suddenly Kel was back on him, forcing his hand away from his dick and flipping him so that he was lying on his stomach. When he immediately went to right himself, he received a hard whack on the right ass cheek. The flash of pain had him growling, but that only earned him another.

With both hands flat on his cheeks, he shoved Rin's ass down and slipped his thumbs between his crease, pulling them apart to expose his hole. He used his elbows to keep Rin pinned by the thighs and then resituated so that he was also lying on the mattress, his face hovering teasingly over Rin's entrance.

"Get off," Rin ordered.

"Oh," Kelevra chuckled, "I'm going to."

"I just want to come and get the hell out of here," Rin said. "Don't you think you've done enough damage?"

"No," he said without skipping a beat. "I think since you're planning on blaming me for taking advantage of you already, I may as well enjoy myself first. Relax, cadet, I'll make it good for you. So good, even, you might beg me for another round in the morning."

"That's never going to happen." Rin liked sex just as much as the next guy, but he'd yet to grow attached to anything or one and he didn't plan on starting now. Especially not with someone as dangerous as the Imperial Prince. "Sexual acts are deemed as transactions on Tibera, but even there, drugging someone is a crime."

"So report me," Kel shrugged. "In the morning."

Rin opened his mouth to lie and say he would be—he knew better—but then something warm and wet was pressing against that tight ring of muscle, cutting off all ability to think.

Kel's tongue explored, pushing lightly at first, the tip circling his entrance. After a moment of that, he wiggled it inside, stretching Rin around his thick tongue as he speared it as deep as it would go.

There was slight resistance, a little pressure and pain, but Rin clenched his jaw through it, practically shaking as he lay there and stopped resisting. On the contrary, he ground down against the mattress, his movements limited by the way Kel held him, stealing most of the control.

Good Light, that felt good. So good, and yet…

"More," he growled, biting into the silk material of the pillow to keep himself from begging. This damn drug was doing a number on him and he was furious about it, but if he didn't get to come soon he was ninety percent convinced he'd literally explode and die.

A finger slipped into him next, the long digit curling up to stroke at his inner walls, clearly seeking out that spot that would send him careening toward the edge. When Kel found his prostate he tapped at it, with just enough force it sent shudders down Rin's spine. He pulled out and eased in two, opening Rin up skillfully, seemingly content to take all night.

Unlike Rin, who was undulating and whimpering.

"Tell me you want it," Kelevra said then, thrusting three fingers in so hard that Rin cried out from the pain, his wrist rattling the chain as he momentarily tried to pull himself free. He merely nipped at the rise of Rin's left ass cheek and ordered again, "Tell me. Say you want my fat cock to replace my fingers and fuck you like the filthy flower you are."

"What," Rin sucked in a breath, "the actual hell does that even mean?" Was the drug making his brain slower than before or did those words make no sense? "What's a filthy flower?"

"You are," Kelevra told him, sounding far too pleased as he continued to work him with those fingers, the pace fast and punishing, as though he was getting off on the sight of his fingers disappearing into Rin and wanted to see it over and over again. "Looks like there's something else your mind can't control, cadet. The way your ass is greedily sucking me down gives you away."

"It's the drug, you garbage, rapist motherfucker!" Rin actually stilled when the words left his mouth, realization that he'd gone too far hitting him a second too late.

He needed to come at this from a different perspective if he was going to make it out of this room in one piece. Get an orgasm and get away. That was the plan and should be the only thing he focused on. Rin didn't need anger, it would do him no good in this situation.

"Since that's what you think of me anyway," Kel's voice was low, deadly, and promising pain, something Rin really wasn't all that interested in. He yanked his hand free and before Rin could so much as consider apologizing to him, lined his dripping cockhead up to his entrance and shoved with one hard thrust.

A pained sound traveled up Rin's throat as he was practically speared in half by that invading member. He hadn't gotten a good look at it, but from the feel of the thing, it was a lot larger than he'd assumed. Too large even. The discomfort cut through the lust caused by the drug and tears prickled at the corners of his eyes. He buried his face against the pillow, refusing to shed them in front of the Imperial.

He wouldn't give Kelevra that satisfaction.

Had he threatened to take the man's eye? That wasn't good enough. He was going to blind him in the other one and then—

Kelevra forced Rin's legs further apart with his knees and grabbed onto his hips, sliding his body down the mattress to meet his next thrust. He drove into him with enough power the bed rattled against the wall, each punch of his cock sending Rin into a tailspin of feelings and sensations.

He hated the guy.
But man was he pretty.
His dick hurt.
But damn did it feel *good.*

His fingers were digging into him too hard.

But also it was kind of hot.

He felt like he was going to be ripped into two pieces.

That part sucked. Full stop.

Kel pulled all the way out to the tip and paused, his harsh panting the only thing that could be made out in the sudden silence for a brief moment.

Rin kept his face hidden, shoulders tense, lying still.

"You're angry," Kelevra noted, sounding less pissed off himself at least.

"And you're a fucking genius," he snapped back, because apparently, Rin hated living.

Sure enough, Kelevra slammed back into him, going as deep as he could go, and then he settled overtop Rin, his skin warm and sticky, the hard plains of his muscles and the heated metal of his body chains digging into Rin's back. He brought his arms up to the sides of Rin's head and then grabbed a fistful of his hair, yanking him away from the pillow so that he gasped from the sting and the surprise.

His mouth latched onto the side of Rin's neck and he sucked, hard. "It's kind of a turn-on when you're angry. You're like this little ball of energy I can't wait to get my hands on. How I managed to keep myself from throwing you down in the gymnasium and taking you right then and there is beyond me."

The most disgusting part about that was it sounded like something Kelevra would do, based solely on the things Rin had heard said about him.

The Imperial Prince had no filter and no conscience. Even if he really did fuck Rin hard enough to tear him down there, he wouldn't feel bad about it. He wouldn't even bother pretending to.

Rin's chest constricted at that thought and he felt the head of his dick twitch, knew another glob of precome had just dripped out of him.

Because of the drug.

Not because he was psychotic and found the idea of Kelevra being an honest monster sexy.

He wasn't even a monster, really. Kelevra Diar was one of the Devils of Vitality.

Rin might be in the midst of getting physically fucked by a Devil, but he refused to allow Kel to mentally screw him as well.

"You're angry again," Kelevra groaned and then pulled back, slamming his cock into him and stilling a second time. "There you go, squeeze me like you want to break my dick off."

Rin hadn't even been aware he was doing that, and he forced himself to stop clenching, not wanting to give the other man any more satisfaction than he had to in order to achieve his own release.

"Don't be petty," Kel said, clearly annoyed.

"If you wanted a willing bed partner," Rin stated, "you should have found yourself one."

"I could make this good for you, cadet," he breathed the words against the curve of his ear and then chomped down on it, not enough to draw blood, but enough to have Rin yelp. "Or you can keep antagonizing me and we can see where that leads."

"Either way you'll be done with me by morning. That's how it goes, right?" If that were the case, he may as well play along and get off on the feeling of a strong body and a big cock. It wasn't easy for Rin to find a suitable male bed partner due to his size. Add that to the fact everyone always assumed he was dominant in bed, when in actuality…He shoved a lid on those thoughts, afraid somehow with his magic-fucking-eye Kelevra would read them.

The last thing he needed was for the Imperial Prince to realize just how much Rin actually was enjoying this. Being pinned down, tossed about a little.

Used.

"I don't have a very long attention span," Kelevra said in agreement. "So, what's it going to be? Should I pluck your pretty petals, or prick myself on those sharp thorns of yours?"

"Stop speaking in tongue," he hissed.

"Tell me what I want to hear," Kelevra insisted, licking a wet stripe down the side of Rin's face. He grabbed onto his jaw and pulled him back, forcing Rin onto his elbows. He held him still so they were facing one another, the wicked, almost evil glimmer in his hazel eyes giving away just how much he was into this.

Since which pill Rin took had been a choice, his choice, he doubted the Imperial needed this type of control to get off. It wasn't pain either. Yeah, his cock had hurt entering the first dozen or so strokes, but he'd stretched Rin enough it was a bearable type of agony. The rough and claiming kind that made Rin's mind narrow down to what was important.

Feeling good.

He lifted his ass a little, pressing against Kelevra's hips to grind that cock in even deeper. Then he looked Kel dead in the eyes and squeezed.

Kelevra reacted instantly, springing forward to capture Rin's mouth in a rough kiss that was more teeth and tongue than lips. He started thrusting at the same time, hard and shallow motions that pounded Rin into the mattress, his dick rubbing against the silky fabric.

The curved tip of that cock hit his prostate and Rin combusted. The orgasm hit him like a tsunami, leaving him gasping for air, hand reaching around to claw at Kel's shoulder as he quaked.

His nails dug in enough to draw blood, and with one final plunge, Kelevra came as well, his cock bathing Rin's insides with hot spunk that only made him writhe even harder.

It had to be because of the drug, but Rin felt like it went on forever, his body twitching and releasing, fireworks exploding in front of his eyes even once he'd collapsed to the bed, boneless.

They stayed like that for a long moment, both of them trying to catch their bearing. At some point, Kelevra reached up and undid the handcuff, allowing Rin's arm to drop down uselessly at the side of his head.

The effects were still lingering, he could feel it in the way he was still flushed all over, but Rin was certain he'd at least be able to make it back to his car before the need to rub one out overcame him. He'd lost this battle and it was time to retreat.

"Move," he elbowed Kel in the side, catching himself at the last second to be sure the move wasn't hard enough to actually hurt. Now that they'd made it to the finish line, it wouldn't be worth setting the guy off. He'd gotten laid so he should be in a fairly decent mood right now. "I'm leaving."

Instead of listening, Kelevra spread out his limbs, trapping Rin beneath him even more firmly.

Rin froze, barely breathing when he felt Kel's tongue lightly suck at his right earlobe.

His mouth trailed down, teeth skating over his jugular and lower to the spot between his neck and shoulder.

"Seriously," Rin said. "Stop."

Kelevra hushed him. A second later, his cock began to fill up.

Rin felt his walls stretching around it to accommodate and he emitted a strangled sound, not liking the way his dick immediately responded. In less time than it took to blink, he was back to being hard and achy.

"You're desperate to be fucked again," Kelevra, the bastard, noted.

"Damn drug."

"I'll have to let Baikal know it's too potent. He can't sell this stuff on Vitality streets," Kelevra chuckled, adding before Rin could even begin to misunderstand his words for concern for his people, "Everyone would be too busy fucking all day and night to get anything done."

Thank the gods he wasn't next in line for the throne, no one wanted a sociopath as their Emperor.

Rin recognized the name. Baikal Void was the heir to the Brumal Mafia. He and Kelevra were apparently close.

"Did you just admit you tested a new drug on me?" A wave of anger threatened to make him see red and he bucked beneath Kelevra, catching the other man off guard enough that he managed to dislodge his cock and wiggle free. He turned and kicked with all his might, sending the Imperial Prince crashing off the bed. "What if I died, you asshole?!"

Kelevra picked himself off the ground, planting his hands on the edge of the mattress, and glared. "You still might, cadet."

"Great, now we're both pissed off," Rin said. "We're even."

The Imperial latched onto his ankle and yanked him down, skillfully aiming his cock at his entrance and impaling him all over again.

They both groaned.

"Look outside," Kelevra ordered.

Rin didn't have to turn to glance over the small strip above the closed blinds that allowed a glimpse of darkness. He understood where the other guy was going with this.

"It's not yet morning, which means," he started thrusting, the same hard and punishing motions as before, "I'm not done with you."

Already overly sensitive and still riding the high of his outburst, Rin cried out and came a second time.

Chapter 5:

Rin was still fuming the next day when he made his way onto Vail University's main campus, shooting off a message to his brother that he'd arrived. He'd called out of classes at the Academy, feigning a mild fever. In reality, he'd needed to meet with his brother to discuss last night.

As much as it pained him to do so.

They shared everything, typically because they had to, so it wouldn't be the first time he was giving Sila Varun the nitty gritty details of his sexual affairs, only this was different. He couldn't leave out the part about how he'd been drugged beforehand.

He also wouldn't be able to leave out how he'd still wanted it.

All last night Rin had blamed the drugs, but this morning when he'd woken, caught up in Kelevra's vice-like arms, ass and muscles sore, his very first thought had been whether or not he should slip his hand down and stroke the Imperial to get him hard again.

Damn it.

He refused to lose his resolve for something as stupid as dick.

With a growl, he slammed a palm onto the door leading into Lab H, where he knew his brother would be. It was a Wednesday and that meant Sila's project was due. He'd be here putting on the finishing touches before he had to submit it later.

Sure enough, a carbon copy of himself was seated in the far corner of the room, a chunky pair of safety goggles on as he leaned over three beakers filled with various liquids. The only way to tell the two of them apart was by their clothing.

Where Rin was dressed in his training uniform—since that's what he'd gone to Kel's in last night—Sila had a lab coat over light gray pants and a button-up in the same shade. The sophomore colors at Vail. There was also a golden star huggie earring in his right ear, and seeing it made Rin subconsciously tug at his earlobe, the same one that Kel had sucked on last night.

"This is delicate," Sila warned at his approach, and Rin rolled his eyes dramatically.

"I'm not going to ruin your experiment, chill."

"You're in a mood."

"I'm—"

"—Always in a mood," his brother concluded for him. He used an eyedropper to place three small pink drops of something into each beaker and then rested back in his chair, pulling the goggles up to the top of his head. "What happened?"

It was just the two of them alone in the room, the rows of other tables set up for some sort of lab but without any students. Trusting they'd be alone for a while, Rin launched into a spiel about the events of last night, only getting more and more frustrated with each passing second.

But not just at Kelevra. At himself.

"You enjoyed it," his brother said the moment Rin stopped talking long enough for him to get a word in. "That upsets you."

"Did you miss the part where he drugged me?" He waved at him. "Get mad. He took advantage of me."

"Even though you liked it?" Sila tilted his head, the question serious.

"Don't give me that bullshit," Rin sneered. "We're twenty. You can differentiate between right and wrong now." Though in his defense, it'd only been a few years since his brother had learned.

Still, he didn't need to be able to *feel* it to understand what constituted breaking the law.

Sila hummed. "He let you go after?"

"I just came from there." He ran a hand through his hair and heaved out a sigh. "He didn't exactly let me anything. He was still asleep."

"But you're sure it's over?"

Rin considered it and shrugged. "I don't see why it wouldn't be. He was curious about it and now that we've done it, that should be that. He's not the type to linger on anything for too long."

"Or you're just a terrible lay."

Rin's eyes narrowed. "I bet I'm better than you, asshole."

"Only one of us takes it up that way," Sila lazily replied, "and it isn't me. So I suppose we'll never know."

Sila had tried it once, but he hadn't been into it. He got off on control where as Rin…Rin's whole life was about putting on an act. The bedroom was the one place he didn't want to have to bother with that crap.

That was probably why he wasn't actually all that angry about being drugged now that it was already done and over with. Hell, he probably would have accepted the pill willingly if he'd been told what it did.

"Things could have been worse," his brother said as if reading his mind. "You could have taken the black one. At least this way you came away with a couple of mind-bending orgasms and a slight limp to your step."

"Fuck off." He wasn't limping.

Much.

Sila was right though. If Rin had taken that other pill and Kel had gotten him to spill all of their secrets…

"You said you'd be done by now," Rin changed the subject, not wanting to dwell. He didn't have to elaborate in order for his brother to know what he was talking about.

There was a flash of something in Sila's eyes, gone in a blink, something anyone else would have missed. But Rin saw it.

Worry.

The two of them were polar opposites, cut from the same cloth, just different parts. Both of them were broken and forced to hide because of it. For Rin, emotions came too quickly, burned too brightly. For Sila, it was a wonder whenever he managed to feel anything at all.

Which was why that little glimmer was so telling.

Rin's brother had a secret. It was tempting to pry, but he didn't. Whatever it was, Sila would tell him eventually. They never kept anything from the other for long. That was part of the agreement.

"Do you really want me to be the one handling the Imperial?" Sila asked.

"Don't try to manage me like I'm someone else," Rin warned. "But fuck you. I hate that you're right." Though, with any luck, he would only ever have to see Kelevra on campus from now on, and as his mentor.

"Temper, brother."

"Eat me, brother."

"I'm not sure your Imperial Prince would approve."

Rin's eyes narrowed. "I will punch you."

"And risk leaving a mark on our face?" He tsked. "Doubtful."

Rin had done it once when they'd been fifteen. He couldn't even recall the reason for it now, something stupid that had set him off for no real reason. They'd both regretted it. Even with their advanced healing, at that age, it'd taken three days for the bruise to completely fade.

Three days. Trapped.

He shuddered remembering it.

"We have to take part in this stupid assignment for the whole semester. Since you're clearly busy with something, I'll have to figure out how to avoid him as much as possible." Rin was confident he could pull it off. The Academy was huge and the senior classes rarely spent any time in the same parts where the sophomores did.

"Do you think he'll pass you since you let him fuck you?" Sila asked absently, shrugging when Rin scowled at him. "Is that a no?"

"The guy is too compulsive to be able to say for sure." There was a lot of time between now and the end of the semester. "Best bet is to stay out of his way and hope he's forgotten all about me."

Sila hummed and then leaned back toward his experiment, checking the contents of the middle beaker filled with purple liquid. "If you were any good in bed he'd remember you."

"Seriously?"

"I remember my past partners," Sila said. "At least, the good ones."

"Really?" Rin crossed his arms. "What were their names?"

"Blue Sky, Soda, and Ribbons," Sila rattled off, shaking the third beaker and then moving to jot down a note on the holo-tablet set nearby.

"Those aren't names," Rin scoffed. "Those aren't even defining features."

Sila thought it over. "Doesn't it still count?"

"No."

Sila nodded but made no further argument in his defense. He was like that. He probably hadn't really cared in the first place, only going along with the motions to help Rin settle his tumultuous nerves.

Rin was antsy, and he hated being antsy. It made keeping his cool on the outside all the more difficult. The seashell in his pocket had gotten as much action as he had last night; his thumb rubbing circles against the smooth mother-of-pearl surface ever since he'd stepped out of his car. He'd brought it from home, from Tibera, the small shell the only item he owned that he never traded off to his brother.

Sila had a grounder as well, a tool they used to help them regulate and calm their minds and emotions. A typical Tiberan thing that they'd been taught from a young age.

Tiberan's were known for being calculative and aloof, perfect for debates and arguments because they very rarely lost their cool. It wasn't because they didn't feel negative emotions like frustration or anger, quite the opposite. They felt them three times stronger than most other species, in fact. But they also filtered through those emotions faster, processing them and coming to grips with them, allowing them to move on to the next.

Except for Rin, who struggled to let go. When he was angry about something, he could carry that shit with him for *days.*

"Do you have any updates for me?" he asked, ready to move on from all of this after all. The sex had been phenomenal, and as messed up and twisted as it was, Rin was starting to realize he was actually a little bit glad he'd been drugged and coerced into it. If he'd been propositioned properly by the Imperial Prince, he would have had to turn him down even though Rin was attracted to him. Involvement with someone in that high of a position was just too risky.

At least this way he'd gotten to sleep with the man and walk away without any strings attached. Though there was nothing Rin could do against Kelevra, maybe Kel would give him a wide berth all on his own afterward. He doubted the guy had any semblance of a conscience, all things considered, but he probably wouldn't want to deal with Rin accusing him of taking advantage either.

"Rabbit Trace's music is very good," Sila said.

Rin stiffened. "Don't."

"It's good," Sila repeated, "that's all I mean."

Rabbit was a musical genius who attended the same school as Sila. He was a bit off-putting and reserved, but underneath that was a loneliness Rin understood all too well.

"He's hiding behind a mask," Rin said to his brother. "We know what that's like."

Sila nodded, still busily at work with his experiment. "He's safe from me."

Rin frowned. "What's that supposed to mean?"

"I'm hardly the only devil on this planet, brother. You should know, you had one pounding—"

Rin threw up a hand and grimaced. "Enough." He straightened from the edge of the desk he'd been leaning on. "I need to go take a shower."

"Would you like to have lunch first? I'm going to be eating in the East Quad today. The weather is nice." Sila didn't give two shits about the weather, which meant he had other reasons for it.

But like before, Rin didn't ask.

It was hard enough for the two of them to be themselves in this universe without getting pressure from each other. They kept one another from stepping out of line. Kept them safe. But they also didn't lock each other out. Sila would tell him if there was anything he needed to know, the same way Rin had rushed over here to warn him about the unwarranted attention from the Imperial Prince. Plain and simple.

"Nah," Rin picked at his shirt and sniffed. It smelled like Kelevra's room, expensive perfume and a hint of something powdery and floral. "I've got to shower before anything else."

"Still feel him inside you, huh?" Sila asked.

"Don't be gross."

"Do you think—"

"I think," Rin's voice firmed in warning, "I just told you not to be gross, brother."

He could tell by the look that had washed over Sila's face whatever he'd been about to ask would definitely fall under that category as well. Sometimes he got this far away, almost crazy glint in his eyes, eyes so like Rin's and yet...different. He could fake it, of course, but when it was just the two of them alone like this, neither of them bothered with the masks, and the blankness in his brother's eyes went unchecked.

"One day I'm going to have someone more fun to play with," Sila stood and stretched his arms over his head, "and then you'll wish I included you."

"Probably not," Rin snorted.

Sila tipped his head. "Probably not."

"I'll see you at the apartment on Friday?" Rin called when his brother went to leave.

In response, his brother held up a hand and then stepped out of the room.

Alone, Rin took a moment to collect himself. They didn't hide the fact they were twins, but the second he stepped foot outside this room, he was going to have to slip back into character, and that sounded every bit as mentally draining as having to interact with Kelevra again did.

And he would have to. There was no getting out of it. The assignment required they meet at least twice a month. What they did during that time was up to the mentor to decide, but the Imperial Prince didn't exactly come off as the teaching type. With any luck, Rin would be able to convince him to just lie on the spreadsheets and claim they met when they didn't. Breaking rules obviously wasn't something Kel was opposed to.

Rin glowered and adjusted his weight, hating the way his sore ass smarted at the tiny movement. He would have showered there, but the idea of staying naked in the Imperial's presence had been a no-go. Survival instincts had kicked in the second he'd woken and seen Kelevra was still asleep.

The emblem on his wrist beeped and he shifted the cover off so he could check the screen, internally groaning when a familiar name flashed over it in neon letters.

Great. Another person he didn't want anything to do with.

The past twenty-four hours sucked.

Straightening his spine, he lifted the device and hit accept, making sure his face remained relaxed, not too happy, but with no hint of the irritation he felt towards the older-looking face that appeared. "Father."

Crate Varun had aged since the last time Rin had seen him in person, his hair now flecked with strands of silver. There were wrinkles at the corners of his mouth and on his prominent forehead. The holographic video image of him flickered once or twice, the distance between them interfering with the signal.

It was tempting to end the call and claim it'd dropped, but Rin refrained.

Barely.

"Where are you?" Crate frowned, glancing over Rin's shoulder. The camera would only show him Rin from the shoulders up and a bit of the background. "Ah, you have regular classes today, don't you."

"Yes." He didn't bother correcting him and letting him know he was on Vail campus. His father would throw a fit if he knew he was skipping. Slacking, he would call it.

"I can't get in touch with your older brother," Crate stated. "He must be hard at work. But you...They let you take calls? What kind of military school is this?"

"It's an Academy," Rin reminded. "Technically not a military school, sir. And we're actually between classes at the moment. I'll need to leave for my next one in a moment. Is there something I can help you with?"

"Just checking in," his father stated. "You're still on course?"

"Yes, sir."

"And your grades?"

"Still fine, sir."

He grunted. "Meaning you're still placed in the middle of your class."

His father hated that he wasn't doing better, but Rin and his brother had already agreed this was what was best for them. They'd deal with listening to their father's complaints from afar. Freedom never came without strings, after all.

They just had to make it through the next three years and then they'd be out from underneath this tyrant's thumb for good.

To be fair, their father wasn't the worst. But he'd certainly raised his boys with an iron fist, controlling and dead set on getting his way in everything. As a Tiberan Royal, Crate Varun had a high-standing position on the Tiberan Council, and that came with a reputation. If he ever discovered neither of his sons was what their planet deemed normal...

"I'll continue doing my best," Rin promised, leaving out the part about how he'd be doing what was best for himself and his brother.

"You better," he said. "If I feel like either of you are slacking off, I'll order you home. There are perfectly acceptable schools on planet that you boys could have attended."

"Vitality is the only one that offers everything we need," Rin pointed out. Their father wanted them to fill certain positions back home once they were done with schooling, and that meant one of them had to attend a regular university while the other was destined for the Academy.

Didn't matter that neither of them wanted that path.

Their father's word was law.

Always had been.

"Tell your brother to call me." He didn't wait for a response, ending the video call instantly.

Rin blew out a breath. He still really wanted a shower, but warning Sila about their dad now took precedence. With a growl of annoyance, he shut the emblem multi-slate and stormed out of the room, settling a friendly smile on his face when he immediately encountered a group of Vail students dressed in the telling freshman white.

He nodded politely at the three girls and they giggled.

Gods. He was so sick of this farce.

Chapter 6:

"You're where?" Zane Solace, second highest standing member in Kelevra's Retinue, asked. His voice came through the hovercar speakers as Kel pulled the vehicle into the parking lot.

"Vail," he repeated, taking the nearest empty spot. His car, a Zale 54, was worth more than all the cars currently in the lot put together, but he wasn't overly concerned about it getting damaged.

"What are you doing there?"

Kelevra shut the vehicle off and climbed out, using his Insight Eye to lock the doors as he strode away. "Someone told Madden he saw him here."

"Saw who?" Zane, used to Kel's spur-of-the-moment decisions, didn't sound all that concerned. Technically, someone in the Retinue was meant to be with the Imperial Prince wherever he went to help ensure his safety, but that was a rule very rarely enforced.

In part, because Kelevra didn't stop to wait for anyone once he'd decided to do something, and also because everyone knew he could take care of himself. He'd been in intensive training since he was seven, learning how to defend himself against any possible attacks. His IQ also happened to be well above average, and coupled with his electronic eye, he could typically sense a threat from a mile away.

Which was why he was livid that he hadn't seen Rin's escape coming.

He'd woken less than two hours ago to find himself alone, tangled in the sheets. The spot next to him had already been cold, meaning his flower had slipped past his notice sometime before. He was a deep sleeper. That was the one weakness Kel had, but it'd never interfered with anything he deemed important up until now.

"Since when did you go chasing after people?" Zane asked when Kelevra didn't reply quickly enough. "Instead of worrying about getting your dick wet, you should be thinking about missing class again. The professor is about to walk in and if she sees you're skipping, she'll fail you for the day."

He snorted. "So?"

"Your sister—"

"Fuck my sister," he said, then paused just as his feet stepped onto a winding stone path that led between two towering brick buildings. "Actually, don't even look at her."

"Stop getting pissed at your own words. Shit. The professors here. Got to go." Zane ended the call.

Kelevra scowled, but he wasn't annoyed for long. The attention he was drawing his way became apparent suddenly, and he smiled at a group of passing students, noting their crisp dress shirts and the shiny pins showcasing the Vail Crest attached to their bags or their belts. Technically, like them, Academy cadets were meant to have the Academy crest on them at all times, but Kelevra didn't like the wristbands—they didn't match any of his outfits—and there was no way in hell he was going to be poking holes in any of his designer corsets so that was a no. He'd gotten special permission to wave that rule, and no one had ever called him out on it.

"East Quad?" he asked the next passing group, a couple of freshmen if his color coding was accurate.

Both boys seemed nervous, but one cleared his throat and pointed over his shoulder to the left. "It's that way, majesty."

Kelevra didn't bother thanking him, the boys all but forgotten the second they stepped out of his peripheral vision. Amongst all the white, gray, and black—the colors assigned to all school uniforms at Vail—he stood out in his black corset vest, even though the boning and the rest of his suit was ruby, to match the rest of the suit. His hair looked windswept, a thick curl partially covering the top of his scar, and he'd chosen a tie made up of broken shards of red. The only reason he'd bothered with a suit jacket at all was because the forecast said it might rain.

As he made his way down the path, he thought about why he was there. Zane was right in regards to sex not being a high priority at the moment. And it wasn't. Sure, Kel was disappointed that his flower hadn't been there for a quickie, certain Rin's sandy-gold hair would look amazing in the sunlight, but that's not why he'd followed him all the way across the city.

Honestly, he wasn't entirely sure *why* he was doing this. All he knew was he didn't like the fact Rin was no longer by his side, and because of that he'd called Madden and ordered him to find his cadet posthaste. Madden, as per usual, had come through and sent over a location within twenty minutes, just long enough for Kel to get dressed for the occasion.

He figured he'd know what it was he wanted once he saw Rin again. Overthinking it beforehand would be a waste of time and energy, so he didn't bother, scanning the somewhat familiar grounds for any sign of Rin as he went.

Kelevra had been to Vail before for Baikal, but he hadn't spent much time there, usually just picking up or dropping the Brumal Prince off. The two were friends, but they lived vastly different lives, and there was a silent agreement between them not to step on each other's toes. He probably should have contacted Kal to tell him he was coming, but it'd slipped his mind, and since he was already here it seemed pointless to send one now.

If Baikal found out and got mad?

Whatever. What was he going to do? Cry to the Emperor? Please.

He was so sick of everyone using that threat against him as if it was anything other than the paper-mâché crap it was. Contessa Diar, Emperor of Vitality, treated her baby brother like he was made of solid gold. The most he'd get was a firm talking to and a family dinner where, sure, maybe he'd feel like he was dying of boredom, but that was it.

His second eldest sister, Lyra, wasn't any different. She was a bit firmer with him, since the two of them were closer in age, and she'd had fewer responsibilities than Tessa growing up, but she would—and did—let him get away with murder over punishing him.

Most of it stemmed from the fact they doted on him, but he understood at least some of their reasoning was his friendship with Baikal. As the next in line for the Brumal Mafia throne, who Baikal chose to side with made a difference, and he and Kel were thick as thieves, something neither of the Diar women could say.

Power on Vitality was split pretty evenly between the Brumal and the official Imperial government. The Void family also happened to run the largest conglomerate on this side of the galaxy, bringing legal funds to help keep the planet as one of the richest in Dual Galaxy. The mafia portion of their business handled things discreetly and under the table, with the strict understanding that the Diar's didn't know, and didn't want to know, any details.

If Kelevra ever decided to try for the throne and mess with the line of succession, there was a very real chance he would be able to with Baikal in his corner. His sisters knew this.

They also knew, so long as they kept him satiated, he would never bother. Heavy lies the head that bears the crown and all that other nonsense. Kelevra was allergic to things like responsibility, and good rulers cared for their people, something he simply wasn't capable of. So, understandably, he wasn't a great candidate for the job. Thank Light.

Too bad no one had taught Rin that little trick of keeping the prince pleased. If he'd been smarter, he would have known better than to sneak off, leaving Kel's mind left to come up with all sorts of irritating possibilities.

Like, for instance, what if Rin was dating a student here? What if he'd run off to cry to them about how last night he'd been forced to fuck against his will? What if he told them all about how he hadn't wanted to, how he hadn't wanted Kelevra?

His fists clenched and he lost some of the luster to the veneer he'd had settled in place. The posh, devilish prince, the part he played whenever he was out and about and surrounded by potential paparazzi and cameras. Already he'd caught sight of over a dozen students taking his picture, and he hadn't even been paying attention, too caught up in trying to figure out *why*.

Why did the idea of Rin having someone bother him so much? When he'd asked, Rin had told him he was single, and his eye hadn't picked up on any physical changes to alert him to that having been a lie. But he hadn't asked if he was messing around with someone.

A girl then, perhaps? Since it'd been a while since Rin had last taken a cock—definitely the truth, because Kelevra had had to squeeze himself inside his tight little body and had almost come from that alone.

Kel could maybe let him keep a girl. So long as it didn't interfere with…Well, whatever he planned for them to be from here on out. If he planned for them to be anything at all. A part of him was still convinced he'd take one glance at Rin and realize that spark had died and he was over it, like he'd assumed last night he would be.

Rin had come to the same conclusion. That, coupled with the drug, had been the only reason he'd eventually given into his lust and fucked Kelevra back.

Those last two times he'd been a bit more fickle, struggling against him so that Kel had been forced to pin his wrists down and screw him fast and hard. He'd hurt him a little in the process, and now he found himself curious how many marks he'd inadvertently left painted over that golden skin.

Everything about Rin sparkled, from his sandy hair to his sun-kissed skin tone. His eyes, those pretty pastel colors, were the only soft thing about him, and even then, whenever Rin got angry there was a flash of something hard and electric behind them. He covered it quickly, but Kelevra had caught it, a part of him having grown a tiny bit obsessed with bringing it out so he could see it again.

Fucking the man had been just as interesting. He couldn't recall the last time he'd been eager to bury his cock into the same hole, but the very thought of driving into Rin again had him twitching in his silk pants.

Correction. Rin was not allowed to keep any others, whether they were male or female.

Kelevra finally made it to the East Quad, a part of the university which had been built over a sprawling mangrove field. Bridges had been built overtop it, planks crisscrossing and leading to various parts of campus. At the heart of it all was a curved row of gazebos meant for studying and hanging out. Most of them were currently occupied, and he swept his gaze over them quickly, coming to an abrupt stop the moment his gaze settled on his reason for coming all the way here.

Rin was seated in the last one, elbows propped on the edge of the wooden table. He was grinning at another student sitting on the bench across from him, a younger male dressed in white who was shyly in the process of tucking a strand of his black hair behind his ear.

Kelevra saw red.

The next thing he knew, he was standing at the side of the table, yanking Rin up by the collar of his shirt. He slammed him back against one of the poles holding the roof of the structure up and opened his mouth to demand an explanation.

Only for the words to die on his tongue.

Rin hadn't reacted to being tossed around, his arms still down at his sides, head resting back against the wooden beam, casually, as though it'd been his idea to stand there all along. His outfit didn't make sense either, the black ensemble suddenly processing in Kelevra's mind as a Vail University uniform and not the Academy's.

That wasn't the part that had stopped Kel in his tracks, however.

It was his eyes. Those same mismatched eyes were staring back at him and they were…empty. It wasn't like he didn't recognize him, because it was obvious he did, but there was no emotion behind the gaze, and most notably, a complete and total lack of anger.

Rin would be furious to be tossed around like this by anyone. Even if he tried to hide it his body temperature would be fluctuating and his heart rate would be going through the roof. But the guy currently in Kel's hold was calm, not just portraying a false sense of it.

He actually was.

Kelevra blinked. "You're not my flower."

The first sign of a crack on the other man's face came then, the corners of his full mouth drawing down ever so slightly in clear displeasure, but that was all he gave.

Before Kel could press him about it, something hard slammed into his side, forcing him to release the Rin imposter. He spun but his attacker was already moving, shoving himself between the two of them.

Rin. The real Rin.

In all his pissed-off glory.

"What the actual fuck do you think you're doing?" Rin growled, voice low despite the fact he'd already drawn attention their way by accosting the Imperial Prince in public.

Kelevra eased his hands into his pockets and glanced between the two of them, trying to find any other differences that would help tell them apart in the future. Aside from the emotion in their eyes, however, there was only the obvious. Their uniforms and the small golden earring the imposter was wearing.

The imposter, who was currently smirking behind Rin's shoulder at Kel smugly.

His eyes narrowed.

Rin shifted so he was standing more in front of the imposter.

"He's not you," Kelevra said, still undecided whether or not he should try to make a grab for the imposter and bash his face in for that look.

"Who's to say." The imposter's grinned wide, but he dropped the expression completely when Rin turned to send him a glare. "I was minding my business, I swear."

"Really?" Rin quirked a brow. "Is that why I showed up to find you about to—"

"I kept my manors," the imposter cut him off.

After another moment where the two stared at one another, almost as if they were having some freaky mental conversation, Rin let out a growl and then spun back on Kelevra. "What were you doing with my brother?"

"Twins." Kel couldn't stop looking at the two of them together. "You didn't mention that."

"There's a lot about me you don't know," Rin stated. "And it's not like you really gave me the time to share."

Kelevra licked his lips, taking an idle step closer. "I don't know, I think we shared a lot."

"Do bodily fluids count now?" the imposter leaned in and asked his brother, quiet enough no one else could overhear aside from them and Kel.

"No," Rin said.

"We got to know one another carnally," Kelevra corrected. "I think that matters."

"I *think* you shouldn't be here."

"I concur," a new voice, dark and deep, interrupted, and Kel groaned before turning to watch as Baikal walked up to them.

The man was every bit the cliché mafia prince one would envision, from his dark hair to the mysterious teal eyes. He was the same height as Kelevra, and just as broad, though he dressed in uniform and wore his school's pin like a good little princeling should.

Barf.

There was an intensity to Baikal, a sense he gave off warning people he wasn't to be messed with. He moved like a predator and even though he didn't need it to take a life, he carried a blaster on him no matter where he went.

"Lost, Imperial?" Kal came to a stop a few feet away from their group. He spared a glance toward Rin, but spent a second longer taking in the brother.

"You know him?" Kelevra asked, tipping his chin toward the imposter.

"Sila Varun," Baikal replied. "He's friends with Rabbit."

"Ah," he hummed in understanding, "your little bunny, was it?"

"Excuse you?" Rin asked, but he was glaring at Kel.

His brother, Sila, moved then, resting a hand on Rin's shoulder. He leaned in and whispered something, this time low enough that not even Kelevra could hear.

Rin sneered but nodded.

Sila stepped away, but the two remained quiet.

Kel didn't like it. He liked it even less than he'd liked the thought of the dark-haired freshman flirting with what was his. Didn't matter that they were identical twins. The fact that someone else on this planet had a connection with Rin made him livid, maybe even enough to—

"You cause trouble in my territory and we're going to have problems," Baikal said then, cutting into Kel's red haze.

Kelevra took a deep breath. "I'm just here to collect what's mine and then I'll be on my way."

An odd look passed over Rin's face, but he smoothed it out and it was gone in a flash.

"Does sex on this planet constitute as a claim?" Sila asked, his voice deadpan.

But when Kelevra looked at him, he was certain he could tell the other guy was messing with him. Or, maybe not him at all…

"No, it does not," Rin told his brother, lobbing yet another warning glare his way, almost as though he were afraid Sila had been serious.

Did he not like the idea of belonging to Kelevra that much?

They would have to remedy that.

Immediately.

Kelevra reached for Rin's arm, latching onto his wrist, but before he could pull him away, Sila moved, grabbing onto the sleeve of his suit jacket. Instincts told him to punch the guy, but the fact he looked identical to Rin had Kel hesitating.

Sila said something in another language then, something that must not be in the Interstellar Conferences database because Kelevra's translating device that was embedded behind his ear didn't pick up on it.

"No," Rin responded, choosing to stick to their language. He eased Sila's hand off of Kel's arm but didn't pull his wrist away. "No, I'll handle it."

"Are you sure?" Sila asked, though he stepped back, leaning against the beam once more. It was clear he was teasing when he added, "Shouldn't I play the part of big brother?"

"You should jump off this pathway, stick your face in the water, and not come back up," Rin told him tightly, then seeming to catch himself, sighed. "I'm fine. I can handle this."

Kelevra laughed, liking the way it felt when that furiously intense mismatched gaze met his once more. "For your sake, I hope you're right, Flower."

Because this interaction had just taught him something very important, settling that burning question he'd had earlier about what he planned on doing and why.

Just the notion that someone out here could even think they had the right to touch or talk to or flirt with

Rin Varun pissed Kelevra off so much that he thought he'd reach for Baikal's blaster and start shooting.

Kelevra Diar, the man who'd never been interested in even sleeping with the same person twice, was smitten.

Rin Varun was *his*.

Whether his flower agreed or not.

Chapter 7:

Don't panic.

He was a Varun, and Varun's didn't show weakness. Although, it helped that they also happened to be Tiberan and Tiberan's were trained on how to bury their emotions.

Training that had never fully taken with Rin.

Fuck.

He ran a hand through his hair as he led the Imperial Prince away from the East Quad and his brother. The two of them being in the same location was dangerous for everyone involved, so as much as Rin hated the idea of being alone with Kelevra again he needed to take the hit to keep them protected.

His and his brother's overall safety came before everything else. That was the agreement. The rule they'd lived by practically their entire lives. It was the reason his brother was currently busy dealing with a situation of his own—to ensure their security.

It was the whole damn reason they'd traveled all the way to this galaxy, and so far it'd been one mess after the other. Rin was tempted to speed up their plans, not sure waiting another three years until graduation was even doable at the rate they were going.

Mindlessly, he headed toward the library on the west side, a building that was close with a lot of side pathways that would keep him and the Imperial off of the more popularly used sidewalks during this time of day. They'd already drawn far too much notice in the quad, and as much as he wanted to go straight to the parking lot and demand Kelevra get in his fancy car and leave, he knew better.

The Imperial Prince wouldn't go until he'd had his say, so Rin would listen, and with any luck, they could come to an agreement afterward where the both of them went their separate ways.

The back entrance to the library required a code, and Rin typed it in quickly, feeling the buzzing sensation of Kelevra's intense gaze on the back of his neck like a livewire was poking him.

Tiberan's felt things ten times more strongly than most other species, but they'd developed strategies to combat this, mental wards taught and set in place when they were children that would help them filter through from one intense feeling to the next in a matter of seconds. They burned brightly but quickly, allowing them to remain stoic and present a strong sense of composure to the rest of the universe that had earned them a reputation for making good advisors and diplomats.

Level-headed people were the best for those sorts of high-pressure jobs.

Their father expected them to return home and for one of them to take over his position on the council, mistakenly believing his sons were the same as the rest of their population in this sense.

Rin almost laughed.

His father was a blind idiot. If he'd had even a modicum of interest in his children, he would have gathered that a long time ago. But Crate Varun only cared about his career. Even his sons had been born out of necessity because he'd needed heirs to take over his responsibilities when he passed—which probably wouldn't be for decades, the bastard.

He'd ruin their lives for something that wouldn't even take place for another forty or fifty years.

A spark of anger slipped through the fear hounding him, but the panic was stronger, banking it back down so the pounding in Rin's chest started making him uncomfortable. There was blood rushing to his ears as well, the instinctual need to flee gripping him, even as he ignored it and continued leading the Imperial Prince up a set of winding metal stairs to the top floor.

This section of the library held most of the older books, paper, and leather tomes that hadn't been scanned into the computer system for how ancient and obsolete they were. It was a space very rarely visited by other students, and sure enough when they reached the landing and he caught sight of the wide open space, there wasn't anyone else around.

The walls bore heavy, packed shelves that stretched from floor to ceiling, with wide windows set between every four. Three long wooden tables with warped places over their surfaces were set in rows in the center, slightly dusty.

Rin would prefer sticking close to the stairs, but if anyone noticed the Imperial had come up here, they'd draw unwanted attention and possible eavesdroppers. He ended up moving toward the nearest table, turning to perch on the edge, his arms crossed over his chest. The easy, enigmatic expression he was used to presenting—when he wasn't in a situation where he needed to smile like some overly happy loon—was somewhat harder to conjure given his nerves, but he managed.

Negative emotions always tended to last longer for him, things like anger, fear, and anxiety able to get a chokehold on him and cling. Half the time, it felt like he was possessed, like some demon had wriggled its way into his bloodstream and infected him. He hated it, hated that instead of being able to give in, he was required to fight against it and keep it bottled inside where no one else could see.

His brother knew who he was.

That had always been enough.

Until recently.

Yes, this planet had been a mistake.

"Looking a little too lax in front of your commanding officer," Kelevra spoke first, breaking the silence for the first time, as he did, he moved forward, dropping a hand on either side of Rin's hips before he could even think to shove him away.

"Move," he said, his voice coming out flat despite the way his heart leapt in his chest. Something felt wrong here, and while he couldn't quite put his finger on it, he was certain it wasn't just his emotions getting the best of him. He needed to be cautious. "Please."

"Are you uncomfortable with me so close?" Kelevra asked, gaze dropping down to linger on Rin's mouth.

He barely resisted the urge to lick his lips, keeping himself still. That was always the best course of action when face to face with a predator. So he'd keep still, hold his anger and his unease in, and get through this the same way he got through everything. By faking it.

"We're at Vail University," Rin replied calmly. "As representatives of the Academy, we can't do anything that could be considered unfavorable." He swallowed and then managed, "Why are you here? Did you come for Baikal?"

Kelevra's eyes narrowed. "Are you two acquainted? I didn't think you were, but then he obviously knows your brother, a man I didn't even know existed."

"That sounds accusatory," Rin pointed out. He really wished the Imperial would step back and give him some breathing room. The warm and slightly sweet scent to his perfume was starting to wrap around him, almost like a coaxing lover, and Rin decided he didn't like it.

It smelled fucking fantastic, that's why.

"You should have told me," Kelevra said.

"I didn't have the chance if you recall."

"Oh," he grinned suddenly, "I do."

"Move," Rin repeated.

"I've decided against it."

He caught himself just before a frown could furrow his brow. "Didn't you mention before you hate wasting time?"

"This doesn't count," Kelevra told him. "I'm here with you. Time with you is never wasted."

That... Sounded dangerous.

Kel tipped his head. "That scares you."

Yes. "No. I'm just curious why you'd say something like that. We're relative strangers."

"I've been inside of you."

"You forced yourself inside of me," Rin corrected, swallowing the bile that threatened to rise and leak all over his resolve. He wouldn't crack. Not in front of this man. Not again. Seeing his brother had reminded him of what was important. Of what was at stake.

"Is it considered wrong that I enjoyed that part of it?" Kelevra asked then, and for a split second it was almost as though Rin were talking with his brother instead. The seriousness on his face gave away he wasn't just asking to be snarky or mean. He legitimately wanted to know.

And that was the other reminder he needed.

Kelevra was a sociopath. Like Rin's brother, he'd struggle to grasp common social concepts. Still, as the Imperial Prince, surely he'd been taught how to handle his own urges and blend with society...

Wait. Actually. He most likely wouldn't have been. If everything Rin had heard about the guy was correct, Kelevra was coddled by his siblings, just as he had been by his parents.

His brother's problem was he had to keep his true self hidden from their father.

Kelevra's issue was the opposite. He'd been allowed to exist unchecked, and the results were a devil running rampant in the streets.

Would that happen with his brother if their plan was fruitful and they managed to escape?

"Consent is an important factor in any relationship," Rin said, trying not to think about his brother or what might one day come to pass. "It shows respect."

"There are other ways to show respect."

"No," he stated. "There aren't."

Kelevra hummed thoughtfully. "Are you saying you didn't like it?"

"It was the drug." Not a full lie.

"Ah," he didn't sound convinced, "so, you're telling me if I threw you down and mounted you right here and now, you wouldn't be turned on by my show of dominance?"

Considering there was no door and the stairwell was right there where anyone could walk up and see? "No."

Some of Kelevra's good mood noticeably vanished. "You're telling the truth."

Rin felt his spine stiffen.

"That's not going to work for me." Suddenly, Kel spun Rin around, slamming his front down over the table.

He captured his wrists and tied something around them, securing them together at Rin's narrow back.

Rin coughed as a cloud of dust from the surface gusted up into his face, then growled and tried to kick back at the large body pinning him. He managed to land a kick to Kelevra's shin, but then his legs were forced apart, spread wide enough to accommodate the other man between them. A hand settled on his hip and then Kelevra humped against his ass, causing him to immediately freeze when he felt the hard bulge behind his pants.

"Relax," Kelevra drawled, slowly dragging his confined cock back and forth over Rin. "I'm testing a theory. Believe it or not, I'm attempting something out of character, trying to see the bigger picture before I make an irrational decision based solely on my dick."

"I am not having sex with you again," Rin said firmly. "Ever."

"As I've just proven, I can easily overpower you, Flower. You aren't used to that, are you? I bet you're typically the one with the most physical strength in your relationships. Maybe that's why you get so hard for me when I take control like this."

"I do not!" some of that fear and anger slipped through his tone and Rin internally cursed at himself.

"That so?" Kelevra shifted, and in the next instant his hand was slapping against Rin's junk, squeezing him hard enough to have him hissing. "What do you call this then? Pretty sure it's a boner."

"I hate you!" Rin pressed his forehead against the solid wood and focused on his breathing, desperate to get his body to cooperate and calm down before he gave more away.

It wasn't even that he liked the Imperial Prince—he didn't. He was deplorable, arrogant, and neurotic. But he was pretty, and big, and last night Rin had experienced the best orgasms he'd ever had in his entire life.

Because of the drug.

He refused to believe it had anything real to do with the man currently feeling him up against his will. He wasn't into being manhandled, and he'd never had a rape fantasy in his life. Hell, kinky sex, aside from the occasional mild domination, was more his brother's style than his.

That was probably why the handcuff last night had done it for him. Because it'd been the first time he'd tried it out, and the drug had him so revved up and ready he'd come with enough force it was a wonder his head hadn't exploded between his shoulders.

Kelevra had gone quiet after Rin's outburst, but he didn't move away. When he finally spoke again, his voice was deep and threaded with warning. The kind of tone Rin imagined he used for official princely business—whatever the hell that entailed.

"That isn't going to work for me either," he stated darkly. Grabbing a fistful of Rin's hair, he yanked him up, his other arm wrapping around his waist to keep him close as he gnashed his teeth close to Rin's right ear. "That comment actually pissed me off. Go figure. Usually, I couldn't care less how people feel about me. Lucky you."

"Let go," Rin struggled to free himself but with his hands bound behind him still, there wasn't much he could do. He sucked in a breath when Kelevra resituated them so that his hard-on was pressed against Rin's palms.

It was tempting to handle him the same way he'd just handled Rin, but he refrained, survival instincts saving him from what would definitely be a mistake.

Kelevra was dangerous when he was calm.

But when he was angry?

Rin shivered, and the sick bastard must have liked that because his growl turned into a groan.

He lapped underneath Rin's jaw, licking at him like he was some kind of ice cream cone. Ignoring the way that had him squirming. His fingers merely tightened and he tugged, forcing Rin's head to the side to expose his neck better to his teeth and his tongue.

"You taste good," Kelevra murmured. "Did you know that?"

"Of course not." None of his past lovers were insane. He'd always been careful with who he interacted with. His sexual partners were all people who knew not to get attached and were just looking for a fun time. They didn't get too close, and most importantly, they didn't even want to.

He'd assumed Kelevra would be like that, having gotten what he wanted. This, what was happening right now, made no sense to Rin no matter which way he spun it.

"If this is a control thing," he tried to reason with him since it was clear he couldn't force the other guy to stop, "there are plenty of people on campus who are into that. I could help you find someone even, set you up. One of my friends is pretty into bondage."

His roommate, Daylen, would be open to rolling around in the sheets with the Imperial Prince too.

"Not interested." Kelevra trailed a little lower, his tongue tracing the spot where his neck met his shoulder.

"That's what I'm saying." Rin didn't like the way all that attention was making his dick ache. "I'm not interested. I don't want this or you, Imperial Prince, so if you could just back up—"

"What if I fail you, cadet?" Kelevra's arm loosened, his hips pressing forward to keep Rin's thighs pinned to the table. His hand started to trace circles over his stomach, the thin black material of the t-shirt Rin was wearing not providing much of a barrier.

Right. If he failed his father would have a conniption and both he and his brother would have to deal with the aftermath. They'd been able to talk Crate out of ordering them home before, but that would only work so many times, and as it was only the start of their second year, playing that card too early would be foolish.

But then Kelevra rocked against him, that hot and heavy cock massive against Rin's trapped palms, and all thought of keeping his father happy went out the window.

Screw that guy. He wasn't the one currently being humped like a damn dog.

"Do it," Rin stated resolutely, Kel's lips freezing over his pulse point, "Fail me. Anything would be better than this." Another lie. But not by much. If circumstances were different, if Kelevra was anyone other than the Imperial Prince, Rin might have given into this twisted attraction and gone for it. On Tibera, sex wasn't frowned upon, and there weren't any kinks or fetishes that weren't considered socially acceptable either.

Rin had never been embarrassed that he liked to be controlled in the bedroom, he simply hadn't been capable of finding a good enough bed partner to satisfy his needs before. But last night...It was almost disappointing, really, that he had to end things with Kelevra when there was a lot left to be desired.

The man's temper notwithstanding.

"Not good enough?" Kelevra didn't seem deterred. His hand dropped away for a split second as he grabbed something from his front pocket, and then he brought it up in front of Rin's face. The tiny white pill glittered in the sunlight pouring in from the nearest window. "What about this then? Is this threat more *motivational*?"

Rin's eyes went wide and he tried to shake his head and pull away, only to be forced forward an inch closer to the pill.

Last night, Rin had three orgasms, and even then exhaustion was the only reason he hadn't begged for more. The drug was far too potent, and he knew without a shadow of a doubt if he was forced to take it again he wouldn't be able to resist its pull for nearly as long as he'd somehow managed in Kelevra's room.

Hell, half the reason he'd asked to be tied up was to keep himself from giving away just how badly arousal was eating at him. He hadn't wanted to jump the Imperial Prince, wanted to be able to walk away in the morning with his head held high.

"Did you know," Kelevra said, his voice dripping with mal intent, giving away that even though he had the upper hand, he was still pissed at Rin, "on some planets, there are species called alphas and omegas? They experience things like heats and ruts, like animals almost." He stared at the pill, rolling it between his forefinger and thumb. "Isn't that kind of hot?"

Rin shook his head but didn't dare speak, keeping his mouth firmly shut seemed like the smartest thing he could do right now.

"I asked Kal earlier. He didn't know anything about this drug, but apparently whichever Brumal concocted it was trying to imitate an omega heat. It's too bad they hadn't also come up with a way for it to replicate an omega's slick, don't you think?"

Another shake of his head in the negative. Rin knew enough about omegas to catch Kelevra's meaning though. Apparently, they entered a heat when their bodies were ready for breeding. They'd exude an attractive scent to lure alphas, and their sexual organs produced something called slick to lubricate their passages.

"I'm not some bitch in heat," Rin growled, internally wincing afterward when the hand in his hair yanked again, smarting his scalp.

"Let's show a little more respect, shall we?" Kelevra suggested. "That's an entire species you're insulting. Besides, the second I slip this past your lips, be real, you'll be no better than one. Want to make bets? I'm thinking you'll beg me for it this time. Maybe even get down on your knees for me, like a good little subject should. How does that sound, Flower? Want to worship my cock like it's your emperor?" He let out a groan. "I like that idea actually. Like the thought of you submitting."

"This is wrong," Rin whispered, unable to keep the fear from entering his voice now. Keeping his composure hadn't exactly helped him in this situation anyway.

"I'm thinking," Kel nuzzled under his jaw, "if I drug you enough times, eventually you'll change that tune of yours all on your own and spread for me without needing it. Don't you agree?"

"Why?" Rin leaned back when that pill was brought closer, though Kelevra didn't try and put it in his mouth. Yet. The danger was very real. He could sense it. This wasn't a bad joke. Kel fully intended to follow through with his threats. "Why me? I haven't done anything to you." Up until the other day, the two of them hadn't even known one another.

"Honestly?" Kelevra said. "I'm just as surprised as you are. I thought for sure I'd fuck you and move on. Maybe it was because I woke up and you were gone? I didn't like that. I should have. It's always better when they've left the morning after and I don't have to bother trying to remember their names. But with you…It felt like an insult. Felt a lot like you were trying to run away and put distance between us." He pressed an open mouth kiss to his jugular. "I'd rather keep you close, Flower. Isn't that interesting?"

"No." It was terrifying. How had he gotten here? How had things escalated so quickly?

Rin had been mistaken in thinking he could handle someone like Kelevra simply because he was similar to his brother. His brother was a psychopath, not a sociopath. He played the long game, could keep a rouse going for years even. He didn't act impulsively the same way Kel did, even when he wasn't hiding and was giving into his true nature.

Kelevra sighed as though Rin's response was disappointing. "You're afraid. Are you used to fear?"

Yes. "No. Do me a favor and stop making me feel this way." It was too open and raw, but Rin needed to say it. Not that he had high hopes it would make a difference. Kelevra wouldn't care that this wasn't something he wanted.

He only cared about himself.

Sure enough, the Imperial Prince tipped Rin's head back and brought the pill closer. "You'll feel better in a moment. I was told the effects happen much quicker on the second dose."

Rin was in the process of struggling the best he could when the sound of approaching footsteps caught both of their attention. A couple of female voices soon followed, their whispers low and quiet due to the fact they were in the library, making it harder to correctly gauge just how far they were from reaching the top and seeing—

"Please," Rin pleaded, he couldn't see the stairs, his body turned away from them, but he tried turning his head in that direction as much as possible, the panic growing tenfold. "Please, don't."

If they saw this word would spread. And if word got around, people would take notice. Not just of him, but of his identical brother. There'd be nowhere left for them to hide, and eventually, with all of that attention, someone would catch one of them slipping, would see something they shouldn't.

"Please," Rin turned back, barely processing when Kelevra's hand loosened its grip on his hair to allow him, locking eyes with him. "They're coming."

Kelevra searched his face for a moment, and little by little, something like understanding morphed his expression from one of determination to something else.

Possibly something even darker.

The Imperial Prince seemed…gratified.

He released Rin, shoving him away with enough force to send him stumbling back several steps.

Rin found his footing just as two girls dressed in dark gray—the shade for juniors at the university—arrived. He turned, keeping his bound hands out of view and offered them a polite smile that had them giggling and rushing off to the back.

They went straight to one of the stacks, but did nothing to hide the fact they were stealing glances at both him and Kelevra.

Great. This was going to be talked about anyway. Though, at least all that would be said was the Imperial

Prince had been spotted on campus. They most likely wouldn't mention him in any capacity other than calling him a hot Academy cadet.

The relief that washed over him was enough to have his shoulders slumping, but he stiffened all over again when Kel took a step closer and leaned in, his hot breath blowing against his cheek as he delivered one last warning.

"Come back to the Academy. If I've found you've lingered here flirting it up, there will be repercussions, cadet." He pulled back and stared at Rin for a moment, seemingly searching for something. "You should have told me you were worried about a possible scandal. That can easily be fixed." He pocketed the pill and then winked.

Rin opened his mouth to tell him that wasn't it at all—even though that had been part of the problem—but then he realized his wrists were still bound.

Kelevra, the absolute prick, left him standing there without so much as a backward glance.

And no way to undo the binding.

Chapter 8:

Ever since he was six, Kelevra had been obsessed with blood. There was something about it that excited him, that instantly had anticipation brewing and thumping at his ribcage.

A few days after the incident in the library, he found himself at Friction, slipping out of his buttery yellow suit jacket, reaching back to leisurely undo the strings holding his corset in place. He'd gone without a shirt, and while it'd make sense to take a moment to head into the changing rooms and slip into sweatpants, that buzzing sensation spurring him toward violence wouldn't allow even that much hesitation.

Zane was already waiting for him in the ring, eyeing him as Kel provided a striptease of sorts, racking up the tension. The rest of the Retinue stood around the center ring and at the bar, along with a couple of Brumal members.

Typically, if he was in here fighting, Kelevra chose Kazimir, Baikal's cousin, or Madden. The first, because he didn't care if he "accidentally" took things too far, and the second because Madden could get crafty in the ring, and that kept things interesting. Zane was a good third option, however, and since he was the only one of the three currently there, Kel had settled.

The upside to Zane was he allowed more than simple fists. Already, he was tossing a star crystal knife in the air. The blade was double-edged, shaped like a long raindrop with a fine tip and a handle carved out of crystal as clear as glass. The material was native to Vitality, and used to make many different items due to how tough it was. This particular blade had been a gift from Kel two years ago and had come in a set.

The other one was currently resting on the edge of the ring closest to Kelevra, and once he was in nothing but his pants, he snatched it up and slipped beneath the rope.

Friction was located on the grounds of Club Vigor, and though he didn't often allow himself to partake, his doing so wasn't exactly out of the norm. Considering the week he'd had, and the piss poor mood he'd been in and hadn't bothered trying to hide, no one had seemed surprised when he'd stormed in fifteen minutes ago and demanded a match.

Zane was almost as tall as him, with hair the color of freshly tilled dirt and eyes so dark brown they were practically black. He had a thick scar just beneath the left underside of his jaw, but otherwise was unmarked, his face angelic upon first glance. He'd chosen Vail University over the Academy, and was considered one of the campus princes—the Prince of Medicine or something like that, Kel could never get it right.

The two of them were the same age, exactly one month apart, and Zane had moved in with him and his sister Lyra years ago. He had a dorm room on Vail campus, but otherwise still stayed at the Little Palace whenever there was a longer school break. He'd been offered an apartment somewhere of his choosing but had refused time and time again until Kelevra had stopped offering.

Kelevra had never asked, and Zane had never said as much himself, but he got the feeling that his friend had a crush on his sister. The age gap between them wasn't terrible, and Kel personally wouldn't give a shit if the two chose to date, but as far as he knew, his sister had never returned Zane's interest.

If Zane had been born as the Imperial Prince instead of merely the Prince of Medicine, he could make Lyra his whether she returned his affections or not, but alas.

"You were at the Little Palace for a long time the other day," Zane said as Kelevra got ready. "Anything important?"

He snorted. "Do you mean is there anything you should be made aware of? No. If there was, I would have told you already, wouldn't I have?"

"Don't know. Would you have? Madden mentioned something about a cadet you—"

Kelevra always tried to keep to the rules of the ring when he was here, mostly because the people he fought against were friends—or the cousin of a friend—

but at the mention of Rin all of those restrictions faded to the background in a blink.

He shot forward, arm extending with the knife aimed right for Zane's heart. It was easily blocked, and he twisted and spun to the right to evade Zane's return attack. Having trained together for years, the two of them understood each other's moves better than most, putting them on a more even playing field despite Kel's extra muscle mass and higher skill level.

Zane was the attentive sort, the type who got someone water before they could ask, or purchased extra tickets to a popular event in case any last-minute additions wished to join them. That also made him keen in other ways, always catching the little things others thought no one noticed. As a senior, he was close to graduating with his degree and was already set to continue his training at High Tower Hospital, the largest hospital in the city. Eventually, when the time came for the Diar family doctor to retire, he would take over the position.

Everything and everyone in Kelevra's life had a place and a purpose.

His flower would learn that lesson soon, even if it had to be done the hard way.

Kel had never cared what others thought of him, so it was a concept he struggled a bit more to grasp than some others. But he'd recognized the hint of fear that had come over Rin in the library. He'd been annoyed when Kelevra had threatened him with the pill, but not afraid.

The second they'd heard footsteps on the stairs, however, that had changed.

He may have been offended if he hadn't already known Rin preferred staying out of the limelight, and therefore his reaction most likely had nothing to do with being seen with Kelevra personally. Getting caught being publicly indisposed was a big deal, and even though they were Academy cadets and not students of Vail, there would have been repercussions if they'd been caught and tattled on.

Considering how phenomenal Kelevra looked naked, there was no way those girls wouldn't have immediately told everyone and anything who would listen what they'd witnessed.

And his flower…

A low rumble traveled up the back of his throat as he pictured Rin splayed out on his bed, lying on his stomach, his thighs spread wide to accommodate Kelevra kneeling between them. He had the perfect body, slim waist, toned back, those muscles bunching as he'd wrapped them around the pillow and buried his face to muffle his scream as he'd come for the third time. His tight hole gripping around Kel's cock like it wanted to break it off and keep it as a memento…

Zane's knife glinted in the harsh overhead lights as he swung it in an arch toward Kelevra's side.

He blocked and then kneed Zane in the gut, slashing at his arm to draw blood.

Zane hissed and shot back out of range, twisting his arm to check the damage. A thin line of red was welling, a bead rolling down his arm. It wasn't deep, and with the man's quickened healing, would most likely be gone by nightfall.

Kelevra watched that single drop and licked his lips, eager for more.

"Just not the face," Zane felt the need to remind, but Kel was already shooting forward a second time.

He feinted left then dropped, slicing across Zane's right upper thigh. He came up behind him, latching onto his throat with one hand to pull him into an upright position, the blade then placed beneath his chin.

"Check yourself," Zane said a second later, and when Kel glanced down, he saw Zane's blade turned and pressed against his side.

He chuckled and released him, shoving him a couple of feet away before backing up to lean against the thick ropes surrounding the ring.

"Feel any better?" his friend asked, dabbing at the blood trickling from his thigh, seeping into the dark material of his pants. He scowled at it. "This is the fourth one you've ruined, by the way. I'm going to start charging you for my clothes."

Kel waved his hand. "I'll have some new ones delivered tomorrow."

"I was joking."

"I wasn't." He may be self-absorbed, but he took care of his things, and besides, it wasn't like he'd miss the couple hundred coin it would take to restock Zane's wardrobe.

If someone asked how he felt about the other man, Kel would say it was above indifference. He cared for him to the extent he was capable of and enjoyed their time together. Zane was witty and intelligent, so talks with him were always fruitful, and there was a quiet intensity to him that he only did away with when he was in a crowd and allowing himself to let loose.

They'd known each other for years, and he was loyal, a perfect member of Kelevra's Retinue.

But if it came down between the two of them, Kel would save himself each and every time. He'd make sure they were well fed and had above what their basic needs required, but at the end of the day, none of that was a sacrifice for him. It didn't take work or effort to maintain these friendships. Even getting a new wardrobe wouldn't take more than a single phone call and a couple of instructions spoken to whoever picked up and was listening on the other end.

Kelevra wasn't blind. He understood he was spoiled rotten, and that was the exact reason he'd opted to stay away from his flower for so long after the incident in the library. It'd been days already. He'd wanted to see if the allure would wear off with time and distance. If perhaps he was overthinking this need swirling in his gut. He'd known what Rin was thinking that night at the penthouse. He'd expected to give in and fuck Kel and then for the two of them to go their own ways, never to speak again.

Honestly, Kel had anticipated the same. But the next day when he'd woken to find Rin gone, that side of the bed cold to the touch…something in him had snapped. It'd felt…wrong. Like something vital was missing. He'd even wandered aimlessly throughout the house, even knowing he wasn't going to find Rin snooping in any of the rooms. It'd been strange and out of character.

Anything that could shake up his otherwise mundane existence was worth further exploration, which was why he'd gotten dressed and gone after the cadet. He'd slipped the pill into his pocket as an afterthought, not actually thinking he was going to use it or even bring it up. But then he'd mistaken the imposter for his flower, and the lingering jealousy over believing Rin had been caught flirting with someone else had eaten away at him.

He'd propositioned Rin in the library in the hopes fucking him again would accomplish what having him the once clearly hadn't. But they'd been interrupted, and now even with more time between them, nothing had changed. Kelevra craved him the same way he craved a new three-piece suit when he saw one.

If he had his way, he'd climb inside of Rin and keep him forever. He'd realized that if he had to buy, barter, or beg to have him, he would do so.

Rin Varun was going to be his. No matter what he had to do, or how low he had to get to make that so. Some things were worth putting in the extra effort, and even though Kelevra had never personally needed to go that far, he'd found that only added to the excitement of it.

All his life he'd lacked one thing and one thing only. Purpose.

Perhaps cultivating a particular flower could be his.

His sisters had sent him away this morning without an answer, but he knew what they were going to say, even if they wanted to drag things out and make him wait for it.

They'd give him what he'd asked for. They always did, just like everyone else.

Just like Rin was going to.

"What do you think about sacrifice?" Kelevra asked absently, inspecting the stain of blood on the edge of his knife.

Zane grunted. "I think you don't know anything about it."

He hummed. "Up until a couple of hours ago, I would have agreed with you."

His friend and future doctor frowned. "What are you trying to tell me? Does this have to do with why you were at the Little Palace?"

"I was asking for a present."

The stiffness that'd come over him eased at that, and Zane laughed. "That means you'll be getting something," he pointed out. "Sacrifice is about giving, Kel. You've got things backward."

"Even if I'm only getting something by giving something in return?" he asked. Could he call what he'd asked of his sisters a partial sacrifice on his part? The choice had come from him and would mean giving up any future chances at making it differently. Didn't that count?

"What did you give?"

"You'll find out soon enough." Technically, Kelevra didn't even have a set answer yet. The last thing he was going to do was talk about it with his friends before the official announcement from his sisters arrived. He wouldn't risk word getting back to them before and them taking it as a sign he was too cocky and denying him in the end after all out of spite. Sometimes they did things like that to "teach him a lesson". It never worked, and eventually, he ended up with what he'd wanted anyway, but that could be after some time and he found he wasn't willing to wait any longer than he already had.

His bed, which he used to love, was now far too cold on one side for his liking. He wanted that remedied. Immediately. He'd even considered fucking someone else, had gone to Fornication, the club, in search of a potential bedmate, only to leave empty-handed.

No one had been appealing. None of them could even hold a candle to his flower.

Kelevra Diar was an Imperial Prince. He demanded only the best, and Rin Varun was it.

"Tag me in," a new, gruff voice said from the side a second before a large man with inky hair jumped into the ring. Kazimir grinned challengingly at Kelevra before making his way to Zane to share a fist bump.

The two shared a weird love-hate relationship wherein no one else could know what stage they were currently in at any given moment. Considering the way

Zane nodded at him and allowed him to stand so close, they were obviously in one of their love stages.

Kel rolled his eyes and motioned between the two of them. "Let's see what you've got."

"Two against one?" Kazimir whistled. "Someone's feeling cocky today."

"I've got a lot of pent-up energy." Energy he'd much rather be expending burying himself in Rin's tight heat, but since that was out… "Giving the two of you matching friendship scars should do the trick."

Zane didn't seem to like that idea, but Kaz, ever the asshole, simply barked out a harsh laugh.

"Bring it on," Kazimir stated, yanking a thick blade from a sheath attached to his narrow back.

Kelevra grinned and charged forward.

By the end of the fight, he was bleeding from several small cuts, but it was nothing compared to the large gashes he'd delivered to the backs of Kazimir's and Zane's right shoulders, deep enough they'd leave a mark for a long time to come.

Matching scars for the sometimes besties, just as he'd promised.

Kel always got what he wanted.

Chapter 9:

The gymnasium was sweltering, the heat causing all of their shirts to stick to their bodies uncomfortably. Everywhere Rin glanced, another cadet was trying to discreetly peel the cotton material away from their backs and sides, fanning themselves with their hands as they waited for the Active to arrive.

His gaze accidentally landed on an intense hazel one and he turned away quickly, trying to tell himself he imagined the light chuckle coming from that direction afterward. There was too much distance between them right now for him to have heard any sounds the Imperial Prince might have made.

It'd been five days since the encounter at the library and just when Rin had started to think that maybe he was out of the woods and Kelevra had gotten bored after all, their two classes had been summoned together. In his constant state of anxiousness—thanks to said prince—Rin had completely forgotten about the group assignment.

Every year the senior classes were paired with sophomores to act as mentors. Both were graded, and to help break the ice an assignment in the form of a case was typically given for them to solve. It was a competition, something that would ensure the seniors did their job and interacted with their sophomores, and that the sophomores weren't left scrambling trailing after them begging for attention like lost puppies.

No matter what it ended up being, this assignment had already put a damper on Rin's plans to avoid the Imperial Prince at all costs. He'd been doing so well, too, extra careful what areas he traveled to on campus, avoiding the main cafeteria in favor of pre-prepared meals bought at the convenience store just down the road. Living under the radar was nothing new to him, and he'd slipped back into that mindset easily enough that it hadn't taken all that much out of him to bother.

And if he'd spent the nights waking in a cold sweat, rock hard, with the lingering memories of deft fingers circling his cock as a rich voice laughed in his ear? Well screw Kel, those could have been dreams about anyone since Rin never saw his dream lover's face.

Maybe he should give Arlet a call and see if anything could come of that after all. She didn't attend the Academy and the two had met through mutual friends at a bar a couple of months ago, but she seemed sweet. Fun. Rin wasn't looking for anything permanent, but maybe the two of them could have a good time.

Before he could change his mind, he lifted his emblem multi-slate and scrolled through his contacts, sending her a quick message just as Active Banks stepped in from the adjoining office.

Everyone quieted around Rin and straightened, both classes taking position with their wrists crossed and settled behind their backs.

He clenched his jaw when it reminded him of how he'd been abandoned in the library, left tied up with no means of freeing himself. He'd had to wait a full twenty minutes for those girls to finally leave so he could take a proper look around for anything that could have been useful. Eventually, he'd found a jagged edge of one of the bookshelves—the thing must have been damaged for a while, since it was definitely sharp enough to constitute a safety hazard.

By the time he'd made it out the door, the sun had already begun to set and he'd half expected Kelevra to be in the parking lot waiting for him with a stopwatch and mocking shake of his head.

Fortunately, that hadn't been the case. Even better, the following days had been peaceful with no hint of the Imperial Prince in sight.

They hadn't been instructed to line up based on age, so seniors and sophomores were mingled into the three tidy rows of eight, with Kel all the way down the line and in the far back from Rin.

Since he hadn't approached him, he could take that as a positive sign, right?

Maybe he really had gotten over it, and if Rin felt a little disappointed by that notion? It was only because the dick had been good.

"Good afternoon, cadets," Banks addressed them and Rin put all those chaotic musings on the backburner.

He waited for them to repeat the greeting and then got straight to the point. "As I'm sure you're all aware, the group case assignment is an important part of this program. Those of you who are able to solve it will be allowed to choose your focus for next semester. Getting ahead like this will help you decide where you hope to be placed before junior year starts."

Everyone had to choose a major of sorts their junior year at the Academy. There were four options, detective, inspector, coast, and guide.

Detectives headed teams of two to four in the field. They took on cases and were given a spaceship and ID badges that allowed them to move about their designated galaxy freely. Sometimes they even got assigned to things in other parts of the universe. Their main training focus was learning how to think with a critical eye, how to defend themselves, and minor interrogation, as well as other things.

Inspectors were the second in command in any given unit. They answered to the detective in charge of their team but weren't technically governed by then. Their jobs were to help solve cases, but also to ensure the team stayed within the legal parameters of whatever planet or world ship their case took place on. Since every planet had its own set of laws, this was an important position and required tons of study.

Coasts consisted of other members of the team, those who hadn't placed high enough to be considered for detective or inspector roles. They could earn the title by climbing the ranks and doing a good job helping with their assigned teams, though many chose to remain in this position their whole lives.

Guides were a fairly broad category, including everything from Actives to diplomats. When a person was officially signed with the Intergalactic Police Force—better known as the I.P.F—they cut citizenship ties with their home planet. Unless they were a guide.

Crate Varun had ordered the brothers before the start that they were to go for a guide position. His grand plan was to have his youngest son graduate from the Academy and return home to act as a diplomat between Tibera and neighboring planets in the name of the Interstellar Conference. Up until now, they'd done a good job of staying in the middle ground in order to ensure this was where they ended up.

But that wouldn't last.

Rin couldn't draw attention to himself, sure, but he also didn't want to be stuck on his home planet, letting his father pull his strings for the rest of his life. That wasn't in his plan or his brothers. All he had to do was make it to junior year, and then he could start really working toward his goal, and to ensure he wasn't automatically placed in the guide training program he needed to get a high enough score on this assignment to be able to choose himself.

Which meant he couldn't let Kelevra fuck things up for him by throwing the competition—because it was a competition.

"The first five groups to solve the case will be allowed to choose their major from any of the four branches," Banks said then, almost as in confirmation to Rin's thoughts. "The next three will be able to choose from the two lower branches, coast or guide. If the rest of your grades throughout the year are high enough to get you automatically placed in detective or inspector, this assignment won't affect that. However, for those of you worried about your futures, I suggest you take this seriously and treat it like a real case with real stakes."

Banks hit a button on the tablet he was holding and a second later all of their emblem-slates dinged with an incoming message alert. "I've sent each of you the same packet of information. No one here has a leg up on anyone else, so I don't want to hear any whining later if you don't place high enough to have earned the choice of placement."

None of them checked their devices, knowing better than to do so until given the go-ahead.

"This year's case is loosely based on a real one that took place in another galaxy. A serial murder investigation. Your job is to find the killer. Once you're certain you've solved it, you can come find me and explain your reasoning. If you're correct, you pass. If you're incorrect, you fail. No second chances, you got that? In the real world, you peg a crime on the wrong guy and you've just destroyed an innocent life."

Calder raised his hand, and Banks nodded his chin at him to speak. "So, it's basically like a board game? We just sort through the information in the file you sent, figure out who did it, and then give you our answer?"

"There will be active fieldwork involved," Banks corrected, eyes narrowing slightly at the usage of the word game, though he didn't call him out on it. "Locations have been set up all over the city, made to look like kill sights. Though they've been inspected already, and information on all of the finds at each kill have been given to you, a good I.P.F agent does his due diligence."

Great, meaning they were expected to wander all over the place with their partner. Rin internally cringed thinking about having to spend any kind of one on one time with Kelevra.

It seemed like the universe was out to get him, though. He couldn't afford to be failed, and he needed to place high enough in this assignment to be able to choose inspector. A lot was riding on solving this case, and not just for Rin.

"And for the seniors?" Madden asked, not bothering to lift a hand and wait to be called on, another thing that had a vein in Bank's temple twitching. "We don't get an extra incentive?"

"Since you're already familiar with the way this goes having been through it yourselves when you were sophomores," Banks replied, "your incentive is to aid your partner. You are their superior, and a good superior takes care of their team." He rolled his eyes like he already knew none of them cared about that. "You'll also be exempt from the final exam."

A couple of the seniors—those standing with Kelevra—let out a hoot, but everyone else kept their respectable pose and their mouths shut.

Pricks.

Rin's anger had subsided over the past few days, but that still didn't mean he was over being tossed around and played by the Imperial Prince. He wasn't a toy to be used and discarded at his majesty's whim, no matter how happy Rin was at finally having been left alone.

"This year we're adding an extra layer to the case," Banks announced. "Throughout the semester, the killer will be conducting more 'murders'. These staged crime scenes will take place at random and you'll receive a notification the same way you would if you were official I.P.F agents. Your job will be to look for clues at these specific scenes. And for those of you who are wondering why bother doing all that extra leg work," he sent a pointed glance to Madden, but knew better than to outwardly scold him, "the team that catches the killer on-site—if a team can—will be awarded. For sophomores, this will include a free year of tuition covered by the Academy, including room and board. For seniors, your apartment will be paid for, in full, on Percy."

That was a big deal. They were basically saying they'd buy them a place outright. Percy was the man-made planet where I.P.F agents lived between cases, since they generally had to sever ties with their home world. Aside from being a planet created specifically for those in this field, it still operated the same as any other, with bills and grocery runs and the like.

"That's insane," Brennon risked tilting his head in Rin's direction to whisper. "That's worth like five times the amount of a year of tuition here."

Someone must have thought the seniors this year wouldn't give the case their all without something bright and shiny dangling over their heads on a stick.

Rin couldn't blame them.

The only problem was, whoever had picked this prize hadn't taken the members of class A-12 into account. Madden was a Royal and Kelevra was the Imperial Prince. They could buy a planet on their own dime, let alone an apartment. And not just, everyone here knew Kelevra had no intentions of becoming either a detective or an inspector. His home was Vitality, and that's where he'd be staying, nice and cushy in his penthouse tower. Madden, as his second, would be doing the same.

This wasn't going to make either of them want to help their sophomores win, and a quick glance in their direction proved as much.

Madden was staring at his cuticles, clearly bored, and Kel—

Rin sucked in a breath and looked away. The bastard had been watching him. Again.

"There's an actual killer?" another cadet, Rose, asked.

Banks nodded. "The murderer was selected and told in secret at the beginning of the semester. They've been given a separate information packet with all of the locations and things they need to do and had a few extra weeks to go over it. Their assignment is to keep their identity hidden and not get caught. The case needs to be solved, of course, and we've ensured that it's doable, if you're smart. So there won't be any repercussions for the murderer when it is. However, if one of you happens to physically catch him on one of the crime scenes...this cadet fails the assignment."

"It's one of us?" Brennon turned to look over his shoulder. "And they'll be flunked? That doesn't seem fair."

"You're overestimating yourself, cadet," Banks stated wryly. "This student was chosen specifically for their ability to blend. Here are the rules, before any of you get any bright ideas. The murderer is not allowed to tell anyone who they are. Period. Doing so will result in immediate failure and a demerit. If your team is able to solve the case and report a name, you are forbidden from sharing this with any of your class, unless you worked together from the start. Doing so will result in the same punishment. We take this very seriously. It's an important part of your training and you will respect the process or I will ensure you are swiftly, and sufficiently, punished, is that understood?"

"Yes, sir," they all agreed.

"You may begin. Remember this can last for the entire semester, but only those teams who place within the top eight will receive benefits." Banks headed straight for his office, as though he couldn't wait to get the hell away from them. He slammed the door behind him for good measure, and as soon as he did, the tension in the room burst like a flimsy bubble.

"Yikes," Brennon turned to Rin. "I'd hate to be the murderer."

"Banks is right," Calder rolled his eyes, "You don't stand a chance of catching him."

"I might!"

"You won't," Rin joined in with a laugh, sticking his tongue out when that earned him a glare. He chuckled and was in the process of opening the file on his device when a familiar shadow settled over him and he tensed a second before a heavy arm dropped across his shoulders.

Kelevra smiled at his friend's shocked expressions, tucking Rin against his side, clearly ignoring the way he'd gone stiff upon contact. "Should we go over the case file with Madden and his cadet?"

"Uh," Calder glanced between them and then stepped back, searching for his senior. The second he spotted him, he sent them a wave. "Later."

Brennon lingered a moment longer but ended up doing the same, ditching Rin.

With a low growl, he shook Kelevra's hold off him and turned, glare already set in place.

Madden and Tine were standing just behind him, the two watching the exchange the same way many of the other people in the room were. Meaning Rin had to keep up appearances or risk rumors spreading throughout the school.

Damn it.

His expression eased into one of false friendliness. "Sure, why not."

The rules were they couldn't share the results, not that they couldn't help each other out.

Not that either senior ended up being much help.

The four of them took a corner of the gymnasium, seated high up on the bleachers while the rest of the cadets fanned out. There was no time limit, so technically they were all free to go whenever they pleased, but it seemed like most people had the same idea as Rin and wanted to at least go over the material and get a feel for their mentors.

The feeling with both his and Tine was they were going to be pretty useless.

Madden spent the entire time playing some shooting game on his emblem-slate, humming noncommittally whenever Tine asked him about a specific detail in the case file he and Rin were combing over.

At least that was better than what Kelevra was doing.

The Imperial Prince was leaning forward, an elbow propped on his thigh as he watched Rin. Not in the paying attention sort of way either. In the creepy, stalker kind of way.

Rin would have snapped at him for it if they'd been alone, but as it were, he was forced to act like it didn't bother him. He went over the material with Tine, trying to focus so they could get this over with and he'd have a good enough reason to leave.

"You think he's only going after female students?" Tine asked, scrolling through the holographic file so that a stream of text rolled by before he stopped at a certain paragraph. "They're all from Guest. Aren't you friends with some of them?"

Guest was the fine arts academy Arlet and some other people Rin had met over the summer attended.

He's received a reply back from her saying she was free later tonight to get drinks, but with Kel watching him so closely, Rin hadn't messaged her to confirm yet.

Rin nodded in the affirmative to Tine's question and then clicked on an image in the case file projected from his own emblem-slate. It was a photo of one of the "killings", a brunette girl around their age staring into the camera with a smattering of bruises across her delicate throat. "Looks like they all happen at random, too. The location is always different, sometimes it's public, other times it's in a more secluded area."

"So whoever he is, he's not too worried about being caught," Tine said. "Think checking in with your friends would help, or no?"

Rin considered it. "I'm guessing the Academy just asked for some of their students to get involved because of the cosmetics." The whole thing was staged, after all, and someone had to have applied the makeup on the girl pretending to be dead in the photo. It looked pretty realistic, meaning they'd pulled out all the stops for this to simulate an actual case. "Unless they're listed as a witness in the files, I doubt they've been told anything."

Tine sighed, disappointed. "Yeah, you're probably right. I bet they're getting extra credit for volunteering even."

Before Rin could respond to that, the holo-file flickered and vanished, replaced by a wavy line and a staccato rhythm indicating he was receiving a video communication. He frowned when he read the name and then stood, heading down three of the bleacher steps before thinking to turn back. Purposefully, he looked directly at Tine, ignoring the Imperial Prince as he said, "I've got to take this. I'll be back."

"Sure," Tine waved him off, distracted with the case file.

Rin tried to pretend he didn't feel Kelevra's gaze on him while he crossed the gym and entered through the door that led down the hall to the locker room. He accepted the call just as he entered, giving a quick look around to see that he was alone. Since they'd only met here to receive the assignment, no one had changed out of their uniforms.

"It's about time, you ungrateful shit," Crate hissed the second his image appeared, the hostility momentarily catching Rin off guard. His father was a tried and true asshole, but he didn't typically lead with juvenile name-calling.

He moved over toward his locker automatically, stopping just before the bench. "I'm not sure what this is about."

"Like hell you aren't," his father snapped. "If you think this type of insubordination is going to go unchecked, think again. You may have ruined my plans for you, but I'll have your brother on the first ship home within the hour. I knew sending you boys to Dual Galaxy was a mistake, even more so since neither of you would shut up about it."

What had his brother done now? It certainly hadn't been *him*, since he couldn't think up a single thing that could have set their father off like this. Hell, the past week he'd been going out of his way to stick to the sidelines and stay *out* of trouble.

"I only agreed to this because the Empress happened to be in the room when I initially took the call."

The Empress of Tibera? Seriously, what the fuck had his brother done to enrage their old man to this degree, and why hadn't he warned him about it?

"I'll find someone else to take over the hospital," his father continued, still seething. "Sila will have to return immediately and be sent to start over on Status. It'll put us behind schedule, but that's entirely your fault and I'll be sure your brother knows where to place the blame."

Status was the planet in their home galaxy, the Crystal Sea, where the Academy was located. Whatever his brother had done, it was bad enough for Crate to uproot one of them and force them to start over. Since Sila Varun was a student at Vail University, he'd have no Academy credit to his name and therefore would have to begin as a freshman.

Rin would be upset that their dad was acting like this, ordering them about like they were still teenagers sleeping down the hall, under his roof, but he couldn't bank down the confusion. Like with most intense emotions, it was strong enough that he was finding it difficult to latch onto any other feeling, and his hand slipped into his left pocket so he could run his thumb over the smooth surface of his grounding shell.

"Father, I apologize, but I honestly don't understand. What did I do?" Supposedly. What had he *supposedly* done? Because for the life of him, he couldn't figure it out. Even if his brother had done something, given the nature of his proclivities, if he'd been caught in the act it would have made national news. But Rin hadn't heard anything from anyone about any sort of major crimes having been committed.

His brother knew better anyway, was careful. They both were. So what—

"Don't play the fool, son, it's unbecoming. You may think I don't know you, but I do. You're a petty creature. I bet you seduced him just so you could get out of your responsibilities toward this family, isn't that right?"

Rin blinked. "I…What?" Had he said seduced? Plus he'd called him petty. As if he truly believed he knew the first thing about what type of person Rin was. It was laughable. But that confusion was still there, maybe even thicker than before, and until he was able to shake it, nothing else was going to be able to get through.

He hated this about himself. Hated his inability to process intense emotion the same way the rest of his people did. His brother had the opposite problem, and there were days when Rin was actually envious of that fact. As if not having emotion would somehow be better.

Maybe it would.

At least if it were his brother here having this conversation he'd be able to follow the plot.

"I hope you're happy," Crate said. "I approved your betrothal because the Empress thinks it'll be a great way to pave future transactions between our planets. You may have gotten what you wanted, but heed this, you better not screw this up. This has become a political alliance and if you cause any more damage to this family's name I'll disown you faster than you can blink those ridiculous fucking eyes of yours!"

Rin was only partly listening to the insults now, a wave of pure, undiluted dread crashing over him, causing black spots to wink in front of his vision. It was amazing he managed to stay on his feet, though he did sway a little, not that his father seemed to notice.

Or maybe he just didn't care. The bastard probably thought Rin's physical reaction was due to his comments about disownment. What a load of shit.

"Betrothal," he managed to get the word out but it was difficult and he had to pause before finishing with, "To who?"

His father sneered. "How you managed to persuade an Imperial Prince to fall for you is beyond me. Remember, Rin, everything that happens from here on out is on you and your selfish actions!" Crate cut the call.

Rin's arm dropped lifelessly to his side as his mind scrambled to piece together this new bit of information. His father thought he was betrothed—no, no since he'd said betrothed and not engaged, that meant he *was* betrothed. To get married. To an Imperial Prince.

The Imperial Prince.

Chapter 10:

There was only one currently on planet and that was Vitality's third in line for the throne.

He wouldn't…

Rin spun on his heels, not even sure what he intended to do, but he only got a step forward before he lurched to a halt.

Kelevra was standing in front of the door, leaning back against it with his ankles crossed and his hands tucked into his front pockets. He was in another one of his fancy getups, the suit a dark forest green. He'd gone without a dress shirt, the green and gold velvet corset vest dipping low to expose the hard lines of his upper chest. After a moment he straightened, quirking a brow when Rin automatically shuffled back three steps.

Rin bumped against the bench, forced to a standstill, and shook his head. "You didn't."

"You were afraid of a scandal," Kelevra said matter-of-factly, as though they weren't speaking about a binding contract that would last for *the rest of their lives*. "As my fiancé, there's no longer a need to be. The announcement will be made tomorrow but I should have known your father would inform you beforehand. I was hoping to tell you myself, but it's been a series of hoops, one after the other, in order to make this happen so I've been understandably busy."

Nothing about this was understandable. If anything, Rin felt even more lost than he had during the conversation with his father. Heightened levels of stress made everything worse, and this...It didn't get more stressful than being told he'd apparently been handed off for marriage like cheap livestock.

Kel clicked a few buttons on his multi-slate and a second later Rin's dinged. "There's the official notice, in case you wanted to see it for yourself."

Robotically, Rin opened the file and stared at the screen, it took five times longer than it should for his brain to process the words he was reading.

Imperial Prince Kelevra Diar has been betrothed to Rin Varun, future Royal Consort.

It went on to congratulate them, and he realized he was reading an actual statement meant to be released by the palace tomorrow, but he didn't bother with the rest. The name got him the most, taunting him as he read it over and over again.

Rin Varun.

Rin. Varun.

What had he done? How had he gotten them into this mess? All he'd meant to do was satisfy his lust that night—thanks mostly to having been drugged—and then both he and the Imperial Prince were meant to go their separate ways. Sure, they'd have to interact on campus because of this whole assignment, but he'd never in a million years imagined *this* could happen.

His brother was going to kill him.

Maybe even literally.

Maybe he should do them a favor, cut to the chase, and get it over with now.

"It's interesting that your family chose to send the younger twin to the Academy and the older to Vail. Usually in families with a strong military presence, it's the opposite. I was surprised when my sister told me after speaking with your father to make arrangements," Kelevra made his way over as he spoke. "Should you tell your older brother before the news gets out? It just occurred to me you may want to."

Right, because the twins were still categorized in a hierarchy just like everything else in this universe. Older by a single minute and yet that meant one of them was called younger. And he was suggesting he tell him.

Tell his older brother.

Tell Sila Varun that Rin Varun was now officially betrothed to an Imperial Prince, against his will, without any prior discussion beforehand.

That was hilarious.

Tell his older brother.

It was quite possible Rin was coming apart at the seams.

A sound slipped past his lips and Rin was too late to recognize it for the manic anger it was. "That's what just occurred to you?"

The fury was swift, all-consuming, and even if they'd been in a crowd of people, Rin didn't think he would have been able to contain it. His arm was already swinging before he knew it, his fist connecting with Kelevra's jaw hard enough to send his head jerking to the side.

Kel stumbled, pressing against his injury, eyes flashing with the same kind of anger Rin still felt bubbling in his chest.

If he'd been anyone else or in any other state of being, Rin would have recognized the danger for what it was and backed off. As it were, his emotional dysregulation issue kept him distracted, too hyper-focused on the tightness in his chest and the way his skin felt like it was on literal fire. He hated anger. Hated experiencing it and hated what it did to him. Hated having to hide and control himself.

And he fucking hated Kelevra Diar.

He swung again, but this time Kel was ready, latching onto him to pull him forward off his feet. One hand grabbed Rin by the scruff of the neck and shoved, sending him sprawling through the open entranceway that attached to the showers.

Rin righted himself and spun, but before he could react at all, Kelevra was there, pushing him into one of the stalls. His right shoulder whacked against the solid tile and he winced, the anger still driving him when he tried to fight his way out only to be cornered in the small cubicle. He hissed and growled, seeming more animal at the moment than anything else, but that frustration was so raw he couldn't be bothered to care about appearances.

Which was a mistake.

He didn't have that luxury.

They *always* had to care about appearances.

Rin froze all at once, his wrists painfully captured in Kelevra's hands, his back pressed against the shower wall. The space kept them close, their bodies practically rubbing together, and—he sucked in a sharp breath when the Imperial Prince shifted and his hard-on rubbed against Rin's stomach.

He couldn't be serious? He was turned on at a time like this?

"Deep breaths," Kelevra instructed, a thread of anger still in his tone as he cautiously released Rin's wrists. When he wasn't immediately hit again, he dropped his hands lower, tugging the black t-shirt Rin was wearing out of his waistband. He had it over Rin's head in a flash, chucking it straight into the empty stall across from them before moving to his pants.

The sound of the zipper snapped him out of it and Rin shoved at his shoulders, forcing him back, but Kelevra didn't let go, the move only jostling them both.

"Fine," the Imperial Prince stated darkly, "ruin your clothes, I don't fucking care." He switched on the shower in a flash, ice cold water pouring down on them, Rin taking the brunt of it when he was shoved beneath the spray.

He sputtered and floundered, but he was no match against Kelevra's strength, and the fingers digging into the sides of his neck warningly finally had him still a second time.

"You need to cool down," Kelevra told him, free hand reaching around to resume undoing Rin's pants. He bucked forward when Rin tried to stop him, the hard bulge bumping against Rin's ass. "Consider this an order, cadet."

The anger leeched out of him all at once, but Rin remained tense as his now wet pants and briefs were dropped to the floor and left there around his ankles to soak up whatever didn't swirl down the drain. He shivered when he felt Kel's hand roam up his stomach, fingers gliding over his chest.

He wanted to tell him to stop, but the words caught in his throat like lead, the sinking feeling of panic overwhelming him. Because he knew if he could just stop and think he'd know exactly what to say to stop Kelevra from whatever he intended—the same way he always knew what to say to his brother whenever he was triggered and out for blood.

But Rin couldn't think. He couldn't do anything but stand there while the Imperial Prince felt him up and took liberties he shouldn't be allowed to take. He sucked in a deep breath, the air burning his lungs, and tried to focus on the icy water pelting his chest. It wasn't enough though. Water was typically his go-to, that and his shell. The latter was in his pocket on the ground and the shower wasn't doing enough to drown out his emotional response.

Blindly, Rin slapped a palm against the tiled wall to his right, thumb brushing against the smooth surface. He needed grounding before he made things worse for them. He needed—

Rin jerked when one of Kelevra's hands suddenly wrapped around his flaccid dick.

"The anger is gone," Kel noted as he started pumping him, clearly undeterred by the fact Rin wasn't in the mood. "But you're still shaking." He hummed like that was interesting and not a tell-tale sign he should back off and give Rin space. A normal person would have picked up on that fact.

The Imperial Prince wasn't normal though.

Rin Varun wasn't normal either.

And Sila...Sila might be the worst of all three.

What the actual hell was wrong with his life?

"We're going to fuck," Kelevra announced.

Rin shook his head, but he had no way of knowing if the other man saw and chose to ignore it or if he was looking elsewhere since he was standing behind him. Either way, his opinion on the matter clearly wasn't something the Imperial Prince cared about.

"Do you know how hard it's been these past few days without you?" Kelevra licked at the back of Rin's shoulder, his hand working more vigorously around his dick. "I kept waiting for the disinterest to settle in, but it never came. Every waking minute was spent wondering what you were doing, who you were with, why it wasn't me. And sleep...don't even get me started. You owe me for every night I woke up jerking off to the thought of you wrapped around my cock."

Rin didn't see how that was his fault. He also didn't think to share how he'd had a similar—though not as aggressive—problem. The Imperial Prince didn't deserve it, and if anything, this whole ordeal had taught Rin things were better when he kept his mouth closed where the other guy was concerned.

He needed this to be over so he could get to his brother. They had to come up with a plan. If their father contacted him before Rin got a chance…He didn't even know what his brother would do.

That was the scary part.

He didn't know.

He hadn't known. He'd underestimated Kelevra when he should have minded the warning. The guy was a predator who didn't feel empathy or remorse. Hell, he was already so pleased with himself that Rin was getting hard in his hand, he didn't even notice how he was currently in the throes of an anxiety attack.

Rin couldn't settle it either, it was taking him for a spin much the same way Kelevra was, forcing his body to react to outside stimuli despite his internal need to curl up into a ball, take a deep breath, and just *focus*.

But he couldn't.

All he felt was the clawing desperation in his chest cavity telling him to run. Run from all of it. Only, he couldn't because Kelevra was blocking the exit and Rin couldn't get his tongue to work long enough to tell him to back off, and even if he did, there was very little chance the Imperial Prince would even listen.

Then there was the pounding of cold water and the hot hands on his body and the press of warm lips over his shoulders and to the back of his neck. There was the way his dick, now swollen and aching, sent pangs of need skittering throughout him. That was somewhat easier to focus on, that arousal churning in his gut, and even though it also added shame to the cocktail of negative emotions he was currently drowning in, at least part of him felt good at the same time.

Thinking with his dick was what had gotten him into this mess, and at least then he'd had the drug as an excuse. But even knowing that Rin couldn't seem to stop himself from angling his hips back, bumping against that bulge in Kelevra's pants. He moaned and tipped his head, dropping it against the curve of Kel's shoulder, realizing just how close they were actually standing to one another.

"There you are, Flower," Kelevra praised fondly, grinning at him as a spark of wicked satisfaction entered his hazel eyes. "Unfurl for me."

Rin gasped when suddenly that hand dropped away and he was bent forward, his arms coming up to brace himself just before his forehead would have connected with the wall. His legs were kicked apart, the sound of another zipper drawing down almost imperceptible beneath the loud spray of the shower.

A moment later, something prodded at his entrance, too thin to be a finger, and he tried to jerk away only to have his hips roughly handled and yanked back.

That something returned, pushed inside, but it was small and he barely felt it. Something gushed forward, filling him up, and he made a sound of surprise as one of Kelevra's arms wrapped around his waist to keep him still.

"It's lube," Kel explained, squeezing the bottle, emptying what must be the entire contents into Rin's hole.

It felt like a violation, to be moved around and prepped like a damn sex toy. If Rin were in his right mind, he'd be furious—probably. When he could only muster a small inkling of disgust, he let out a whimper.

The now empty bottle of lube dropped to the floor at their feet with a light clatter, the plastic pinging and rolling to the back, directly into Rin's line of sight. It wasn't that big, maybe a couple of inches long at most. Something Kelevra could easily carry around in his pocket without it being noticed.

His cheeks being spread brought him back to attention, a low growl emitted at his back causing a shiver to roll up his spine. The fear he felt was palpable, but the arousal never diminished, his dick still thick with need.

Kelevra lined his cockhead up to Rin's hole, not even bothering to open him with a finger or two first, and then with one deep inhale, thrust all eight inches inside of Rin's body.

He wailed, hands curling into fists, nails digging into the tender flesh of his palms as Kel pummeled his insides, setting a hard and steady pace that had their bodies coming together with harsh slaps.

"Good Light, you feel so tight," Kelevra groaned, reaching around to tweak one of Rin's nipples, pinching it roughly when that got him a gasp. He rocked into Rin even harder, burying himself deep and holding his cock there for a second with each inward thrust. Like the other times they'd been together, he seemed to get off on just being inside of him. "No one's ever clung to me the way you do. It's like you're desperate to keep me."

Rin was not. The pain was subsiding at least, the sensation of feeling that fact cockhead drag against his inner walls chasing the sharp zaps of agony the initial, brutal entering had been to dissipate. He hadn't been properly stretched to take a cock of that size, and it wasn't like he went around leisurely fucking people. The last night had been that night at the penthouse in Kelevra's bed five days ago. His body was not prepared, and while he didn't think there'd been any real damage done, that didn't make this okay.

Even if he kind of liked it.

The only times in his entire life he'd been able to breathe properly had been those moments when he'd been forced to give up complete and total control. They were few and far between, like snippets of joy that were there and gone in a flash, but he held onto them when he could.

This was not a situation he should be deriving any sort of joy from.

The Imperial Prince had him pinned up against a dirty shower wall, his cock pounding into him like he had a right to, fingers digging divots into his hips that were sure to leave bruises…This was an act of pure and total domination. Kelevra hadn't even asked how Rin felt or if he wanted to. He'd simply touched him and manipulated his body into giving him the reaction he wanted.

But…as he was fucked, some of that anxiety finally started to dissipate, and before long he was pushing back to meet those thrusts, widening his stance to help that cock spear in deeper. He moaned when Kelevra's teeth nipped at his shoulders and lapped at his skin, always seeming like he wanted to feast on him when they were joined like this.

And Rin got the distinct feeling that he was not right in the head. That he was even more twisted and wrong than he'd previously believed. Because he couldn't stop thinking about how all of this had begun.

With Kelevra seeing him at the competition.

With Kelevra. *Seeing* him.

Rin wasn't used to being seen, not by anybody, not even himself or his brother. Hell, the two of them were the worst at seeing one another even, bleeding too close together for that to still be possible. The two of them were just that. A them. For as long as Rin could remember, there wasn't a him, only a them. No me, just us. He wouldn't change it—couldn't even if he tried—but this…

Being taken like an animal in a shower stall felt so intrinsically like a him moment that for a brief second it all snapped into place.

For one spectacularly clear blip in time, he was Rin Varun, just Rin Varun, no strings, no brother, no emotional issues.

"Flower," Kelevra growled, wrapping those fingers around Rin's wet length all over again. He twisted his palm as he stroked him, fast and harried, clearly trying to get him to orgasm before he did. "Flower." He pressed his lips to the curve of Rin's ear, blew a sharp, hot gust of air against it. "Come for me."

Yes, something was very, very wrong with him.

His body followed the command like it'd been conditioned to do so, his balls tightening a second before they released and he was panting and coming apart in Kelevra's arms like a puppet with their strings pulled.

Kelevra continued to work him as he came, painting the shower floor with his spunk. His thrusts increased in speed, getting clunky and less precise, and then he was shoving himself deep, pulling Rin's hips back and holding him there.

Hot waves of come filled him and Rin moaned at the sensation, clawing at the wall as his own release finally came to an end. He watched as the evidence circled the drain and disappeared through the small grate, his lower muscles still milking Kelevra as he continued to gush inside him.

Chapter 11:

When Kel was finally finished, Rin continued to tighten as he pulled himself free, sucking in a deep breath at the feeling of emptiness the moment their bodies were separated.

He managed to remain upright for less than a minute once it was over, wobbling on his feet a second before he found himself sitting on the ground, the harsh spray of the shower still going.

Kelevra flicked it off, wordlessly looking down at him.

Rin caught the exact moment the Imperial Prince realized there was something wrong, though Rin didn't tear his gaze off the cracked spot in the tile he'd been sightlessly staring at.

"Hey." Kel pulled his pants back up and then knelt next to him, reaching out to rest a hand on Rin's shoulder. He shook lightly. "Hey."

Out of the two of them, Rin's brother had always been the bigger monster. They could both claim the title, in some way shape, or form, of course, and sometimes they traded, for fun or out of necessity, but it'd always been a silent understanding between them that while one was a demon, the other was a devil.

Except, here Rin was, having just been used by an actual devil, a Devil of Vitality no less, and…

That'd been the best orgasm he'd ever experienced in his entire life. Even better than the ones at the penthouse.

The panic and anxiety he'd felt earlier? Gone. There were still snippets, sure, of anger as well, but there were other things. Guilt. Shame. Indignation. Nothing was all-consuming. Rin sat there and sorted through them and picked them apart and not once did he feel like he was about to die or punch a hole through the wall and that was…

Terrifying, actually.

A lifetime of feeling trapped by his inability to control his emotions.

A decade of learning how to hide that from the world.

And all it'd taken was one cock to completely shatter him.

Although, in his defense, Kelevra was hung in a way few people were capable of claiming.

But still.

Here Rin was, basking in the afterglow of…whatever the actual fuck that had been, because it certainly couldn't be considered consensual, when he should be three steps away from bashing in the Imperial Prince's skull and going to prison.

He should want to bash in Kelevra's skull.

So…why didn't he?

He still loathed the other guy and yet a part of him felt stretched and pliable and calm.

Calm wasn't a word Rin was all that familiar with. He didn't experience calm. He faked it.

Was he faking it now?

Absently, he pressed a hand to his bare chest, over his heart, but the beats had slowed and turned steady. His skin was no longer buzzing like a livewire had been slipped beneath it, and his head…He could focus. Clearly. He was having this whole crisis of identity without any interruptions, wasn't he?

Kelevra grabbed his chin between two fingers and roughly twisted his head to the side so he was facing him. The worry pinching his brow was ironic, all things considered. "Rin? Talk to me."

He snorted, but the sound came out empty. "Now you want to talk? Kind of late for that, don't you think?"

The Imperial Prince frowned.

"I'm not marrying you," Rin said.

Any semblance of concern was wiped from Kel's expression at that.

Now that he was coming to his senses, Rin was able to sort through his priorities and phenomenal orgasms? Yeah, unfortunately, those weren't high on his list. They couldn't be. Nipping this whole betrothal thing in the bud, however, was.

He needed to pick himself off this bathroom floor, end things with Kelevra, and go find his brother. In that order. And he needed to do it now.

If only his legs didn't still feel like jelly. His mind may have settled, but his body was still a hot wreck after the rough fucking. Whether he liked it or not, he was staying on the ground for at least another five minutes.

"Come again?" Kelevra asked, lip sneering in the process. He looked coiled and ready to strike, clearly not having the same problem as Rin when it came to controlling his body. Since he'd been the aggressor in all of this, that wasn't surprising.

"You heard me," Rin barreled forward despite the visceral warning. Pissing off the Imperial Prince a second time could cost him, and his ass smarted as though in protest even as he continued to mouth off. "I'm rejecting your proposal. I won't marry you."

Kelevra stared at him for a lengthy moment, then he was hauling Rin up, propping him against the wall. He stooped and freed his ankles from the soaked pants, leaving them in a heap on the ground. "Stay."

Rin bristled but didn't respond, using all of his energy to remain upright instead as he waited.

It wasn't long before Kel returned carrying a pair of gray sweatpants he must have gotten from Rin's locker.

"It was locked," he said dumbly as Kelvera knelt once more, easing first one foot and then the next into the pants.

"I know the code," Kel replied, rising as he tugged the pants into place. He pulled a shirt Rin hadn't noticed from beneath his arm and got him into that next, smoothing down the wayward strands of sandy-gold hair after.

Rin's earlier thought came back to him and he smiled wryly, shaking his head at Kelevra's questioning look. "Nothing. You're just set on taking this all the way. It's amusing."

"This?" His eyes narrowed.

"Treating me like a doll. You positioned me like one, dressed me like one, and now you're even brushing my hair? It's like you think I'm a shiny new toy bought by your sisters for your birthday."

"You are."

Rin froze. "What?"

"Not the toy part," Kelevra corrected, adjusting the collar of the new t-shirt he'd put Rin in. "I asked them to let me pick my Royal Consort as their gift to me. It's in a month, didn't you know?"

No, he did not, because up until this point, Rin's goal had been to avoid anyone with high-standing authority.

"You're telling me," he bit out, "you consider me a birthday gift?"

Kelevra shrugged. "For my eighteenth, I was given Zane. It's not uncommon for an Imperial to receive a person as a present."

Royal Zane Solace. Rin recognized the name. He was part of Kelevra's Retinue.

"I'm going to punch you again," Rin threatened. "As soon as I get the feeling back in my legs."

That frown returned. "What's wrong with your legs?"

"Oh, I don't know, maybe we should shove an eight-inch dick up your ass without any warning and see how well you can stand afterward, prick!" Ah, there was the anger. Rin almost sighed in relief when he felt it. If nothing else, it was familiar.

"Are you injured?" Kelevra, the complete and total fucker, actually looked legitimately concerned.

Rin was tempted to call bullshit, but then he realized it actually panned out. "Worried you broke your new plaything already?" He clicked his tongue derisively.

"I take care of what's mine," Kelevra said.

"Don't include me on that list," Rin told him. "I am not, and will never be, yours."

Kel's grabbed a fistful of the hair he'd just painstakingly combed and straightened and pulled Rin off the wall. Chest to chest, he secured him with an arm around his waist, his free hand cupping one of Rin's ass cheeks and squeezing hard enough it would most likely bruise there as well.

Rin would have shot off some other snide remarks, but self-preservation finally clicked into gear, and he recognized the darkness in Kel's eyes. It wasn't empty like his brothers or heated like he knew his own got sometimes.

Kelevra's gaze was smoldering, promising pain and retribution.

He might have dressed Rin just now, treated him gently, but it'd been because he'd wanted to, not out of any actual kindness toward Rin. Kel did what he pleased when it pleased him, which meant if he chose to strangle Rin right here and now, he could do it without batting an eyelash.

And he'd get away with it afterward too.

This wasn't the first time Rin was recalling this, reminded of the power imbalance between them at the last second, just before he tipped over the proverbial line and took things too far. He had to do a better job of remembering that he and his brother weren't the only ones on this planet pretending to be something they weren't.

"There," Kel tilted his head, staring him down as he kept him close, "that. That flash of fear you just felt. I'm sorry you're not happy with my plan for you. I'm sorry if I hurt you just now."

"Liar."

"I'm not finished," he said tightly. "I am sorry you don't seem to have grasped the situation you're in, so allow me to show you some kindness and help you out." He walked forward a step, the move bringing Rin's back to the wall for the third time. Kel settled over him, using his entire body to keep him pinned so there was almost nowhere they didn't touch, and then he pulled his hand out of his hair and captured his jaw instead. "I didn't mean to hurt you. But do I care that I did? Not really. You didn't bleed and you're in one piece. That's good enough for me.

"It's unfortunate that you aren't satisfied with the betrothal, it would have been better if you were," he continued. "But does that make me reconsider? No, not at all. You'll be well kept, and now a million doors that were once closed to you will be opened."

"I don't want it," Rin stated, but his voice had dropped and the words came out nothing more than a harsh whisper, little more than air spoken an inch away from Kel's hovering lips.

The Imperial Prince grinned, viciously, beautifully, and then he licked at the seam of Rin's mouth, just a single flick of his tongue, there and gone. "If you didn't want to be plucked, you shouldn't have stood out in a crowd. If you didn't want me to crave that sweet, sweet ass of yours, you shouldn't have been so good at taking my dick."

"Neither of those things were in my control!"

"And neither is this," he replied. "I'm not used to wanting things because everything has always been handed to me before I even have to ask. But our time in the library made it clear to me that I want you. Which means I'll have you. I *have* you," he corrected.

"The time in the library where you almost drugged me against my will?" Rin reminded coldly. But if he thought putting things into perspective was going to get through to someone like Kel, he was a moron of the highest degree.

"I didn't have to drug you today," Kelevra said. "Progress."

"That's—" He gave him a blank stare. "You're certifiably insane."

"You already know what I am," Kelevra corrected. "I'm acting according to my nature. It's not my fault you've found yourself bound to a Devil."

"Yeah," he pushed at his chest but Kel didn't let up, "it actually is. All of this? Your fault. So do me a favor and release me, then give your sister a call and cancel this whole sham of a betrothal before—" Rin didn't get to finish, crying out when his hair was pulled again, this time harder than the last. He growled and glared, his head still tipped back forcefully. "Fucking prick."

"Devil, Flower," Kelevra drawled. "Your Devil."

"I've already got one of those, thanks anyway."

Wrong. Thing. To. Say.

Rin found himself on the ground, right in the middle of the shower section, in full view if anyone chose to enter the locker room.

The Imperial Prince was on top of him, securing him to the tiled floor with his muscular body, seemingly uncaring that he was ruining his suit between this and the water from the shower.

The ridiculousness of that notion—that here he was, thinking about the guy's expensive clothes—was not lost on Rin.

"If you tell me who they are," Kelevra said, and his voice was off, deeper than Rin had ever heard it before, "I promise to make it quick."

"Make what quick?" Why was he asking?! He didn't want to know. He already knew that was a thing he did not want to know.

"Their death."

Yeah. Hadn't needed to hear that. Rin gulped and Kel's gaze shot toward the motion, taking in the movement of his throat with more intensity than was necessary. If this were his brother, Rin would know exactly what fucked up thought was going through his head, but with Kelevra...He'd thought he'd pegged him. How wrong he'd been.

"Let me up," he forced himself to make his tone gentle, easy, the exact opposite of everything he was currently feeling. The alarm bells were full-on blaring now, even more so than when he'd realized Kel planned to screw him in the stall. Thank Light no one had come in while they'd been doing it.

Wait.

No one had, right?

Rin inwardly cursed. Focus.

"Kelevra," he tried again, "you're hurting me." It wasn't a complete lie. The guy was heavy and Rin's shoulder blades were pressing into the floor painfully.

"If you don't give me a name," Kelevra growled, "when I find them myself it won't be pretty. I'll string them up in the middle of campus for the entire student body to gawk at. At least," he leaned in, his nose brushing against Rin's, "half of them, anyway."

He wasn't kidding.

"There's no one," Rin admitted, and when that didn't seem to do the trick, risked wiggling his hands out from where they were pinned on his stomach so he could rest them on the other man's hips. "Really. I told you that already, remember? That night in your room. You asked if I was with anyone."

"You said you were not."

"I'm not."

Kel searched his gaze. "Who's the devil then, Rin? I also recall explaining to you that same night that you can't get away with lying to me. I'll know. I'll always know. So, who are you protecting? A past lover? A crush? Someone you wish you were fucking instead of—"

"Myself," Rin blurted, not seeing any other way out of this. At the rate they were going, Kelevra was two seconds away from taking a wild guess and going on a mad rampage. His friends wouldn't be safe then, and neither would his brother. A little honesty to protect the people he cared about? Sure, whatever.

He'd survive it.

Hopefully.

"I'm the Devil, Kelevra."

The Imperial Prince paused, and before he could think better of it, Rin took the opening.

He rolled them, catching Kel off guard, and kneed him in the side on his way up. The whole time he retreated into the locker room, he kept his eyes locked on Kelevra, keeping the danger in sight as he escaped.

The Imperial Prince stayed on the ground, clutching his side, but he was pissed, that barely contained rage aimed directly at Rin.

Which was good. Better him than an innocent person.

Better him than his brother.

"If you take one step out that door," Kelevra wheezed, "you will regret it."

Even knowing that was true, Rin bolted. He almost crashed into Brennon on the way down the hall, throwing an arm around his friend's shoulders to turn him toward the exit.

"Daylen just called and said he needs to see you in your room," Rin rattled off the lie, glancing over his shoulder, relieved to see they weren't being followed, "it's an emergency."

"Yeah?" Brennon frowned. "What happened?"

"No clue." He let him go once they were in the main area of the building. "I'll catch you later."

"Where are you going?" Brennon yelled after him, but he didn't stop to explain.

Rin pulled the small attachment from beneath his emblem-slate and stuck it in his ear, hitting the first number in his contacts list as he raced away from Training Building 5. He didn't waste time on pleasantries when the person on the other end of the line picked up his call.

"SOS. Meet me at the Brick. Now."

Chapter 12:

"You put us at risk."

"I fucking know, asshole." Rin hung his head and kicked at one of the wooden boxes that littered the floor. They were in the middle of the woods close to their apartment, in a small shack they'd found randomly last year. It'd been abandoned a while ago, empty aside from a rickety bench and a couple of old farm tools.

His brother was perched on another box in the corner, leaning back against the cold gray stone walls, arms crossed over his chest. He was dressed casually, in black jeans with a red leather jacket over one of Rin's black t-shirts. Not up to the school dress code, which meant he hadn't come from Vail.

Rin was tempted to ask where he'd been and what he'd been doing but didn't. They already had one mess to clean up. Whatever his brother had gotten involved in, hopefully, he could handle it on his own.

"Do you feel better now?" His brother asked after a moment, indicating the now smashed box at Rin's feet.

"No. Do you feel at all?"

"Yes," Sila said. "I'm annoyed. Stop throwing a tantrum like a three-year-old."

"Go blow yourself, at least one of us has experienced that!" There was silence immediately following Rin's words.

His brother broke it finally with a sharp burst of laughter. "Did you mean the blowing part or the tantrum part?"

"Tantrum," Rin mumbled, dropping down on the bench. "I'm sorry. I fucked up."

"He made you angry." Sila shrugged like the fact Rin had accosted an Imperial Prince—twice—was no big deal.

"There's a name attached to the decree, brother," he said softly.

They stared at each other a moment, and then Sila nodded.

"No one makes us do anything."

"You should be more concerned," Rin stated.

"You mean if I wasn't a psychopath, I would be."

"That's not—" He blew out a breath. "I know you have feelings, okay? I was just being an ass."

"Well, there's nothing all that new there."

"Dick." Rin chuckled.

"What do you want to do?" Sila asked a moment later.

"You don't do anything," he said. "I'll figure something out."

"Brother."

"He's an Imperial and as soon as they make that announcement tomorrow, all eyes are going to be on us. We can't afford for the two of you to go at it."

"Sure that isn't just jealousy speaking? Since you've already…" Sila gave him a pointed once over, "gone at it?"

Rin pinched the bridge of his nose. "Sometimes I really want to drown you."

"Sometimes I'm curious what you look like on the inside."

They both meant it.

"We're fucked up." Rin had stopped feeling bad about that fact a long time ago. Being normal meant the two of them ending up as their father's perfect pawns, and that sounded far worse than anything they'd been through together.

This wasn't like anything they'd faced before, though, and admittedly, Rin was worried.

"Always have been," his brother grunted. "But I love us."

"Do you?"

"Of course."

"Us," Rin said, "plural?"

Sila sent him an odd look. "There is no singular us, brother. That's not how the word works." He snorted. "What are they teaching you at the Academy? I don't remember it being that lax."

"Eat me."

"Temper," Sila smiled and shook his head.

"You wouldn't be saying that if it'd been you who took that call from Crate earlier today," Rin stated, and like it always did, mention of their father wiped any semblance of a good mood from the both of them. "It was a complete ambush."

"Do you think he's serious?" Sila asked. "The Imperial?"

"I don't know." He ran a hand through his hair. "He certainly believes he is."

He hummed. "We could wait it out. If he's as sporadic as you've heard, he might lose interest eventually."

"Fantastic plan. Gold star."

"That was sarcasm."

"Yes."

Sila nodded like he was taking mental notes.

Rin rolled his eyes. "Seriously. What do you think we should do?"

"Didn't you just say you'd handle it?"

"Not about Kel." He would handle it…somehow. "About Crate."

"I dismissed his call earlier, so I haven't spoken to him yet."

"You've got to stop doing that," Rin said. "Eventually he's going to catch on."

"He'd have to pay attention to us first."

He opened his mouth to argue, but that was a fair assessment.

"If he orders me home," Sila told him, "I'll say no."

"Yeah, that'll work."

"Why not?"

"He pays for our tuition," Rin reminded. "We can't stay on planet unless we're attending school, and even if we pooled our savings, we wouldn't even have enough to cover a semester."

"Then I'll quit. I'm fine with that."

"*I'm* not."

Sila ran the pad of his middle finger beneath his bottom lip in thought. "What about your Imperial?"

"One, he isn't my anything—except maybe the bane of my existence—and two, what about him?"

"He wants to marry you. That'll make us family. Tell him to pay for me."

Rin blinked at him. "You can't be serious."

"Why not?" Sila tipped his head.

"I'm not selling myself for money."

"Just taking it up the ass for free then."

Rin leaped to his feet, but Sila remained calm and stoic as ever. He inhaled slowly, letting the air pool into his lungs, and then exhaled even slower.

"Better?" Sila asked.

"Quiet," he snapped. "I'm trying to recall how awful the repercussions were that time we were fifteen." Trapped in his own skin. For days. He shuddered and made a face. "Nope, not going to hit you. Not worth it."

"So glad we could come to that conclusion," Sila said, then, "What if I asked him?"

"What?"

"I asked this Imperial to pay my tuition."

Rin tensed. "Don't get involved with the Devils. That's a rule, remember?"

"You broke it first, brother."

"Not on purpose."

"Irrelevant." Sila rose and stretched, his movements languid, like a cat.

Very different from the tight and nervous way Rin carried himself whenever they were alone like this and they got to drop the act.

"Baikal Void and Kelevra Diar are dangerous," Sila agreed. "But they aren't a threat to us."

"Oh yeah? You stay here and get hitched and I'll take the ship back to Tibera then." Rin rubbed at his temples. He'd been nursing a headache since Kel had tossed him to the floor.

"Neither of us is returning to Tibera," Sila said, an edge slipping into his tone that he typically tried not to use. "Ever."

"Hey, relax," he held up a hand. "I was joking."

"It was a shitty joke."

"I'll find a way to break this whole betrothal thing and then we'll be back on track. Stick to the plan, right?"

A shutter dropped over his brother's eyes, morphing his expression into an enigmatic one, and this time Rin did push.

"What was that?" He frowned. "We're still sticking to the plan…right?"

"Free ourselves from our father." Sila gave a sharp nod.

"…And get off this planet and find somewhere new where we can both be ourselves," Rin added, watching him, waiting for his brother to agree. Only, he didn't. "What the actual fuck is going on, man?"

"Don't panic."

"Fuck you!"

"Or get angry."

"Again, fuck you!" Rin clutched at his hair and pulled it slightly, the burn to his already abused scalp—thanks to that other prick in his life Kelevra—helping to center him before he could completely lose it. "Explain. Right now."

"I'm just not sure I want to leave. That's all."

"Don't tell me you like Vitality?"

"You do, too," Sila said. "We have friends, beds to sleep in…This planet has its appeal."

Rin groaned and slammed his hands down on the bench, the thing almost collapsing beneath him. He hardly noticed, too pissed off and confused. Why was this the literal worst day ever?

"We fake our way through every day," Rin stated. "Are you forgetting that part?" It was the whole reason they'd wanted to leave after graduation, to begin with. That had been the plan since they'd concocted this whole scheme back in middle school, huddled underneath the single ratty blanket their father had tossed them out the upstairs window when he'd locked them out for the night.

Again.

"We're supposed to find somewhere we belong," he continued. "Where we can be *ourselves*."

Sila was watching him closely. "Maybe we can do that here."

"We fucking cannot!"

"Maybe we just haven't found the right person yet."

Rin froze. "Hell no. Absolutely not. If you're about to tell me you're abandoning me for dick I swear I'm going to drown you for real." He might go all sorts of ways, but his brother, like with everything else, was particular in his tastes.

He was only attracted to men, but he hadn't been in many relationships. They didn't last and they were too risky.

"I could never leave you," Sila made a face, "just like you could never leave me."

A sharp, humorless bark of laughter escaped him before he could help it.

Sila frowned.

"Nothing," Rin said. "It's just the two of you sounded similar for a second there."

"Who?" He got it a second later. "Ah. The Imperial. You think he's a sociopath."

"Yeah."

He tilted his head. "I'm not a sociopath."

"Same dif."

"It is not."

"Sure." It wasn't, hadn't been for a while since the Intergalactic State of Medicine had officially split them into separate categories, but Rin was having fun getting a rise out of him and after the blunt way his brother had all but suggested he sell himself for his tuition fee, he deserved it.

"If that's the case, then you and I are the same thing as well."

"Of course we're the same." He waved at him, noticing Sila's droll look a moment later. "We are."

"You know that's not true," Sila said. "You and I are different sides of the same coin. We might trick everyone else into believing otherwise, but we've always known the truth, big brother."

Rin winced. "Whatever."

"There's nothing wrong with you," he insisted then, in complete juxtaposition to their earlier discussion about how they were both fucked up. "Mood disorders, of all different types, have been a thing for centuries on most planets. People who have them are different, but they aren't bad."

"Then why have we been hiding? Hmm?" Rin countered.

Sila looked away. "Because if we don't hide, our differences are too noticeable. And we were unfortunate to have grown up on Tibera, which is a far less accepting planet when it comes to the inability to properly regulate or feel emotion the same way everyone else does."

And by less accepting, he meant banishment kinds of levels. Hell, their Heir Imperial, the crown prince, had been rejected by his own mother for being imperfect, and he'd had an organ disease.

The twins simply had different brain chemistry than the rest of the people on their home world. It shouldn't be enough, and maybe if they'd been born to someone other than Crate Varun or another political figure it wouldn't have been. But they'd always known, from the moment Rin had shoved Stax Hyuk off the cliffs, resulting in a broken arm, they'd known.

He hadn't felt any guilt.

Any remorse.

And the empty look in his eyes afterward...

"We also can't be compared to other species who suffer from similar diagnoses," his brother cut into his thoughts. "Tiberans were built to feel at extremely heightened levels and to process those emotions more quickly. We've got several dozen more neural transmitters that act as emotional breaks than the average being."

"So we should be praised for not having already turned into crazed serial killers, is that it?" Rin drawled.

"You suffer from emotional dysregulation," Sila said. "Parts of your prefrontal cortex shuts off during moments of intense stress and you're forced into a prolonged state of flight or fight mode, which typically for you means you either want to bash someone's face in or run. Kind of fun that you did both today with the Imperial. My point is, you don't have what it takes to become a serial killer, brother. In fact, it's insulting to regular people who have mood disorders to assume that you would."

Rin heaved a sigh. "Stop acting like a med student with me. Why do we have to put a label on it at all?" What difference did it make? At the end of the day they were who they were no matter what name they went by or which of them felt more than the other.

Sila cocked his head. "You're the one who first diagnosed me with psychopathic tendencies."

"Right. It's my fault. Everything is."

"Don't be dramatic."

"I'm not!" He was. Rin crossed his arms, then to lighten the mood again said, "Hey. Do you really believe you're not bad?"

"Oh, I meant you," Sila stated without hesitation. "I'm a fucking monster." As if to prove it he grinned, the expression drawing attention to his sharp gaze and the slightly chaotic twist of his full lips.

"Devil," Rin corrected, glancing away. Not because it was hard to look at his brother when he was showing his true colors. But because it wasn't. He was starting to think he'd gotten a little too used to dealing with both psychopaths and sociopaths. Wasn't that why he'd miscalculated and foolishly believed he could handle Kelevra? "This is Vitality. If the shoe fits."

Sila considered it. "I like it."

"And this planet?" Rin didn't want to, but he brought the conversation back around to that. "You like it too? That much? Enough to stay?"

"It's only a consideration," Sila corrected. "We have three years left before graduation. I'm only suggesting we keep an open mind. Let's not force ourselves onto a predetermined path. Isn't that what we're trying to escape from in the first place?"

"Is it?" Rin clicked his tongue. "And here I was thinking we were trying to escape from Crate Varun and his abuse."

Sila huffed. "That guy has a personality disorder."

"Yeah, it's called being a massive dick."

There wasn't anything medically wrong with their father, as far as they knew. He was just an asshole. On Tibera, relationships weren't really a thing, so they'd never had a mother. If their dad wanted some, he went out for a night and came home in the early hours of the morning, same as most other people on the planet.

Sex was an exchange, a way to relieve stress. Something without strings.

His upbringing with that understanding, and having heard Kelevra slept around, had given him a false sense of comfort that night at the penthouse.

Rin's emblem lit up and he groaned, flicking the device open to check the new message. He swore when he saw it was from Kelevra, taping to open it and turning so his brother could read it at the same time.

Kelevra: Come to this address. It's time to get to know your betrothed.

"Hell no," Rin shook his head. "The last time he sent a message like this I got—"

"Fucked," Sila finished.

He glared. "Drugged."

His brother scoffed. "Are you still pretending you didn't like that?"

"I didn't," Rin snapped.

"Brother, I mean this in the nicest way, you get off when someone else—who isn't our father—takes control from you. That's nothing to be ashamed about."

"Coming from the guy who can't feel shame," this time he was telling the truth, "that doesn't mean all that much."

"Is it a shitty feeling?" Sila asked. "I read it was."

"It pretty much sucks, yeah."

"Wouldn't you prefer to just accept it then? Wouldn't that make the shame go away?"

"It's not that easy." Rin's device went off again, putting an end to what was most likely about to be another exhausting argument about really nothing.

Kelevra: If you don't present yourself to me in the next twenty minutes, someone is going to have an unfortunate accident.

There was an image attached and Rin clicked it open, eyes going wide when he recognized Arlet standing in the corner by some bar. She was smiling and talking with a guy turned away from the camera.

"That's Madden," Sila said, pointing at the guy's back. "Look at his hair."

Rin only just got the chance to glance at it before another text interrupted.

Kelevra: Tick tock, Flower. Unless you don't mind having her blood on your conscience.

Sila grunted. "Does he think that's going to work?"

When Rin didn't reply, he glanced up at him.

"Oh," Sila said. "Right. You have one of those."

"That's not something you should forget," he warned.

"I don't."

"You just did."

"Yeah, because we're alone and in a safe space. Relax, brother. I promise I'm being a good little," he chucked his chin toward the device, "*flower* when you're not around."

"Where's the nearest body of water?" he asked. "I'm going to drown you in it."

"Fratricide will have to wait," Sila drawled. "Unless you really don't care if he kills her."

Rin hesitated. "Do you think he really would?"

Sila gave him a pointed stare. "I would."

"Right." He clicked on the GPS link Kelevra had included and turned toward the exit.

"I'm coming with you," Sila announced, falling into step at his side as they made their way through the woods toward the street. "The last time you went you were…drugged."

"Take this seriously."

"I am."

"You aren't."

"Hey." Sila pulled him to a stop just before they made it to the road. It was rare for them to touch, physical contact another uncommon thing on Tibera, so the fact he was doing so now made it clear he meant whatever he was about to say next. "Did you really not like that he drugged you? I know it's technically not socially acceptable behavior and would be classified as rape or sexual assault. But you didn't seem traumatized."

"No," Rin said, and then sighed. "Kind of. A little. I don't know, all right?"

Sila waited a moment, but when he didn't tack on anything else asked, "And you're sure you don't want me to handle it?"

"You're still working on handling that other problem of mine, remember?"

He dropped his hand. "It's my problem now, I already told you that. Don't even waste time thinking about it."

Why did that sound possessive?

The GPS pinged letting them know they'd been standing in one place for too long and Rin dropped it and started walking again.

"From one fucked up person to another," Sila said as they crossed toward the small parking lot attached to their apartment where his white hovercar was parked, "I don't think there's anything wrong with you being into it. But if you aren't into it, tell me, and I'll step in. I'd never stand back and allow anyone to hurt us."

"Thanks," Rin circled to the passenger side, meeting his brother's mismatched eyes, identical to his own, over the hood. "That's super comforting."

Not even Sila had to ask if that was sarcasm to know it was.

Chapter 13:

"You invited him *here*?" Madden let out a low whistle. "Ballsy move."

Kelevra motioned toward the man on the stool next to him with his half-empty glass. "Kal suggested it."

"That's not at all what happened," Baikal corrected, sipping his drink with a shake of his head. He was wearing those dark-framed glasses he was obsessed with, the Inspire 3.0, tech that one of his daddy's many companies had created.

It operated a lot like Kel's eye, so as much as he wanted to rag the guy for them, he understood the appeal. He'd lost his eye when he'd been a child and had gotten the implant shortly after. The tech in his face was as much a part of him as his actual working eye was at this point.

"I told you to find something that could be beneficial to him and offer it up as an apology," Baikal reiterated. "I did not tell you to invite the object of your obsession to an underground fight club."

"Apology for what?" Madden asked, out of the loop.

Kelevra didn't want to tell him, and one quick warning look in Kal's direction had the Brumal Prince shrugging in disinterest. They didn't tread on one another's toes, even when it came to the small stuff. That's what made this work.

Knowing Baikal had an obsession of his own was what had drawn Kelevra to him after the incident with Rin in the locker room. He'd been fuming the entire drive over to the Void estate before he'd thought to call ahead and had been forced to change trajectory when he'd discovered Kal was here at Friction.

Baikal didn't come here often, not as keen on bloodshed as Kelevra was, at least, not in the same sense. Kal wouldn't hesitate to resort to it, as the prince of the Brumal mafia, violence was second nature to him, but he typically thought things through before acting on them.

Kelevra didn't like to bother with thinking, he'd rather react. This wasn't due to a lack of intelligence, but a lack of consequence. When you were an Imperial Prince with no real responsibility and an entire planet willing to cater to and kiss your ass, there weren't really any repercussions.

Which was probably why he was so lost with how to approach Rin from here.

Baikal was better at playing people than Kel was. Manipulation had never been his style. People either gave him what he wanted or…they gave him what he wanted. But after what had happened in the shower, seeing Rin shut down so completely like that…Maybe learning how to handle people wouldn't be such an epic waste of time after all. Not that he wasn't loathe to admit he needed the other guy's help.

Because he was.

Kelevra scowled and downed the rest of his drink, slamming the glass onto the bar countertop with a little more force than necessary.

"Whatever," Madden rolled his eyes and crossed the room toward the ring, never one to feel left out.

"Baby," Kel grumbled under his breath, but Baikal caught it and chuckled.

They were standing at the long bar—a slab of shiny mahogany wood that was polished to such a fine finish Kel could—and had—stare at his reflection on it. Their personal bartender, a man who was loyal to both Brumal and the Imperial family, stood behind it polishing a glass, not paying either of them any mind. He never spoke to any of them, merely nodded his head in the affirmative or negative.

Probably because he didn't have a tongue but...Now that he thought about it, Kelevra wasn't exactly aware of why or when the guy had lost it.

Friction was a single-level building built on the property of Club Vigor, set off to the side, half hidden within a copse of dense trees. Initially built to house a private spaceship for the upper tier of the club, it'd been abandoned and later taken on by Kel. The building itself was privately owned, and invitation-only on a night-to-night basis. Only members of the Satellite—those within Baikal's inner circle—and Kelevra's Retinue had the code to the place. If cleaning personnel from the club wanted in to do their job, even they had to wait for someone with the code to let them in.

Even though it was on club grounds, there was a separate parking lot, located down a narrow windy backroad almost no one ever traveled on. That was where most of them parked when they came here to hang out and blow off steam. It was safe territory, a place where politics and corporate jargon played no part.

"Still mad?" Baikal had been nursing the same drink since Kelevra had gotten there, leading him to believe the man had other plans for the evening. He kept his eyes on two of the guys horsing around in the large ring across from them, though it was clear he was only mildly interested in their antics.

Kal was good at playing people.

But Kelevra wasn't too keen on being played.

"I shouldn't have asked you," he grunted. "Won't make that mistake again."

The corner of Baikal's mouth tipped up. "Are you upset that he kicked you, that you let him get the upper hand, or that you ruined a suit by rolling around on a grimy gym locker room floor?"

"It was one of my favorites," Kel said, tapping the bar to get June, the bartender's, attention. "I can't believe I lost my senses that deeply that I ruined it."

Kal quirked a brow.

"Fine, spur-of-the-moment sexcapades are my thing, it's not that surprising. Still. His reaction…He was into it. He's into me!" He snatched the drink and drained the glass a second time, immediately motioning for another.

"Everyone's into you," Baikal bit out, his gaze hardening a little.

"You say that like being pretty is a crime."

"No, but your ego should be considered one." Kal tipped his head. "Speaking of crime—"

"Good Light," Kelevra cut him off, "don't tell me you're about to spout some bullshit about consent. Madden got the drugs from one of yours if you recall."

Baikal snorted. "Consent? If he doesn't want you now, make him change his mind." He lifted a single shoulder in a shrug. "Simple as that."

Simple. Right. Kelevra had never been very good at paying attention to other people's needs. He had his own desires to contend with, after all. But there'd been something odd in his chest when he'd seen Rin crumple like that.

Kelevra had wanted to make him feel better.

Somehow, he'd ended up getting angry and tossing the guy onto the ground like some bitch.

Rin wasn't a bitch.

He was a flower, perfect and pretty and in full bloom, ready for the picking.

The idea of him wilting, and worse yet, for Kel being the reason for it…It didn't sit right with him.

Which pissed him off.

Caring about other people was a bore, and tedious, and not something he'd ever thought he'd have to bother wasting his time with, and yet, here he was. Inviting Rin to Friction, not so he could toss him down and fill him up and order him to want him back—like he wanted to—but because Baikal Void had told him to find out what Rin needed most and become the sole provider of it.

Rin needed an outlet, that much was obvious.

And since mind-numbing sex hadn't been enough for him, Kelevra figured this, Friction, might be.

He was so riled up he needed Baikal to tap his shoulder and point toward the entrance to realize the object of his fascination had just walked through the door.

The building had insanely high ceilings and a glass dome that opened at the touch of a button. Someone had it that way already when Kel had arrived, the chilly air filling the place with the scent of pine from the forest. It'd grown dark, an inky star-studded sky staring down at them.

Kelevra only noticed because Rin paused for a brief second in the doorway, head tipped back so he could look at it, a strange, almost nostalgic expression shifting his features.

An identical copy of Rin stepped up behind him and leaned in, whispering something against the curve of his ear, far too close for Kel's liking.

The copy, his twin Sila, also happened to be looking back at Kelevra, holding his gaze unwaveringly. He had to have heard what'd been done to his brother—both the night at the penthouse and earlier in the locker room—but if that bothered him in any way, he didn't show it.

Rin had mentioned something about being acquainted with a devil earlier…

As badly as he wanted to, Kelevra held his ground, even going so far as to lean back and sprawl out his arms on the bar as he waited. His instructions had been clear. He wanted Rin to present himself, which meant waiting the torturous minutes it took for his flower to locate him and cross the expanse of the room.

Had this place always been massive? It was a single level, a wide open space with some bleachers set against the same wall where the entrance was, the bar to the far right, and another door to the far left that led to another locker room and showers. There were three rings total, two smaller ones flanking a larger one set dead center on the concrete floor. Blood stains, spilled beer, and a few other questionable substances stained the ground, but aside from that, it was all kept clean and ready for use.

Rin was still in his uniform from earlier, the Academy pin attached to the leather belt cinched at his tapered waist. He looked wary, mismatched eyes pinging between Kel and Baikal who tipped his head in greeting at their approach.

His brother had ditched the school outfit, dressed casually in a red leather jacket that Kelevra was a little covetous of on sight, and sleek black jeans that hugged his long legs in all the right places. He trailed his eyes down them, making a note to put his flower in tighter pants the second they'd moved past this little dilemma and there was less of a risk of being punched for "treating him like a doll".

There was one upside to them being twins. At least he got to see what Rin might look like in other clothes, even if Rin wasn't the one currently wearing them.

"What?" Rin practically barked the second the two of them came to a stop some ten feet or so away.

Kelevra motioned with a finger for him to come closer, grinning when Rin opened his mouth to so obviously refuse, only to have his brother lean in a second time.

Whatever he said, it had Rin's spine straightening. "You're the fucking worst," he said, loud enough for both Kelevra and Kal to hear.

Sila chuckled, maintaining eye contact with Kelevra when he replied, "You love me."

"Yeah," Rin agreed tightly. "I do."

Kelevra emitted a low growl before he could help it, and Baikal chuckled at his side.

"It's literally his brother," Kal reminded quietly, but Kelevra didn't care.

The idea of his flower loving anyone else—loving someone when he didn't even yet *like* Kelevra—had him seeing red.

Rin walked closer and repeated in the same suspicious tone, "What?"

Someone laughed by the small ring, and his head turned to see who it was. Arlet was standing with Madden and a couple of Baikal's Satellite.

"I'm so sick of her," Baikal said. "Who invited the clingy music student?"

"Not me," Kelevra stated, eyes narrowing at the way Rin was still watching her. He snapped his fingers in front of his face and Rin blinked at him as though surprised. "What do you think you're doing, Flower?"

He scoffed. "Checking to make sure you didn't do anything to her. That was your threat, remember?"

No, not really.

Oh. Right.

Kelevra waved his hand absently. "I picked the most innocent-looking person in this joint."

Sila, who'd followed Rin closer, leaned into his brother's back, but before he could get a word out Kelevra shot him a warning glare.

"Don't even think about it, Imposter," he snapped.

Sila's brow winged up, his mouth twitching as he held back a smirk.

Rin's reaction was the complete opposite, his brow dipping low in distaste as he slid his hands into his front pockets and shifted his stance. As if he was preparing to take Kelevra on. Again.

"I'm curious—" Sila began, this time directing his comment to Kel, only to have Rin send him a warning look over his shoulder, shutting him up.

"No," Rin said, in a voice that left no room for argument, "You aren't."

"Apparently, I'm not," Sila agreed, standing down, just like that. He shifted his attention toward the room, almost as though he was dismissing Kelevra and

Baikal. Like now that he'd been ordered off participating, he was willingly separating himself from the goings on of present company.

All because Rin had given him a dirty look.

Why was that so…sexy?

It occurred to Kelevra then, that if Sila really was the Devil Rin had been referring to earlier, *this* was why Rin had been so confident that night at the penthouse. It was impossible to glean from a single interaction the dynamics of his relationship with his brother, but it was obvious that he at least maintained some control.

Suddenly, Kelevra was one hundred percent positive inviting his flower here had been the right call.

"Hey," a blond guy with hair close to Rin's golden shade—but not nearly as shiny—called from the center ring, drawing all of their attention his way. He waved an arm. "Someone fight me. I've got some serious steam to blow off."

"Berga almost blew up the science lab at school," Baikal drawled at Kelevra's side.

"Again?" Kelevra chuckled.

"Flix," he motioned to the guy still waving them over, "had to clean up the mess."

"That was one of yours?" Sila asked, tilting his head. Most people struggled to hold the Brumal Prince's gaze, the intensity, and darkness in his eyes too much for them, but Sila didn't so much as blink as he waited for a response.

"Yeah," Baikal said.

Sila turned to stare at Flix for a moment and then took a step toward the ring.

Faster than Kelevra knew he was capable of moving, Rin's hand shot out, grabbing onto his brother's elbow to yank him back. "No."

"You've been saying that word a lot, brother," Sila replied, but he didn't try to pull away. His eyes wandered over Rin's shoulder to Kelevra for a brief moment before returning to Rin, a slight glimmer there that had been absent before. "All right. You do it or I do it."

"This isn't the place—"

"This is exactly the place," he disagreed.

"Which of you is the older twin again?" Baikal asked, even though they all must have known he was well aware.

"Sila Varun was born one minute and two seconds before Rin Varun on the day of the Summer Solstice," Sila answered without skipping a beat.

"Don't be robotic," Rin scolded. "No one is going to fall for that."

"I'm being factual," he corrected.

"The younger twin should listen to the older twin," Baikal pointed between them. "Looks like you're up, Rin."

Kelevra sent Baikal a glare, even though he knew his friend was only trying to help him out. He'd brought Rin here specifically so the other guy could get into the ring and blow off some steam.

He'd prefer him hitting someone else before they hooked up again, get it out of his system.

"Seriously? Is someone coming or am I going to have to go burn something down to get my kicks tonight?" Flix called, losing his patience.

"Keep your firebug in line," Kelevra said before straightening from the bar. He rested a hand on Rin's narrow back, easing him toward the ring, and though his flower stiffened at the contact, he was smart enough not to pull away in the presence of their current audience. Once they'd moved far enough he was certain Baikal wouldn't be able to eavesdrop, he pressed his mouth to the curve of Rin's ear and whispered, "I'll reward you for this later."

Rin didn't ask what this was, but his tight expression never loosened. "You can do so by leaving me the fuck alone."

Punishment it would be.

He shoved Rin toward the ring when they got there, crossing his arms and shrugging when that earned him a scowl.

"What's up?" Flix peered over the edge of the ring, his arms propped on the velvet ropes surrounding it. "Don't think I know you."

"Rin," he drawled, tugging his t-shirt out from where it'd been tucked into his pants. In one swift movement, he had it over his head and discarded onto the ground, then he reached for the ropes and hauled himself up.

Kelevra was aware of Sila's presence coming up to his side, but he couldn't tear his eyes off Rin's toned body. Flix's gaze swept over him and he had a flash, an image of him taking the Brumal member by the skull and bashing his face into the concrete at his feet.

Maybe this hadn't been a good plan after all.

"Are there rules?" Rin asked when Flix picked up a pair of extra black fingerless gloves from the floor and handed them over. He slipped them on, nonplused about all of this despite his earlier resistance to his brother's suggestion.

They were drawing a crowd, several other people heading over to circle the ring, sensing blood in the water before the match had even begun.

Kelevra watched Rin closely, trying to gauge his reaction to having an audience since that seemed to be his biggest turn-off, but if it bothered him this time, he didn't show it. In fact, he was a completely blank slate. It was impossible to tell what he was feeling, whether he was excited or nervous. It was the exact opposite of how he'd been in the shower stall after they'd fucked. Then, he'd been so clearly overrun by emotion his body had shut down in order to protect itself from overstimulation. But now?

He'd made a comment to Sila about playing a robot.

He should look in a mirror.

Kel wasn't sure how he felt about it. On the one hand, logically he understood Rin's reaction wasn't specifically meant for him, but on the other, the idea that

Rin was locking him out made him seethe inside. What gave his flower the right to build up walls against him?

"You can tap out if you've had enough," Flix was explaining. "Otherwise, whoever passes out first loses. Who'd you say you were again?"

"I go to the Academy," Rin replied. "I'm a sophomore."

"Younger than me."

He smiled wryly. "That seems to get pointed out a lot."

"If you guys want to get to know one another I suggest a date instead," Zane called out from the opposite side of the ring. Until he saw Kelevra's angry look. He cleared his throat. "Never mind. You, uh, ready?"

No referee was standing in the ring with them or off to the side, but Madden hung close, ready to play intermediate at any given moment.

"You sure about this?" Baikal stepped up on Kelevra's other side. He'd brought his drink with him, staring into the ring as he swirled the dark blue contents in the glass. "You can't go flying off the handles when Flix inevitably hurts him."

Sila snorted, but when they both turned to look at him, his expression was as empty as Rin's.

Zane called the start, a bell clanging, and then everyone went quiet. It was obvious that Baikal wasn't the only one who expected this to go a certain way, some of the others sending Kelevra nervous glances.

He'd already promised himself he wouldn't retaliate. Flix was a Brumal member who stood on the mafia prince's Satellite. He was heavily trained and a fierce fighter who was quick on his feet. Kelevra didn't expect a sophomore Academy agent, someone who had only just barely started combat training, to beat a man like Flix.

This wasn't about winning anyway. It was about getting Rin to that sweet spot. That mental place where the body was too damn exhausted to care about anything other than feeling good. Physical satisfaction. Craving and need. He wanted his flower stripped down to his basic instincts.

Flix tested the waters at first, jabbing forward lightly to see how quickly Rin could evade before picking it up a notch. As soon as he started firing punches, Rin began getting pummeled.

Kelevra watched, growing more and more uneasy with each passing hit. Watching as Flix's fists connected with Rin's jaw, his sides, over his eyebrow. He split his lip and a growl rumbled up Kel's throat at the sight of the blood.

He loved blood. He thought it was sexy watching someone bleed. But this? Knowing the blood was there because of someone else? That just infuriated him. Not to mention, sure, he hadn't expected Rin to win, but he also hadn't anticipated this.

Rin was barely able to get in hits himself, too busy playing defense. He wasn't the worst fighter, the fact he was still standing after a few minutes a testament to that fact, but at this rate, if he didn't tap out, he'd surely get knocked out.

"You can't see it, can you," Sila's voice, light and low, cut through Kelevra's agitation and he frowned over at the twin. He still didn't look concerned. Not even a little bit. "He made it sound like you were interesting," Sila continued, clearly knowing he had Kel's attention. "I'm not involving myself because he asked. Because I got the impression you made him feel seen. But you don't," he finally turned and caught Kelevra's gaze with a bored one of his own, "see. Do you?"

Kelevra frowned, torn between being pissed off at the obvious insult and curious over the cryptic comments.

"He's faking," Baikal was the one who replied, drink held low, forgotten. His eyes followed the fight closely, a sparkle of intrigue there that Kel didn't like.

"Always." Sila grinned, the smile cutting across his face in a way that was somehow the opposite of everything it should be. It wasn't friendly or open or kind. It was cold and twisted, with an edge to it that up until this point, Kelevra had only seen staring back at himself in the mirror.

Rin was getting beat to a pulp *on purpose*?

"My brother is all about control. He lives it. Breathes it. Caged and confined. He'll suffocate himself like that, but he doesn't seem to care enough to stop."

What the hell?

"Would you like to?" Sila suddenly asked. "See, I mean?"

Without waiting for a reply, Sila stepped a little closer to the ring, lifting his voice so it would carry and be heard over the rough sounds of the fight. "The damage to the face has become noticeable, brother."

It made no sense. Coded words spoken seemingly at random.

But it was like a switch flicked for Rin. His whole body tightened and then went easy all at once, the look in his gaze shifting. When Flix swung, Rin dipped and evaded, twisting on his heels in a move far more graceful than any he'd shown prior.

Sila clearly wasn't satisfied. "Should I take over for you?"

"Shut," Rin exploded, switching from defense to offense so fast Flix couldn't keep up, "the fuck," he feinted a right hook then delivered a left, "up!"

The blow was hard enough that it took Flix down, and while he worked on getting back to his feet, Rin stormed over to the edge where Kelevra and they were standing and spat a mixture of blood and saliva down between his brother's feet.

Sila gave his face a pointed once over. "Forget three days. That's going to take at least a week to heal. Well done."

"You're the one who told me to get in here, asshole."

"I don't recall suggesting you forget about the rules," Sila replied.

"I pulled back enough and you know it, so don't give me any lip."

Flix had risen and was coming up behind him, but Rin didn't seem to notice, still glowering down at his twin.

Kelevra tensed, but his worry was for nothing.

Just as Flix was about to lash out, Rin gave Sila one last dark look and spun, dropping to his knees. Flix's arms ended up swinging over his shoulders, leaving him open for Rin's attack lower.

He punched him in the side, right over the liver, and then shifted behind him while Flix sputtered and grabbed at the injury.

Flix growled and tried hard to regain the upper hand, barreling forward, delivering as many attacks as he could. But each and every one was deflected. It became painfully apparent that Sila had been right earlier.

Rin had been faking it, taking all those hits to make it seem like he was weaker and less skilled when in reality…

He was toying with a Brumal member like this was a beginners class for children and Flix was some wide-eyed five-year-old kid who'd mouthed off to his trainer. Only, Rin wasn't glaring or trying to teach him a lesson like a pissed-off trainer would be.

No, he was grinning. A real grin too, the elation on his face mixed with the hard steel of his eyes taking Kelevra's breath away.

His hair was matted from sweat and there was blood still dripping from a cut over his left eyebrow and the side of his lip. But his muscles bunched as he moved, clipped and steady, well-thought-out motions that looked as though they'd been choreographed for how accurately delivered they were.

It seemed like Rin could go all night, but after a particularly hard blow to the side of his head, Flix did the unthinkable.

The asshole tapped out.

Sila met Rin at the side, standing still when his brother jumped down and slapped a palm against his shoulder, jostling him. But they were both smiling, laughing. Sharing a moment.

"Someone is pretending not to be a devil," Baikal said at Kelevra's side, watching the twins same as him.

"You think somethings off about Sila too?" Kel didn't like how weirdly close he was to his brother. But also, he recognized the signs for what they were. Saw that in some ways he and the older twin were similar.

Baikal gave him a look. "I wasn't talking about Sila."

Chapter 14:

Kelevra and Sila were having a standoff.

Rin had disappeared into the locker room a few minutes ago with his brother, but then Sila had exited just as Kel was about to enter, blocking the door with his broad frame.

"Move." Kelevra was two seconds away from rearranging his face. Literally. He hated how alike to his flower the other man appeared. When he'd first discovered they were twins, he'd taken a moment to consider if that excited him. The possibility of bedding identical people was everyone's fantasy, right?

Apparently not his.

It wasn't just because the very idea of Sila's hand wandering over Rin's bared flesh—flesh that belonged to Kel—made him see red. He also wasn't physically attracted to him. Go figure. Identical, and yet Kelevra's dick didn't so much as twitch as he stared Sila down.

"You don't like me very much." Sila tilted his head, inspecting him.

"I see the feeling is mutual." He glanced over his shoulder to the closed bright red door pointedly. "I gave you an order."

"We aren't at the Academy right now," Sila replied.

"I'm your Imperial," Kelevra reminded, baring his teeth. "We don't have to be anywhere but on this damn planet for you to have to listen to me."

"Rin wouldn't like it if you tried to hurt me." The corner of his lips turned up tauntingly.

"What he doesn't know and all that jazz." Kel was trying to figure out if he should swing, or simply shove him aside. He was a little bit bigger than Sila, and he was able to overpower Rin easily enough so…with how similar the two were, he was guessing he'd be able to do the same with him.

"I'm not as easy to hide as a pill in your pocket," Sila said. He glanced pointedly down at Kelevra's pants but then seemed to consider something. "Trade you."

Some of his anger subsided, replaced with curiosity. "What?"

"I've got somewhere to be anyway." He held out his palm. "Give me the pill and not only will I move out of the way, I'll leave entirely. There's something more interesting waiting for me downtown."

He was going to ditch his brother? In exchange for a single drug? Kelevra almost asked him who he intended it for, but then he realized he didn't care.

"Deal." Kel dropped the small white pill into Sila's hand.

Sila smiled and slipped it into his own pocket, stepping to the side. "Care to make another?"

Kelevra canted his head, waiting.

"I'll give you some advice, and you promise to do me a favor someday."

"That's fairly open-ended." And dangerous. Kel grinned. "I like it. You just can't use it to ask me to let him go. I won't."

Sila grunted. "I wouldn't waste a favor with an Imperial on that. My brother can more than take care of himself. No. It'll be something else. I just haven't ironed out all the kinks yet, so to speak."

"Deal." Kelevra didn't much care what he was going to ask him for, so long as it wasn't about Rin.

Sila sidled a little closer. "Offer to pay our tuition fees."

He frowned, a bit disappointed. "That's all?"

"Father is threatening to cut us off thanks to that stunt you pulled with the imposed marriage," Sila said. "My brother's been stressing all day over how to keep him off our backs and keep us both here, on planet."

"He isn't going anywhere," Kel growled.

"On that, we are in agreement." Sila gave him one last knowing look and then headed away without another word. If he was concerned about leaving Rin alone with a man who'd already forced himself on him in the past, he didn't seem it.

Maybe they weren't as close as Kelevra had believed?

He waited for a moment to see if it was a trap of some sort, if perhaps Sila was merely messing with him and would storm back and rage about how he couldn't believe Kel actually thought he'd abandon his brother. But nope.

Interesting.

Kelevra slipped into the locker room quietly, flicking the lock behind him so they wouldn't be disturbed. The room was setup with the entranceway facing an alcove where they stored some gear—boxing gloves they seldom used, old sandbags, and stuff like that. The right opened up to the main area where a wall of red lockers was. Their names had been added, one for each of them, some bullshit thing Baikal's future butcher, Berga, had done. Floor-to-ceiling mirrors made up the rest of the wall with the entrance.

The showers were attached to the side of that, but unlike back at the Academy, they had doors. There was also a sauna, which was where Kel typically spent his time unwinding.

Rin hadn't bothered entering that section, however, standing instead at the end of the lockers, between the metal and a low, polished bench. He was rifling through an empty locker, having changed his pants already, though he was still shirtless.

His brother had helped him with his face, patching him up somewhat so there was a bandage across his eyebrow and the blood had been scrubbed from him.

Kelevra couldn't believe he was getting jealous over the guy's brother, and yet here he was, annoyed at the thought of Sila touching Rin's face, tipping his chin up to the light and blowing across his wounds like some—

"What the fuck are you wearing?" He'd made it halfway into the room before the new pants Rin was in finally registered. Rin hadn't come here with anything but the clothes on his back, which meant... "Whose fucking clothes are those?"

Rin scowled at him but tugged loosely at the stretchy material of the dark gray sweatpants. "Think they're Madden's." He hummed. "No, actually, Kazimir handed them to me. Maybe they're his."

God damn Kazimir.

Baikal's cousin, and the bane of Kel's existence. He hated that fucker with a passion. Even more, now that he'd had the audacity to slink in here and offer up clothing to *his* flower.

"Take them off," he growled.

"I just put them on," Rin argued.

Kelevra stormed forward, intent on tearing the offending pants off himself. "You're mine. I won't have you walking around in some other man's—" The soft tick of a blade springing free was the only warning he got before the sharp and cool edge of one was being pressed against his neck, right over his carotid artery.

The bench was still between them, and Rin didn't seem too perturbed holding a weapon to his Imperial Prince's throat.

"Threatening the life of your prince is grounds for execution," Kelevra drawled, nice and low, ignoring the way a fire was licking at his insides. He didn't have a death wish or anything, but something about the confidence on Rin's face was sexy as all hell.

Rin lifted a shoulder. "I guess that's one way for me to get out of this betrothal."

His mood soured instantly. "You aren't getting out of it. Period."

"Want to bet?"

"You'll lose." Kelevra wasn't letting him go. He was going to keep him and tie him to him completely and eternally. Hadn't Rin been the one to suggest it first even? Restrain him. Tie him down. Subdue him.

Quick as a whip, Kel struck, shoving Rin's wrist to the side, the blade slicing slightly but not deep enough to cause any real harm. He twisted in the process, elbowing Rin in the stomach as he wrenched the wrist holding the weapon.

Rin lost hold and it clattered to the floor, Kel snatching it up, leaped over the bench, and shoved Rin up against the lockers with a loud bang that had probably been heard outside by anyone close enough to the doors.

He angled the blade toward Rin and used the tip to lift his chin, chuckling at the anger snapping behind those mismatched eyes.

And the mirroring heat.

Oh yeah. Kel wasn't the only one who got off on that fight against Flix.

"Like hurting people, Flower?"

"I'm going to seriously enjoy hurting you," Rin snapped, only for Kelevra to laugh again.

"I'm the one holding the knife now."

"Keyword, now. There's always later."

"That a threat?" Kelevra, surprisingly, didn't get many of those.

"Just imagine how vulnerable you'll be when you're sleeping in that ridiculously massive bed of yours," Rin said. "All I'll have to do is reach for a weapon, a blade, or a blaster, and I could end you before you'd even see it coming."

He let out a low groan. "I see what you're doing," Kel told him, "trying to make me distrust you so I'll leave you alone and give you space. But it isn't going to work, sweetheart. Want to know why?"

Rin pressed his lips together, refusing to speak, not that Kelevra needed him to.

It'd been a rhetorical question anyway.

"Now all I can picture is you in my bed, naked, strung up all pretty for me." His cock pressed uncomfortably against the seam of his dress pants. "It's where you belong."

"No," Rin said.

"Even your defiance gets me going," Kelevra informed him. "Makes me want to wrestle you down to the ground and force my cock into that sweet ass of yours. Make you grind against me and beg for it, all while you pretend your dick's not leaking for me. Are you dripping for me right now?" He cupped him, biting down on his lower lip to keep in another groan when he found Rin was in fact hard as a rock in his hand.

"It was the fight," he spat. "It's got nothing to do with you."

"I was the one who invited you here," Kelevra corrected. "I'm the one who let you step into that ring."

"You didn't let me do shit. I make my own choices."

Something dark pricked at Kelevra's arousal, worming its way in until he was grimacing and his grip on Rin's dick tightened too much.

Rin sucked in a breath and reached down to try and pull him away, but when the knife was pressed in closer, he froze.

"You make your own choices unless it's your brother telling you to do something, that it?" He hated thinking about how easy it'd been for Sila. All he'd done was taken a single step closer, lobbed off one sentence, and Rin had dropped the act for him instantly. "He had you shedding your fake skin, turning into a wild, feral thing. For. *Him*."

Some of Rin's steal-like exterior cracked, his confusion and sudden uncertainty shining in his gaze as he stared back at Kel. "Are you...You're not jealous of my brother, right? Because look, I get you're certifiably insane, but that's just looney on another level."

"You don't mind when he touches you." Kelevra had noticed that too. How with everyone else—even that Brennon guy at school—Rin tended to tense up just a tiny bit when they got too close, but Sila had put his hands on him several times tonight and gotten no negative reactions whatsoever.

"He's my identical twin," Rin huffed. "Not all of us are into katoptronophilia. Don't think I didn't notice your bedroom ceiling is made entirely of mirrors. I did."

So Kel liked to watch himself fuck. So what?

He was gorgeous. Who wouldn't want to watch him go at it?

"I've got no interest in screwing myself, or seeing myself screwed," Rin scowled and pressed lightly at Kel's wrist, the one holding the knife. "Back off."

"He wouldn't fuck like you," Kel said, barely catching the way Rin went stiff at that comment, too caught up trying to conjure an image of what Sila Varun might look like during sex.

"Don't," Rin's voice was deadly soft, barely a whisper spoken between them. "Doing this to one of us is enough. If you so much as lift a finger toward my brother—"

This wasn't exactly how Kelevra had anticipated things going down. He'd hoped he'd invite Rin, have the guy blow off some steam, and then coax him back onto his cock. Coax being the important part of the plan.

Kel had never been very good at following plans.

His flower had just exposed a weakness, and while he'd been trying to play things nice, he wasn't above using this newfound information to his advantage.

Screw Baikal's way of doing mental gymnastics. Kelevra preferred to do things the Imperial way. Bribery and your everyday run-of-the-mill extortion. More his style.

"What if I did?" He wouldn't. He had literally no sexual interest in Sila, but Rin didn't have to know that. "What if I went to my sister right now and told her I'd changed my mind? It's not unheard of you know. An Imperial taking *two* consorts instead of one."

"We'll kill you first," he hissed, but that wasn't the reaction Kelevra was after.

He squeezed his junk again until Rin's lips were twisting in barely veiled pain, then he eased up and began tracing circles with his thumb over his hard dick behind the pants. "Maybe you're right, I'm already discovering one of you is enough of a handful to manage. I could always have him banished instead. Shipped off planet and sent back home. What was it called again? Started with a T…" He remembered. Kel couldn't forget anything when it came to his flower, but he could tell by the way Rin was holding his breath this tactic was working.

Forget Baikal's shitty advice. Give him what he needs?

This was what Rin needed. A shove in the right direction.

Kelevra's direction.

He pressed the flat part of the knife beneath his jaw. "Breathe, sweetheart."

Rin sucked in a sharp breath, eyes wide and frantic.

He was starting to panic; Kel recognized it this time, saw all the signs when earlier he'd been too blinded by lust to bother.

That had been messed up of him, he admitted. He wanted Rin, wasn't above forcefully taking him against his will, but that didn't mean he wanted him damaged in the process. Emotions were funny things, things that someone like Kelevra didn't fully comprehend all the time. Still, he got the gist. They were important and fragile yada yada yada.

"Or," Kelevra made it sound like he was just coming up with the idea, "I could pay for him to stay."

Some of the faraway look in Rin's eyes dissipated. "What?"

Huh. Maybe Sila was onto something after all.

"You'd like that, wouldn't you?" Kel released his dick and reached up to brush strands of his sandy-gold hair from his forehead. It was still damp from the fight, clinging to the tips of his fingers the way he wished Rin would cling to him.

Soon.

"All it would take is one phone call," he continued, keeping his tone gentle and lax, a sharp juxtaposition to the knife he still wielded. "I could pay off all three remaining years in one go even." It was tempting to try and milk it, to offer only the first year and then make Rin give him something else down the line to pay off the others, but Kel was starting to learn.

Sila had mentioned Rin was all about control, and that was something Kelevra had already picked up on. It was part of what had enthralled him so much. Watching all of that tight-knit command over himself slip through

Rin's fingers as he'd come apart beneath Kel that night in the penthouse?

The most beautiful thing he'd ever seen.

And he wanted to see it again.

He *would* see it again, for as many times as he wanted to. Possibly for forever if this thing he was feeling never went away.

Rin was the type of personality that carefully thought through everything, down to the minute details. Past, present, future? He'd account for them all, and any potential bumps that could occur down the road. Which was why offering to pay for all three years, to take away the burden of having to fret over something that wouldn't come to pass for months yet, was the smart play.

Rin searched his expression for a moment before finally asking, "What would I have to do in return?"

Hook. Line. And sinker.

Maybe this whole reading people bullshit was easier than Kelevra had thought.

"That's simple, Flower." Kel's hand slipped from his hair to settle on his shoulder. He pulled the knife away at the same time, but kept it close, the threat still apparent. "All you've got to do," he pressed, lightly though, a clear indicator he expected Rin to go all on his own, "is get on your knees for me."

He hesitated, that defiance returning to his multicolored gaze for a few seconds before he was doing it, dropping down before Kelevra, maintaining eye contact the whole way.

Good Light, seeing someone kneel for him had never been so erotic before in his life, but Kelevra somehow kept his cool. He waited for a tick, letting Rin start to wonder what might happen next, what Kel might ask for. Letting it ruminate until the first stirrings of doubt had his flower's brow furrowing ever so slightly in the middle.

Then Kelevra lowered onto the bench. He held the knife loosely in his left hand as he spread his thighs wide, settling them at either side of Rin who remained motionless all the while. He leaned back on the bench, resting himself on his palms, and then he jutted his chin at the obvious bulge pressing behind the ruby-red pants he was wearing.

"Suck."

Rin flinched as though Kelevra had let off a gunshot instead of simply delivered a one word order. He shifted on his knees, clearly trying to weigh his options before finally settling on this being his best one.

Of course it was. He was going to marry Kelevra, that was already a done deal, but that didn't mean Rin couldn't get a few things out of it himself. Kel was willing to give him whatever he wanted.

He just wouldn't be telling him as much. Not just yet. Not until he had his flower tamed, those sharp vines of his so twisted around Kel it would take a lifetime just to untangle them from one another.

Rin slowly lifted his hands, reaching for the button on Kelevra's pants, glaring up at him.

"That's it, Flower," Kel urged. "Dig those thorns of yours deep into me. The same way I'll be burying my cock in that pretty mouth of yours in a moment."

"You're fucked up," Rin told him as he undid the zipper, leaning back a bit when Kelevra's fully erect cock sprung free.

"Oh, you don't know the half of it." But he would. Soon. Kelevra had never wanted to own something so completely and entirely before, hadn't even realized that was a feeling he was capable of.

He wanted Rin though. Wanted all of him. Wanted him crying and raging beneath him. Wanted him giving and taking. Soothing and hurting. The cut on Kel's throat from the knife stung but in the most delicious way imaginable. A tiny prick of a thorn.

A gift from his flower.

When Rin's hand finally wrapped around the base of his cock, Kel's head fell back and he moaned.

"Light," Rin cursed. "You're huge."

"Don't need to butter me up, sweetheart." He lifted his head to meet his gaze. "I'm already a sure thing. And so are you." He motioned again. "Get to work."

He could practically feel the animosity snapping off of Rin like a live thing, but he kept it contained, giving Kel an exploratory pump of his fist as he got more comfortable on his knees.

Kelevra realized with a smirk that Rin was approaching this the same way he did everything else. "It doesn't need to be perfect," he said. "It just needs to be inside you."

Rin scowled. "I don't do anything in half measures."

He chuckled. "Suit yourself. Make it good for me then."

Almost as though he was taking it as a challenge, Rin finally leaned forward, tongue tentatively sweeping out to lap at the thick, swollen cockhead once before he wrapped those lips around the girth of him and bobbed down in one slick glide.

Kelevra felt himself bump against the back of Rin's throat and honestly, it was a miracle he didn't come right then and there.

Rin flattened his tongue and brushed it against the underside of his cock as he pulled off, smacking his lips in this obscene gesture before he swallowed him all over again. He set an even rhythm, head bobbing up and down, sucking as he drew back, humming whenever his crown hit the back of his throat.

Movement in the corner of his eye caught Kelevra's attention and he turned his head, taking in the reflection of him propped up on the bench, his flower between his legs, satisfying him. Worshiping his cock so good.

Maybe too good.

Rin knew exactly what to do with his tongue, knew exactly how much teeth he was allowed to skate over the sensitive skin at the top of his dick to send electric waves jolting through Kel's hips. He knew when to hollow his cheeks, and when it was safe for him to take a breath.

The whole thing was incredibly controlled. Amazing as all hell, but controlled.

It wasn't even the fact that, in a way, Rin was the one with the power now, the one leading Kel—literally by the balls. He didn't really care about that, didn't mind a little power struggle between them.

No, what Kelevra couldn't shake from his mind was how perfect Rin was at this. The kind of skill level that had to be taught and learned through experience to achieve.

His right hand lifted from the bench and the next thing he knew, he'd grabbed onto the back of Rin's head and shoved, his hips lifting at the same time so he could drive himself as deep into that skilled mouth as he could get.

Rin sputtered and choked, his palms coming up to brace against Kelevra's powerful thighs.

Kel watched it all happen in the mirror, entranced by Rin's reflection, struggling as he ground himself against his face. Rin's nose rubbed against the trail of dark hairs leading to his dick, and Kelevra hissed at the contact, liking it.

He'd never killed a person this way before, but he could, and that concept....Thrilling.

Not that he'd do that here, with Rin.

Murder wasn't in the cards for his flower. He kept good care of his things. Even if he broke them a little from vigorous use, he was always sure to polish them back to a shine afterward. Call him a spoiled prince, it was true, but his sisters had made sure to instill a sense of pride in his belongings.

He yanked Rin off his cock, watching a string of saliva trail from his lips to his flushed crown.

Rin gasped and coughed, his eyes filled with tears, cheeks ruddy.

Kelevra's face was red too, but not nearly as much. His chest was rising and falling quickly, the suit jacket stretched taught against his back. He looked sexy.

"Tell me I look good, sweetheart," he ordered, tearing his gaze off the mirror to meet Rin's eyes.

His flower was pissed, but when he rubbed his thighs together, the bulge between his legs was obvious.

"Tell me I look edible," Kelevra insisted, fingers tightening in Rin's hair.

"You look," he swallowed and looked like he'd rather swallow nails, "edible."

"Then be a good filthy fucking flower," Kel grinned, "and eat me up."

Rin was smart enough to suck in a lungful of oxygen a second before he was forced back down onto his cock.

Kelevra rammed it into his throat, growling at the tight squeeze, holding himself there with a strong hand at the back of Rin's skull. It seemed to be like this whenever it came to the younger guy. This unexplainable urge to be inside of him, to burry himself so deep Rin wouldn't be able to separate them, no matter how hard or long he struggled.

Maybe Rin finally got the memo, finally realized just how crazed about him Kelevra actually was, because the second he loosened his hold, Rin started bobbing all over again, sucking him in an almost frenzied state.

Almost like he wanted Kel buried deep inside of him too.

Chapter 15:

The second he felt it coming, Kelevra yanked Rin off of him and shoved.

His shoulders hit the lockers, rattling the metal, and he blinked at Kel, as if in a daze.

It was lust. The guy was totally gone.

"Lean back," he ordered tightly, taking himself in his fist so he could pump his cock. The orgasm came quick and he aimed at Rin's face. He exploded, come shooting out to land all over Rin's red lips and his chin. A thick glob hung there for a second before plopping down onto his chest, the sight making Kelevra go crazy, his palm working himself even harder, desperate to see every last drop painted across his flower's skin.

When he was finished, he took in the view.

Rin's hair was mussed, and he was still out of breath, his chest covered in come, looking every bit like he belonged to Kelevra. If he'd been told to conjure the perfect man from his fantasies, Kel wouldn't have been able to even come close to this level of perfection. Rin was staring back at him, raw and open, that feral glint he'd had in the ring shining back at Kelevra full force, like he'd set him ablaze telekinetically if he could.

His little flower was pissed off but impossibly turned on, his dick having made a huge wet spot in the center of those sweatpants.

Those damn sweatpants.

Kazimir's.

It was almost as though Rin sensed the change in him before Kelevera even did, his shoulders tensing as he set his feet flat against the floor, clearly about to make a run for it.

Kel was faster, hand shooting forward to grab him by the arm and pull him up so he was standing. Though not for long. He tore the pants down his long legs, lifting Rin out of them roughly so he could toss them as far away as possible. Then he was bringing Rin's left leg over the bench and shifting him closer to one side of it.

"What are you doing?" Rin gasped as he was pushed down with one hard hand on his shoulder, suddenly straddling the bench, facing the mirrors. His eyes lifted so he could watch Kel's reflection, but Kelevra was already watching him back.

He tracked the rise and fall of his throat muscles when Rin swallowed, remembered how close to all of that his cock had just been. That was enough to have him lengthening all over again, his dick so hard it was like the blowjob had never happened.

Planting a hand on the back of Rin's neck, he folded him forward so his head was hanging off the end of the bench.

Rin's hands scrabbled for purchase as Kelevra continued to position him, lifting his hips so Kel could slide a knee beneath him. He moaned when he was lowered onto Kel's thigh, his kneecap bumping against the underside of Rin's balls.

Satisfied for now, Kelevra reached around, scraping his seed off of Rin's chest. With this angle, Rin's ass was forced upward, his fluttering hole visible between his spread cheeks. Kel smeared his come over it, pinning Rin down with his arm across his lower back when he made as though to climb off the bench.

"I could go in with no prep like earlier," Kelevra warned, even as he corkscrewed a finger past that tight ring of muscle. "Or, you can stay still and take it like you should."

Rin didn't seem to struggle with acceptance as much this time around, his body only staying clenched up for a second before he relaxed. He eased his chest down to the bench, hands going to the floor to help steady himself as Kelevra worked in a second finger. He didn't make any sounds, kept impressively still.

But Kel saw the truth reflected in the mirror.

Rin was focusing on his breathing, clearly counting his breaths as he inhaled and exhaled, his brow pinched. When Kel shoved in a third finger with a little more force, his mouth popped open on a silent oh, his glazed expression jumping up as though he'd just recalled Kelevra could be watching.

As soon as their eyes met, Kelevra curled all three fingers, scrapping his trimmed nails lightly against Rin's inner walls as he pulled out. He pumped them back in, and Rin pressed back into him ever so slightly, almost like his body had reacted without his approval.

Sure enough, his frown deepened.

"You're adorable, you know that?" Kel grinned when that earned him a silent glare. "There's nothing for you to think about in here, sweetheart. No reason for you to torture yourself. Stop working that pretty little head into exhaustion and," he removed his fingers and then brushed them lightly across the underside of Rin's balls, "let this take over instead. I've got you. I'm in charge. All you have to do is sit back and enjoy the ride."

He reached into his pocket and pulled out a packet of lube. He'd been in a rush earlier and had absently thought to take one from the stash in his car.

"Do you always carry that shit around?" Rin asked, but it was spoken in an accusatory tone.

"I told you," Kelevra tore the packet with his teeth, "I got you, Flower. Be grateful I'm bothering with it at all." He'd stretched him nice and open, and there was enough of his spunk it wouldn't be a dry glide in, but... "You can never have too much lubrication."

He slathered his cock, biting the inside of his cheek when the feel of his own hands over his oversensitive skin had his member twitching. Once that was ready, he grabbed Rin by the hips, lifting him so he could slide his thigh free and take up position behind him. At the last second, he paused, glancing up to meet his gaze in the mirror.

Kel held them like that for a tense moment to see if Rin would seize the opportunity to complain or lie to him again and say he didn't want it.

But Rin merely stared back, unblinkingly. Waiting.

Kelevra flicked his hips forward, finding his target and slipping inside. He groaned as he watched Rin's hole stretch around his cock, accommodating him as he sunk deeper and deeper until he'd completely disappeared. He undulated, relishing the feeling of those hot, velvety walls griping him tight.

Draping his body forward, he held Rin close as he started fucking into him, shallow thrusts at first that started to grow more urgent the longer he stayed nestled within that heat. He licked up Rin's spine and then buried his nose against the crook of his neck, breathing in that sea salt scent. Beneath them, the bench shook, the metal legs rattling against the concrete, the sound accompanied by the slapping of flesh against flesh and Rin's sharp intakes as he struggled to contain himself even with Kelevra balls deep inside of him.

Kel cupped his jaw and forced his head to tip up, the move also causing Rin's body to bow, his hips tipping so that on the next stroke forward, he slipped in even deeper. He groaned.

Rin ground his teeth together.

"Unfurl, Flower," he demanded, clipped as he felt himself get closer to the edge. He wouldn't let himself drop though, not until he forced Rin over first. Kel latched his teeth between Rin's shoulder and neck and bit down, licking at the light wound only after Rin cried out. "Come apart for me."

Kelevra slid his other hand around the curve of Rin's waist and captured his dick, timing his movements with the tempo of his hips.

Rin's mouth opened with a gasp, and Kelevra grinned.

"Come for me," he commanded.

Just like that, Rin obeyed. He jerked in his hold, his dick spasming as it emptied into Kelevra's palm.

Kel pulled him upright so he was practically seated on him, his whole body sinking onto Kelevra's cock. He jerked up into him, watching as Rin whined as he tapped against his prostate repeatedly.

The look on his flower's face was pure euphoria.

Seeing it sent Kelevra toppling, and he shoved himself in as deep as he could go, arms coming around Rin to keep him in place as he pumped him full. Full of his come, in his building, at his club.

His. His. His.

"I'm never letting you go," he didn't realize he was speaking, the words tumbling out of him as quickly as his spunk was spilling from his cock. "You were made for me. You were made to be mine."

He tugged Rin's face back, tongue pressing between his lips so he could feast on him, grinding into him the same way he was still rocking up into his hole. He tasted like a mixture of salt and sweat, a hint of musk, probably left over from the wild blowjob he'd given.

It was the best damn taste Kel had ever tasted.

If he could turn it into a lollipop flavor he would.

There was no need to though, was there.

He could have this taste whenever he pleased. Have this ass too. And this smell.

He groaned and nuzzled his cheek against Rin's, pealing his eyes open to find those mismatched eyes, wide and filled with something he couldn't place, on him in the mirror.

It didn't matter what Rin was feeling at the moment, to be honest. Kel was too much a slave to what *he* was feeling. To this intense ownership and rightness he now felt toward the man in his arms.

He'd asked his sister to grant his betrothal so Rin would get over that pesky embarrassment issue and stop not wanting to be seen with him. Carrying around drugs wasn't his style and he didn't like the thought of having to drug him every time he wanted to get laid. But now he was seeing how smart that move had actually been. How perfect.

Kelevra lowered his head so that his face was hovering right next to Rin's in the mirror, their reflections looking well fucked, all rosy skin and frantic breaths. "You're my Royal Consort," he said, testing it out, liking the way it rolled off his tongue and seemed to explode into the room like fireworks. His face split into a wolfish grin, the one that sent people scurrying, but with Rin so caught up in his hold, still impaled on his dick, there was no fear of him getting away.

"Say it, Consort," he ordered. "Tell me you're mine. Don't—" He pressed his cheek against Rin's before the other man could speak, "ruin this. If you tarnish this moment, I'm not sure what I'll do. Just give control over to me. Don't think. Just do. Tell me."

Rin obviously wanted to argue, wanted to spit and claw his way out of Kelevra's hold, it was written clear as day in his harsh gaze and the set of his shoulders. But he must have seen something on Kel's face as well because he ended up doing none of that.

In a tone that was only slightly sarcastic, he held his eyes and complied. "Yes. I'm yours." A second later his expression turned panicked.

Kelevra's cock was hard again.

"Hold on," Rin started, but Kel didn't listen.

He bent him back over the bench and fucked him until both of their voices were raw.

Chapter 16:

Rin grumbled when something tickled his cheek and tried to brush it away.

"Quit it," Kelevra said, unamused. "We're almost there."

There, where?

He'd barely managed to lift his head from the Imperial's shoulder—why was he carrying Rin on his back?—when he felt himself tumble backward, letting out a yelp. He came awake all at once the second his ass hit the mattress, a pained sound slipping past his lips.

"Mother fucker," he growled, rolling onto his side, glaring daggers at Kelevra who was making quick work of the buttoned sleeves on his dress shirt. "Prick."

"Yeah," Kel agreed. "I used mine and it turned you to mush. Literally. Do you remember passing out on me?"

Rin frowned. They'd been doing it against the lockers—for the fourth time—and he'd orgasmed and...

"How much water did you drink today?" Kelevra asked absently as he removed his shirt and walked over to a door. He disappeared inside, and Rin got the impression it was a walk-in closet. When he came back a second later, his pants were gone as well, leaving him in a pair of tight black boxer-briefs.

Rin slapped his hand away when he went to press it to his forehead.

"Don't be childish," Kel told him. "You're dehydrated and exhausted. Wait here."

"Where are you going?"

"To get you something that'll pump you full of electrolytes."

"That's the only thing you'll be pumping me full of from here on out," Rin promised darkly.

Kel paused by the door, tipping his head. "For tonight, yes."

"Asshole!" If there was something nearby he could throw, he would have. Instead, he slumped down on the bed, tossing his arm over his eyes when he was immediately greeted by his own reflection showcased all over Kelevra's mirrored ceiling. "Damn mirrors."

He should be furious that he'd been brought here against his will, but he couldn't muster that familiar spark of anger, too drained from the day. Finding out about the betrothal, sex, his talk with his brother, sparring, then more sex…Yeah, it made sense he was too exhausted to bother with wrathfulness at the moment. Maybe tomorrow.

It beat having to crawl back to his dorm at the Academy and explain to his roommate Daylen why he couldn't feel his legs.

This had been irresponsible.

His brother was partially to blame.

It didn't take a genius to guess that he'd told Kelevra about the tuition costs, or that he'd left Rin alone at Friction shortly thereafter, completely at the Imperial Prince's mercy—which they both knew he didn't possess. Tomorrow, once he'd recovered, he was going to give his brother a piece of his mind.

Maybe even punch him for real this time. He dabbed lightly at his busted lip, wincing. Yeah, it wasn't like it would hurt them now that he'd already ended up like this. When he grinned, not even the pain of having his broken skin stretching was enough to wipe the expression off his face.

"Thinking about making good on that threat earlier?" Kelevra returned, a serving tray in hand. He placed it on the end table and pulled Rin up into a sitting positon, ignoring his mild struggles. There was a ceramic jade teapot and a matching mug, and he poured in steaming contents from the pot, blowing on it a few times before holding it out to Rin.

He stared at it and then up at the Imperial. "Is it drugged?"

"Does it need to be?"

"I'll behave," Rin grumbled, snatching the mug. He sipped at it, testing the temperature, an earthly flavor greeting his tongue. "What is this?"

"Aura tea," Kelevra said. "It'll help replenish your system." He disappeared into the bathroom next, the sound of running water coming a moment later.

Rin drank the tea—because it was delicious, and he was thirsty, not because he'd been told to—but braced himself when Kelevra returned with the water still running in the background. "I'm not going in there."

"I love watching you guess what's coming," Kel smirked, grabbing a large gray t-shirt from the top dresser drawer. He tossed it over his shoulder and turned back. "I can carry you, or you can enter of your own volition. The choice is yours. The fact I'm even giving you options at all is generous of me."

He was going to kill his brother the next time he saw him. Turning himself into the brunt of a joke with Daylen and the guys was starting to seem more appealing than his current predicament.

"Seriously, I really can't anymore." Rin was hoping the Imperial Prince would act out of character for once and listen. He didn't care about Rin, he just wanted what he wanted when he wanted it. That was another reason this would never work between the two of them, no matter how good the orgasms were.

No matter how on the nose those comments Kelevra had made about him being able to be himself had gotten to him. He hadn't meant them anyway. It'd just been heat-of-the-moment bullshit. Kel had been talking with his dick, plain and simple, and Rin needed to remember that.

"I've only been your betrothed for a day," Rin continued when Kel didn't say anything, "and I passed out. This is too much for me." He almost added that Kelevra was too much for him, but that would be a blatant lie, and with his all-seeing fucking eye, there was a great chance the Imperial Prince would pick up on that.

As far as stimulus went, Kelevra actually provided the exact kind of twisted cocktail Rin needed to escape his headspace and let loose. Things between them were rough and electric and all-consuming. But it wasn't real and it wouldn't last. Rin was a shiny new toy, and as soon as he lost his luster, Kel would toss him like he did everything else he no longer felt compelled to keep.

"Plus," he added, "I have to check out the crime scenes for the case, which involves me walking. I can't afford not to be able to move."

Kelevra's gaze zoned in on him like a laser. "How many times do you think I'll have to dick you down to cripple you with my cock?"

Rin recognized that expression. His brother got it sometimes. "Hell no. We are not about to find out. Get those thoughts out of your pervy head."

"I wouldn't break you permanently," Kel mused, but Rin let out a sound of warning.

"I *will* toss this hot tea at you." It'd be worth it too. For a few seconds, anyway.

Kelevra sighed. "I'm running the bath. The warm water will help with the aches."

"Not falling for it." Rin could picture it now, walking in there expecting to have a nice relaxing soak, only for Kel to bend him over the edge of the tub and force himself inside.

Again.

His muscles clenched in protest just thinking about it.

"I already have you where I want you," Kelevra said. "The official announcement will broadcast by the time we wake in the morning, and then the whole planet will know you're spoken for. You're already mine, Flower. I won't hurt you if you don't give me a reason to."

"Liar." Although, there'd been pain, yes, but it was almost always followed swiftly by intense pleasure. Kelevra knew how to keep him dancing on the edge, pulling him back just before he was about to fall too far over the side.

"It's arousing," Kel offered, "seeing you angry, watching that spark come alive. I like knowing I'm seeing something few people get to. Even from the beginning, you've let me in, accidentally or not. You exposed your true self to me, and of course, I covet it. Covet you." He stalked forward, keeping Rin frozen in place with the dark promise in his gaze.

"I know this is sudden, Flower, but you'll adjust. You're good at that, aren't you? Adapting. I can tell. That's how you're able to play people so easily. But not me. You can't lie to me. Maybe I didn't before. But I do now. I see you." He was close, almost to the side of the bed where Rin was still sitting, still as a statue. "More importantly, I see my name written all over your skin. See it in the way you look at me. The way you arch into my touch even as you're cursing and spitting mad. You may not be a doll or a toy, but you're right about one thing. I do own you. You are mine. Correction, two things. You called me a Devil, and I am a Devil, sweetheart. I'm the worst kind of devil. Do you know why?"

Kelevra was standing between his legs now, leaning in to speak directly against the curve of Rin's ear. "I'm not like Baikal, all devious and patient. No. I'm forthright, and I'm overeager. I'll have you branded and conceding, even if I have to actually cripple you to make it so. I don't play. I take."

When his fingers captured Rin's chin, the spell broke and he tried to pull away, only to find himself dragged off the bed and tossed over Kelevra's shoulder like he weighed about the same as the t-shirt he was rested over. The carefully spoken and not-so-thinly veiled threats pinged inside of his head as he was carried into the bathroom, stunning him into momentary silence.

Kel dropped him back to his feet in front of the clawed tub that was large enough to fit two grown men easy, but only so he could strip Rin's clothes off. Then he was lifting him all over again, settling him into the heated water and lowering his body until he had Rin resting with his back against the porcelain.

It wasn't until the Imperial Prince was moving around him, settling on a stool positioned behind him that Rin realized at some point he must have taken the half-empty teacup from his hand all without him noticing.

Since when was Rin *that* inattentive? He could walk into his dorm, see his desk lamp slightly askew, and instantly tell that Daylen had been messing with his things.

Kelevra stretched his arm over Rin's shoulder, dipping his fingers in the water to test it as he shut off the tap. His other hand trailed up the length of Rin's neck, nails dragging slightly through the short hairs at the base of his skull. "Should I wash you, Consort?"

The words were breathed against Rin's ear and for the life of him, he couldn't come up with a single witty reply suitable enough, his mind still reeling over those other things he'd said.

"Is it happening again?" Kel asked quietly, a hint of displeasure entering his tone, even as his hand in the water continued to lazily spin circles over the surface. "What happened in the shower earlier?"

Rin gave the faintest shake of his head. This was different. He didn't feel overwhelmed by emotion, and his fight or flight response hadn't been activated, even though it most certainly should have been.

But he *was* drowning though.

Instead of anxiety or anger, it felt like he was choking on the Imperial Prince, much in the same way he'd been choked on his cock earlier. Rin had never been handled that savagely before. There'd been a few moments where he'd feared Kelevra intended to suffocate him for real. That he was literally going to experience death by dick. His chest had seized up, tears running down his face and…

It'd had him so hard he'd been seconds away from coming in his pants with no stimulation to his junk whatsoever.

Kelevra's hands pulled away, returning a second later with a washcloth. He dipped it into the water and then began running it over Rin's chest, gently scrubbing him. There wasn't soap, but Rin got the impression he'd been cleaned back at Friction, since he hadn't come to with any uncomfortable stickiness or dried come on his thighs. Any signs of the spunk that had been unloaded on his chest were already gone as well.

For all his huff and puff about not being interested in playing anyone, Kel was certainly doing a good job of it now.

"You're pulling my strings," Rin whispered, barely managing to get his voice to work that much for him. There was still something lodged there, something foreign and raw. The steam wafting up from the warm bath and the feel of the Imperial Prince's body heat behind him doing a fine job of lulling him into a relaxed state of being that logically he knew he couldn't afford.

Kel brought the cloth lower, disappearing beneath the water line as he rubbed it against Rin's lower abs. "I'm trying to subdue you," he confessed. "Is it working?"

"I'm too tired to fight," he said. The lighting had been left low purposefully, and he peered around the expansive bathroom, taking in the glass shower stall in the corner and the immaculate gold and white marble double sink. "For a guy who's never been interested in a serious relationship, you certainly ensured you'd have enough space for more than one person when you purchased this place."

"Jealous?"

"No." He wasn't. Even if he did care about Kelevra having brought other people here to fuck before, it didn't make a difference.

"Because you're the only one I've ever wanted to make my consort?" Kel guessed.

"Because I don't want you," he stated, tensing as soon as the words were out.

Kelevra dragged the cloth lower, still at that same steady pace, but with a clear goal in mind this time.

Rin latched onto his wrist just before he could swipe over his dick. "Don't."

"Why not?" Kel shifted closer, settling his chin on Rin's shoulder, his lips tickling the side of his neck. "If you don't want me, why should I bother with this charade? Hmm? If it's as you say, and I can't win you over anyway, isn't it smarter for me to cut my losses and simply use you the way I see fit?"

He inhaled.

Kelevra chuckled against his skin. "All that griping about being treated like a toy, yet here you are getting hard over the word use?"

"I'm not." He was. Fucking damn it.

"If you'd stop being so obstinate you'd realize you can only benefit from being mine. I can touch you how you like, take you how you like. Fuck you hard and dirty and make you forget all about trying to maintain control. Aren't you stressed? Don't you want a break from that mask you're always hiding behind?"

"Not really the right person to be talking to me about control," Rin stated.

"I'm an Imperial Prince. Your Imperial Prince. I'm the only one in this entire universe who gets to control you, Flower. Tame you and bend you to my will. Bath you, clothe you, and treat you right. Or bad. Think. Rin Varun has no power, and therefore, for whatever reason, he has to hide. But Royal Consort Rin? He can shed the mask completely. I'm the only one who can make you an offer like that."

And there in lay the crux of the matter.

"I can't be what I need to be and be yours," he said. "I won't survive it."

Kelevra took him by the chin and tipped his head back so their eyes could meet. "You believe that to be true. Why?"

"My mask means survival," he answered, "and you want to take that away."

"I want you to be yourself," Kel corrected. "I don't want you locking up that fire inside of you when you have the potential to set this whole planet ablaze. I'll confiscate everything from you, Flower, your control, your future, your body, and your mind. But I won't strip you of that. I won't take your sense of self."

"What do you think you've been doing this entire time?"

"Oh, sweetheart," he smiled viciously, "we both know whether I meant to or not, I've been doing the exact opposite." He licked at the seam of Rin's lips. "Even your brother noticed. You're more yourself with me than you've possibly ever been. I might be uprooting you, but it's only because you've outgrown your pot. It's time to stop clinging to whatever old fears have been holding you back." Kel kissed him, soft and sweet. "It's time to flourish and be what you were meant to be all along. Unequivocally you."

Chapter 17:

"Tell me about your home world."

They'd moved into the bedroom, where Rin had demanded he be given some sort of clothing before he'd stay put in the massive bed. Kelevra eventually relented and given him a pair of boxer briefs. And nothing else, not even the t-shirt he'd carried before.

The prick.

He was curled around Rin's back now, one arm wrapped around his middle, a leg thrown over Rin's thighs to keep him in place. He'd argued and complained about the heat, but Kel had merely grunted and turned on the air conditioning. Just when Rin had begun to think at least he'd be able to escape by falling asleep, the Imperial had buried his face in his hair and started making demands.

"I'm tired," Rin said.

"It isn't my fault you didn't think to take care of your basic needs properly," Kelevra told him, holding him tighter when Rin tried to jostle himself free.

It'd mostly been for show, so he settled back down a second later with a huff. "It is actually your fault. First, you dropped this bomb on me and then you—"

"Fucked you into oblivion?"

"I didn't have time to eat anything after breakfast," he finished.

"You have to keep yourself in shape," Kel stated. "I don't want a weak consort, and I don't want to worry about you potentially passing out on me again."

Rin snorted. "As if you'd worry about something like that. You'd probably just keep fucking me through it. Unconscious? Like that would stop you."

Kelevra went quiet and he realized his mistake.

"That wasn't a suggestion," Rin quickly affirmed.

"For the record," Kelevra said, "I did stop earlier. Then I cleaned you up, got you dressed, and carried you to my hovercar."

"Sorry for the inconvenience, Imperial," Rin drawled sarcastically. "My bad for not having realized you were planning on using me so thoroughly."

"You should always be prepared to take my cock," he replied, and it was hard to tell if the sarcasm had gone over his head or if he was simply ignoring it. "And don't call me that. You'll give me my name or—"

"Nothing at all?" Rin cut him off. "Can I go with that option?"

Kel's hand trailed up the length of Rin's chest, settling loosely around his throat in warning. "Keep pushing me, Flower. You're forgetting you aren't the only one with a temper here, and while I rather enjoy when you lose yours, you won't like it if I do the same."

"Because you'll hurt me?" He had no clue what possessed him to ask that.

Kelevra ran his tongue over his neck and across the side of his jaw. "Because I'll eat you alive."

"That's…" He didn't know what to say back to that.

"Tell me about your home world," Kelevra repeated, settling in the bed once more, though he kept his hand where it was, ready to squeeze at a moment's notice. "Did you not like it there? Is that why you left?"

Rin swallowed, feeling the press of that large palm against him with the movement, and opted to just go with the flow. "It's not that. Tibera is a beautiful planet, all sand beaches and blue ocean for miles and miles. Everyone there is born in pairs, and while they aren't always identical, my brother and I weren't considered novelties like we are here."

"Why leave then? From the sounds of it, you'd have better luck blending in there."

"My father." A wash of unease swept through him, same as it always did, but with how spent his body was, it didn't linger. That was a nice surprise. A happy accidental result of their time spent at Friction. "He decided to have children out of necessity. He needed one to take over the family-owned hospital, and one to inherit his position on the Royal Council. The original plan was to separate us, but we begged him to allow us to come here instead, to Vitality."

"You wore him down."

"We're good at getting what we want when we put our minds together." They'd gotten their teachers involved, their friends' parents, talked about it loudly whenever they were forced to go to the summit building with their father, where they knew the Empress was. Once the seeds had been planted in everyone else's minds, it'd been difficult for their father to argue.

"Is that why he was so cross on the call earlier?" Kelevra asked. "You marrying me means you're no longer allowed to leave the planet. You won't be returning home to take over his position like he'd always intended."

"I'm honestly shocked he agreed to the betrothal at all," Rin replied.

"My sister can be convincing as well." He grinned against the crook of Rin's neck. "There was never any doubt she would be able to secure our betrothal once I asked it of her."

"And me?" Rin risked pulling away slightly, just enough so he could look over his shoulder. The lights were off, the only source coming through the large window, strings of light from the rooftop below providing enough he could just make out the bridge of Kel's nose and the arch of his dark brow. "Did you even consider asking me my opinion on the matter?"

"No," he surprised him by saying without skipping a beat. "You made your stance clear at the library. You didn't want to be caught with me. It would have drawn attention if there was a scandal. Now there won't be one. The attention is unavoidable, but at least now everyone will be talking about how you're my fiancé and not just about us fucking in the library."

Rin frowned. "Why would that matter to you?"

"It matters," he said firmly. "I'm not sure why. But it does. I didn't like thinking about it, in any case. However, the idea of everyone looking at you and knowing you're claimed? That I liked."

"I won't marry you." Marriage had never been in the cards for him, at least not while he was still on this planet or under his father's thumb.

Although, with how his brother acted today, it was starting to seem like he'd been serious when he'd mentioned them staying on Vitality.

Damn it.

"As you've pointed out, Flower, I didn't ask." He kissed him beneath the jaw. "You will. When the time comes, you'll stand up there with me and you'll exchange the vows. You'll wear my crest instead of the Academy's. You'll bear my name."

"Children?" Rin really didn't want to know. "We can't have them. Couldn't even if I was female. Tiberan's can't procreate with those native born to Vitality. We are incompatible."

"I don't need children," Kelevra said. "Can you imagine me putting anything else above myself? Babies need attention and care, neither of which I'm willing to give to something that will only steal all of yours from me."

"I'll never care for you."

"You will," he disagreed. "I'm not patient, but I'm trying to be understanding here. This is sudden. I've reset the entire course of your life. You need time."

"All the time in the world can't make someone love you, Kelevra." If it were that easy, their father would have loved them. Then maybe none of this would have happened in the first place.

Maybe Rin could have really been himself instead of the man behind the mask.

Maybe he would be able to breathe and let go, hand control over to someone else, even someone like the Imperial Prince.

"I always get what I want," Kel told him, unbothered by Rin's comments.

"And if *I* want children?" He didn't. But that was beside the point.

Kelevra stilled around him. "Do you?"

"I asked first."

He considered it. "We can speak with the Imperial doctor and find a way to make it happen—a clinical way, that does not include either one of us putting our dicks in a female body. I also insist we hire a nanny because I wasn't joking about not being pleased over the idea of having to share you, even with our own child. But if that's really something you want, sure."

Rin blinked, certain he'd misheard or he'd fallen asleep and this was a dream. "What?"

"This is a good time to bring up," Kel continued, completely oblivious to Rin's shock, "that you are forbidden from allowing anyone other than me to touch you from here on out. I don't share. And I won't be made a fool. If someone flirts with you, they'll pay. If you flirt back..." That hand tightened once before loosening as if he couldn't control himself. "Female, male, doesn't matter. If I catch you being unfaithful, I'll strip you down, tan your hide, and fuck you in the middle of Center Point."

The Academy had been constructed to form a circle, the buildings placed in a way they formed rings. At the center was Center Point, a sort of hang-out spot for cadets, and also where the most foot traffic was directed, since traveling from one side of the Academy to the other almost always involved taking a path through Center Point.

"I'm not into exhibitionism," Rin said dumbly, because it was the only thing he could think to say.

"I'm aware." Kel nuzzled against him. "So behave, so that neither of us has to experience any of that unpleasantness, hmm?"

Rin was way over his head. The day had been a blur, one horrible event after the other, but he'd still held onto the belief this was all a game to the Imperial Prince. That they'd wake up, maybe tomorrow, maybe the day after, and he'd tell Rin he'd grown bored after all…

It was starting to look like that wasn't going to happen, like maybe, just maybe, Kelevra was serious about all of this.

What would a lifetime of being chained to this man entail?

As third in line, Kelevra was only at risk of taking the throne if both his sisters tragically died without leaving any heirs of their own. Unlikely, since the Emperor had recently announced she was pregnant. There was no fear of being thrust into that kind of power, which was a relief. Kel was also on track to becoming the diplomatic advisor on planet. He'd greet all the incoming dignitaries who visited that his sister, the Emperor, didn't want to bother with, as well as keep the other Royals who looked after other countries in the Emperor's name in line.

Basically, he wouldn't become a bum prince twiddling his thumbs and demanding to be fed grapes all day long. He had the one thing Rin had always dreamed of having. Stability. A stable and set future.

An identity all his own.

"I don't want children," Rin said quietly.

"Then we won't have them," Kel smirked in the dark. "I'll keep you all to myself."

"And the Academy?" He was only a sophomore. Earlier, Kelevra had promised he'd pay for his brother's tuition, but there'd been no mention of paying off his debts as well. "I won't quit." It was an empty statement. If the Imperial Prince wanted him booted from the school, Rin wouldn't be able to stop him. He'd be tossed on the streets with nowhere else to go, in the perfect predicament for Kel to swoop in and corner him—

"Who said anything about quitting?" he sounded genuinely perplexed. "Unless it interferes with you being mine, I have no intentions to involve myself in your other affairs. Stay at the Academy, don't stay at the Academy—actually. I still have a year left. Stay. I just pictured sneaking off to make out behind the Trajectory."

Kelevra didn't want to waste his own time he meant. That's why he wouldn't get involved, not out of some sense of respect toward Rin and the things he wanted, but because it didn't affect the Imperial Prince one way or the other.

He had to keep correcting himself when his emotions tried to make him believe otherwise. It'd been too easy to fall for this false charm the Imperial Prince was feeding him.

"If you make me do this, I'll eventually find a way to—"

Kel coiled around him all at once, his voice darkening as he dragged his bottom lip up the rise of Rin's cheek. "Say *escape*, I dare you."

Rin was proud, but he wasn't so proud he couldn't recognize the danger for what it was.

"I'll put you on the no-fly list," Kelevra said when Rin remained quiet. "They'll have your picture, which means your brother won't be able to leave either."

"We don't go anywhere without the other," Rin whispered.

"Ah." He chuckled and the sound sent a shiver rushing down Rin's spine. "Is that it then? The magic code to crack your golden shell? How about this then, Flower. I'll ship him off world, to an undisclosed galaxy you won't know the name of. It'll be far though, so far he won't be able to find his way back even if he spent the next three decades trying."

"Kelevra."

"Afraid?" he asked. "Funny how you only seem to really get that way whenever your brother's involved. You care for him more than you do yourself, that it?"

They were one in the same.

"You promised if I blew you, you would help him stay," Rin reminded, grasping at straws.

"That's the great thing about being the Imperial Prince," he said. "I can always change my mind."

"So I'm just supposed to never trust you? The man who I'm apparently going to spend the rest of my life with?" Rin couldn't live like that. He'd done it before, been a slave to the whims of another person. It wasn't the same, his father would have been a permanent presence, but he never would have forced the brothers to marry. Only because it wasn't common on their planet though. "I ran to another galaxy to avoid that fate."

"Would you like to?" Kelevra asked, and some of the harsh edge had left his voice. "Trust me?"

Rin licked his lips. "Yes." There was no other alternative.

Their number one rule was to do what they had to to keep them both safe. His brother couldn't be used as a pawn against him. He'd do what he had to to ensure that he wasn't.

"Then I'll make you a deal, Consort," Kelevra replied silkily, lapping at the curve of Rin's ear, a sure sign his anger was ebbing.

He swallowed. "I'm listening."

"You will not contest this betrothal," Kel said. "You will give yourself to me, in whole."

"You can't make someone love you," Rin interrupted.

"I'm not asking for your love," he told him, "not yet. I'll claim that on my own, as surely as I've claimed your hand. But you will be mine. You'll answer to no one but me. You'll move in here and share my bed and when I tell you to spread for me, you will do so. You can still curse me and argue though. You can even still threaten me with knives and your fists—when we are alone. Outside, in front of others, you'll be my Royal Consort, and you'll like it. Is that understood, cadet?"

"And in return?"

"I'll keep my promise and pay off your brother's tuition fees. I'll even sweeten the pot and give him an allowance if you'd like. You don't have to worry about the Academy expenses, I've covered those for you already."

"What?"

"It was taken care of this morning," he said. "I didn't see the need in telling you before, now I can see it'll bother you if I don't. Your brother will be granted permanent citizenship, and I won't threaten to off-world him again. He can come and go as he pleases, so long as he never tries to take you from me. So long as you never try it either. You're all in, Flower. Or I show you, unapologetically, why I'm a Devil of Vitality."

Trapped. Rin waited for the same sinking, twisting panic to consume him, that flustered almost frantic sensation that came over him whenever he and his brother were cornered by their father or an obvious injury. He waited. But it didn't come.

There was a chance he was simply numb to it by now, too tired and mentally drained. If he allowed himself to really think about it though, if he was honest, he knew that wasn't the case.

Kelevra was promising not to separate them. That meant he and his brother still had time. He'd said so earlier himself at their hideaway in the woods. No one made either of them do anything they didn't want to.

Rin would agree, for now, and he would plot. If there was a way out of this mess, he would find it, and if there wasn't…

At least the two of them would be free of their father.

"Tick-tock, Flower," Kelevra cut through his thoughts. "You know I'm not very patient."

"All right," he blurted before he could change his mind. "But the second you break your end of things, I'm gone. My brother isn't a pawn." *He* wasn't a pawn.

"Trust goes both ways," Kel told him. "I'm willing to buy yours with my own."

"Then," Rin inhaled, "we have a deal?"

"We have a deal, Consort." His hand finally slipped from his neck, arm settling back around his waist. "And I have you."

Sure, but who exactly did the Imperial Prince think he caught? Was it really him?

Or was it someone else?

* * *

Sometime in the morning, with the sun just barely cresting outside, bathing the room in a golden glow, Rin was woken. He was on his stomach, his face pressed into the silk pillow.

"Awake?" Kelevra asked from behind him, grinding his hips against Rin's backside, his hard cock driven in deep with the movement.

That's what had pulled him from sleep. The feeling of something hot pressing against his entrance, forcing itself inside.

Rin cried out and wrapped his arms around the pillow to help keep himself from sliding up the bed as Kelevra thrust into him. The Imperial's movements weren't as frantic as usual, almost like he was attempting to be gentle as he stretched Rin's hole around his wide member.

"Does it hurt, sweetheart?" Kel brushed Rin's hair off the side of his face and stared down at him.

Testing, Rin shifted, lifting his ass a little on the next inward stroke. Pings of electricity shot through him and his toes curled as his dick rubbed against the smooth silk sheets. He shook his head. It didn't hurt, he'd merely been startled.

"Are you disappointed?" Kelevra kept pace with ease.

Rin frowned and moaned when he felt his thick crown bump against his prostate. He shook his head a second time. He was grateful it wasn't hurting, maybe that made him pathetic. He should probably be angry and fighting back, but...Everything felt warm and pleasant, and he found he just didn't want to struggle when there was another option.

When he could just lay here and feel good instead.

"I'm glad," Kel said. "Sometimes I like it soft, but that isn't your style, is it, Flower? You're all thorns all the time, ready to prick me a dozen times over when you're awake. But like this?" He ran his fingers through his hair and made a pleased sound. "Sleepy and docile, willing to behave for me. Show me. Show me how good you can behave. Come, sweetheart."

He pressed in as deep as he could go and that mixed with the words was enough to have Rin coming.

The orgasm sent shockwaves throughout his system, nothing world-shattering this time, but still enough to have him groaning and jerking against the mattress.

Kelevra came soon after, settling his large body over Rin's back, painting his shoulders and neck with licks of his tongue and open-mouth kisses. He kept it up until Rin went boneless beneath him.

"Go back to sleep," Kel told him. "I'll wake you with my cock again in an hour."

Rin grumbled something, a curse word maybe, he couldn't be sure, but then he was slipping back into that comfortable darkness, drifting away more relaxed than he'd been in years.

Chapter 18:

"Stop staring at me." Rin didn't bother glancing over at his friends, though it was tempting to send them a glare. A real one too, not one of those fake, slightly upset expressions he used whenever he was out in public. It wouldn't do to never show any negative emotion, so he'd perfected the balance, both he and his brother experts at getting people to see exactly what they wanted them to.

Unless they were the fucking Imperial Prince.

He ground his teeth and flicked the information on his emblem-slate with a little more force than necessary, sending the digital document to the holographic screen set in the center of the round table he and his friends were hovering around.

They'd met up in the library to go over their case notes for the assignment, thankfully without any of the seniors there to hound them. The three-story, two-hundred-year-old building, housed an upload center, five computer rooms, three classrooms, and over ten thousand physical books. The information had all been uploaded into the Academy's database and was accessible from all of the computers, but there were still books spread out on tables, students actively using them to study.

There were a lot of other cadets in the library, and Rin had felt almost every single one of them staring at him as soon as he'd entered through the double glass doors. He'd found his friends waiting on the third floor, meaning he'd had to pass by even more prying eyes, but even they'd looked at him like he was a zoo animal as he approached their table.

That settled it.

Rin was going to kill the Imperial Prince. Preferably by drowning. Maybe even in that ridiculous clawed bathtub of his.

Just as he'd promised, the announcement had already been made by the time Rin had peeled himself out of bed. He'd been furious and achy and still too exhausted to deal, so had mostly been quiet on the drive back to the Academy. It'd been thrilling when Kelevra had followed him to his dorm room, only for Rin to slam the door in his face and lock him outside. He'd laughed the whole way to his dresser, picturing the pinched look on Kel's face when he'd realized what was happening.

But Rin would pay for it later, he was sure.

"What are you doing here?" He turned to his roommate, Daylen.

Daylen smiled mysteriously. "Yeah, like I would miss out on this."

The two of them had gotten along fairly quickly, though he was more the type of personality his brother preferred. Stoic, and a bit too observant. His brother got off on trying to fool people like that, whereas he felt it was extra work. Daylen wore his dark blue hair cropped short, and his tongue was poking at the empty hole in the corner of his bottom lip where his piercing was whenever he went off Academy grounds. He had to remove the facial jewelry when in uniform, something he complained about constantly.

Rin sighed and rubbed at the bridge of his nose. "Fine. Three minutes. Ask me."

"Dude, what the hell?" Calder asked first, propping his elbows against the table to lean forward. He was seated directly across from Rin, the corners of his mouth turned up despite the mild confusion in his gaze.

"Seriously, were you two even dating?" Brennon was the only one scowling.

Rin lifted a single shoulder absently. He'd been quiet on the drive over mostly because he'd been too distracted formulating a game plan. He may have no say in this betrothal, but he could put a spin on it, turn things more in his favor and put an end to the constant questioning.

"We barely know one another," he told them, organizing the notes the other guys had already sent to the tabletop screen. "It was a political alliance set up by our families."

"Whoa, for real?" Calder's shoulders slumped. "Man, I'm sorry, that sucks."

"They just sold you out like a piece of meat?" Brennon shifted. He was seated on Rin's right and he reached out and rested a comforting hand on his arm. "Do you want me to see if my mom can do anything about it?"

Brennon was technically a Royal, but unlike Madden and Zane, he'd never gotten an invite to join Kelevra's little band of assholes, either because of the age difference or something else.

Rin shook his head. "Thanks, but no can do. Already tried."

"What about your brother?" Daylen asked. "Why couldn't he do it?"

"He's studying to be a doctor," Rin reminded.

"And you're training to be a detective, not seeing how one is more important than the other."

"I have experience in hand-to-hand combat," he replied.

Brennon made a face. "You're supposed to be his Royal Consort, not his bodyguard."

"Why would Tibera want to ally with Vitality?" Calder frowned. "We're in different galaxies."

"Not sure," Rin said. He'd tried to come up with something but had realized that would be overkill. The best sorts of lies were the ones easily remembered and not so easily traced. "I'm not privy to that information. I just do as I'm told."

"You're too nice, man," Daylen ran a hand over his head and clicked his tongue, the flash of metal catching Rin's attention briefly. Clearly he'd kept that one in thinking he wouldn't get caught. "Like, what era is this anyway? Arranged marriages? Yikes."

"Imperials." Calder shuddered. "Scary."

"Entitled," Brennon spat, "that's what you mean. And you're not going to contest it?"

Daylen hummed in agreement. "That is your right, whether your families set it up or not."

The Interstellar Conference tried to avoid involvement in how planets were individually run, so long as none of the other treaty rules were broken, but they'd instated the Arrangement Act a few decades ago. It allowed anyone who was being traded by their parents and forced into a marriage contract they didn't want to legally contest it by submitting a form to the I.P.F. There'd be an investigation and eventually the Intergalactic Conference would either step in to put a stop to it or allow it to happen.

It was messy and time-consuming and considering both he and his brother planned on remaining on this planet for at least another three years, pissing off the entire Imperial family by publically announcing Rin didn't want to be a part of them? Yeah. No.

Rin's conversation with Kelevra last night came to mind and he forced himself to smile at his friends, easily burying the unease and the anger he still felt. "Relax, guys. It's really not that big of a deal. So I have to marry a prince? Boohoo."

"Do you...like him?" Brennon asked.

"I think," he wasn't touching that with a thousand-foot pole, "it doesn't matter. It's already been decided. Anyway, that's what's up, sorry it's not as exciting as my secretly having been dating Kelevra this whole time, but can we get to work now?"

They grumbled but dropped it, letting him steer the conversation onto the case. Daylen was part of another class and therefore his case was completely different, but he helped them go over their findings and the notes anyway, taking it just as seriously as they were. He liked puzzles so that wasn't too surprising. He also happened to be a pretty decent friend.

Rin glanced around at the three of them and remembered what his brother had said yesterday about possibly staying. About how they had friends here. He'd specifically chosen his words—because his brother didn't *care* about any of these people—but…It was true, wasn't it? What they had going on Vitality was good. At least here they were able to carry on separate lives. They'd even stopped telling one another their entire daily schedule; Rin had no clue where his brother was at this moment.

Back on Tibera, there hadn't been a second out of any day that he hadn't known exactly where his brother was and roughly what he was doing and vice versa.

"Have either of you checked out one of the mock crime scenes?" Calder asked. "I couldn't find anything when I went."

"Nope," Brennon said. "My mentor has been busy."

"It's only been a day since it's been assigned," Daylen rolled his eyes at them. "Chill."

"Some of us haven't been gifted with top marks." Calder stuck his tongue out.

"Hey, I earned those," Daylen argued.

"Why don't we go to one now?" Rin suggested. "Maybe together we'll be able to catch something we'd miss on our own."

"Sounds like a plan." Brennon closed his portion of the table screen as Daylen rose to his feet. "You coming with?"

"Nah," Daylen shook his head, "leg work isn't appealing. If I wanted to bother with all that, I'd be working on my own case. I'm going to head to the café. Grab some brunch."

"Oh, I like that way better." Calder gathered his things quickly. "I'll go with you instead."

"We aren't sharing our findings," Brennon warned, but Calder merely waved and then bounded off with Daylen.

"Forget them." Rin had just pushed in his chair when both of their emblem-slates dinged.

"Shit." Brennon's brow winged up. "There's been another murder."

"Don't be so dramatic," Rin said as he scanned the new message. It'd been made to look like an actual notice from an I.P.F branch to their agent, giving them a brief summary of who had been killed and where. "There's an address."

"It's close," Brennon sounded excited. "Let's go. Maybe we can get there before anyone else."

They practically raced from the library, running into Calder on the steps.

"What happened to brunch?" Brennon teased as they fell into formation, heading toward the parking lot where his hovercar was parked.

"And let you discover something without me?" he grunted. "No way."

* * *

It was Arlet.

Rin tried not to keep looking, but his eyes constantly wandered over toward where she was slumped against the alley wall, her head tilted to the side to expose her throat and the wide slash that had been painted on there.

"Hey," Calder was having the same problem, standing only a few feet away from her, "you sure you're all right? We won't tell anyone if you want to just sit up and take a break."

"There's no one else here," Rin agreed, feeling bad.

"What are they paying you for this gig anyway?" Brennon asked. Out of the three of them, he was the only one picking through the scene, snapping photos with his emblem-slate and logging notes along the way.

The alley had been left mostly untouched, meaning there were bits of trash and debris scattered about, along with a large orange dumpster. It was narrow, enough so that Arlet's stretched-out legs were only a foot or so away from reaching the other side, and set between a deli and an insurance office of a quiet area in the city.

There was blood splatter on the floor and sprayed across the wall opposite where she was sitting.

"Looks like he got her good the one time," Brennon announced as he checked out the marking. "See the splatter? How it arches? Bet he's right-handed."

Calder snorted. "You have no idea what you're talking about. Stop trying to sound smart in front of her."

"You mean the dead girl?"

"Guys," Rin shook his head and then knelt by Arlet's side. "Are you really okay?" She'd been frozen in that position since they'd gotten there and it couldn't be comfortable.

"I'm fine," her eyes moved to meet his, "thanks. Just act like I'm a corpse and do your thing."

If she insisted.

"Why don't they use dummies or holographic displays," Calder asked as Rin straightened and started searching like Brennon. "Why ask for volunteers at all?"

He thought it over. "Maybe it's to shake us up. Think about it, sure it's not the same as having to be around an actual dead body, but you and I both wasted time checking if she was all right."

"And I still feel bad that she has to just, sit there," Calder grimaced. "Okay, I get it."

"If you get it, then shut up and help," Brennon said.

"The blood is still wet," Rin pointed to the spots on the ground. "Let's take some samples."

"It's paint, man," Calder reminded.

"We're supposed to treat this like a real crime scene." There was a chance their superiors had used specific kinds of paint just to see if they would bother checking. "No half measures."

"Whatever, over-achiever."

"He doesn't need to be now that he's engaged to the Imperial Prince," Brennon stated.

"What?" Arlet's head whipped up. "You're engaged to Kelevra?"

"You haven't heard?" Calder was the one to ask. "It's been all over the news all morning."

"I've been here setting this up with—" She clamped her mouth shut.

Rin and Brennon shared a look.

"Was the cadet who's playing the murderer here with you?" Rin took a closer look at the scene. If that were the case, he may have left clues behind, either purposefully or accidentally. It wouldn't matter which it was, their assignment was simply to solve the crime and catch the killer.

She stared at him for a moment before pointedly resting her head back, body going limp a second later.

"She's dead, man," Calder bumped his arm. "The dead can't talk."

"The dead talk all the time," Brennon corrected, pointing to her left arm. "See?"

It was sprawled out on the pavement, but stretched a little away from her body, almost like she'd been trying to reach for something when she'd "died".

Rin walked over to the dumpster and peered behind it. "Help me move this."

Calder and he slid it to the side so there was enough room for Rin to reach behind it. He pulled out a multi-slate, standard issue, black. The screen was cracked and when he tried to power it on, it flickered and then shut off.

"Just to be sure," Calder turned to Arlet, "that's not yours, right? It's part of the mock case? I just don't want us to take it if it is. Don't say anything if it's not."

They stared at her for a bit, but she was silent.

"Cool." He turned back to Rin. "It's broken?"

"We'll have to get it fixed," Rin said, pulling a plastic bag from his front pocket to slip the device inside.

Calder quirked a brow.

"What? They told us what to expect." Of course he'd come prepared.

"Promise you won't apologize to the killer when we catch them," Calder joked, rolling his eyes. "You're too nice and an overachiever. How are you not top of the class?"

"Because he's constantly being weighed down by you," Brennon joked, laughing when Calder scowled. "We've got to take these 'blood' samples in too. Let's head back to the Academy before—"

Footsteps came at the end of the alley and a second later Ives and his mentor entered.

Rin casually slipped the multi-slate they'd found into his front pocket, keeping his hands there to help make it seem like he wasn't hiding anything.

"How did you get here already?" Ives glanced between them and briefly down at Arlet. "Geez, they're making students actually play the bodies too?"

"Right?" Brennon made to leave. "It's all yours."

"What'd you find?"

"No cheating," Calder said, winking as they passed.

"Hey," Ives stopped Rin. "Come on. Did you find anything?"

Both Brennon and Calder groaned, expecting friendly Rin to cave and share the evidence they'd collected.

He probably would have too, but he was still annoyed about being woken—three times—by dick this morning, and hadn't forgotten about that stunt Ives had pulled during their competition. In fact, if Ives hadn't been such a major asshole that day, Rin never would have revealed himself to Kelevra in the first place.

He plastered on a smile and shrugged. "We didn't get anything. Hopefully you'll have more luck."

Brennon tossed an arm around his shoulders as they made it back toward the car.

"So much for friendly Rin," Calder laughed and then fist-bumped him.

If only they knew.

Chapter 19:

Calder ditched them the second they were told by the forensics department it would take a few hours for them to process the "blood" samples. The students who headed it were all juniors and seniors. They'd be graded on how well they worked with the sophomores on their case assignments, so in a way, handing in the fake samples helped them out as well.

Brennon and Rin had gone to the other side of campus to see the technicians about fixing the multi-slate, another department also made up of juniors and seniors. That was going to take even longer than the samples.

It was pretty late in the afternoon by the time they settled down at the on-campus coffee shop and ordered large drinks to sip on while they passed the time.

"You grew up with him, right?" Rin tentatively asked, staring out the window to his right to try and feign a disinterest he wasn't feeling. Attempting to make it seem like it'd only just occurred to him to ask, and only in passing since they had nothing else to do. "Kelevra?"

"I mean," Brennon shifted in his seat, "yeah. We've never been close or anything, but he's hung out with my older brother a few times at events and dinners that both our families are dragged to. Why? Want to know more about him?"

"Sure," he ran a hand through his hair, "if you've got anything. Might as well find out more since I'll be spending the rest of my life with him and all."

Brennon's brow furrowed. "You really aren't going to contest it? Seriously? Marrying someone you don't know is insane already, but marrying a guy like Kelevra..." He shook his head. "He's not right, Rin. You're too...nice, to be forced to be with someone like that."

He grunted. "I'm not that nice."

"Why, because you lied to Ives back there?" he scoffed. "Come on. We're helping each other out but it's still a competition. Of course you didn't want to share our findings, and neither did Calder or I. Like, look. One time in the fifth grade, Kelevra got mad at some kid for buying the last soda flavor he liked so he beat him with a metal lunch tray. He needed to be hospitalized for over a week after. Did Kelevra get in trouble? Nope."

Sounded like something the Imperial Prince would do. He was quick to react and didn't bother stopping to think things through beforehand.

Like getting engaged to a guy he'd only known a handful of days.

"Another time, he was racing—"

"Racing?" Rin interrupted.

"Yeah, down by the north docks, hoverbike races. I'm not surprised you haven't heard about them. It's a big deal though, pretty underground and invite only. Brings in a lot of money."

"And he participates?" Rin couldn't picture it no matter how hard he tried. Kel on a bike? In one of his ridiculously fancy suits with the laces of his corset tightened to the point he couldn't breathe? The potential grease stains alone should be enough to turn the pompous Imperial Prince off the whole thing. "No way."

"Not him," Brennon confirmed, "Madden. The guy is nuts. He rarely, if ever, loses. One time he beat a guy from that small fry gang, the Shepherds? The Shepherd had words to say about it and he ended up insulting Kelevra in the process."

"Let me guess," Rin drawled, "he hit him with something heavy?"

"Nope." Brennon sipped his drink to pause for anticipation. "He ran the dude's bike over with his hovercar. Thing was worth over fifty thousand coin."

Rin let out a low whistle.

"He's not a good guy," Brennon said. "He's a Devil of Vitality for a reason."

"He's got rage issues. I already knew that." He still had the bruises to show it. Though, the damage to his face had been all on him. Rin had been trying not to give himself away with all the attention from both Kelevra and Baikal, but then his brother had to go and open his big trap.

It wasn't like a single busted lip or a cut eyebrow really mattered. They were both pretty set at the moment. If not for his brother, he most likely would have let Flix beat him a little longer and then would have tapped out. He would have laughed and joked that he had a lot more training to do as a sophomore, and then he would have made up an excuse to get the hell out of there.

Instead, he'd slipped up and revealed his skill level, and then had hooked up with Kel.

Things got weird every time they had sex. Confusing. Part of him understood it was pure sensation, endorphins firing off in his brain, making him enjoy something he shouldn't. But the other part, the part that was starting to get addicted to that high, was excited whenever Kelevra initiated things.

He should probably be grateful, really. If he couldn't find a way out of it—and Kelevra never grew tired of him, which Rin still thought was a strong possibility—then at least their sex life would be worth it.

How messed up did that make him? They'd yet to have one encounter where Rin hadn't been either blackmailed or drugged into it, and yet here he was thinking about how great the orgasms were as though that somehow made everything fine. He needed to get a grip. It was one thing to try and find the positive in an otherwise shitty situation, but it was another to sit here and wax poetic about what had to be the most toxic relationship he'd ever heard of.

Great. And now he was thinking about them as a *relationship.*

Fuck Kelevra.

And Fuck his stupid flashy clothes.

That looked sexy as all hell on him.

Damn it.

His brother would get a kick out of things if he knew this was what Rin was wasting his time thinking about. Another surprise, really. He'd expected his brother to throw a fit and threaten to murder the Imperial Prince as soon as he found out about the betrothal. Instead, he'd not only told Rin to milk it for all it was worth, he'd also abandoned him at Friction, knowing full well what Kelevra intended to do.

"Are you going to ask for a replacement mentor at least?" Brennon asked. "It's got to be weird to be paired with your fiancé. The power imbalance is already through the roof, but he can also decide whether or not to pass or fail you? Doesn't seem right. Besides, he can't be happy about this either."

Rin frowned. "What do you mean?"

"Kelevra's never been with anyone long-term before. He's never even shown an interest. If this was set up by your families, I doubt he's pleased." Brennon reached across the table and rested a hand over Rin's. "I'm worried about you. He's not the type of person you can afford to piss off. He's dangerous. Like, really dangerous. It's a well-known fact that he's killed before, even if there's never any evidence left behind to prove it. The last girl who tried to tie him down ended up dead."

"You think Kel is responsible?" Rin had heard rumors about a girl dying over the summer break. He and his brother had stayed since a trip to their galaxy was pricey and far, and they hadn't wanted to go anyway. It'd supposedly happened at one of the Royal parties, much too high class for either of them, so they hadn't been invited, and neither of them had known the girl in question. "Didn't she fall?"

"Yeah," Brennon said, "from the rooftop of Kelevra's penthouse."

It should have terrified him—a normal person would have been scared but... "That's unfortunate."

Brennon gave him an incredulous look.

"Like you said, there's no proof he did anything. What? You think he pushed her?"

"How can you not?"

He wasn't like his brother. His range of emotions was a lot broader, and he could experience things like guilt and empathy. It was sad a girl died, and if Kel had done it, that was awful.

Did Rin hate him for it though?

No, not really.

His brother wasn't exactly squeaky clean either, yet another reason why they'd needed to leave Tibera. There were more secrets belonging to the two of them buried in the sand on that planet than there were shells.

"He's a murderer, Rin," Brennon insisted. "What if—"

"He's not going to kill me," Rin snorted. Oddly, he wholeheartedly believed that. Kel would probably hurt him some more in the future, there was no doubt about that, but he wouldn't take his life. He'd already pushed the Imperial many times, and somehow he'd held his anger in check each and every one of those occasions. Besides. "I can hold my own. Trust me. I'll be all right."

"He's not a normal person."

"I'll let you in on a secret," Rin said. "There are no normal people, Brenn. There's just the mask and the true face hidden behind it. Everyone's got demons, and the Devils? They're no different from us in that respect."

"Sure, except they're rich, powerful, and above the law. Last I checked, I only fit under one of those categories, and you..."

Rin smiled humorlessly. His dad might be wealthy on their planet, but none of that had ever transferred over to his sons. Giving them money would mean allowing them the opportunity to slip through his grasp, and he never would have done that.

Only, somehow, they'd managed to do it anyway, hadn't they? And a whole three years sooner than they'd originally planned to.

For the first time, Rin considered things from his brother's perspective. From the outside, it didn't look all that bad. Kelevra was gorgeous, filthy rich, and powerful enough all he'd had to do was whine to his sister and she'd granted him a full person, as a birthday gift no less. Attaching himself to him meant Rin would be set for the rest of his days. He could even quit the Academy and—

No. Those were dangerous thoughts. He had to stay focused. Just because Kel was showing an intense interest now didn't mean it would last. Rin couldn't risk dropping his guard and falling into the trap of glitz and glamour. He needed to think about what was best for him and his brother.

His emblem-slate went off then and he checked it, barely controlling the urge to roll his eyes when he saw who it was from, the contact details Rin had changed that morning the only thing holding him back.

His Imperial Prick: You aren't where you belong, Flower.

"Who is it?" Brennon asked, finishing off his coffee. The other tables in the small shop were empty, and outside the sky had darkened dramatically since their arrival. "Whoever it is, ask if they want to grab a drink with us somewhere. Let's forget about the results today. We've spent the whole day running around for this dumb case."

"Can't," Rin said absently, distracted as he sent a reply off to Kelevra.

Rin: I'm on campus. You know, where I go to school?

The response came back almost instantly.

His Imperial Prick: It's dinner time. School is over.

Rin: We aren't in elementary. There's such a thing as late classes.

His Imperial Prick: Your only late class is on Friday. It's not Friday, Flower.

That was…

"What?" Brennon cocked his head. "What's up?"

"Nothing." He'd memorized his schedule? Why? His skin started to feel tight and he adjusted his collar. He hated feeling like there was someone keeping tabs on him other than his brother. It felt…suffocating. Their father had done it and it'd driven them both mad.

Rin: Are you stalking me?

His Imperial Prick: If I was, I wouldn't be texting to complain about how you're not here. Come home.

That…didn't make him feel much better. Did it? Maybe they needed to talk about boundaries—Rin laughed, this time unable to hold the reaction in. Their first interaction he'd been forced to take a random drug, but *now* he was worried about boundaries?

His Imperial Prick: Come home, Consort.

Rin: Can't. I'm working on the case. I'll probably be at it late into the night. Makes more sense for me to just sleep in my dorm.

Where all of his stuff was. Seriously. He couldn't believe the guy thought he was going to move in with him in less than twenty-four hours. He'd barely wrapped his mind around the whole engagement thing, now he wanted him to leave his dorm too?

Rin: I'm uncomfortable.

It sucked admitting it, and it was risky but…It was a little easier to be vulnerable through this mode of communication. Nothing else seemed to work either. Kel apparently liked it when Rin got mad, and when it'd been something else, he'd overpowered Rin in other ways. Even his damn senses weren't immune to the Imperial Prince.

Honesty might be the only course of action left, so why not give it a try? The worst that could happen is it failed and he felt like a bigger idiot than he already did, but so what. Pride had never really been a burden of his. You had to care what people thought about you first, and Rin only cared about appearances when he needed to use them to protect himself and his brother.

Rin: It's stifling. I just...I need some time.

"Everything good?" Brennon asked, reminding Rin that he was even there.

"Yeah, just trying to figure this whole fiancé thing out." He laughed, but the sound was hollow even to his own ears. "Can you do me a favor and grab me another coffee while I deal with this?"

"Sure thing." Brennon took his empty cup and headed over to the counter to order refills.

Rin's multi-slate rang then, signaling a communication and not a message. He inhaled in an attempt to calm his nerves and then answered, slipping the small earbud attachment in and hitting the green button. "Hey."

"Are you shutting down?" Kelevra's voice came through the line steady and strong.

"Am I...What?"

"Like you did in the shower," he elaborated. "It's a regulation issue, isn't it? You struggle to maintain control over your emotions and they can sometimes overwhelm and overload your system, causing you to shut down."

His eyes narrowed. "I'm not a damn computer."

"And now you're getting angry because I've gotten close. Another effect of a mood disorder. If you recall, I have one as well."

"I'm not like you," Rin stated.

"Of course not. But your brother…He and I are similar, aren't we, Flower? That's the devil you were really talking about. He doesn't share the same problems as you, but you both share your problems, that it?"

"We share everything." This was making him uncomfortable. He needed to end this call and—

"Not everything," Kelevra said. "Not me. Not the things I can do to you. For you."

"Kel. Stop."

"You're mentally and emotionally overstimulated," he ignored him. "Physical stimulation, exhausting your body, helps. But you knew that already, didn't you?"

"It's my damn body." Duh, he'd known.

"You like shutting off that part of you that overthinks things. Like not having to worry about being in control all the time. You can let go when you're with me. Don't be scared. Even if I use this knowledge against you, you know I'll make you feel good in the process."

That was the problem.

"Anyway," Kel changed the topic in that annoying way he sometimes did, with no leeway or warning, "I didn't call to convince you of that."

"Didn't you?" Because it felt an awful lot like he had. It wouldn't be beneath Kelevra either, to call Rin just to rub his nose in the fact that he'd uncovered one of his secrets.

It was one he'd already partially figured out from the start though. He'd been able to tell from the beginning that Rin held back when it came to pretty much everything. When he stopped to think about it, it didn't really bother him that Kelevra figured out it was a mood disorder.

Rin wasn't embarrassed about it either. He was what he was, plain and simple.

"No. I wanted to make sure you were okay. The way you were in the shower? I don't want anyone else to see you like that, ever."

"I'm careful." Rin hadn't had a lapse that bad in a while. "It's only because I was ambushed. It's your fault."

"I'm taking responsibility, aren't I?"

Was he? Rin ran hand through his hair and nodded at Brennon when he came back.

"I got you something with cinnamon this time," Brennon told him, setting the cup down in front of him. "It helps with stress and you seem like you could use it."

"Who the hell is that?" Kelevra's tone dropped.

"A friend," Rin said, sipping at the coffee. It was hot and burned his tongue but he couldn't be bothered to care about that at the moment. "I told you, I'm on campus working on the case."

"You're refusing to keep your end of the deal," Kelevra stated.

"I'm just asking for you not to rush this, I'm not saying I'll never come." Anger prickled and he rubbed at the center of his chest, trying to remember that with Brennon here, he couldn't let it loose and curse out the Imperial like he wanted to. "You offered to give me time. That's all I'm asking for right now."

"Time? So you can get something with cinnamon with another man?"

"Good Light." This was futile. "It's just Brennon!"

"Ouch," Brennon mumbled, but it was loud enough that Rin knew Kelevra caught it when the other end of the line went dead quiet.

"Kelevra…"

Brennon's device beeped. "Oh, the results of the blood samples are in."

"Did you hear that?" Rin asked stubbornly. "I told you. We're working on the assignment. That's all."

"What's his deal?" Brennon smartly lowered his voice to a whisper.

Rin debated whether or not to answer and then figured what the hell. "He wants me to come over."

"Don't!" Brennon's hand whipped out again, clamping over Rin's wrist. "What if this is it? What if he's trying to get rid of you so he doesn't have to bother with the betrothal?!"

"What is he sniveling on about?" Kelevra drawled through the comms.

"He thinks you're going to throw me off the roof," Rin said lightly, chuckling when Brennon gasped.

"And why would he think that?"

"Because I told him that our families set us up." There was a lengthy pause and Rin frowned. "Kelevra?"

"Tell your friend to check Imagine," Kelevra said, then in a clipped voice added, "I'll give you the time you want, Flower. But there will be a cost, and you will be paying it in full soon enough."

"I—" The call ended and he tapped his multi-slate. It hadn't dropped. "He hung up on me." That asshole! At least it sounded like he wasn't going to force Rin into going back to the penthouse tonight. That was something. "Hey, do you follow Kelevra on Imagine?"

Imagine was a social media app that pretty much everyone in the galaxy used. They could share photos, videos, and captions, and there was a follow feature. Rin's account was mostly just pics of him goofing off with the guys—a carefully constructed front to keep up the appearance of a social butterfly who could do no wrong. He never posted anything of substance, and he didn't spend that much time on it.

He was still in the middle of scrolling to find the app on his multi-slate when Brennon sucked in a breath, drawing his attention.

"Holy hell, dude." Brennon was shaking his head, his eyes tore from his screen and he stared at Rin wide-eyed. "You're epically fucked."

"What?" He frowned and giving up on his own, waved his fingers so that Brennon would turn his wrist and show him. Kelevra's account was pulled up. He'd made a post two minutes ago.

Of Rin.

Sleeping.

In his fucking bed.

The silk sheets and the fact he was shirtless pretty much summed up for everyone what had transpired before the photo had been taken, but as if that wasn't enough to appease Kelevra's twisted sense of ownership, he'd gone and added a caption just in case anyone was too slow on the uptake.

Where my Consort belongs.

"I'm going to kill him," Rin said darkly, completely losing the plot for a minute. "He's dead. He's so dead."

"Whoa," Brennon pulled his arm back. "Calm down. Yikes, Rin. I was just kidding. It's not that big a deal. It's only been seen by—" he glanced down and paled.

"How many?" Rin asked, slamming his fist down on the table when Brennon refused to tell him.

"Five hundred," he blurted.

"It hasn't even been up for five minutes and it already has that many views?" He groaned and dropped his head into his hands.

"Have you never checked his account before?" Brennon asked. "Practically the whole planet follows him. Don't you?"

"No."

"...Shouldn't you? He tagged you and everything."

"Fuck."

"Okay, seriously, you're starting to freak me out. What happened to rolling with the punches and this not being a thing? You seemed fine with it before."

Yeah. Because *he'd been faking*. But Rin couldn't say that. He could only dig his nails into his palms under the table, drawing blood, waiting for the prick of pain to help steady him and pull him off the edge. Fight or flight was starting and if he entered that state of being, he'd definitely lean toward fight and be in his car heading straight to Kelevra.

Which was no doubt exactly what that prick was hoping for.

He inhaled, held it, and slowly let it out.

"It's the PDA of it, isn't it?" Brennon guessed, thankfully giving Rin a believable excuse.

He grabbed at it like a lifeline. "Yes! Public displays of affection aren't common where I come from and that…He may as well have posted a picture of my bare ass!"

Brennon laughed. "It's not that extreme. If anything, it's kind of sweet? In a twisted, shitty he didn't ask you first, kind of way? I mean, I've never seen him show an interest in anyone like this before. At least there's that, right?"

"You mean maybe he won't off me or beg his sisters to call off the engagement after all?" Rin drawled.

"Yeah." Brennon smiled like that should be the most comforting thing Rin had ever heard.

He hated that a small part of himself actually took it that way.

Chapter 20:

Club Vigor was the largest country club in the country, a place where only the richest of the rich were allowed admittance. Which mostly just meant everyone here was either boring or a kiss-ass. Still, it was quiet, and whenever Kelevra needed a break from the limelight—not often, but it happened—the club was his go-to place to wind down away from the flashing lights of paparazzi.

The Devils paid for a private room on the upper level. Sometimes they held official meetings, where Kelevra and his Retinue might congregate with Baikal and his Satellite, the topic of discussion varying in degrees of actual importance.

The last time they'd gone over Kel's twenty-first birthday party plans, for example.

Fortunately, there was just him and Madden at the moment, the two of them sprawled out on opposite leather couches, Kelevra taking up most of the rectangular coffee table set low between them. He was using the holo-screen feature, notes about the sophomore class case carefully organized into separate piles from most important to only mildly so.

Madden was lying across the length of the other couch, his red and white leather racing jacket open to expose his toned bare chest as he idly tossed a hoover ball up into the air over and over again.

"Are you going to do anything about the recent string of murders?" Madden asked absently.

Kelevra grunted. "Two murders hardly counts as a 'string'."

"It's three now."

He paused. "Where'd they find the last one?"

"Yesterday," Madden said. "In the park on Grand. We almost had to call off the race at the docks. Would have been hell to pay."

Grand Street was close to where the races were held.

"Who's covering the case?" Kel wondered if he'd been too caught up with his personal plans to have noticed, or if the news was being contained by someone.

"Officer Adair. It's been listed as a serial murder, but between you and me, they're not really taking the investigation all that seriously."

"Why not?" Kelevra switched to a new file of information.

"They were all members of that gang, for one, the Shepherds? And there was talk that they may have been into something super shady."

"Aren't we all." Though it made sense to Kel. Adair was in the Void's pocket, and the Brumal was experiencing some issues with the Shepherds, though he didn't know all the details. He didn't care, so long as

Baikal kept mafia business from spilling out into the streets.

Madden shrugged. "Just what I heard. You didn't have anything to do with it?"

"With their deaths? If I had you would have been the first one I called to come clean up the mess."

"I really wish you'd stop doing that," he frowned, "we have cleaners for a reason."

The Imperial family had never been above getting their hands dirty. Kelevra had only ever lost his cool and caused an accident of that magnitude once—or twice—before however. He didn't make it his mission to go around killing people for the hell of it. He loved blood, sure, but when it was carefully contained and there was no risk of it spraying all over one of his suits.

"Why are you wasting your time on this?" Madden switched topics now that he'd gleaned Kel had nothing to do with it, and glanced over at the information and grunted. "Who cares about this stupid assignment?"

"Why aren't you wearing a shirt?" Kelevra countered.

"It was hot outside."

"It's pouring out."

Madden shrugged. "I got wet."

"Which is it?"

He sighed. "Does it matter? It's not like you can't tell when I'm lying anyway. Why bother being truthful?"

"Because lying to your Imperial Prince is dangerous?" Kel suggested dryly.

"Fine." In one swift motion, Madden sat up. "But honestly. I've never seen you this dedicated to anything before."

"That's because school is easy." Kelevra had a high IQ and found learning only somewhat entertaining. He managed to maintain his GPA by simply half-assing the work. If he actually put his mind to something, he'd no doubt shock his professors into a stupor with his intelligence. When he'd been a child that had been fun for a while. Until they'd started refusing to teach him at all, and his sister had been stressed with the burden of trying to find someone qualified who would.

Kelevra was spoiled, entitled, and arrogant. But his sisters cared for him, and the least he could do in return, even if he didn't necessarily love them back, was make himself less of a nightmare.

Less of one.

Like hell he'd become some angelic daydream bullshit though. Even for them.

"Yeah but we won't even really get anything out of this," Madden waved to the case files.

"Rin will." Kelevra's mood soured. He was livid that his flower had opted to work the case without him the other day. Even more so when he thought about Rin spending time with Brennon.

"So…" Madden blinked slowly, "You're doing this for him? To….make him happy?"

Kel scrunched up his face. "Don't be ridiculous. I'm doing this to put him in my debt." Obviously.

Madden blew out a relieved breath and leaned back, tossing an arm over the back of the couch. "Had me worried for a second there. But also, kind of surprised you're still invested in that. Haven't you been ignoring him for the past week?"

Yes, but that wasn't because Kelevra had lost interest. On the contrary.

"I'm stepping up my game," he said. "Apparently, there are some things even I have to work for."

"Pretty sure you don't," Madden replied. "Couldn't you just lock him up or something? Sure, it wouldn't look great appearances-wise, but it's not like anyone would call you out on it."

"My sisters might," he drawled. Lyra especially. She'd been oddly excited when Kel had gone to them to make his request. The only reason she hadn't insisted on meeting Rin yet was because she was attending business on the other side of the globe. "Besides, locking him up is too easy. Dull. What I'm doing is much more entertaining."

"Avoiding him?" Madden didn't sound convinced. "Come on. Everyone at the Academy is talking about it now. Your absence hasn't gone unnoticed. You post that photo of the guy in your bed, and then nothing. People are starting to feel sorry for him. The rumor is you're already bored with him."

Kelevra smirked as he jotted down another note in the holo-pad propped on his thigh. "I bet that's driving him crazy."

Madden lifted a questioning brow.

"He doesn't like attention," Kel filled him in. "Whether they're making fun of him or showing him pity, everyone's looking his way. They're curious why he was chosen as my Consort and they're curious if I'm pleased or not about that fact."

"So you know some people are saying shitty things about him then, right?" Madden said. "Like how he's hot, but not hot enough for you. Or how you gave him a spin the night you took that photo but found out he was terrible in bed. He's had to have heard most of it. Won't that upset him?"

Rin was made out of tougher stuff than that.

"No," Kel replied. "It'll only add to his ire. All that pent-up aggression with nowhere to direct it? He'll cave shortly." He was impressed Rin had lasted this long even. He'd been certain he'd stay away for three days, max, before Rin was seeking him out. So far though, that hadn't happened. "He's stubborn, but the more exposed he becomes, the more frustrated he'll be and he's no pushover."

"Are you really telling me you're doing all of this to piss your Consort off?" Madden rolled his eyes.

"Angering him is just a part of it," he said. Once that died down, Rin would be forced to admit that things were better with Kelevra around. That the only one who could protect him from all the gossip and nonsense was Kel. That he needed him.

And, with any luck, that he wanted him as well.

He'd seen the way Rin had gone to mush beneath him after a rough fucking. Saw the blissed-out state he entered. It was a reprieve from the constant barrage of overthinking he suffered on a daily basis. Kelevra had also realized Rin didn't just do that for himself. He thought ahead for his brother, too. Worried for them both. Prepared for them both. It was like the guy thought his life was some epic chess match, and if he made one wrong move, he'd lose the entire board.

If Kel guessed correctly, up until this point, Rin had convinced himself that the sex wasn't worth all the baggage that came along with it. He'd agreed not to contest the betrothal, and to move in, and yet a whole week had passed since Kel had called to ask where he was and Rin was still spending his nights at the dorms.

Was he racking his brain trying to figure out what Kelevra's angle was? Had he gone from relieved that he was getting that space he so desperately craved, to anxious? Were those rumors that Kel was bored with him getting to him?

Rin was an overthinker.

Just by staying away, Kelevra had given him a lot to think about.

He bet Rin was missing it by now, the way Kel could touch him and wipe all those pesky thoughts from his mind. How he could force himself in deep and shove that overanalyzing nonsense out.

"Random suggestion," Madden twirled a hand in the air, "but have you considered trying to romance him instead? If you're really into him, and don't just want to trap him—"

"Who said I didn't?" Kel interrupted. "I don't want to lock him up. There's a difference. There are two parts to everyone, the physical and the mental. I don't just want to conquer one. I want both. I want all of him. And I'll have all of him. He's good at telling people what they want to hear, but there's no way of knowing whether or not he'll follow through. I can't just shove him behind a locked door and throw away the key. The rest of our lives will be a constant battle, and eventually, one or both of us would get tired of that kind of drama.

"If I want to keep all of him, I need to do more than simply catch him. I need to tame him, and the start of that happens," he tapped his temple, "right here. My flower's main issue is he feels too much. He's ruled by his emotions. It doesn't take much to make him feel resentful."

Madden frowned. "Pretty sure he's the Academy's resident nice guy."

"It's a façade." Kelevra didn't like outing Rin, especially since he still didn't understand why it was so important for him to stay hidden. He'd figure it out eventually, but it wasn't the highest on his list of priorities.

Rin wasn't the only one he was learning new things about through this.

"It turns out," he continued, "I can be patient when I want to be. Taking his body was the easy part, infecting his mind is harder. It's a process. I can't just force my way in all at once."

Madden stared at him for a long moment before, "Have I mentioned recently that you're terrifying?"

"Not recently, no."

"I spilled coffee on my shirt, that's why I took it off."

Kelevra gave him a droll look. "I don't actually give a shit."

"So you want him thinking about you?" Madden brought them back to the topic.

"I'm going to use his issues against him. He's emotional and a control freak. Not knowing what I'm planning, having to deal with the constant barrage from the public…Eventually, he'll torture himself enough and he'll break for me all on his own."

"That's why you haven't ordered him back to your side."

"There's no need." Once Rin had enough, he'd find his way back, most likely fuming and chomping at the bit. They might even get into a physical altercation wherein Kelevra would be given an excuse to subdue him. He enjoyed that. Got a real kick out of subjugating his flower whenever he was in a particularly foul mood. It somehow made the conquest all the sweeter.

"And the brother?" Madden began tossing the ball once more. "He's not giving you any grief?"

"He hasn't, why?"

"I see him around the docks sometimes." Madden shrugged. "The guy looks different at night, that's all."

"Devils tend to flourish in the dark," Kel hummed, and at his friend's confused glance added,

"How do you expect to be a good head of guard for me if you're this obtuse? The twins aren't normal. But normal is overrated anyway. I'm too good for normal."

"Yeah, because you aren't," Madden replied, laughing. "And you still don't think this has escalated too quickly? You banged the guy a couple of times. That usually doesn't make a person want to rush out to marry them. You're aware it's forever, right? You only get one shot at naming a Royal Consort. That's a tradition not even your sisters will be able to change for you. I get impulsive is your middle name but…?"

"The Imperial decree has already been made," Kelevra reminded.

"Sure, but until the actual wedding, there's still time to change your mind."

"I won't be changing it," he stated, annoyance flickering in his sharp gaze when he set it on his friend. His sisters might be elated that he was willing to settle down with someone, but his Retinue were less enthusiastic. That was going to have to be dealt with, but right now his main focus was on his flower and edging him to the conclusion that he was already plucked.

Rin Varun belonged to Kelevra. Body and mind. If his flower also happened to have a soul? Kel would take that too. He was going to leave nothing behind.

"He's mine. He'll always be mine."

"It hasn't even been a month since you met him," Madden said. Then he seemed to recall something and blew out a breath. "Actually, this is very on-brand for you. You may be spontaneous, but you're also obsessive.

Like these damn corset vests you're always in," he motioned to the glittery black and gray one Kel was currently wearing. "You saw one in an AD and boom. By the next day, you'd changed your entire wardrobe. And the roses." Kelevra's tattoos were covered by his suit jacket, but Madden looked at his arms pointedly. "How many do you have delivered to your penthouse weekly again?"

"It's daily," he corrected. "I have two dozen fresh roses brought in. It spruces up the place. And they smell nice." And if he sometimes passed his time by pricking his fingers on their sharp thorns and watching the blood roll...That only added to their functionality and appeal.

Madden rubbed his face and snorted. "Yeah, not sure how I didn't see it before. Maybe you're right. Maybe I am too oblivious for a job as important as your head of guard." It's what he was attending the Academy to become. Every member of Kel's Retinue already had their future positions selected.

"It's a good thing nothing slips past my Consort's notice." Kelevra was even sure Rin knew what was going on right now. That's most likely why he'd managed to last this long. But knowing wouldn't help him forever. Eventually, he'd crack and give in, no matter how illogical it seemed.

"Wow, are you saying he'll protect you if I can't?" Madden snorted. "Last I checked, he doesn't even like you. What makes you so sure he'll do that?"

"Who says he doesn't like me?" And even if Rin didn't, he would. Kelevra was confident of that. "You should see how he treats his brother. How much he cares for him." Despite the fact his brother was a psychopath.

Kelevra guessed therein laid the difference between the two of them, but that was fine. He didn't want to be like Sila Varun, he just wanted what he had.

Kel's sisters loved him, and his Retinue were genuinely friends of his, but he knew even they walked the line, too afraid to push him and suffer his wrath. His flower didn't hesitate to tell his brother off. It didn't matter to him what Sila was capable of or the types of things he no doubt dreamed about doing to others— Kelevra had figured that part out about the imposter as well. He'd always been interested in blood. Seemed like Sila was probably the same in that retrospect.

"Rin is perfect for me," Kelevra said. "It's almost as though he was made for me even. He grew up with a Devil so he's already accustomed to us. He'll learn to accept me the same way he's accepted his brother. Step by step. I'll fill him up until he can no longer tell where he begins and ends. Until he's so used to having me around, life without me will be an unbearable prospect."

"Your obsession is noted, but it's important to point out that things are different this time around than they were with your corsets and your roses," Madden told him. "Those things are inanimate. Easily controlled. Rin is an entire person. He has his own thoughts, his own wants, and his own desires."

"I'll simply become all of those for him," Kel shrugged.

"You're not even slightly concerned you'll fail," he noted. "That's one serious god complex you have, my friend."

"I'm an Imperial Prince," Kelevra corrected. "I'll have him on his knees just like I have everyone else." And if he also happened to have those full lips wrapped around his cock again as well?

All the better.

Using the drug on his flower had been exciting.

But his nectar was going to be all the sweeter once Kelevra made him want it without drugs or threats.

If all went to plan, he was going to have Rin Varun begging to be his by the end of this.

Chapter 21:

Rin's arms cut through the water. He'd lost count of how many laps he'd done around one hundred, and he couldn't recall when he'd taken his last full breath either. Tiberan's were born for water, with the ability to hold their breath longer than most other species. Even though they'd left their home world, he and his brother still made regular trips to the pool, though Sila more so than Rin.

Which was technically why Rin was there now, swimming in the Vail University pool. Three days ago, his brother had come to him asking to swap places, and seeing as how he'd been on his last thread of patience when it'd come to surviving on the Academy campus, Rin had eagerly agreed. It'd been a small reprieve.

Too small.

He'd expected to show up to the university, playing the part of Sila Varun, and get to relax, instead, he'd been screening questions about his brother's engagement to the Imperial Prince. At least as Rin the student body whispered—loudly—behind his back, but as Sila, people were bolder.

Being identical twins meant no one could tell them apart, and they'd been using this trick for so long, slipping into the role of Sila and shedding Rin had been simple. If only he could shake his emotional baggage with the same kind of ease.

Rin was two steps from going off on everyone, which he couldn't afford. His brother had fucked with the process and upped Sila's personality since returning from their summer break. Now he had friends and a reputation on campus as a flirty, fun-loving guy, a major change from the quiet and reserved freshmen he'd been last year. No matter how many times Rin asked, his brother wouldn't explain either. He'd simply say there was a reason and eventually he'd tell him. That was it.

They'd split their "personalities" for a reason, to make it easier for them to switch places and keep up the rouse. His brother had never messed with that on his own before.

Cursing in his head, Rin tapped the wall and rolled in the water, pushing off to shoot across the pool. Three times a week, like clockwork, Sila could be found at this pool doing laps for at least an hour. Rin had been looking forward to it since swimming had always helped him alleviate stress and get his head on straight, but he'd been in here for at least two and was still seething.

How dare Kelevra treat him like this? Who the hell did he think he was?

First he had the audacity to make a public announcement and post that way too personal picture, and the next he's ghosting? And not just. He was making a public statement by avoiding Rin, and Rin hated that he was aware of that fact. Why couldn't he be dumb?

Ignorance was sometimes bliss, and this would have been the perfect occasion for that. Instead, he was pissed off that the Imperial Prince was messing with him, and stressed out that everyone kept staring at him, and anxious over the rumors being spread attached to Rin Varun's name.

If their father got word...

That was another nightmare. Rin had taken a page out of his brother's playbook and ignored every single call his father had sent to Sila's multi-slate, but that could only go on for so long. When he asked his brother about it, he'd mentioned he'd been doing the same with Rin's device. So basically they were both icing out their father, who no doubt would realize—if he hadn't already—that their tuitions had been paid for and they no longer needed him.

Except, Rin couldn't even be excited that they could finally cut their father off, because he was too busy freaking out about potentially having the rug pulled out from under him. On the one hand, he was pretty certain this was all a game to Kelevra, a punishment of sorts for refusing to spend the night at the penthouse. But on the other...

What if the rumors weren't actually rumors? What if Kel really had grown tired of him already? The tuition had been paid, Rin had checked, and he didn't think there was a way the money could be refunded but...If they blew off their father indefinitely now, and then later Kelevra tossed them aside like used goods...

Which meant Rin had to keep his interest, whether he wanted to or not.

Did he want to?

He swore, this time out loud, as he reached the other end of the pool and came up, slapping an arm against the water as a burst of fury coursed through him.

"Breathe, brother."

Rin wiped water droplets from his eyes and looked up to find his brother standing a couple of feet away.

He was dressed in the Academy uniform, his spine straight as he held himself with poise and authority the way Rin Varun was known for. His face was unmarked, but so was Rin's, the cuts he'd received during the fight with Flix having healed a lot sooner than everyone else had assumed.

Mostly because Rin had been easing ever so slightly away from the impacts. He'd taken the hits, sure, but that hadn't meant he'd been willing to suffer the long-lasting consequences. It'd irked him that his brother hadn't realized.

"What?" Rin tugged at the golden earring cuff he was wearing—Sila's earring—and glared.

"You're doing it all wrong," his brother said. "Anyone who glances in here will easily see you're in a mood."

"I'm allowed to be every now and again." If his brother hadn't recreated Sila's personality, this wouldn't be such a problem anyway. "There are too many eyes on us here. I hope you're pleased."

"It was necessary."

"Yeah, sure, but for what?"

"To handle my problem."

He meant Rin's problem, but fine. Rolling his eyes, he moved over to the steps and climbed out, water pooling at his feet as he rested his hands on his hips. "What are you doing here?"

His brother turned ever so slightly to the left, almost as though he'd seen something in that direction but didn't want to alert whatever—or whoever—it was that they'd been caught. The only reason Rin caught on was because he was so used to his movements. Still, he didn't verbally point it out.

"I came to check up on you. See how you're doing," his brother motioned toward the door that lead into the locker room, "Why don't you get dressed?"

"Ah," Rin nodded, "checking up to see if your problem is affecting me?"

His brother shrugged. "The betrothal is all anyone can talk about, it seems."

That's not what Rin had been referring to and they both knew it. He rolled his eyes and started for the gray door, not bothering to hold it open for his brother when he passed through. It was childish, but he really was in a mood.

He stripped out of his wet swim trunks as soon as he was standing by his locker, glancing over at his brother when he stopped in the center of the room. "Aren't you going to check?"

"It's empty," his brother said confidently.

Whatever. If he said there was no one else in there, Rin believed him. "Why'd you actually come?"

He started to remove his clothing as well. "Let's switch back."

"Right now?" Rin paused with one leg through the gray pants.

"It's not like being here instead of the Academy is helping you," his brother pointed out, handing over his combat pants before curling his fingers indicating Rin should switch.

With a huff, he did. But he wasn't happy about it.

"This couldn't have lasted anyway," his brother continued. "Your Imperial can tell us apart. Swapping places on him isn't going to work."

"Fucking computer eye." Although, Rin had to admit the accompanying scar was pretty sexy. "You seem to have forgotten how there's a name attached to the decree. That's kind of an important detail, brother."

"We'll burn down that bridge when we come to it," he stated absently, holding out the t-shirt he'd been wearing next. "It's only been a couple of weeks."

"Tell him that!"

"He's obsessed with you." His brother came over himself to remove the earring from Rin's ear. "You can't blame him. We're awesome."

"We," Rin growled, "aren't exactly in this together when he can tell us apart on sight."

He snorted. "We're always in everything together."

"Oh, really?" Rin crossed his arms. "Why'd you want to switch for? And what—"

"Fine," his brother conceded. "You have your thing with the Imperial Prince, and I have my thing with…" He grinned.

"I hate you." Rin hated that he was being so damn secretive. "We've never kept things from the other before."

"Isn't this part of the reason we came to this galaxy? To develop individually?"

"Is that why Sila Varun is suddenly friendly? Sounds a lot like Rin."

"And *flirty*," his brother emphasized. "Not like Rin at all."

"Yeah, what's up with that?" Rin made a face. "I was hit on by like eleven people in the past three days. What, are you suddenly sleeping around?"

"Maybe I'm looking for my own prince," the way he said it made it clear he was full of shit. "You have to meet the guys at Fornication in an hour."

"What the hell?" That was the real reason his brother wanted to switch back, wasn't it. "You're the one who agreed, you go!"

"Rin agreed," he stepped back and gave him a once over, "and you, brother, are currently him."

"You're lucky this feels better." Rin tugged on the pants.

His brother quirked a brow, seemingly surprised.
Shit.
"That's not—"

"Preferences are good," his brother cut him off. "I happen to have one as well."

His eyes narrowed. "You're not telling me...Is this why you're not mad about the betrothal?"

"That and the fact it'll set us both for life?" His brother nodded. "Yes. I don't see why you are. We've both spent the week completely ignoring Crate and what's happened? Nothing. There've been no repercussions because he has no hold over us anymore. That's all thanks to your—"

Rin held up his hand, not wanting to hear him call Kelevra his again. "I knew you were a dick, but pimping out your brother, seriously?"

He went still, his whole demeanor changing at the drop of a hat. The room seemed to chill, and when he spoke, his voice was deadpan and hollow. "Is he not good to you? Do you not like it?"

"No." Rin ran a hand through his hair, seeing his mistake. "That's not it."

"He took advantage of you," his brother tipped his head, darkness flickering in his gaze, a look he often kept hidden since Rin wasn't capable of conjuring it himself, "but since you're into that sort of thing, I let it pass. Was that a mistake? If someone hurts us—"

"Enough," he exhaled. "I didn't mean it, okay? Besides, the second he actually does something I don't like, you know I'll handle it myself."

"You don't have what it takes to be a killer, brother."

"If someone hurts us?" Rin countered. "Hell yeah, I do."

"Well, considering only one of us is getting fucked by him—"

"And I'm going to stop you there before the person I end up murdering is you. The pool isn't too far if you recall."

"You and your obsession with drowning people." His brother slid his hands into his front pockets, dropping the scary vibe all at once. "Almost do it accidentally the one time and suddenly it's all you can think about. Surely you can be more creative?"

In high school, Rin had lost his cool once and almost killed a kid in their grade. The kid had made inappropriate comments about a female friend and he'd lost it. Their father had been able to get them off the hook with the guy's parents, and Rin had pretended it'd been an accident. He'd been convincing enough that everyone had bought it.

He was used to people only seeing what he wanted them to see.

Damn Kelevra and his fucking eye.

"Any progress on the case?" He asked before he forgot. The only problem with switching places was they needed to keep each other updated. Since this was pretty par for the course, they mostly had that down pat.

"Nothing groundbreaking," his brother said. "The blood results showed there were two different samples found at the scene with Arlet, one hers and the other belonging to who we assume is the killer. Since no other samples were found at past sites, Calder and I are guessing the Actives plan to divulge more clues with fresh crime scenes. We haven't had one all week though."

"And the multi-slate?" That still hadn't been cracked when Rin and agreed to this.

"Messages and calls were all wiped, as well as search history, but there were photos of each of the victims so far."

"Any that haven't been murdered yet?"

His brother shook his head.

"And here I was hoping you were going tell me you solved it so I could just coast the rest of the semester."

"You mean so you could keep avoiding Kelevra," his brother corrected with a knowing smirk. "Admit it, you're about to cave. If I hadn't asked for us to swap, you would have by now."

Being in Sila Varun's shoes had certainly helped. He couldn't very well have rushed over there and demanded answers from the guy dressed in Vail University's uniform.

"I know what he's trying to pull," Rin stated dryly.

"Of course you do," his brother agreed. "That's what he's counting on."

"You think?"

"It's how I would play things. Wear you down mentally until resistance feels like too much of a chore to bother with. He gets you to give in now, and it's game over. He can avoid numerous battles and simply end the war in one move. Clever."

"You find him so appealing, you marry him."

His brother shook his head. "I would never try to steal what's rightfully yours. It's one of the rules."

Rin opened his mouth but then snapped it shut again.

"You like him," his brother said.

"I'm partial to his dick."

"You're deflecting by being crass. You only do that when you're uncomfortable."

"And you're goading me on purpose," Rin countered. "You only do that when you're trying to distract me."

They stared at each other silently for a moment.

"All right," his brother held up both hands, "let's agree not to root around in each other's proverbial closets. You want to pretend like you aren't falling for the Imperial Prince? So be it."

"And if you want to pretend like I don't know exactly what you've been up to, go ahead." Rin wasn't as blind as his brother believed. "Or are you going to tell me that was something you wanted me to know, the same way Kel wants me to know he's tugging on my strings?"

His jaw clenched, almost imperceptibly, but Rin caught it.

"Relax," Rin said before his brother could respond. "I'm not going to get in your way. When have I ever?"

"You stopped trying to save me a long time ago," he agreed.

"Us," Rin corrected, moving to clap him on the shoulder. "If we're going to be devils, we may as well be them together." What one of them was responsible for, so was the other. They were accomplices. Always.

"It's Devils," his brother grinned wickedly. "Devils of Vitality."

"Pretty sure we're not part of that little group."

"That's only because we're better at it than they are," his brother explained. "True Devils know it's safer in the shadows. In the dark, you can get away with anything."

Rin hummed. "Can I get away with not going to Fornication?"

His brother shoved him lightly toward the door. "Not a chance."

"Sila doesn't have to go," he complained.

"Maybe, but *you* do."

Rin flipped him the bird as he exited the locker room.

Chapter 22:

"What's up with you?" Calder bumped shoulders against Rin as he came up to the circular table they were all crowded around. "You've been in such a good mood all week. Something happen this afternoon?"

Rin ground his teeth and forced a smile, shaking his head in the negative as he took a deep drag from his beer. He should probably slow down, this being his fourth already, but his nerves were shot and the loud beat music blaring through the speakers and the stifling heat from the packed club were playing on his last nerve.

Fornication was a club located between all three main campuses in the city, so students from the Academy, Vail, and Gift constantly flooded the place. The music changed every week, but the drink menu was a classic and they carried alcoholic brands from all over the galaxy.

The overstimulation of the club always gave Rin a migraine, and over the summer whenever he'd been asked to come, he'd convinced his brother to go in his stead. Which was why he was so irked that he'd been tricked into switching back and being forced to come here. And all while his brother had apparently been playing the part of happy-go-lucky-idiot all week.

"Did you hear more of the rumors?" Daylen asked sympathetically. "Thought you said you weren't going to let those get to you?"

"Yeah," Calder clapped him on the back. "Kelevra's just busy, right?"

Is that what his brother had told them?

Fucking hell.

"To be honest, I'm still shocked you're interested in him," Brennon joined in.

The four of them kept coming and going, heading away to meet up with other people only to return to their main table when they were done. They'd already been here for over an hour.

Rin downed the rest of his beer and then popped open another. He was drinking Scan, a brand exclusive to the planet and three times stronger than any beer he'd had back home. It was only a matter of time before he got wasted, but even knowing that he couldn't bring himself to care or stop.

"Dude," Calder twisted his mouth in displeasure, "stop pestering him about that."

"Yeah," Daylen jumped in. "So what if he fell for the Imperial Prince?" He leaned his elbows on the table and tapped his bottle against Rin's. "If you're happy, man, I'm happy for you."

"Plus you have loads of time to change your mind anyway," Calder reminded. "It's cool he agreed not to rush the wedding."

Rin didn't actually have a choice and couldn't change his mind, but sure. Although, maybe the talk on campus wasn't just talk after all. Maybe Kel really had gotten bored of him and he was finally willing to leave him alone.

And if that bothered Rin? Well, it was only because he was worried about what that'd mean for him and his brother.

Obviously.

"What does being a Royal Consort even entail?" Daylen asked.

"It's a fancy title for the partner of an Imperial," Calder explained. "How much actual involvement they have with the government or with the Retinue is up to Kelevra. Considering his personality though, he'll most likely want Rin to be a part of it. Having him considered Retinue means he can keep him close. Like an excuse to invite his boyfriend even before the wedding."

"You're going to have a ton of royal duties. What's that mean for your future?" Brennon finished off the hard liquor he'd been drinking and poured himself another.

"He told me the other day he wasn't planning on going for detective or inspector anyway," Calder said.

Had he? He was going to have to have a serious talk with his brother later. Usually, the way this went down was they filled one another in on all the important details when they'd been switched, that way things like this didn't happen. What was his brother playing at?

The only reason Rin had wanted to bother with the Academy had been to learn how to stay hidden, and even though he was only a sophomore, he felt like he and his brother already had that part down pat. And if Kelevra was just messing with him right now and he did still intend for them to be together…Rin didn't want to quit going, but as far as his future went, there was nothing specific he'd had his heart set on.

His only real goal had been to learn enough and get a job that would pay for him and his brother to flee without telling their father where they were going. They were going to disappear and never look back, another reason why he hadn't gone out of his way to make real friends.

His brother's earlier words about wanting to stay echoed in his mind and he took a longer look around at the table. He'd tried not to get attached to anyone, but clearly that had been a failure of epic proportions.

Sort of like how he'd been trying to convince himself he wasn't interested in Kelevra.

"Maybe I'll just act as a bodyguard or something," Rin joked, laughing it off to help sell it.

"Isn't that him?" a girl whispered nearby, loudly enough her voice carried over the music.

Rin didn't have to turn to know she was referring to him.

"Do you think they're going to call it off? I heard that's why Kelevra's been M.I.A. He's at the palace begging the Emperor to let him change the rules and cancel it," another voice, this one male answered.

"Why? He's cute," the girl said.

The guy snorted. "You think he's cute?"

"Hey, assholes," Daylen glared over Rin's shoulder at them. "Move along. No one's interested in your shitty rumors."

"What are you guys eleven?" Calder added shaking his head at them. "Ignore jerks like that, Rin. They're just bored."

"I can't believe he's left you to deal with shit like this," Brennon stated.

"He has his reasons." Rin left out the part about how this was most likely a manipulation. One he was probably about to fall for. Even the week as his brother hadn't been enough to quell this unease within him. Any second now he was going to cave and rush over to wherever the Imperial Prince was and he knew it.

The funny thing was he didn't even feel all that bad about it. At first, he'd been annoyed and determined to hold out, thinking Kel would actually get bored of him once he realized Rin wasn't going to cave and fall for his crap. But that resolve had been chipped at nonstop all week and now it seemed stupid of him to hold out.

For what?

He liked Kelevra. At least, he liked how the guy made him feel, and sometimes that was enough. So what if he was abrasive and arrogant and frustrating as all hell? No one had ever paid Rin the type of attention Kelevra did. No one had ever been able to look at him next to his twin and instantly tell them apart. Most of that was his eye, but Rin had the feeling even without it Kelevra would be able to tell the difference, and that—

He chugged his beer.

"Is he nice to you?" Brennon said then.

"He tries to be," Rin answered honestly. Must be the alcohol.

He frowned. "What does that even mean?"

As the Imperial Prince, they all knew who held the power here, but aside from forcing his hand—both literally and figuratively—Kelevra had been surprisingly…lax as far as abuse of power went. If he'd wanted, he could have ordered Rin dragged before him and locked in the penthouse like some damsel. No one would have been able to do a damn thing, but instead, he'd opted to try out a mental play instead.

He was using Rin's need for anonymity against him by ensuring the entire city was talking about him, gossiping over whether or not he was going to be made Royal Consort after all or kicked to the curb like used goods. Instead of having Rin dragged home, he was attempting to rile him up, antagonize him to the point Rin stormed through the doors on his own two feet.

Clever.

Manipulative.

Sexy.

There was something severely wrong with Rin for thinking so, but then, that was old news. He may feel more than his brother, but there were other proclivities they shared. Sila liked doing the manipulation, but Rin? There was something wholly arousing about another person willing to put themselves through mental gymnastics just to obtain him.

His father couldn't even tell him and his brother apart, so he'd never done anything for either of them specifically. They had different roles to fulfill for the family, sure, but they were still treated the same. It's not like they'd have preferred if he'd played favorites, but a little attention, personal attention, now and again wouldn't have killed the old man.

The only time Rin felt unique was when he was with Kelevra, and maybe that made him a bit off and a lot psychotic, but the truth was the truth.

"It means he cares what I think," he said finally when he realized his friend was still waiting for his response. "That's…nice."

"We care what you think." Brennon scowled.

"Dude." Calder rolled his eyes.

"Pathetic," Daylen said under his breath.

"What?" Brennon glared at them. "Can't I be worried for our friend? A month ago he was single, and now suddenly he's engaged? Several steps were skipped, and if you ask me—"

"That's the thing, Brenn," Calder cut him off. "No one did. Just let the guy be happy, damn.

"He could be forcing Rin into it," Brennon refused to back down. "Rin is so kind, of course he'd roll over if an Imperial ordered him to. You really think he'd tell us if that's what was going on? No. He'd grin and bear it because that's the type of friendly person he is."

The other two hesitated, finally starting to see where he was coming from.

Which wasn't good, because Rin couldn't afford to fight off all of them second-guessing things.

Rin made himself laugh lightly, slapping his hand on the table for good measure. "Guys! Come on, stop it. I told you, our families agreed because it's a mutually beneficial merger, and since Kel and I already knew one another, we decided why not go for it."

He was such a liar, and if he really were the kind and caring person Brennon had just painted him out to be, he'd feel at least a little bit bad about that too.

But he didn't.

If they kept being suspicious about this, they'd try to investigate. They were all cadets at the Academy, after all. And if they did that, they ran the risk of discovering he and his brother sometimes switch places and *that* Rin could not allow.

When it came to keeping his brother safe, there was nothing Rin wasn't capable of doing. Be it lie, steal, cheat, maim, kill, or torture. They came first. It was a rule.

"Seriously, I appreciate the concern, but everything is really okay. I'm not being forced to do anything." That was less of a lie, considering Kelevra was making him come on his own. Which Rin would be doing. Soon, if not tonight. He could feel the last bit of his resolve snapping, those comments from the other patrons hitting too harshly.

With everyone looking their way, it was honestly a wonder no one else had realized they'd switched all week. Go figure. Suddenly, his friends crowded around the table didn't seem as sweet and endearing as they had a second ago. It wasn't fair to them, and yet Rin couldn't help but feel that way. He was a hypocrite on top of everything else it seemed.

Yeah, he really was the worst.

Chapter 23:

He was wasted. He knew that for a fact because he found himself standing outside of the penthouse suit, on the rooftop where it had all started. Rin laughed, the sound tight and a bit manic, and rubbed at his face, trying to get everything to stop spinning around him.

How'd he even get up here?

His brow furrowed as he tried to piece together the night up until this point, only vaguely able to recall walking into the bar where his friends were already waiting and being handed drink after drink. It'd been their poor attempt to cheer him up and get his mind off the whole Kelevra thing, but clearly it hadn't worked, because here he was, outside the prick's door.

Focus. He was trying to figure out how he'd gotten here. There'd been the drinking, dancing like idiots to some shitty live rock band, and hands on—

Rin blinked and almost fell over, catching himself on the wall. He was certain someone had touched him, but for the life of him, he couldn't recall who. He'd swung at them though, he was pretty sure…

"Fuck." He dropped his forehead against the cool glass of the door. It was the same side entrance that

Kelevra had led him up that night of the party, only now it was locked and with the blackout mode activated so he couldn't see inside. Was there a damn doorbell?

No, wait, that wasn't important right now. Figuring out who he'd decked was. He inhaled through his nose and held it for a beat, playing back the night like a movie reel. Brennon, Daylen, Calder, and he had been on the dance floor, and…Arlet had come over. Had she—

She'd made out with Calder in the corner. Daylen had noticed first and hollered like some juvenile delinquent urging his buddy on.

Then Calder had gone to get another round and Daylen had gone with to help carry it back and—

Brennon had put both hands on Rin's ass and leaned in for a kiss as soon as their friends weren't looking.

Like a fucking creep.

"Fuck me." Rin shifted around so he could lean against the wall next to the door, sliding to the ground. He hung his head and pressed against his eyes when that caused a wave of dizziness to wash over him. This was bad. Real bad. They'd been in a crowded place, and with all the attention that had been on him, what were the chances no one had seen or seized the opportunity to snap a photo?

Thinking about it, he wanted to break his friend's nose a second time, but that wasn't even the worst part. If he was this angry, he couldn't even begin to imagine how livid Kel—

"You're late," Kelevra's voice interrupted Rin's thoughts.

Blearily, he lifted his head, glancing over to find the door was now open and the Imperial Prince was propped up against the stile.

"And drunk, apparently," Kelevra added once they locked eyes. "What's wrong, Flower, needed liquid courage to get yourself to admit defeat?"

"Screw you." He groaned and pressed to the spot that was thumping between his brow, trying, and failing, to lift himself from the ground. He stumbled and Kel caught him, steadying him against the opposite stile of the doorway.

The Imperial Prince left his hands on Rin's waist, taking him in from head to toe.

"It's been a week," Rin complained. "Stop acting like you haven't seen me in years."

"It certainly feels like that," he replied. "You kept me waiting longer than I expected."

"That's why you like me, right?" Rin snorted. "Gotta keep you on your toes. Keep things interesting so you don't get bored of me and toss me out."

Kelevra lifted a dark brow. "Is that so? That the conclusion you came to during our time apart, Flower? You decide from now on you're going to," he sidled in closer, voice lowering suggestively, "keep things interesting for me?"

"Back off." Rin shoved him, and even though he was drunk, he wasn't too drunk to note Kel let him put space between them.

He *was* too drunk to think about why that might be, however. Or recognize the potential danger in that fact.

"You're a real prick, you know that?" Rin wagged a finger at him in displeasure. "Vanishing so the whole dame city only has me to look at. The next person who offers to teach me how to show you a better time in the bedroom is getting their head held under a large body of water."

Kelevra's eyes narrowed, but Rin was too busy scowling at the recollection of this afternoon when he'd passed a group of senior guys at the university and they'd shot that one off to him. They'd thought they were original, but he'd already heard that offer from at least six other assholes.

"I should have fucked each and every one of them to prove—" His sentence ended with a curse as he was suddenly yanked into the penthouse, the door slammed shut behind him a split second before he was roughly shoved up against it.

"By all means," Kelevra's hot breath fanned against the side of Rin's face, causing him to shiver, "keep talking. I dare you."

"I…." He frowned. "What was I saying again?"

Kel chuckled darkly. "You were telling me how badly you missed me."

Rin blinked and leaned to the side so he could meet his gaze. "I don't think that was it."

"No?" Kelevra feigned innocent. "Sure you weren't just working your way up to it?"

Had Rin missed him? His gaze inadvertently dropped, lowering down the expanse of Kelevra's torso, down to the slight bulge in his pants. "Why are you always so fucking flashy?"

He hated it. Hated it because he liked it. There was something attractive about Kelevra getting to be one hundred percent himself without holding back. He didn't have to lie or pretend or hide behind a mask.

Rin wanted that.

The Imperial Prince was dressed in another one of his famous suits, though he'd done without the jacket and the shirt. The corset, some velvety material in pastel pink with glittery gold detailing, hugged his form as tightly as the matching pants. He wasn't wearing any shoes or socks though.

"Were you getting ready for bed?" Rin guessed. His hand reached up and the next thing he knew, he was touching Kelevra's curls. "You haven't showered yet."

Kel watched him closely, allowing him to run his fingers through his dark strands. "Is that an invitation, Flower?"

Rin scowled and dropped his arm. "You and I near water right now isn't a good mix."

"Because?"

"I'll try to drown you."

He tilted his head. "Is that so?"

"Definitely."

Kelevra nodded once. "Are you that angry with me?"

"I'm furious with you," he corrected.

"Because I set you up? Let everyone spread those awful rumors about how you can't please me and I'm already sick of you?"

"Sure," he shrugged, "that was shitty."

Kel's gaze sharpened, clearly catching something either in Rin's tone or from his body. "That's not the reason you may try to drown me."

"Not try," he corrected, "I don't do anything in half measures. If I go to drown you, Imperial Prince, I will. But no. It was shitty, but as my annoying asshole of a brother has pointed out already, it was also clever. Clever is sexy."

"Is it?" Kelevra obviously hadn't anticipated that response, but he seemed pleased.

For some inexplicable reason, that pissed Rin off even more.

Before the other guy could react, Rin shoved him, hard enough to send him stumbling back. Kelevra knocked into the banister, but Rin followed, grabbing onto his hips to roughly drag him back, grinding against him at the same moment as he sealed their mouths together.

Rin moaned at the first taste of Kelevra's tongue, rich, with a hint of alcohol. His hands left his waist to dive into his curly hair, all those silky strands making him crazy with want. There was something so impossibly sexy about the Imperial's contrasting hard edges and soft accents. His hair, the velvet of his outfit, his ass…

Kelevra's teeth nipped into him then, hard enough to draw blood and Rin gasped and pulled away.

He brought a finger to his bottom lip, drawing it away with a spot of red. "Ouch."

Kel laughed. "Did you really just say that? *Ouch?*"

"It stung!"

"Oh, sweetheart, that's the least painful thing I've done to you yet, and *now* you're complaining?"

Rin frowned. "Haven't I been this whole time?"

Kelevra sighed. "This won't do. You're way too drunk. It'll be no fun if you can't remember it in the morning."

"Remember what?"

"All the things I'm going to do to you." Kel's expression altered, but Rin couldn't place it in his current state. "Up for one last game tonight?"

"I'm not taking any pills," he stated firmly. With his luck, he'd end up choosing wrong and spilling all their secrets. Then his brother would make good on all those threats and Rin would lose—

What would he lose? Had he really been about to think about losing Kelevra?

"Another drink then," Kel conceded easily enough, but when Rin nodded and went to take the stairs up to the other level, he stopped him. "No, this way."

He took Rin's hand, and even though he thought he should pull away, Rin let him, eyes locked on their linked fingers as if in a trance as they walked beneath an archway leading into the living room. From the outside, the wall of windows in here had been blacked out as well, but inside he could see the patio and the pool crystal clear.

Kelevra left him standing in the middle of the beige carpet, staring out at the city skyline, and went to a small bar catty set behind one of the three large couches. The sound of clanking ice and liquid being poured came, and then he was back, offering a glass to Rin.

Rin glanced at the identical glass Kel lifted to his own lips. As soon as the Imperial Prince sipped and gave him a challenging smirk, he rolled his eyes. He downed his drink in one go, coughing at the slight burn.

"What the—" He abruptly stopped talking, the room seemingly spinning even more than it had been a moment ago. When his legs started to lose sensation, he realized what was going on. A whole slew of insults came to mind, but he couldn't get his tongue to work, and he ended up falling before he was able to get a single one past his lips.

Kelevra reached for him on the way down, catching up his body to hold him close. He pressed a row of feather-light kisses across Rin's forehead and smiled down at him smugly. "Welcome home, Consort."

It was the last thing Rin heard before he sunk into the dark embrace of unconsciousness.

* * *

Rin felt funny. His mouth was dry and wherever he was it, was dark.

He blinked and it took him longer than it should have to process his eyelashes brushing against cloth. His wrists were up by his head, and he was pretty sure he was vertical but he wasn't standing. The blindfold kept him from seeing what was going on, and when he tested it, he could only move his arms and legs a fraction, and it was hard, almost as though he was fighting against secure chains.

"Awake?" Kelevra's voice came from behind him a moment before the sound of him entering whatever room they were in followed. He set something down—probably something metallic from the way it clattered slightly—and then moved up to Rin's side.

"What—" Rin sucked in a breath when Kel's hand pushed lightly against his shoulder, spinning his body until he was practically hanging upside down.

"I'm doing my duty as your mentor," Kelevra told him silkily while Rin's brain scrambled to figure out what was going on. "You're currently experiencing what it's like to use the G-Tester 450."

"The—" He frowned. That was tech used by the school for training. He'd seen the room they were kept in. Each station consisted of two circular power pads, one on the floor and one on the ceiling directly above it. Cadets were given cuffs for their wrists and ankles that were connected to the remote controls for the device. When activated, the space between the top and bottom panels altered, simulating a zero gravity experience where the cadet felt weightless.

"You wouldn't get to train on them until next year," Kelevra said, walking around him as he spoke. "Your Active encouraged us to share our knowledge and prepare you, and this," he tapped on the side of Rin's left leg, effectively sending his body spinning again until he was hovering over the ground on his stomach, "is one of my specialties."

The Academy prepared students for their future roles as agents in the I.P.F, which would require spaceship travel. Since there wasn't always a mechanic on those assigned ships, all cadets were given basic repair training which would require them to exit the ship while they were in space.

"I don't think this is what Banks meant," Rin growled, realizing that his dick was hanging which meant he was also naked. "Take this thing off and put me down."

"The blindfold stays on," Kelevra said. "And as for the rest," his hand came down on Rin's calf, causing him to jolt, and he skated his palm up his leg, over the curve of his ass, and across his spine, "I like you where you are."

"Tell me we aren't at the Academy." Rin would absolutely lose it.

"Don't fret. We're home. I had the equipment installed over the weekend. You came just in time." He shifted, his hand traveling up the length of Rin's neck before he captured his jaw firmly and tilted his head up.

Rin glared behind the thick black cloth.

"Don't you like it?" Kel cooed, stroking the pad of his thumb over Rin's bottom lip. "I was thinking of you when I bought it. A week trapped in that head of yours, you must be itching to get out of your own skin and let loose. Were you worried the rumors were true, Flower? Did the thought of me being done with you keep you up at night?"

"You're such a prick." Rin tugged his head out of Kel's hold, but that only earned him a chiding click of the Imperial Prince's tongue.

"I'm your caretaker, actually." Kelevra stepped away, and Rin struggled to follow him by sound alone as he moved about the room. "Do you know anything about roses?"

"What kind of random question is that?"

"Not so random, Flower."

Rin paused and then, "You are not comparing me to an actual plant right now. I'm a *person*, Kel. Not a bush. Let me down."

"If left unchecked," he continued, ignoring him, "roses can suffer from all kinds of diseases. It's important to prune them, to cut away all the rot before it can infect the body."

Something cold settled at the base of Rin's spine and he stiffened. "Kelevra."

He shushed him. "There's nothing to be afraid of, sweetheart. I've got you. Are you thinking it's a chilly blade? It's just an ice cube, you're the only one here who's drawn the other's blood with a weapon."

Rin had nicked him with the knife in the locker room and carved up his back their first night when Kelevra had refused to stop on their third time. "Only one of us likes bleeding," he countered.

"Want to know why roses are my favorite?"

"No."

"It's the thorns. Things are dull without a little resistance. A little danger." He shifted the ice up the slope of Rin's spine slowly. "A little bloodshed. Flowers on their own are pretty, but so many things are. What use is there in being pretty but nothing else? Imagine if I consisted purely of this shell and nothing more. If my only standing was that I look good in a suit."

"You're really bragging about being psychotic?" Rin ground his teeth when the ice hovered at the base of his skull. "That's cold. Cut it out."

"Stop overthinking everything," Kelevra sighed. "I want you to feel."

"I want you to put me down."

The ice was pulled away, but before Rin could feel relieved, he felt it poking lower. Without warning, Kelevra pressed the cube against his hole and pushed it in, the tip of his finger going with it to ensure it stayed in place.

It burned at first, an uncomfortable and sudden intrusion that automatically had his body trying to push it out. His internal temperature had the ice melting right away though, water trickling past Kel's finger, dripping down Rin's taint and his balls, causing him to shiver.

Rin jerked against the cuffs holding him in place, the anti-gravity unit keeping him pinned in the exact place he was settled. Only Kelevra, who had the remote, could move the cuffs around, which he did now, activating them so he could reposition Rin with his head lower and his ass up in the air.

His legs were pulled further apart, and he felt Kelevra step between his thighs, the heat from his bare flesh instantly warming Rin wherever they touched.

The Imperial Prince was also naked.

There was clanking, and Rin easily placed that Kel had grabbed something from a glass nearby. It must have been one of the items he'd brought in when he'd entered the room. He was about to ask if there was anything else, and what exactly Kelevra intended to do here, but then he felt Kel's palms smoothing up the outside of his thighs.

The Imperial's hands reached Rin's hips and turned, traveling over the sides of his ass to spread his cheeks wide. A second later, Kelevra's tongue prodded at his entrance, the organ almost as cold as the ice. He licked and nipped around his hole, barely allowing the tip of his tongue to slip inside before pulling away.

Rin's breathing increased, and he tightened his hands into fists as he struggled to maintain some semblance of control over this situation in which he logically had none. His balls hung heavy and he felt his dick, swollen now from just that minor bit of anal play, bob beneath him. He hated to admit it, but the other guy had been right. He had spent the past week horny and desperate for some type of release from it all.

The kind he'd only been able to experience at the Imperial Prince's hands.

Maybe that's what had finally had him cracking tonight after all. Brennon had come on to him and he'd been pissed, but it might have also sparked the lust that'd been swirling in his gut. How else could he explain coming here of his own volition? Like he hadn't known this was exactly where he would end up if he did.

Well…maybe not exactly like this, but still.

Kelevra slapped him on his right ass cheek, hard enough the sound echoed in the room. "Concentrate."

"You're the one who told me not to think—" Rin's complaint ended on a long, drawn-out moan when Kel used his tongue to push another, smaller piece of ice past that tight ring of muscle. He followed it, spearing into him in slow, languid strokes that had Rin writhing within seconds.

Kelevra pulled out and dragged the flat of his tongue up over his left cheek and then bit down.

"Ow!" Rin made a sound of frustration when he was slapped yet again, this time directly over the fresh bite. He doubted it'd broken skin, but it'd stung. The irritation didn't last, however, quickly washed away by anxiousness when he felt Kel move from between his legs and travel back up his side.

"Have you figured out I'm a bit cross with you?" Kelevra asked, his voice dropping ever so slightly as he came to stand in front of Rin. He pulled his shoulders up, so Rin's body was completely horizontal once more, and then he pressed down.

Rin felt himself lower a couple of feet, a hint of musk tickling his nose a second before he felt the fat, wet head of Kel's erect cock slap lightly against his cheek.

Everything was pitch black, so he had no way of knowing what expression was written on Kelevra's face. No way to gauge how angry or not he actually was and how much was simply a fear tactic. He also felt nothing on his body aside from the metal of the cuffs, trapped in a weird state of floating. It was similar to when he dove to the bottom of a pool and allowed himself to go weightless, a tactic he'd used since young to help empty his mind. Only, there were differences as well.

Like, for one, the fact he was still every bit in control of what happened to him next.

Unlike now.

"Keeping me waiting again, Consort?" Kel tsked. "Not a wise move."

Right. He'd asked a question.

Rin gulped. "Considering you've got me strung up in some twisted version of a sex swing? Yeah. I've gathered."

He chuckled darkly. "Interesting take. Here's the thing though, only good boys get to come, and you, Flower, haven't been very good as of late, have you."

Rin was about to snap that he didn't want to come, catching himself at the last second before he could make what would most definitely be a horrible mistake.

Kelevra laughed, somehow knowing exactly what had just gone through Rin's mind. "That's better. We made a deal, you and I, and the very next day you refused to keep your end of it. As a result, my bed has been cold for six days. You owe me for every one of those lonely nights. You'll pay, won't you, Flower?"

Rin felt the press of fingers beneath his chin, his head lifted yet again, though he couldn't exactly make eye contact with the blindfold firmly in place. He wanted to argue. Lash out. Curse the guy and tell him to go fuck himself but...

"Overthinking again," Kelevra pointed out. "Why do you feel the need to analyze every single thing? Would it really kill you to just give in to the moment and allow yourself to simply *be*?"

"Honestly?" Because he had a feeling honesty was required right now. "It might."

If Rin did that, gave into his urges and his primal instincts, he'd leave himself and his brother vulnerable to attack and discovery. And if something awful happened to the two of them because of him? Because of his mistake? His inability to keep himself contained?

"If I screw up," he said, tentatively, not sure why he was being *this* honest, yet unable to stop the words from flowing, "the guilt will eat me alive."

"Sweetheart," Kelevra's fingers shifted through his hair gently, "the only thing allowed to eat you is me. How entirely ingenious of you to have ensnared the only person on this entire planet who can ensure your safety from anything and everything. I'm the Imperial Prince, the Emperor, my sister, even goes so far as to bury the bodies for me. You are mine, and I protect what's mine. If that's your biggest doubt, I'll set the record straight."

"Allowing everyone to spread rumors about how you don't want me and I'm awful in bed is protecting me, is it?" Rin drawled bitterly.

"A few nobodies talked shit behind your back," Kelevra snorted. "We both know, at most, it made you angry. It didn't hurt your feelings, don't pretend that it did. I see you. I know where to push and where to prod. That's another important aspect of being an owner, didn't you know? I have to know everything about you in order to keep you safe."

"You mean," he licked his lips, "to keep me yours?"

"Do you think there's another option?" Kel asked. "Did you spend the week trying to think up a way to escape from me? There's nowhere you can run to that I can't follow. This planet bows to me and you're no different. I do not permit insubordination. That's why you're being punished now. Why you'll take my cock between those pretty lips of yours and suck like it's your greatest duty to please me—because, Flower?" Those fingers tugged at his hair then, causing Rin to cry out. "It is."

He stubbornly clenched his jaw when he felt the bump of Kel's flushed crown against the seam of his mouth, but then those fingers twisted in his hair and pulled again, harder this time, and when he gasped the Imperial Prince didn't hesitate to slip himself inside.

Rin's lips stretched around his girth as he sucked in oxygen through his nose. His tongue shifted around, rubbing against that hard member, the taste of salty precome exploding on his taste buds, causing a fresh way of arousal to sweep through him.

Kelevra's hand settled behind his head, cupping his skull for purchase as he eased himself in inch by torturous inch. He groaned when he finally bumped against the back of Rin's throat, pausing with his cock buried deep, blocking off his airflow despite that little speech he'd just made about keeping Rin safe.

If not for the blindfold, he'd glare at the guy.

Finally, just when Rin thought for sure his lungs were about to explode, Kelevra extricated himself, stopping with the tip balanced on his full bottom lip.

"Get to work," Kelevra said after he'd given him a moment to suck in a few breaths. "Obey, Consort. Take your punishment like you should, and maybe I'll reward you after."

In the back of his mind, Rin recalled that passing comment about not allowing him to come. He really wasn't a fan of that idea. There also happened to be worse things he could do than suck a cock, and weirdly, having that solid heat in his mouth was grounding him in a way. It helped provide something tangible he could cling to amidst the otherwise weightless sensation his body was being subjected to.

Rin pressed his lips around his cockhead and sucked, hollowing his cheeks as he took him all the way in, letting him poke at the back of his throat again, his tongue swirling around all the while.

"I dreamed about you like this while you were away," Kel said breathlessly, his hips undulating. "Kept desperately trying to guess when I could get back inside of you. You were made for my cock. Made for me."

Rin bobbed his head, focused on pleasuring him as much as possible. The Imperial Prince was always more generous when he was in a good mood, and Rin had passed the stage of mild arousal, his whole being hot and burning. He still didn't fully trust that Kelevra would protect him, but he was starting to buy that maybe he did actually want to. Those rumors, while they hadn't cut him or anything, had messed with his head on some level. Rin was loathe to admit it, but he had spent a few nights tossing and turning in bed, wondering how long Kel would keep this up, and whether or not he'd eventually grow tired of waiting and forget Rin for real.

With his cock as hard as it currently was, however, it certainly didn't feel like he'd forgotten him. On the contrary, it felt exactly as he'd said.

Like he'd missed him and he'd been waiting in agony.

It happened a lot faster than it had that time in the locker room. Rin felt Kelevra tense up a second before he buried himself all the way.

"Swallow," Kelevra ordered as he came, jerking against Rin's mouth as he emptied his load down his throat.

Rin did as he was told, even going so far as to lick him clean afterward. Vaguely, he recognized that Kel's plan was working this time as well. Taking away his agency like this, ensuring he was completely at Kelevra's mercy…It was doing it for him.

He cried out when suddenly he was flipped, his body spinning until he was in a more seated position. One of those strong hands traveled up his stomach, over his abs to tweak at a nipple and Rin whined shamelessly, too caught up in the electricity shooting off to bother with pride.

There were a million and one reasons why he shouldn't give in, why he should resist and fight, but with each new touch, they fled his mind one by one until all that was left was the fire in his gut and the urgency to come.

Chapter 24:

Kelevra drank in the sight, his Consort hovering in the air, his wrists up by his head, legs angled and parted so he could get an eyeful of everything.

It hadn't taken much to get Rin hard, streams of precome dripping from his slit, rolling down his shaft. A small puddle of it had stained the bottom power panel from when he'd been sucking Kel off, and the sight of it was almost enough to make Kelevra blow a second load. He contained himself though, intending for the next round to end up deep inside Rin's plush ass.

"I'm going to fill you up so good, sweetheart," he promised, recognizing the needy way Rin was rolling his hips, the cuffs restricting his movements too much for him to get any good thrusts in, even if he'd only be humping at air. "But first..."

He'd set a metal tray close by, near enough he could reach the items laid out on its shiny surface. Most of the ice he'd brought had already metaled but that was fine, he was done with that particular type of play. The goal here wasn't to focus on any one thing anyway. He was curious about what his flower liked best, what would make him whine and howl for him.

What would most efficiently force all other thoughts from Rin's brain, until the only thing he was capable of thinking about was Kelevra and only Kelevra.

Up until a few days ago, this room had acted as a dining area that went unused. He held parties outside but only allowed guests as far as the living room when it came to the actual house itself. The table and chairs had all been removed so the device could be installed, and he'd come in here on more than one occasion to check the controls, test everything out and make sure it was in perfect working order. He hadn't wanted anything to go wrong tonight, had even stroked himself off in the shower picturing what Rin might look like when he used it on him.

His fantasies paled in comparison to the real deal, though he was used to that being the case when it came to his Consort.

Rin was hovering at an obtuse angle, his breathing labored. Everything but the cuffs had been removed, and his toned body was glistening from a fine sheen of sweat under the bright overhead orb lights Kel had kept on.

He wanted to see everything. Every twitch of muscle, every furrow of Rin's brow.

His gaze wandered over to the massive wall made entirely of mirror to his right. He wanted to see himself too.

Kelevra stood between Rin's spread thighs, holding a flickering candle over his chest. Bringing the end to the nipple he'd just pinched, Kel tipped it, watching as melted wax spilled.

Rin hissed when it pooled over his sensitive bud, throwing his head back. A vein in the side of his neck bulged, and his dick bounced, the tip just barely brushing against Kelevra's navel.

He moved in closer, pressing against Rin so he could feel his cock settle between his ass cheeks. Soon, Kel would slip inside and make a home of all that welcoming, velvety, heat.

Soon. But not yet.

"Is it better than the ice?" Kelevra asked, pouring more onto the opposite nipple, watching as Rin tensed upon contact. It should be hot, but not enough to cause any damage or leave any marks. That was for Kel to do himself.

"It's better," Rin answered, and he was a bit surprised that he had, accidentally spilling more wax over between Rin's pecs than he meant to.

"How is it better?" He was curious.

"It feels…" Rin's brow furrowed. "Tingly. I can feel the wax hardening."

"Ah, it's grounding you. Is that because you're Tiberan or because—"

"I'm in a zero gravity device and feel like I'm floating with nothing to hold onto," Rin cut him off, though it lacked any of the usual sarcastic bite his comebacks held.

Interesting. This appeared to be working far better than Kelevra had even hoped.

He set the candle aside and took in the other objects on the metal table, recalling Rin's earlier statement. "Am I to believe you're not interested in being bled?"

Rin froze, but the fear didn't last long, there and gone, Kel's eye picking up on the minor fluctuations of his body and processing just as quickly. "Some pain is fine," he began tentatively, clearly trying to decide how much he wanted to divulge, how much could be used against him later.

Which meant he was still thinking too much after all.

Kelevra would have to remedy that. He wanted him so mindless, not only would Rin be unable to guard against him, he wouldn't even think to try.

"It's not the pain that does it for me," Rin continued. "It's—"

"Lack of control." Kel nodded even though he couldn't see it with the blindfold on. A part of him had been determined to hold himself back, had spent days trying to convince himself that since he'd bought the machine outright, they'd use it again and there was no need for him to rush.

Seeing Rin's naked body like this though, knowing that he was fully at Kelevra's mercy...

Kelevra skipped over the leather whip and picked up the short knife on the table.

"That doesn't mean I'll be okay with you doing whatever the hell you like," Rin said, and it was obvious by the way he paled slightly and tipped his head in the table's direction that he'd heard the slight clatter of the handle as it'd been lifted.

Kel had intended for that to be the case, gaze dropping to between his thighs to take in his dick. For what he intended to do, he needed Rin to calm down some.

"That's exactly what it means," he corrected sternly as he walked around, stopping at his left shoulder. "That's what a lack of control is, Flower. It's when I have all of it," he brought the sharp tip of the blade to the spot just beneath Rin's nipple, "and you have none."

Rin cursed when his skin was nicked, the wound only small enough for a single drop of blood to well. "Asshole!"

"Quit acting like I cut it off," Kel drawled, then pretended to consider. "Should I?" He tilted the blade so Rin would feel it against him. "Just slice it off?"

"That's…" He shook his head ever so slightly. "This is too far."

Kelevra sent another look to Rin's dick but it was still hard as a rock. He rolled his eyes, honestly torn between being impressed with his prowess and annoyed he was being pushed into scaring the man further. He didn't like Rin afraid, it brought him too close to that head space he'd witnessed in the locker room and that wouldn't do. But he also couldn't proceed with him fully erect, not without risking injury, and he would never.

"Seriously," Rin spoke again, "Kel?"

He shushed him and just barely stopped himself from petting his hair comfortingly. "I won't mutilate you, sweetheart. It was just a joke."

"I didn't like it."

"I'm going to do a lot of things you don't like," Kelevra said. "But you're going to take it, aren't you, Consort?"

"You say that like it's my duty to let you hurt me."

"I'm not trying to hurt you," he corrected. "I'm trying to own you, and in order to do that, I first have to help you escape from whatever demons have sunk their claws into your mind. Besides, I don't think you're really in a position to talk."

"Kelevra."

"I don't mean because I have you restrained." He'd really been trying hard to curb his own urges, to avoid unleashing his true self onto Rin. Things may have even gone differently if his flower had come home even a day sooner. Alas... "I got a message while you were passed out."

"You knocked me out," Rin stated, but some of that fighting edge was missing. Even without the ability to see him, it was obvious he was tuned into Kel enough to recognize when his mood altered.

Knowing that had Kelevra preening and was almost enough to have him change his mind after all.

Almost.

"There were image attachments." He walked back over to the table and set the knife down as quietly as he could, so Rin wouldn't be able to pick up on the fact he was no longer wielding it. Cutting him hadn't done a damn thing to ebb his arousal, meaning as much as Kel enjoyed seeing blood, for his purpose that wasn't going to work. "Aren't you going to ask me what they were of?"

Rin was quiet for a while, but Kelevra allowed him his silence, staring at his dick so intensely it was a miracle his flower didn't somehow sense what he was doing. He deflated some during that pregnant pause, clearly sensing the impending danger.

Kelevra carefully reached for the bottle of lube. He'd already opened it ahead of time, so there was no sound of the cap popping open. His other hand picked up the long, thin metallic object he'd selected yesterday, and he started to apply a generous amount of lubricant as he waited.

"What…" Rin hesitated. "What were the photos?"

"Brennon was in them," he hinted, smirking when Rin's dick got softer. It was less than at half-mast now, good enough.

"Kel, I can explain—" He was startled when Kelevra grabbed his dick and squirted a massive amount of lube over the top of his cockhead. His hips jerked, but there was no shaking his hold and they both knew it.

"Stay still," Kelevra warned, "or this could injure you. I don't want that. Do you want that, Flower?"

"No." He shook his head. "Kel, really, whatever this is, don't do it. It's not what you think! I didn't—"

"Have that disgusting sheep's mouth all over yours five hours ago?" He resituated himself between Rin's legs, pulling the skin around his slit down to expose the hole on his dick more. "Don't lie. I already know it happened. You don't need to tell me. What I don't know, is whether or not you've ever played with sounding before. Have you?"

Rin frowned.

"I'll take that as a no." And if he got a little excitement over being his first? He was a Devil. He'd never claimed to be a saint. "Since you can't see, should I explain it to you, or would you rather it be a surprise?"

"No!" Rin was panicking a little now.

"I'll be descriptive then," Kelevra promised, understanding the panic was coming from the unknown factor of it all. Rin wanted to give up control, but he still had a long way to go before he could feel one hundred percent safe with him. It irked his ego, but he understood. A lifetime of bad habits and learning to guard against every single person in the universe wasn't exactly something easy to overcome.

He brought the end of the metal rod to the tip of Rin's dick, slowly easing it into his slit, just a little so Rin would know it was there.

His entire body locked up.

"Relax, sweetheart," Kelevra said. "This is perfectly safe. So long as you don't try moving around, nothing bad will happen. I'm holding a sounding rod. I picked it out specifically for you. Aren't I kind?"

"I..." He wanted to curse at him but was too afraid to risk it, it was obvious.

"I'll let you yell at me all you want tomorrow." Kelevra liked it when Rin got angry. Liked that spark and that fire and feeling like at any moment he might spontaneously combust from keeping it trapped inside. It was a little cliché, but no one dared fight with Kel, not in any real capacity. And yet Rin had hit him, kicked him, and drawn blood more times than he could count.

"I've got you nice and lubed up but this will still feel weird, breathe through it." He lowered the rod further down, taking things slow. Kelevra groaned as he watched the thin metal disappear into Rin's dick, holding him carefully as he inserted it.

Rin made a strangled sound. "Stop. Please, stop!"

"I told you to breathe through it," he reminded, but he pulled an inch of the metal out before slowly slipping it back in.

"I can't!"

"All right, sweetheart," Kelevra coaxed, shocked he could manage to formulate full sentences with how turned on he suddenly was. Watching that metal disappear into Rin's body, knowing he was taking it because Kel was making him…Thinking about how pissed off he was going to be come morning…He groaned and shook his head. Focus. "Let's do this instead. Tell me what you feel. How does it feel, Flower?"

"What the hell is that?"

"We've been through that part already. It's a sounding rod. It's a metal rod that's inserted into the urethra. This particular one has grooves. It'll stimulate nerve endings in a way you've never experienced before. Can you feel them?"

"I hate it!"

"Rin."

If possible, the use of his name had him going even more still in fear than he'd been a moment prior.

Now Kelevra was the one frowning, and he paused with the sound only halfway inside, debating whether or not he should remove the blindfold to get a better idea of what was going on in Rin's head.

Just as he was reaching to do that, his flower spoke.

"It was cold at first but now…" his voice was thready and he seemed to be feeling it out.

"It's adjusting to your body heat," Kelevra said. "That's good. What else?"

"It's…unnatural. I feel full in a way I shouldn't. I want it out."

"Does it hurt?"

"Yes." He nibbled on his lower lip. "No. It feels like I have to take a piss."

Kelevra chuckled then went back to inserting the toy. "Unfortunately, that's not one of my kinks."

"Mine either," Rin grumbled, though in his current state, it came out tight and clipped.

He slid the sound all the way in and then leaned back to get a good look at it.

Rin's dick was pointing straight up to the ceiling, flushed and shiny from the precome and the copious amounts of lube. The curved end of the sound poked out, the golden metal winking at Kelevra suggestively.

"Thoughts on getting a piercing?" he asked without really meaning to.

"Don't you dare."

"All right."

"...Really?"

"No body modifications without your consent," Kelevra reassured. "I'm a Devil but I'm not pure evil." There was a line, he'd edge as close to it as he could without pushing Rin too far, but he knew better than to cross it. He may like it when the guy was spitting mad, but he didn't want his hatred. So far, despite how often Rin tossed that particular insult around, he didn't really mean it. Not entirely.

If he did, he wouldn't have come all the way here in the middle of the night during a downpour.

Rin had known exactly what he was doing when he'd shown up at Kel's doorstep, and that in itself was sort of a form of trust.

"Please," he begged then, snapping Kelevra out of it. "Take it out."

"I told you before I'd buy your trust with my own," he reminded. "I'm still willing, are you? Tell me what happened at Friction tonight, Flower. Explain." He looped a finger under that curved end and began easing the sound in and out, fucking him with it gently as Rin struggled to obey past the foreign sensations.

"W-we were drinking," Rin's breathing increased as his body warmed up to the feeling, "Brennon was drunk. I was drunk."

"You, my pretty Consort, were completely and totally shitfaced."

"Yeah." His dick started to harden and for a moment he grew silent again, scrunching his nose as though in distaste. Like he couldn't believe his own body would betray him like that and start finding any of this pleasurable. "He kissed me, true. But I didn't want it. I didn't even see it coming."

Kelevra had, but he kept that to himself. For now. Instead, he settled the sound in once more and let it go. He slathered lube on his cock and then grabbed Rin beneath the knees so he could angle him better, staring at the metallic shine of the end of the sound all the while.

"Kelevra?" Rin shivered, but his eye picked up on the truth.

It was in anticipation, not fear.

His flower wanted this every bit as much as he did. Wanted to be owned and used.

Claimed.

"Please, Kel," Rin said. "I pushed him away. I hit him."

"He touched what was mine," the flash of anger in his tone was real, something he couldn't hold back. The photos Zane had sent had also included one of Rin busting Brennon's nose. It was the only reason Brennon wasn't dead already.

"I didn't want him to," he repeated. "I've never wanted him like that ever."

"Oh? Who do you want then, Flower? Who do you want pounding this hole of yours? Whose name are you going to scream when you're fucked past oversensitivity and forced to keep taking it despite your protests?"

"...Kel..."

"That's not an answer," he growled, lining his cock up with Rin's entrance.

"Wait."

"You've kept me waiting for an entire week," Kelevra said. "If you'd wanted me to spend time properly prepping you beforehand, you should have considered that and come home sooner."

"Kelevra—"

"You're still keeping me waiting."

"The rod. Take it out first."

He laughed, the sound twisted even to his own ears, but his cock was straining and his patience was so thin it was a wonder it hadn't snapped already. His grip under Rin's knees was tight enough that he was sure there'd be bruises in the shape of his fingers tomorrow, and something about that had a glob of precome rushing out of him, plopping to the floor between his feet loud enough even Rin had surely heard.

"This isn't a negotiation. Punishments aren't meant to be easy," Kelevra said. "You're only making things worse for yourself by refusing me further. Your continued silence isn't going to work for me."

"You!" He dropped his head back. "You. Kel. I want you. I wouldn't have come if I didn't."

Kelevra notched his cockhead into Rin's hole, moaning when that had his flower hissing from the slight burn. He didn't like hurting him, but he got off on controlling Rin every bit as much as Rin enjoyed being controlled. It stroked at something primal within him, something that seemed to come alive whenever his flower reacted to him, in any way, shape, or form.

Knowing he could get Rin to drop the mask?

Sexy as fuck.

"Tell me what you feel," Kelevra ordered, and this time Rin immediately obeyed.

"Too full," he whined as Kel sunk in halfway, taking things slow on purpose to draw it out and give him time to adjust. "My dick aches. It still feels…wrong…but also…"

"You want to come."

"Yes!"

Kelevra hummed. "That's too bad."

"…Kel."

"Keep talking, Flower."

"You're stretching me and—" He gasped when Kelevra stroked against his prostate. "Everything hurts but doesn't at the same time, okay? I can't explain it. I'm trying, but I can't."

"You're doing fine, sweetheart." As if to prove it, he picked up the pace, finally seating himself fully within that velvet heat. Kel adjust his grip and then rolled his hips, relishing the mewling sounds Rin emitted and the way his balls tightened in preparation for the orgasm he was going to be denied.

He didn't think his flower had fully caught onto that part just yet. If he had, he'd be cursing up a storm.

Kelevra started pumping into him with rough, measured strokes, sure to spear in as deep as he could go. He groaned whenever he felt those muscles clench around him, a reaction Rin gave with no extra thought to what he was doing. Whenever Kel got him like this, lust-crazed and mad, Rin dropped everything.

That damn shield he kept around him.

And the hatred, however much that actually amounted to, he held for Kelevra.

Here, like this, Rin was nothing more and nothing less than completely and unequivocally *his*.

Kelevra started pounding faster, enthralled by the sight of Rin's dick slapping against his stomach with each inward thrust. "I wish I could burrow inside of you and stay there."

"That's," he gasped, "so," again, "fucked up."

"Tell me to go deeper."

"You're already too deep." Rin shook his head.

"Do it."

"Please, Kel." His hands clenched into fists, and for a split second Kelevra saw red, thinking he was going to deny him. "Fuck me deeper."

He growled and changed his hold, slipping his hands around to the front of Rin's thighs. He readjusted the cuffs on his ankle so they lifted higher into the air, bending Rin into an acute angle that allowed Kel's cock to drive further into that heated depth.

"You're moving in tomorrow. All of your things. No more excuses." He held him tight, the machine keeping Rin relatively secure and stuck in position for him.

Rin was already wailing, tear tracks streaking past the damp blindfold, but there was nothing he could do about it. He could only hover there and take it however Kel chose to make him. Not because he was a sheep, but because Kelevra had fought him for it and overpowered him.

Kel had won, but he wouldn't be satisfied until he'd taken everything.

"Tell me, Flower!"

"I'll move in tomorrow," Rin agreed. "Kelevra, please, no more."

"Is the sound starting to hurt?"

"Everything hurts!"

Kelevra blinked, activating the functions of his eye so the computer would do a more thorough scan of Rin. "You're fine."

"I feel like I'm coming apart!"

"Good." That's exactly what he wanted. "Do that. Break for me, sweetheart. When I put you together again, it'll be as my Royal Consort. Tell me that's what you want, too."

"Stop say—"

Kelevra slammed his cock inside of his hole and ground his hips.

Rin's sentence died on a sob. "I want to be your consort!"

"Do you?" He was close, fucking into Rin like a man possessed now, only partially aware of the demands he was making.

"Yes!"

"Yes, what?"

"Kelevra," Rin didn't seem to be fairing any better, "marry me. I want to move in and I want to be your Royal consort and I want you to marry me, okay? So, please, for the love of Light, please just—"

He hadn't expected a marriage proposal.

Kelevra's orgasm was so intense he momentarily went blind, white light bursting in front of his vision as his mouth dropped in a silent scream and he pumped Rin's ass full of his come. He rocked against him as he came, wanting to milk himself of every last drop, growling thinking about it buried deep inside of his flower.

Had anything in the history of ever, ever felt this phenomenal? Every moment leading up to this one, this fuck, suddenly felt dull and drab. Colorless. The way Rin's hole spasmed around him, holding him tight, and the small whining sounds his flower emitted while he was filled to the brim…Kelevra truly wanted to know how he'd survived up until now without it.

Without Rin.

He would have stayed buried there all night if not for the obvious distress his Consort was in. With a groan, he forced himself to pull free, come splattered from Rin's ass to make a further mess of the floor. It was tempting to push it all back in, but Kelevra somehow managed to focus on the task at hand, stroking the underside of Rin's tightly drawn balls instead.

Rin hissed at the contact, and Kelevra cooed at him shifting closer so he could reach up and remove the blindfold. Then Kel waited as Rin blinked against the sudden light exposure, his eyes peeling apart, lashes sticky with tears.

As soon as Kelevra had his attention and he knew he could see clearly, he hooked a finger in the end of the sound and carefully eased it out. They both watched as the metal slid free, globs of come coming with it, pouring out of Rin's dick in rivers of opaque white.

"Bet you came at least three times," Kel surmised in awe as he watched it flow out. Considering how deeply he'd set the sound, there must have been some reverse ejaculation. He set the used toy on the metal tray and then gently lowered Rin's feet to the ground before he risked disabling the machine.

Rin cried out as gravity returned for him, his body dropping instantly.

Kelevra was ready for it and caught him, wrapping his arms beneath his legs and back. He lifted him and made a beeline for the door, ignoring how badly he just wanted to drop into bed after that mind-bending orgasm.

"What are you doing?" Rin asked, and he sounded just as exhausted as Kel felt.

"Mad, sweetheart?"

"That you robbed me of my orgasms?" He snorted, a rush of hot air gusting against the curve of Kelevra's neck. "Hell yeah."

"Didn't it still feel good at all?" Kelevra was mostly just trying to keep him distracted as he carried him down the hall to the guest bathroom. He'd prefer they use theirs, but he wasn't confident he'd be able to make it all the way up the stairs with Rin in his arms, and after everything he'd done to him already, the last thing he was going to do was make the guy walk on his own anywhere, least of all up an entire flight of steps.

"It felt…odd. Not the same."

"Would you try it again?"

Rin considered so long Kelevra almost checked to see if he'd actually fallen asleep. "Maybe."

In Rin's language, that meant yes but he was coming to his senses enough to know better than to admit it.

Kelevra reached the bathroom and carried him over to the toilet, setting him down but keeping his arms around him so Rin wouldn't fall. "This may be embarrassing, but you really need to—"

Rin didn't even let him finish, grabbing hold of his dick to aim and then pee without so much as batting an eye. When he felt Kel staring at him, he turned and shrugged. "What? You literally just shoved a piece of metal up it, I think we're past the point of bodily fluids being degrading in any sense of the word."

Kelevra couldn't help it. It felt a little like another win and before he knew it, he was capturing Rin's mouth in a bruising kiss.

"Not while I'm taking a piss!" Rin tried to pull away but Kel wouldn't let him, grabbing him by the chin to force him back.

His tongue stroked in deep, and he sucked on Rin's bottom lip, hard enough it might even leave a mark. When his cock twitched, he winced and pulled away, knowing Rin wouldn't be up for another round for some time.

"Close the lid and sit down," he instructed, helping Rin to do just that. "I'm going to turn on the sauna."

The master bathroom and the largest one on the main level were the only two that included that feature, and he was grateful for that fact as he made his way across the pale white tile to the control panel set at the side of the glass door that led inside. He took a moment to consider which temperature would be most beneficial for Rin, then settled on one and turned back, pausing for a moment.

Rin had propped himself back against the toilet and was watching him from beneath hooded eyes. There was a flash of heat when their gazes met, but he was clearly too tired to put up a fight, so he remained there, silently waiting for Kelevra to break the tension.

"How do you feel?" Kel asked.

"Used."

"So," he grinned, "good then."

"Don't sound so smug. As soon as I have autonomy I'll retaliate for sure."

"Then I'll just pin you down and fuck you all over again," Kelevra promised.

Rin winced and then closed his eyes.

Sighing, he walked over and took him by the arms, easing him back onto his feet. "Can you walk?"

"To there?" Rin motioned the ten or so steps it would take to reach the sauna door. "Of course—" he went to move his foot forward and stumbled, clinging to Kelevra when he held him upright, "—not."

Kel chuckled and tossed his arm over his shoulders, hoisting him up so they could slowly make their way there together. Then he helped him across the small distance within the sauna itself and lowered Rin down onto one of the wooden benches. As soon as he had the door shut, sealing them both inside, he returned, settling down next to him.

Rin shifted down the bench, and Kelevra narrowed his eyes, about to scold him for putting distance between them.

He was shocked into silence instead when Rin ended up lying down, resting his head comfortably in Kel's lap.

His flower gave a contented sigh, his eyes closed, and he noticeably relaxed against him.

Testing, Kelevra brought his hand up, slipping the tips of his fingers through the damp sandy-gold strands of Rin's hair. When he got no reaction, he grew bolder, brushing them off Rin's forehead, then twirled them between his forefinger and thumb.

All the while, Rin simply lay there and let him do as he pleased.

Something inside of Kelevra's chest cracked. He'd thought forcing his control over Rin in the bedroom had been the peak of pleasure, but he'd been wrong.

It was this.

It was being allowed to play with Rin's hair and have him willingly lay in his lap. It was listening to his even breathing, and watching his full mouth curve upward at the ends ever so slightly, as though even Rin didn't realize he was smiling.

It was being let in on something Kelevra was fairly certain no one else had ever been let in on—not even his brother, considering he doubted Sila had ever seen Rin's post-coital glow this soon after he had done the deed.

He wanted to ask Rin if he felt it too, this amazing thing taking place between them, but fear of ruining the moment kept him silent.

Instead, he continued to run his fingers through Rin's hair and fed the newly awakened devil within himself.

The one who seemed to be purring in contentment.

Chapter 25:

He carried Rin up to their room and almost laughed. If anyone had told him even a month ago that this would one day be something he'd do willingly, he wouldn't have believed them. Kelevra didn't do things out of the goodness of his heart, but where his flower was concerned it actually wasn't…entirely unpleasant.

He liked the way the other man tucked into him, his warm breath tickling against the side of Kel's neck. And he liked feeling him, all that power and muscle, and yet here he was, being lugged around by Kelevra with ease. It was a turn-on, but more than that, it made him feel special in a way he'd never experienced in the past. He'd been brought up to take care of his things, sure, but this was different.

Kelevra didn't just want to be gifted Rin. He wanted Rin to choose him. This past week's minor manipulation had been a step in the right direction, but it wasn't enough. He'd seen the way Rabbit Trace looked at Baikal Void and he wanted that for himself. He wanted that with his Consort.

As far as he understood it, there was only one major obstacle between them, and that was Rin's father. But Crate Varun held no power here on Vitality, and with

Kelevra having already bankrolled the twins, he could no longer threaten financial control over them either.

"Tell me something," Rin's voice, soft and quiet cut through the comfortable silence as Kel made it to the top landing.

"Such as?"

"Something personal."

Kel considered as he brought them down the hall toward the bedroom. He wasn't the type to withhold anything, always speaking his mind the second a thought popped into it. Because of that, there'd never really been an instance where someone had asked an open-ended question like that.

"I'm trying to get to know you," Rin added when he'd been silent for too long. "You aren't making this any easier for me."

"Should we play a game?" he suggested, only for his flower to tense up. "Not that kind, I promise. A question for a question." Kelevra had Rin's file, and he had a basic understanding of who he was, but it couldn't hurt to learn more.

Actually, now that it'd been brought to his attention, he realized he wanted to know everything. Everything there was to know about his flower.

"Do you like hurting people?" Rin asked. "My brother…"

It was no great reveal that Sila Varun enjoyed causing pain. Kelevra had pegged that their very first meeting.

"No," he replied honestly. "It doesn't make me feel anything one way or the other when I hurt someone. I like the sight of blood, but it can be my own, it doesn't have to come from another person. I have hurt people before, I've killed. But that's usually when they've pushed me past my breaking point and I've lost control."

"You don't regret afterward," Rin surmised.

"I don't feel things like that, Flower."

"Sometimes," he licked his lips and glanced up at Kel just as he entered the room, "I wish I didn't either."

"What is it exactly?"

"You mean what's wrong with me?"

Kelevra scowled and settled Rin down on his side of the bed, even going so far as to pull the covers over his half-naked form. He'd given him boxer briefs to change into, thinking that would help settle any lingering nerves and it'd seemed to do the trick.

While his flower had clearly enjoyed their experimenting tonight, it also would have taken a lot out of him. Kel didn't want him to feel anxious or scared, not of him, and not now, so soon after that comfortable moment in the sauna. For the first time, he truly felt like he was making progress.

Like maybe there was a chance he could convince Rin to accept and want him with the same level of ferocity that he wanted his flower back.

"There's nothing wrong with you," he chided. "You find regulating your emotions difficult, that's all."

"On my home world, that's practically unheard of. I would have been treated terribly if anyone had found out."

"Is that why you learned to hide it?" Kelevra asked. Eventually, he was going to coax Rin's true nature out in all its brazen glory, but he didn't think now was the correct time to say as much, so he kept it to himself. "And Sila?"

"My brother has the opposite problem. I feel too much, he feels too little. Tibera is a planet that values emotions. Our people tend to feel them at a heightened level, which allows them to process them at a rapid rate. It's why we come off as calm and collected more often than not."

"Ah, so they fake it too."

Rin frowned. "I...No. It's more like they just don't show it. If you asked what they were feeling, they would tell you without hesitation. But it's harder to know. It isn't as simple as it is here or on most other planets, where all you have to do is look closely enough to be able to tell when someone is feeling a certain way. Emotions, especially complex ones, are harder to gauge on Tiberan's. That's why we're taught grounding. It's a way to focus and calm the mind so we're able to move through one feeling to the next without overstimulation setting in."

"You've mentioned grounding before," Kelevra draped an arm over Rin's hips, keeping close as he sat on the edge of the bed. "I've helped you with that? That's what happens when we have sex?"

"Sometimes," Rin admitted.

"Was it always like that?" Kelevra didn't want to, but he forced himself to ask. "Whenever you fucked someone?"

Rin considered. "If you're asking if you're the first person I was able to give up control to in the bedroom, then the answer is no. But, if you're wondering if you're the only person who's made me completely and totally let go? Then yes. I've never felt this way with anyone else before, Kel."

"What way?"

"I don't know," Rin said. "I can't put it into words."

"Try."

He gave him a look. "This was supposed to be a question for a question, and yet I'm the only one doing the talking. It's your turn."

"It wasn't really a question, but you wanted me to tell you something personal." Kelevra trailed his gaze across Rin's face. His cheeks were still rosy from the sauna, his damp hair finger-combed to the side. "I love seeing you here, in my bed. It makes me pleased. I feel like I've managed to acquire something difficult to obtain, but I also struggle to put it into words that make sense. Nothing feels suitable. All I know is, this is your place, Flower. This is where you belong."

"For how long?"

Kel paused.

"You're impulsive and rash," Rin sighed. "You can just as quickly decide to call the betrothal off and toss me aside as you did setting the whole thing up. You expect me to trust you because what? I know you like fucking me?" He chuckled humorlessly. "You aren't the first, but I don't see any of those people beating down the doors."

His initial response was to get angry and jealous—that was the second time Rin was reminding him he'd had past lovers and he hated it. But he hadn't come this far and waited an entire week for this just to blow it by giving in to rage.

"I've never worked for anything a day in my life," Kelevra admitted. "I saw you and decided I wanted you all in the same moment, and you're right. I could just as quickly change my mind. But I won't. I know I won't, Flower, because I know myself. The major difference between us isn't that you feel more and I feel less, it's that you choose to hide while I choose to stand tall. I am who I am and I enjoy being that person. This allows me to understand myself better."

Kel didn't love his sisters. Up until this point, he hadn't grasped the full concept. He knew it meant he would do nice things for them and want to keep them happy, and for the most part, he did. He understood they cared for him and protected him, and that was nice, sure, but if it came down to his life or theirs, there was no question he would save himself.

He'd never tell them that, of course, but he'd always known that was the truth. He cared for them to the extent of his capabilities, but that wasn't love.

But this…

He leaned forward and gently stroked the pad of his thumb against the arch of one golden brow, tracing the fine hairs on Rin's face. "If anyone hurt you, I'd castrate them. If you and I were trapped in a burning building, I would push you out to safety first."

"You sound…surprised," his flower noticed.

Kelevra laughed. "I am."

Rin searched his gaze. "How can you know that won't change tomorrow? You could wake up and—"

"It was a trap, Consort. That's all it was. The rumors that were spread around were just that. They weren't real. I only allowed them to happen to get under your skin, but I never intended for it to bother you this much. Only enough to get you to come to me."

"And if I do something in the future you don't like?" Rin forced Kel's hand away but kept his fingers on his wrist when he placed it on his chest. "If I don't always agree with you? If I want to make my own choices?"

"Outside of the bedroom or in?" Kelevra asked.

"Either."

"I have no problems with you being who you are. If we don't agree, we can discuss it. The only thing that I'm not willing to bend on is our betrothal. You will marry me. You've agreed to be mine, and even if *you* wake up one day and realize that's not what you want, I won't let you go. I'll never let you go."

Rin nibbled his bottom lip, and Kelevra anticipated an argument right then and there, a little caught off guard when instead he said, "Do you swear?" He licked his lips nervously. "No matter what?"

Kel tilted his head. It was obvious he was keeping something from him, but he'd known that from the start. It helped that whatever the big secret was, it was clear Rin kept it from everyone and not just Kelevra. It wasn't personal, and for that reason alone, he'd been able to look the other way.

For now.

It was tempting to force the issue, while he had his flower so forthcoming, but he didn't want to risk tarnishing the moment. Things were going surprisingly well between them after what had taken place downstairs. He'd expected outrage after he'd let Rin down from the device, but instead, he was being soft and open with him.

It was…endearing.

It also made him greedy.

If Kelevra could fill the rest of his life with moments just like this one, he would do anything in exchange.

"Yes, sweetheart," he promised. "You came to me tonight—you came for me," he grinned when that made Rin huff, "I comprehend it must have been a difficult choice for you to make. In exchange, I'll cherish you and keep you always. Forever."

"Cherish me, huh?" The tops of his ears started to darken.

"Is that too much?" Kel laughed. "Am I embarrassing you *now*? You weren't even embarrassed downstairs when—"

"I don't open up to people," Rin cut him off. "Ever. It isn't safe, and I'm not good at trusting. Some of it is just instinct, some of it is habit. I might be...closed off most of the time. I need to know you understand that, that you're sure you won't get bored of me if I'm not always—"

"Tricking your Active into thinking you're not as good a shot as you actually are?" Kelevra teased. "I have this, remember?" He tapped his eye. "I can always see you, the real you."

Rin reached up and ran a finger down the length of the old scar. "How did you get this?"

"You don't know?"

"Is it a well-known story on Vitality?"

Kel was pretty certain it was. "You know my father?"

"The guy who literally just passed the crown onto your sister a couple of weeks ago?" he drawled. "No. Never heard of him."

"Cute." It actually kind of was. Very few people dared get sarcastic with Kelevra, but even from the beginning, Rin hadn't been afraid to. "When I was six, he did something that pissed a few people off—don't ask me what, I don't remember. I was too young to care about politics at the time, and I haven't been told since, most likely because I've never shown an interest in knowing. The why doesn't matter, in any case, only what came next."

He didn't think of that time often, and for a moment he paused to collect his thoughts, trying to decide what details were and weren't important. "I was kidnapped on the way to school by my driver. He was trusted by the family, on payroll even before I was born, and had once driven Lyra to school like he was responsible for doing with me and my little brother."

"Wait," Rin stopped him, "your what?"

Kelevra shrugged. "He's not spoken about."

Aside from the anniversary of his death, his name was practically taboo. It should probably bother him, but he could hardly even recall the kid's face now after so much time had passed.

"He's…dead?" Rin asked.

He nodded.

"I didn't know," Rin murmured.

"Don't, Flower." He gave him a soft smile. "We weren't like you and your brother. It's no great loss."

"That's only because you were never given the chance for it to become that."

Kel pursed his lips, finding he didn't like thinking of it that way, and continued with his story to avoid delving any deeper into the why of that. "Our driver took us to an office building a city over, a seedier location we were unfamiliar with. My brother, Kaiden, cried as soon as he realized we weren't going to make it to school. He had a presentation in his art class he'd been excited about. Something about the planetary alignment in the galaxy if I remember correctly."

If he really tried, he could almost picture the Styrofoam diorama Kaiden had spent the weekend putting together with their sisters.

"What about you?" Rin's voice broke through his thoughts. "How did you feel?"

"Afraid," he replied. "It was the last time I ever felt anything like that. Real fear. We were there for a few days before we were discovered. Baikal's father had helped track us down and the Royal cavalry swooped in like damn idiots, blasters blazing. Our kidnappers—Mr. Juy, our driver, and two other guys I don't know the names of—barely spoke to us the days we were there, so we had no clue what was going on or why we were being held at all."

"Money?" Rin guessed.

"Enough for them to hop off the planet and disappear," he confirmed. "My father refused to give it and they'd been in negotiations all that while. Earlier that morning, they'd threatened to cut my brother's fingers off on camera as an incentive for him to hurry up and concede, but I stepped forward instead." He'd wanted to protect Kaiden…Like a fool.

"You loved him," Rin sounded awed by that realization.

"I suppose." He shrugged. "Maybe. Maybe I was simply trying to play the hero. A dumb six-year-old kid, looking out for his little brother like he'd always been instructed to do. Anyway, I was known for my looks even back then. Not in a creepy way, but in a doting way. Everyone constantly talked about how I would grow up to outshine both my sisters and my father in the looks department. That was why they did it. They made sure I knew before it happened. Mr. Juy, the guy I'd grown up with, the guy I'd trusted, whipped out a blade and slashed me across the face faster than I could realize what was coming. The eye was gone before I even knew there was pain."

And there'd been a lot of it. He'd screamed in agony and dropped to the concrete ground, clutching at his face, rolling around as the pain tore through him.

"My father's men arrived a couple of hours later, storming the place. They killed his two accomplices, but Mr. Juy had been with us at the time and heard them coming. He slit Kaiden's throat right in front of me before he tried to kill himself. He cut, but he must have been too big of a coward to take his own life. It wasn't nearly deep enough. He was captured and made to wish it had been. I was rushed to the hospital, and the last thing I saw in that room was my brother's corpse lying in a pool of his own blood on the ground. There was a funeral, but I hardly recall."

"Kelevra..." Rin shook his head, clearly at a loss for words. A rarity for him.

"Don't feel bad," he told him. "They had the replacement eye created and implanted within six months, and I actually prefer it. I came back different, and they realized it early on, but the damage was already done and they all knew it. Who I am today is the version of myself I am most familiar with. I like who I am. I accept who I am. That day may have been the catalyst, but who cares? It happened, it's over, and there's no changing the past, even if I wanted to."

Why should he though? Kel was awesome. He had everything the Emperor did just without any of the responsibility. His remaining siblings doted on him, and his father had always treated him like a prized possession after he'd been the only son to return.

He bent over as if to divulge some great secret, wanting to lighten the mood even though he'd been the one to darken it. "I used to watch cartoons with the Insight Eye during family dinner and no one knew."

"That's way too normal of you," Rin chuckled, and it was obvious by his expression that he knew exactly what Kel was doing, but he didn't call him on it, allowing things to settle seamlessly. "Especially since I'm fairly certain they would have just let you watch them if you'd asked."

"Probably. They let me get away with anything, still do. Back then, it also helped that I was never intended for the throne. Knowing they wouldn't have to entrust the planet to me allowed them to turn the other cheek, so to speak."

"They know about…?" Rin circled a finger at him.

"Yes. My sister has cleaned many a blood stain out of my proverbial carpets. As long as I don't do anything that could cause a political scandal or start a war with another planet, they don't care what I do or who I hurt. Does that make you upset?"

Rin thought it over. "It should, but no."

"Even though you're capable of feeling empathy?"

"I can feel it," he confirmed. "But I have my own problems to deal with. I'm a bit selfish too, so it seems. We're a pair."

"And your brother?" Kelevra hedged.

A shutter came down over Rin's eyes. "My brother is the most important person to me in the entire universe and that isn't going to change."

"Relax, Consort, that wasn't a threat." Although, he was now determined to make it his mission to out-seat Sila as Rin's number one priority. "I've had one taken. I wouldn't take yours."

"I know we're weird. That we're…too codependent by normal standards. But it is what it is. We're a package deal, Kelevra."

"I have no interest in fucking your brother." Kel got a bad taste in his mouth just thinking about it. Ironic, considering how similar they were in appearance. But Sila was nothing like Rin, and how people struggled to tell them apart was beyond him.

"If you ever did, I would drown you both," Rin replied. "I only mean, where he goes, I go, and vice versa. If he's harmed, I'm harmed. We've only ever had each other. Call us unhealthily codependent, it's true, but it is what it is and I wouldn't change it any more than you'd change yourself. I won't change it. You want anything else from me, I'll do my best to give it. But I won't do that. I won't lose my brother, and I won't stand around and watch anything bad happen to him either."

"I have no intention of harming him," Kelevra reassured. "But I do want you to start adjusting your mindset. Include me, sweetheart. In your plans, in your hopes. I'm part of your future. You have me now, and I'm not going anywhere either."

He could tell it was going to take more time for Rin to fully believe him and open up all the way, but this was progress.

And Kelevra Diar, the man known for his impulsive nature, was discovering that maybe he wasn't entirely as impatient as once believed. For Rin? He could wait.

Chapter 26:

Rin slept most of the next day. He'd rouse every couple of hours and sometimes Kelevra would be there to whisper nonsense at him and muss up his hair, but other times he'd be alone. Kel never tried to get him out of bed, and he didn't try to wake him with sex the way he had the last time Rin had spent the night.

When he finally forced his eyes open and felt rested enough, the clock on his emblem-slate said it was nearing two in the afternoon. He rubbed at his face as he sat up, glancing around the room to find he was alone. Half of him expected his body to ache when he climbed out of bed, but it was the opposite. He felt...Pretty good.

Actually, he couldn't recall the last time he'd felt this relaxed. Even the anger he'd been anticipating was minimal, enough for him to feel properly affronted for everything that had been done to him against his will, but nowhere near catastrophic levels.

Neither of them would ever speak of it, but unlike his brother, Rin had struggled more and more with maintaining his own sense of self over the past few years. That was a large part of the reason his brother had pushed for this plan in the first place, bringing them far enough from their father and the people they'd grown up around so they could be free to develop separately from one another.

They'd managed to go an entire year without switching places, and while his brother had flourished, Rin had still struggled. It'd been better, but he'd been reserved, more interested in learning this new planet and how to best control himself in this environment. Basically, he'd kept up with the act despite not having to.

He'd thought he could use this year to make progress in the personal growth department, then this situation with Kelevra had happened and…

Rin walked into the bathroom and rested his palms against the edge of the sink, staring at his reflection in the large mirror. His hair was a mess, his cheeks still red, and there were love bites on the side of his neck and peppered all over his chest. He pressed at one, the spot tender to the touch, but the pain only helped clear his mind even more.

He looked used.

And happy.

His brother had never come out of the bedroom covered like this. Looking like this. It wasn't their only difference, logically he knew that, but right now seeing himself helped drive that home for Rin.

All he'd ever wanted was to be free. Free from his father and those damn expectations, and free from himself and the impossible ones he set. He didn't want to hide who he was anymore. Maybe…maybe his brother was right. Maybe this was a good thing and he'd just been too stubborn and angry to see it.

What if marrying Kelevra Diar was exactly what Rin needed? He felt more real standing here—more himself—than he ever had before.

They'd never swapped bed partners, but his brother and he had always informed the other who they'd slept with to avoid any misunderstandings or confusion. If they traded places but seemed like they'd forgotten a wild night with someone, it'd hurt feelings and turn into a topic of discussion. Their whole goal had been to stay out of the limelight, so that wouldn't have worked. His brother was also an extremely possessive person. Even if it was a one-night stand, he refused to share the same body with him. Considering their tastes in both people and sexual proclivities had always been vastly different, Rin had never shown an interest in one of his brother's playmates anyway.

But even after the fact, if they switched places the next day, whoever they'd slept with the night before was always none the wiser. Whether they'd been inside of him or had his brother inside of them, they could never tell the difference. To the entire universe, Rin and Sila were one and the same if they chose to play the parts.

Except with Kelevra.

The Imperial Prince would always be able to tell them apart, be it in or out of the bedroom. Over time, Rin had found himself dropping more and more of the guise when he was with him as well, unafraid of poking and insulting him. Sometimes Kel still scared him sure—only a fool wouldn't acknowledge the insanely uneven power dynamics between them—yet on some level, he knew Kelevra didn't plan on hurting him.

That shouldn't be enough to assuage his fears, not while also knowing how mercurial Kel could be but...Of the two of them, Rin had come to the realization he was actually the worse in that regard.

Even last night, blindfolded, Rin had been able to sense Kelevra holding back. For him.

He'd turned what could have been a traumatizing experience into something Rin would never forget—in a good way. Hell, if Kel walked in right now and asked if he wanted to go another round with the G-Tester 450, Rin was ninety percent certain he'd agree.

The Imperial Prince had been right. After a week of panicking, worrying, and being pissed off about the whispers and the rumors, having his control completely stripped away like that had been amazing. It didn't even matter to him that Kelevra was the cause of all of those negative emotions. Honestly, knowing someone like the Imperial Prince, a man who'd never had to plan for anything in his life because it was always handed to him, had taken the time to scheme just for a chance of catching Rin...

He chuckled at himself and hung his head. Oh yeah, he was definitely the worst of them all.

If only Kel had been trying to morph him into something he wasn't, trying to mold him into another person, like he'd mentioned last night briefly. Then at least Rin would have something to cling to, something definitive he could point at and say "this is why he isn't good for me". Kelevra had commented that he would put Rin back together as his Royal Consort.

But he'd asked if Rin was comfortable with bloodletting.

And he'd paused in the middle of sex to check to make sure he was all right.

As often as Kelevra pushed his boundaries and forced him to take things he didn't want, there was an equal amount of instances where he was considerate. The real kicker was Rin wasn't entirely certain Kel was even aware of those moments himself.

The Imperial Prince wasn't turning Rin into a different person, he was helping him flourish as his true self, the self he'd buried deep in order to be able to switch with his brother at the flip of a coin. Part of Rin understood the danger in that, in growing attached when he should still be thinking of ways of escape, but the rest of him...

Rin wanted Kelevra. He wanted to keep him.

Wanted to be kept *by* him.

He was allowed to want one thing for himself, wasn't he? Hadn't that been the whole purpose of coming to Vitality in the first place?

Hadn't that been what his brother had tried to tell him all this time?

He couldn't make any rash decisions, but the possibility of giving in, really and truly, was there, and Rin allowed it to linger as he washed his face and used the spare toothbrush Kel had set aside for him.

After he used the bathroom and returned, he noticed the set of clothes that had been laid out. The sophomore uniform was new, not the set he'd been wearing when he'd arrived, and he vaguely remembered it'd been pouring when he'd gotten out of the taxi and stumbled into the receiving area of the hotel. He'd been soaked clean through, but the doorman had merely directed him toward the private elevator in the back that brought him up to the penthouse rooftop entrance.

The whole planet really did recognize him as their Imperial Prince's fiancé.

He took a moment, standing there in the middle of a bedroom large enough to fit his dorm back at the Academy plus two others, and considered his brother's words more carefully.

If he didn't see a downside to this, why was Rin struggling so much? It wasn't the fact he would have to marry someone he didn't love—he'd never considered marriage or love as possibilities, so it wasn't like he was missing out on anything by suddenly gaining at least one of those things.

How did he feel about Kelevra Diar?

A couple of weeks ago, he would have stated without a shadow of a doubt that he hated the guy with a burning passion but now…The passion part was still applicable, but hatred…Did he hate him? Kel infuriated him and sometimes he frightened him.

But there was all that other stuff to take into account as well. Like how he could wipe Rin's mind blank with a few simple touches and dirty phrases. How he pushed him, too far, and yet, never so far Rin felt there was no coming back from it. Even last night, he'd cut him after Rin had explained he wasn't interested in pain, but logically he understood that'd been because Kelevra had been trying to get him to lose his erection in preparation for the sound.

And the sound.

Rin shivered just thinking about it. He still wasn't sure if he'd enjoyed the toy, but the feeling had been intense. He'd felt things he'd never felt before, the fullness and the brush of the bumps on the rod sending him reeling. It'd all been too much and not enough all at the same time, and while he still fully believed Kelevra owed him a few fully felt orgasms, he wasn't against trying it out again sometime. Seeing Kel pull the rod out of his dick at the end there…At the first stirrings of lust, he cut those thoughts short.

He got dressed quickly, stomach grumbling. When was the last time he ate? Honestly, it was a miracle he hadn't passed out in the middle of their session again, though afterward, in the sauna he'd slipped in and out. The feel of Kelevra's hands in his hair had been too relaxing to resist, his body spent and overused. It'd been almost sweet between them.

The only one who'd ever taken care of Rin before was his brother, and his idea of being caring was…questionable at best. Not murdering the Imperial Prince for slipping Rin a drug? That was his brother's idea of kindness.

Using Kelevra for sex was one thing. If he started savoring those softer moments there was a very real chance Rin would become complacent. Could he afford that? Could he risk letting down his guard around someone in as high of a position as the Imperial Prince? Truthfully, even though he'd told himself he'd only been agreeing that night to buy himself time to come up with an escape plan, he'd spent practically no effort on actually trying to think of one.

If he didn't want out, what *did* he want?

His brother apparently wanted to stay on planet, despite their agreement to the contrary. He'd made it sound like it was a minor suggestion, but Rin knew him better than that. He wouldn't have brought it up if he hadn't already decided, and if he was staying, didn't that mean Rin had no choice but to as well? They would never separate, and while there were some battles of will he could beat his brother at, it was clear this wasn't going to be one of them.

So, if he was staying on Vitality anyway, and the two of them still wanted to slip out of their father's grasp…

He was going to have to make good on the deal and marry Kelevra.

Didn't that mean he was also going to have to come clean?

Rin cursed and pinned the Academy crest to the side of his belt before yanking open the door. He stepped out into the hallway, taking in the long white-tiled path that led to several other rooms he'd yet to explore. While it was tempting to snoop, knowing that he was going to be moving in later today anyway had him opting not to bother, instead turning to take the flight of stairs down to the main level where he assumed Kelevra would be waiting for him.

He was still so caught up in his head and torn over how to approach this whole betrothal thing, that he almost didn't register the sound of multiple voices until it was too late. Coming to a standstill just outside of the entrance to the living room, he tipped his head and listened.

There was a female voice, speaking low enough he couldn't make out what she was saying. And then there was Kel, slightly louder, but clearly trying not to be too much so.

"He's sleeping," the Imperial Prince said casually, and there was clinking glass and the shifting of ice. "Why don't you come back another time?"

Realizing he couldn't stand there all day, Rin inhaled, squared his shoulders, and walked in, pausing as soon as his eyes locked onto the female company.

He'd seen Lyra Diar on TV once or twice but never in person before. She was lithe, with hair the same shade and curly texture as her brother's. She wore it loose, the thick dark brown strands hanging past her elbows. Her eyes were also that same hazel shade, and they were sharp, and intelligent, as they turned to Rin and took him in.

She was seated on the couch that faced the windows looking out over the patio, in a tight cherry red dress, with a chunky black belt. A choker of diamonds sparkled around her neck, and her nails had been painted an inky shade, a single gemstone winking in the center of each. She was both as regal and as flashy as Kelevra, and Rin would have made a joke about seeing where Kel got his style from if not for the fact she was the Heir Imperial Princess.

"Well, well," Lyra drawled, giving Rin a drawn-out perusal, "you never did like things easy, did you, little brother?"

Kelevra was standing over by the mini bar, leaning back against it. One hand was stuffed into his left front pocket, the other was holding a glass decanter. He'd also chosen red for the day, the black pinstripes on his pants matching his sister's outfit. There was no undershirt again, just the tight, fitted corset vest in the same colors, the black lines of the boning making his torso appear to go on for an eternity and—

"Maybe not so difficult after all," Lyra chuckled knowingly, and Rin realized with minor embarrassment that he'd been caught staring at Kel. "From first glance, he doesn't look like the type that'd put up with your bullshit."

"He isn't," Kelevra snorted, sipping lightly from his drink before setting it down. He held out his hand to Rin, palm up, the challenging glint in his eyes impossible to miss as he silently commanded him to go over there.

Rin only hesitated for a moment. If he made a scene in front of his sister, there was no doubt Kel would find a way to make last night's punishment seem like a cakewalk, and so soon after...Not worth it. He crossed the room, but instead of taking the offered hand, he bypassed it, taking up the discarded glass and downing the remaining contents in one swallow.

Lyra laughed and clapped.

Kelevra's eyes narrowed ever so slightly, but he gave no other reaction than that.

To soothe some of the sting, Rin kept close, turning, allowing his shoulder to brush against Kel's chest in the process, one of his legs slipping between the Imperial Prince's. He bowed to Lyra, making sure to hold the position for a few heartbeats as would be tradition before rising and offering a friendly smile.

"Hello," he willed the tension from his shoulders. "It's nice to meet you, Heir Imperial Princess Lyra."

"You are far too polite for my brother." She stood and offered her hand. "I've been dying to meet you, Rin. There's so much to go over, but as per usual, Kelevra was being selfish and refusing to share even a moment of your attention."

"Go over?" They shook and he kept himself composed when she moved back to the couch, but he did not like the sound of that.

"For the wedding," she replied, as if it was the most obvious thing in the world what she was talking about. "How involved in the planning process did you want to be? Kelevra is particular, but I'm already familiar with his tastes. Is there anything specific you don't like or are hoping to avoid? Colors that don't go with your complexion?"

Rin blinked at her and then slowly turned to send Kel a silent look asking for assistance.

Kelevra rested a hand on Rin's hip and smirked. "He doesn't really care about fashion, Lyra. Isn't that a shame?"

"I can't believe you've fallen for someone like that," she said, though it was obvious she was only teasing.

Whatever Rin had been expecting from his family—because he'd known that eventually he was going to have to meet them—it hadn't been this. Lyra was sweet, and while there was an air of regality to her presence, there was none of the overbearing edge that accompanied Kel wherever he went.

Then again, Rin should understand better than most how easy it was to fake a whole personality. Judging anyone from the first encounter was foolish and typically something he knew better than to do.

"I was thinking," Lyra told them, "what about a winter wedding? That gives us a couple of months to plan."

"He's a sophomore, sister," Kelevra drawled. "I intend for us to have a long engagement."

Rin couldn't help but wonder if that was so Kel would have an easy out when he eventually grew bored of him. Was that it? Was he planning ahead so he could toss him aside the first—

Kelevra shifted closer, leaning in to rest his chin on Rin's shoulder, his other arm wrapping around his waist. "Breathe, Consort. It's only so you can focus on your studies and graduate without having to worry about all the official responsibilities that come with being married to me."

How the hell had he known what Rin was thinking? He'd been certain to maintain his friendly expression and not let his spine stiffen even the slightest.

"How unexpected." Lyra was watching their exchange. "I wasn't aware you were capable of being supportive of someone else, little brother. I certainly never took you for the type to be tamed by your consort."

"Am I?" Kel seemed pleased by that notion. "You'll have to take responsibility for me now, Flower."

"Nicknames, too?" She beamed. "I can't wait to tell Tessa. She won't believe me. When will you be bringing him by the hospital?"

"The what?" Rin held his smile, but he was positive Kelevra felt the way his heart skipped a beat from how closely pressed against him he still was.

"Are you afraid of doctors?" Kelevra asked curiously.

"Don't worry," Lyra waved at him. "It's nothing serious. The Royal doctor will just run a few standard tests, that's all. There aren't any health requirements to marry into the family, it's just precautionary to ensure there's an updated medical file on hand in case there are any emergencies in the future."

"Can't you just ask for my file from the Academy?" Rin had undergone extensive testing when they'd been accepted. "I haven't had any major medical complications in the past year and a half since I've been on planet."

"We'd prefer our doctor to do it," Lyra insisted. "He'll be thorough, and he's worked with the family since our parents were our age." She stood up. "How about we go now? Get it over with? I can call him and ask him to prepare a room."

He needed an excuse to say no, something legitimate. If he got caught refusing an Imperial—and the Heir Imperial no less—things could go from pleasant to really bad for him really fast. But this wasn't something he'd considered, and with Kelevra still clinging to him, his damn scent invading Rin's senses, it was proving difficult to think up anything.

Fuck.

"Maybe some other time." That so wasn't going to cut it. Rin could tell them he had classwork. Telling them he was busy would have been a lot more believable if he hadn't spent practically half the day in bed though.

Plus, Kelevra would be able to tell he was lying.

Double fuck.

He just needed to stall. Stall for now and—His emblem-slate dinged and he checked it, almost heaving a sigh of relief when he saw it was from his Active.

"It's the mock case," he said, feigning apology. "There's been a new mock murder. I have to check the scene for clues." When he went to step away from Kel, there was a moment where the Imperial Prince resisted and held him back, but eventually, he released him and straightened.

"Rin takes the Academy very seriously," Kelevra informed his sister. "He's determined to solve this before any of his classmates."

"That's very dedicated." Lyra smiled and nodded. "Of course, school should come first, and since the wedding is being put off now, there's plenty of time to get you to the doctor's beforehand."

"We'll schedule something," Rin promised, walking by her toward the door. He was lying through his teeth, and it was somewhat cowardly, but he avoided looking Kel's way as he did it.

"Are you leaving too?" she asked her brother.

"As his mentor, I should." Kelevra kissed her cheek and then grabbed Rin's hand, linking their fingers as he tugged him into the hall and out the side entrance. He didn't speak again until they were both tucked into the elevator on their way down. "I was able to discover that this killer of yours knows each of the victims."

Rin blinked at him.

"It's looking like they met over the summer, just before the new semester started," Kel added as they came to a stop. He walked them out, ignoring when Rin tried to remove his hand from his.

Somehow, even though he hadn't called ahead, his cherry red hovercar was waiting for them out front.

Giving up, Rin allowed himself to be stuffed into the passenger seat, waiting until the Imperial Prince was inside and had started the vehicle before saying, "So a couple of months ago? How'd you figure?"

He cut him a smirk. "Research."

"You?"

"It seemed like winning this thing was important, considering how much time you spent working it and ignoring me."

"Don't mope," Rin chided, not liking the way something warm and sticky seemed to unfurl in his chest at the sight. "It's unbecoming of a man of your stature."

Kelevra laughed as he drove them toward the crime scene. "That's got to be one of the funniest things you've said to me so far. Are you forgetting about how last night I trussed you up and made you cry? Decorum's not really my thing."

"Says the guy in the fancy outfit," Rin mumbled, but he wasn't in the mood to argue, still too mentally and emotionally drained.

Not to mention internally freaking out over how to deal with this new development regarding the Royal doctor.

Chapter 27:

"Who the fuck thought it was a good idea to set this up in the middle of the forest?" Rin shoved a low-hanging branch out of the way, following the small blinking light on his emblem-slate that told them where the mock crime scene was located. They'd parked on the edge of the Academy campus and had been walking for a good ten minutes already.

It was a lot different from all the other scenes which had been in relatively public, though more off the beaten path, areas.

"Someone's cranky," Kelevra noted, following a few feet behind, clearly not in any sort of rush to get there.

Rin flipped him the middle finger over his shoulder and kept going. So what if he was in a bad mood? Who was there to blame for that?

"How are you feeling, Flower?"

"Fine."

"You're tense."

"Can we just get there and get this over with without the running commentary?"

"I liked you better last night," Kelevra said. "You were softer. It was almost endearing."

He bit the inside of his cheek to keep from snapping something stupid back, sighing in relief when the scene entered his line of sight up ahead.

Like with the others, there was a female student propped on the ground, fake blood painted across her neck. It'd been made to look like she'd been out here camping, a small tent meant for a single person built a few feet away, still intact. There was a fire panel, turned off, but clearly ready for use, and a zipped backpack dropped on the ground. There were no obvious signs of blood splatter like at the one in the alley, or even any signs there'd been a struggle. If not for the body, Rin would assume they had the wrong place.

"Hey, Nila," Rin absently greeted the student who was resting against the thick trunk of a tree. "No, no, don't get up, it's fine."

She hadn't so much as twitched.

"Flower."

"I don't see anything suspicious, do you?" He turned a circle, growing more confused by the second. Why was he out here wasting his time when he should be finding his brother and planning their next move? Who cared about this dumb assignment? If he did end up marrying Kelevra, it wasn't like he was going to be able to pick his future position in the I.P.F anyway.

They hadn't spoken about it, but he doubted he'd be allowed to become an agent. That would entail traveling to other planets in the galaxy. With how possessive the Imperial Prince was, there was no way he'd approve that.

"Flower."

"Seriously, do—"

"Rin," Kelevra stated tightly, finally drawing his attention. His face was pinched. "She's dead."

"Of course she is, that's the whole point."

"No," he shook his head. "She's really dead."

"Don't be ridiculous." Rin stepped closer to Nila. "Hey, I know you're not supposed to break character but can you—" He froze. The slice across her throat was clearly stage makeup, but… He dropped down next to her and leaned in. The makeup covered bruising. Real bruising. "Someone strangled her."

What the actual hell?!

Rin flicked open his emblem-slate, about to report it when a knowing feeling tingled up his spine, giving him pause.

He was in the process of turning toward the right when the sound of a blaster going off ripped through the air, causing his hackles to rise. The bullet zipped past him, a wave of warm air gusting across his face a second before he heard Kel grunt.

Spinning around, he gasped when he saw the Imperial Prince clutching at the side of his right arm.

"Were you just shot?!" He rushed over to see, but whoever was shooting fired again. This time the bullet slammed into a tree nearby, sending bits of bark splintering. "Get down!" Rin shoved Kelevra to his knees and positioned himself in front of him, desperately searching the trees for any sign of the attacker.

A flash of black clothing some distance away stood out, the figure twisting on its heels to retreat.

Before Rin knew what he was doing, he was giving chase, racing through the forest. Anger swept through him, spurring him on, and he ran harder, ignoring the burning in his thighs. Kel had been shot in the arm and from what he could tell when he'd glanced at it, there'd been minimal bleeding, so he'd be okay. Still, someone had been ballsy enough to shoot Rin's Imperial, and all he could picture was stealing that blaster off of them and firing off a dozen rounds straight into their chest.

He was covering good ground but the culprit was still a ways away, and it was looking unlikely that he'd be able to confront him. If he could at least get a look at the person's face he might be able to ID them later though.

Rin leaped over fallen logs with ease and pushed himself, cursing when the culprit suddenly seemed to be getting further and further away. He kept going even after he finally lost sight of them, only stopping when common sense kicked it, reminding him that walking into an ambush would be idiotic.

He twirled around, swearing again when there was nothing but trees and foliage as far as he could see. How—

Someone grabbed him from behind, tossing him against a tree trunk and pinning him by the throat. Rin lifted his arm to swing at his attacker, pausing the second he processed it wasn't whoever had been shooting.

Kelevra's grip tightened around his neck, the darkness swirling in his gaze promising pain. Blood trickled down the side of his arm, but the bullet had merely grazed him.

"Is this why you were strange earlier?" Kel asked him, voice thick with malice, enough to have Rin's spine snapping straight and his shoulders drawing back.

The fear didn't last though, the mixture of confusion and anger still burning acidically in his gut too great.

"What are you talking about?" He grabbed at Kelevra's wrist but the guy wouldn't budge. "You're hurting me."

"You lied to Lyra at the penthouse," he stated. "Didn't want to go to the hospital. You were severely against it, in fact. Was it because of this? Did you have this planned ahead of time? Is that why you came back last night, so you could lure me out here and—"

He thought Rin was behind the assassination attempt just now?

After everything they'd been through last night.

He—

Rin swung after all, his knuckles digging into the rise of Kelevra's left cheek. Since he hadn't even thought to hold back, it had to have hurt, and as soon as the hold around his throat loosened he jabbed Kel in the right side, sending the guy to his knees.

"I cannot fucking believe you!" he snarled, unable to keep in the vitriol. His skin was buzzing, the anger blindsiding him. "I can't believe myself! After last night I really thought—" He stopped and cursed. "Fuck this. And fuck you, Imperial Prick! Good Light, I must have lost my mind to even consider—"

Kelevra rammed into him, taking him down onto his back in the dirt.

"Get the hell off of me!" Rin struggled, but his wrists were captured and pinned along with his legs as Kel flattened overtop him, the weight enough to constrict his lungs and make it difficult to breathe.

"Look me in the eye and tell me you had nothing to do with this," Kelevra commanded, though it was clear he was less certain than he'd been a moment ago.

Not that that made it any better.

Rin was tempted to refuse, but why not let the asshole see just how big of a dick he actually was? He stilled beneath him and growled vehemently, staring directly into the computer eye. "I wish I had something to do with this because right now shooting you sounds like the most fun I'd have all fucking month. But no, Kelevra, I didn't hire a terrible assassin—because let's be real, he missed so he sucks at his job—to kill you in the middle of the forest like some loser."

Kel searched his gaze. "It's the only way you'd escape me. If you had me killed—"

"Good Light!" He dropped his head back, fuming.

"I gave you enough reason last night."

"And you what?" Rin made sure it was clear in his tone that he thought he was a moron. "Thought that between then and now, I somehow orchestrated this whole thing? When, exactly, would I have had the opportunity to do so? Hmm? When we were in the sauna? Or perhaps when I was sleeping like the dead after the absolute wringer you put my body through?"

"You were so soft last night," Kelevra murmured, almost as though he was trying to work things out on his own despite Rin's continued protests. "Then with my sister...You were trying to come up with an excuse to avoid the doctor, I know you were."

"So use that freaky intrusive eye now and get it through your thick skull that I'm not lying." Rin was pretty sure beneath the fury there was a tiny prickle of hurt. He was insulted that he'd been accused, but the fact he was also allowing Kel's opinion to affect him like that...Damn it. "Maybe this is a good thing. It's exactly the reminder I needed."

Yes, that was it. He needed to calm down before he did something stupid like attack the Imperial Prince again, so he latched onto that notion. If anything, this should prove to him he'd let things get too far. Maybe he hadn't come up with a way out yet. There was still time. And all that other nonsense he'd been thinking earlier? A moment of weakness.

He should have known better than to believe even for a second someone like Kel could ever truly see him.

"What do you mean?" Kelevra asked.

"There's only ever been one person in the entire universe I could count on," Rin stated. "And it isn't you."

Kel flinched.

"Get off of me. Report me to the damn authorities if you want. At least they'll use their brains and run an investigation." They'd see right away that Rin had nothing to do with any of this. "A girl is dead and here we are, wasting time. Move."

Kelevra didn't. He stared down at him for a long time and then finally said, "I'm sorry I suspected you."

"Screw your apologizes and screw you." He fumbled to get free again and after a brief hesitation, Kel climbed off of him. Rin sprang to his feet and headed back the way they'd come, needing to release all the pent-up emotion within him before they called the authorities or ran into anyone else. The alert for the crime scene should have gone out to the other groups, and there was a chance they were already there and had discovered Nila's body.

"Consort," Kelevra caught up with him and reached out, touching his wrist, but Rin slapped him away.

"Don't touch me!" he snarled. "And don't call me that! You can't even trust me not to try and murder you. Clearly this isn't going to work." Rin kept walking, crunching debris loudly beneath his boots, barely realizing what he was saying, the words just spewing out of him as the anger kept control. "When we get back, the first thing you're going to do is contact your sister and call this farce of an engagement off. I wouldn't marry you if you were the last—"

Kelevra pulled him back by the collar of his shirt, pinning him to yet another tree. Unlike Rin, he'd lost some of the anger, at least the part that had made him scary, but there was heat swirling in his hazel eyes still, and a determination there that made his stance on the matter of their betrothal clear before he even spoke.

"Repeat that," Kel asserted. "I dare you."

Rin held his gaze unblinkingly. "I would rather die than tie the rest of my life to an egomaniac like you."

"You aren't allowed to die," Kelevra stated. "You're going to stay mine until you're old and gray. When are you going to accept that?"

He snorted. "Is that a joke? You're the one who just accused me of hiring a hitman. So much for buying my trust. Your payment was counterfeit, I don't want it anymore, and I don't want you."

His chest felt tight and it was getting harder to keep his breathing even remotely even. Rin's vision was a bit fuzzy too, the anger causing dark spots to float in front of his eyes. If he wasn't careful, he may even end up blacking out, and then he'd really do something he'd regret. It didn't happen often, but that was because he'd learned how to sense when he was about to snap and get away from whatever was pushing him to that point.

Fight or flight.

With the Imperial Prince pinning him like this flight wasn't an option.

That left only one thing.

"That's what this is?" Kelevra frowned, then tipped his head to the side, something seemingly clicking for him. "I hurt your feelings."

"Quit throwing your weight around and—"

Kel captured his chin, holding firm when Rin tried to shake his head loose. "It's different from that look in the shower, but it's also similar. You're finding it difficult to regulate your emotions."

"The only thing difficult here," he said, "is you."

"You need grounding."

"Are you even listening?" Rin glared. "What I need is for you to stop this. Stop all of this—What are you doing?"

Kelevra moved one hand to Rin's hair, the other sliding down to unbuckle the belt and slip the zipper of his fly down. He palmed at his dick through the thin material of the boxer briefs, keeping his touches light but persistent, somehow managing to call it to action despite the fury eating Rin from the inside out.

"Stop it." Rin ground his teeth as the first sparks of arousal shot through him.

"I'm sorry I hurt your feelings, sweetheart," Kel said softly. "I suffer from a temper, same as you, and that can get the best of me. That's all that was. It was nothing personal."

"It felt personal," Rin argued.

"Like this?" He let go only long enough to slip his hand beneath the waistband of the briefs to pull Rin's now fully erect cock out.

He hissed at the touch, cool air blowing against his bare skin. Rin tried to remember they were standing in the middle of a damn forest, potentially with a murderer, but when Kelevra rolled the pad of his thumb around his cockhead he couldn't help but moan.

"Forgive me?" Kelevra asked.

"Eat me, asshole."

"All right." His hand moved to the center of Rin's chest to keep him pinned as he dropped to his knees in front of Rin and licked his lips.

"Wait, that's not what I meant. I didn't mean *that*!" Rin reached for Kelevra's head, but Kel was quicker, dropping down over him and swallowing him to the root in one go. He sputtered and slammed his head back against the tree, a groan breaking free at the first feel of tongue tracing the vein at the underside of his cock.

Kel bobbed and sucked a couple of times before pulling off of him with a pop, a string of spit connecting his bottom lip and the flushed head as he grinned up at Rin. "Any better yet?"

He clenched his jaw, trying to find the words, but apparently that wasn't the reaction the Imperial Prince wanted.

"Guess not. Let's keep going until you feel better, shall we?"

"No—" Honestly, Rin wasn't even sure why he was complaining anymore, not when the feel of Kelevra sucking him down felt so electrifying. That jittery feeling he'd had since the blaster shot had first fired was finally dimming too, lust slowly but surely washing his anger away until it was nothing more than a dull throb in the back of his mind.

Kel brought him all the way back until he bumped against his throat and then hummed.

Rin cried out and grasped a handful of his curly hair, holding on as if for dear life as he was worked into a frenzy. They could be caught at any moment, or shot at, or any number of other equally terrible things, and yet Rin's dick didn't seem to care. Not even a little. His hips started jutting forward, chasing after that wet heat whenever Kelevra pulled away, his balls already starting to draw up.

Then Kelevra wiggled a hand behind him, just barely breaching Rin's tight hole, and that was enough.

Rin came so suddenly he was honestly shocked into silence, mouth hanging open as his lower half jerked into Kel's mouth. The Imperial Prince continued to suck and lick him through it, that one finger teasing him but never fully entering.

He slumped forward when it finally ended, short of breath. Stars winked in and out of his vision, and if they'd been anywhere else, he would have given in and slunk to the floor.

Kelevra straightened him up, rising to his feet in the process. Tucking Rin away, he took his time redoing his pants, as though to give them both a moment to settle. When there was nothing else left for him to do, he met Rin's gaze, taking in his expression carefully.

"You're centered now," he noted.

Rin didn't bother denying that fact. He could think clearly again and his skin no longer felt like it was about to tear from his body. As far as grounding tools went, the Imperial's mouth had arguably been one of the best he'd ever had, but while it made him feel better, it didn't solve anything in the long run.

"We can't just be this," Rin covered his eyes with his forearm and heaved, trying to control his breathing. If they were going to spend a lifetime together, they couldn't just be about sex. Helping him come down was one thing, but if Kelevra always tried to subdue him this way, eventually Rin would come to resent him for it. Yes, he enjoyed having his control taken away in the bedroom, but he needed to still be his own person at the end of it. "I need more."

"Okay, sweetheart," Kel said, no hesitation.

"I'm serious."

"Okay."

"Kelevra." Rin dropped his arm and sucked in a breath when Kel immediately sealed their mouths together.

The kiss was hot, the flavor of musk and salt still on his tongue, as the Imperial speared it past his lips. It was both frantic and languid at the same time, a rotation of both, almost as though Kelevra couldn't decide how he wanted to do it.

By the time he pulled away, they were both breathless all over again.

He brushed his fingers lightly through Rin's hair and smiled at him. "Okay, sweetheart. I hear you. So," he licked his chin, "forgive me now?"

Rin scoffed and shoved him away, straightening from the tree. "Come on. We've got to call this in."

Kel grinned and fell into step at his side. "That means yes."

"Whatever."

It didn't mean no…
Damn it. What the hell was he going to do now?

Chapter 28:

"She was definitely dead." Rin rubbed at his temples, staring down at the empty space in front of the tree. There was an impression in the dirt, the only indicator that Nila had ever been there. "Bodies don't just get up and walk away."

"Someone moved her," Kelevra agreed.

"You don't sound nearly concerned enough about this."

"Whoever you chased either had help," he said while typing on his multi-slate, "or he doubled back while we were—"

"Fighting." Rin crossed his arms, eyes narrowing when the corner of Kel's mouth tipped up.

"Yeah. While we were *fighting*." He finished with the device. "We can go, unless you want to continue looking for clues. Madden and the others will be here shortly though. They can take over."

"Did you not call the police?"

Kelevra shook his head. "There was an attempt on my life. I wouldn't trust Vitality police. Would you? If so, we'll have to remedy that. Remind me to read you into all the seedy business half the higher-ups are into.

It'll change your mind. My Retinue will handle it. It's what they're for."

"Does this…happen often?" Rin wasn't a fan of how casually he was handling all of this. "You were livid a half hour ago, but now you're…calm? Someone tried to kill you."

"I'm the Imperial Prince, Flower. It's bound to happen now and again. For the record, no, this is probably only the second or third time in my life. Don't worry. Madden won't be alone, my sister will send a senior officer on her staff to help assist. Whoever took a shot at us won't get away."

Rin contacted Calder, a thought crossing his mind. They'd chased after the killer, had a huge blowout—both figuratively and literally—in the woods, and returned and yet…no one else was here. Where was the rest of his class?

"What's up?" Calder's voice came through the speaker on the side of the device since Rin hadn't bothered with the earpiece.

"Hey, where are you?"

"Dorm, why?"

Rin frowned. "Didn't you receive the alert about the new crime scene?"

"What? No." The sound of rustling sheets and papers came and then, "Hey, Brenn. Did you get any messages about another crime scene?"

"Let me double-check," Brennon answered.

Rin spared a glance in Kel's direction. The Imperial Prince was staring at him, but it was impossible to tell what he was thinking. He'd seemed pretty upset last night about the kiss…

"No," Brennon finally said. "Why?"

"Neither of us knows anything about that," Calder told Rin. "What's going on?"

"I'll fill you in later. Thanks." Ending the call, he rested his hands on his hips as he thought through what they knew. "If it was just sent to me, that means we were exclusively targeted."

"I was," Kelevra reminded. "They didn't shoot at you."

That was true. Rin had been standing closer to the shooter, so it was safe to assume if the plan had simply been to kill anyone who arrived, they would have aimed for him instead. This was a direct attack against Kel.

"They had to have known we'd come together because we're partners." That didn't help narrow down the list of suspects, or even help to formulate one. Rin felt a prickle of frustration and breathed through it. He needed to maintain a clear head. "The number shows up as belonging to the Academy. There was no reason for me not to trust it."

Now that he'd calmed some, he could sort of see why Kelevra's initial reaction had been so suspect him. It wasn't like the two of them had partaken in many civil conversations either.

"Since we're already out, let's go get lunch," Kelevra suggested then, clearly not understanding the reason when Rin frowned at that.

"What about Nila?"

"What about her?" Kel slipped his hands into his front pockets.

"…Aren't we going to report her at least? She's dead. Her family and friends should be made aware."

"I suppose."

Rin stared at him quietly for a moment. He recognized that empty expression on Kel's face. His brother wore it whenever he thought no one was looking. "You're not remorseful."

He quirked a brow. "You know I don't feel things like that."

"Then what about your apology before? If you can't feel—"

Kelevra's scowl stopped him short. "Don't compare yourself to a nobody. A girl I've never met before was murdered. Yes, yes, very sad. Maybe the killer had a good reason? Maybe he didn't. Either way, she's already dead, Flower. Getting upset about it won't change anything."

"What if she died because of us?" Rin asked. "To lure us out here?"

"You're smarter than that. That's guilt and empathy talking. If you think about it, logically there was no reason for this person to kill anyone. We were coming anyway since we thought it was organized by the Academy. If anything, it makes more sense that she'd done something specific to piss this person off, and they seized the opportunity and called us out here as well. If you're going to end up with multiple bodies, might as well do it all in one bang. Makes the cleanup a lot easier."

Rin blinked. "That's...dark."

Kelevra cocked his head. "I'm having a hard time telling if you're actually upset or simply believe you should be. Which is it?"

He turned back to the spot where Nila's body had been before they'd gone after the killer. They were assuming the person shooting at them was the same person who murdered her, seemed too coincidental to be otherwise, but he supposed there was no real way for them to know.

Rin didn't enjoy learning about someone's death, and he wouldn't go so far as to say he was like Kel or his brother, completely and totally unaffected by it but...Nila had been a nice girl. He'd hardly known her, but they'd been introduced at the start of the semester and she'd been funny. As far as surface level went, she hadn't deserved to die.

All that being said...

"I can feel things like compassion," he explained. "I feel bad when I've done something wrong, or when my actions have harmed another person. Thinking about how her friends and family will feel when they find out is upsetting."

"But?"

"I won't lose any sleep over it." That had nothing to do with Rin's inability to regulate his emotions. It was just who he was. Years of living with his brother, protecting him, covering for him, understanding him, had helped make him this way, sure. But Rin didn't really mind. Maybe that made him a selfish person. Maybe it made him a bad one.

Maybe he didn't really care all that much one way or the other.

"You know I've killed before," Kelevra said, and even though it wasn't a question, Rin answered.

"I sort of figured, yeah." He'd been meaning to ask about what Brennon had told him. Might as well now. "The girl who fell from the roof at the penthouse. Was that you?"

He snorted. "No. She got drunk and climbed up there like a fool. I wasn't even outside at the time, so I had no idea. Apparently she turned too quickly and ended up slipping. There's security footage that caught the whole thing and I allowed them to open an investigation to give her family closure."

Not because he would have cared, but because it made things easier for him. Rin somehow gathered that on his own.

"I'm a Devil for a reason, Flower."

"You're also an Imperial Prince," Rin pointed out. "Shouldn't you be looking for someone who can help make you a better person or some shit like that? That isn't me."

Kelevra laughed. "Did I break you last night after all? Was it too much? Did you," he waved a hand next to his head, "snap? You keep saying funny things today. No one can make anyone into a different person. That type of change has to come from within, and me? I like who I am just fine. I don't have any interest in changing. So that I can, what? Waste time crying when a stranger gets a boo-boo?" He sneered. "Pass. Things with you are different. I may not be able to *feel* remorse, but I don't feel good about making you feel awful. Hurting you, really hurting you, was never my intention. That? I'm willing to work on that."

"You are?"

"I'm a good communicator, Flower. You'll always know exactly what I want exactly when I want it. I'm not shy. I'll tell you. I'll tell you everything you want to know."

"Let me guess," Rin drawled. "When I want to know it?"

"You're catching on. An over thinker like you needs someone who can properly communicate. Who can say this is how things are and this is how they'll be, so don't fret. I'll work on my anger and make sure it's not wrongfully directed at you next time. I've asked for everything, and so far all you've asked of me is trust, and you were right before. I didn't give it to you. I thought I did, but clearly I hadn't. I can fix that. I've got you. I've got us."

"Us?" Rin had only ever been a part of one *us* before. He'd never considered being a part of another one. That type of thing required a certain level of devotion that he wasn't sure he could muster for anyone other than his brother, and even then, he and his brother were practically the same. All his life, loving his brother meant loving himself.

What would loving Kelevra Diar entail? Because you couldn't be a part of something as serious as an *us* without love eventually becoming a leading factor.

"The Imperial Prince and his Royal Consort," Kel said. "We're a unit. Where I go, you go, and vice versa. Why do you look so conflicted? I've been transparent from the start. I told you before, I'm not Baikal. If I see something I want, I don't waste time pining away or plotting. I simply take. I took you. You belong to me. But, Flower? I'm not opposed to belonging to you in return."

"You thought I tried to kill you," he reminded.

"I was angry," he shrugged. "But I would have gotten over it."

Rin gave him a droll stare.

"What? Do you think I would have gotten rid of you? I would have retaliated, but not like that. I don't break my own things. I can afford not to give a shit about some random girl getting strangled to death, same way I can afford not to off my future Royal Consort for trying to have me killed once."

He snorted without meaning to. "That's ridiculous logic."

Kelevra grinned. "It's fine. Now that I've come to my senses, it's obvious it wasn't you. This wasn't your style. If you did ever try to kill me, it'd be a spur-of-the-moment thing, in a fit of rage. And you'd most likely—"

"Drown you," Rin stated.

"Yes." He laughed. "That. One day, you're going to have to tell me what your obsession with that is."

One day he most likely would.
But that wouldn't be today.

Chapter 29:

The next few days were strangely...simple. They kept low because of the shooter, waiting for the Retinue to come up with some lead as to who the culprit could have been. So far, there'd been nothing, but Kelevra didn't seem all that concerned. Most likely because it'd given him good reason to ask Rin to spend more time with him at the penthouse.

There was only so much they could miss at the Academy before their grades started to be affected, so they'd returned to their regular schedules. It meant the two of them rarely saw each other during the day, but space was healthy in any relationship.

At least, that's what Rin kept telling himself.

It was insane, but after the incident in the forest, he and Kel had seemingly grown closer. He was getting used to the guy's arrogant jokes and being constantly surrounded by the delicate smell of roses and spice. The sex was still electric, but in a shocking turn of events, the Imperial Prince had actually taken Rin's words to heart. They spent just as much time talking over meals and having regular conversations as they did in the bedroom.

It was...nice.

And terrifying.

Rin had never had anything to lose other than his brother, and this growing attachment to Kelevra made him uncomfortable in a way that was difficult to describe. He hadn't tried, not to himself or anyone else, but eventually, it was going to catch up to him and he'd be forced to acknowledge it. That's always how things worked.

Even his father would eventually find a way to force them to accept his calls and speak with him again. Honestly, it was a miracle that Crate Varun hadn't already. His messages continued to come in, but both Rin and his brother had agreed they would no longer accept them.

For some, the concept of cutting off and losing a parent, especially the only one they'd ever known, would be scary. For Rin, it was as though a giant weight had been lifted from his shoulders, and even though he knew logically Kel had done this to further bind them together, he couldn't help but be a little bit grateful.

It was the Imperial Prince's financial backing that allowed them to so boldly cut Crate off, after all. Something else another person might experience guilt over that he didn't. For Rin, in a life that had always been about transactions, this was merely a deal that benefited them both. Kelevra wanted him, so he paid their tuition fees to ensure he'd stay. Rin wanted to stay, so he gave himself over to Kel.

When it was laid out like that, it was all pretty clear-cut. Plain and simple.

Which was why, despite Kelevra's continued insistence that he wouldn't grow bored and kick him out, Rin couldn't help but feel uneasy. That feeling only seemed to get larger and larger with each passing day.

They teased each other still, but they hadn't had another argument since the forest. Kelevra had tied him up and blindfolded him once or twice, but it'd never been against Rin's will. He'd always one hundred percent been onboard with any sexual deviance Kel wanted to experience. And afterward...

Before this, Rin would have said in no uncertain words he was not into cuddling, but...He'd lost track of the number of times he'd woken resting in Kelevra's lap, the Imperial Prince's fingers running through his hair. Or in bed, curled up against him, listening to the pitter-patter of Kel's heart beating in his chest. Those moments always felt warm and safe, as though they were in a bubble of sorts, out of touch with the rest of the universe.

There was no cure for Rin's mood disorder, only ways to cope, and that was another thing that had gotten easier for him. Using Kelevra's body as a grounding tool worked exceptionally well. That, paired with the fact he was physically exhausted each and every time after helped to keep his emotions in check more often than not.

Things felt really...good.

Which made Rin really anxious. Things hadn't exactly started out amicable between the two of them, and from afar, he understood this didn't look so great. "A spoiled prince sets his sights on a love interest and is gifted them by their sister" was not exactly the way most fairytales began. But Rin wasn't looking for a Prince Charming, and he personally didn't care how they'd started.

His emotions might be more stable, but his mind was anything but, and he was constantly lost in thought, only partially paying attention to the world around him. It shouldn't have been surprising when his friends were able to corner him in the stairwell on the way from the library five days after the incident in the forest.

"Dude, where have you been?" Calder clapped him on the back, appearing seemingly out of nowhere.

"Were you sick?" Daylen asked, giving him a once over, frowning when he couldn't find anything. "You look fine."

"Just busy," Rin said. His smile wasn't as fake as it usually was. He'd maybe even actually missed hanging out with them a bit. Go figure. "I'll be coming back to class regularly starting today."

"What about the dorm?" Calder glanced between him and Daylen.

"Don't ask him that," Daylen tugged Calder in and cinched his arm around his neck playfully. "I'm enjoying having a single room!"

"I won't be coming back," Rin laughed at their antics.

"You've moved in with him?" Brennon, who was standing behind the others and had kept a couple of feet away broke his silence. When Rin met his gaze, he dropped his.

Calder snorted. "You two idiots. Just talk it out."

"Yeah," Daylen gave Rin an almost pleading look. "That night was wild and we were all wasted. That's all it was."

"He regrets it," Calder tacked on.

"I do," Brennon immediately agreed.

Rin stared for a moment and then sighed. "Yeah, okay. Let's talk."

"Perfect." Calder bumped by Rin and grabbed onto Daylen's arm to drag him down the next flight of steps. "We'll be in the cafeteria! Join us after!"

Brennon waited until they were truly alone and then came closer, running a hand through the hairs on the back of his skull sheepishly. They were standing on the landing between the first and second flights, in front of a large bay window, sunlight highlighting the pink on his cheeks. "Hey, look, I know I should have messaged you sooner but…I was too embarrassed. I am so sorry. I should never have kissed you."

"We'd both had a lot to drink." It also wasn't lost on Rin how big of a hypocrite he'd be if he couldn't find it in himself to forgive his friend for one stolen kiss when he was actively falling for Kelevra. Who'd done way worse, and all while sober.

"I don't want things to be awkward," Brennon said. "If you've been skipping training because of me, I promise it'll never happen again."

"That wasn't why," Rin told him. "I had something else going on." They'd kept the shooting a secret since Kel hadn't wanted it to make headlines in the news. "But, Brenn," this was uncomfortable, but it had to be mentioned, "I am with Kelevra. I have a fiancé. It may be supper sudden, but it is what it is. I'm sorry, but you and me? That's never going to turn into anything other than friendship."

"I know." He glanced away, then forced himself to look back. "I know. It was stupid. I just, was drunk, and I thought...It doesn't matter. You've made yourself clear and I respect your decision. I just want us to go back to the way things were. Is that possible?"

"Is what possible?" Kel's voice cut through the conversation and Rin turned to find him and Madden making their way up from the first level. He was sucking on a lollipop, but he pulled it out and offered it to Rin as soon as he was close enough.

Rin made a face, but the Imperial Prince laughed and leaned in.

"We're being watched, Consort."

Wherever he went, Kelevra drew attention, and sure enough, cadets had stopped on the upper level to stare down at the two of them.

He rolled his eyes and opened his mouth, allowing Kel to slip the candy onto his tongue. It was sour.

He liked it.

"Shouldn't you thank me?" Kelevra smirked and then turned, offering his cheek next.

"Good Light." Rin took out the candy and quickly pressed his lips to Kel's warm skin. Popping the lollipop back into his mouth just so he'd have a reason not to kiss him anywhere else. The warning look he sent the

Imperial Prince's way hopefully helped to bolster his stance on PDA.

Some of the onlookers giggled and it took everything in him not to elbow Kelevra in the side as hard as he could.

"Where are you off to?" Kel asked.

"Target practice." Rin risked a glance in Brennon's direction. His friend seemed rightfully nervous but hadn't yet excused himself. He wasn't sure if that was brave or idiotic.

"I'll join you," Kelevra said.

"Been a while since we wasted a free period remaining on campus," Madden chimed in, bounding up the stairs. He looped an arm around Brennon's neck, tugging him in close and ignoring his small protests then looked to Kel. "Let's go."

"Wait, I'm not—" Brennon shut his mouth when he received a sharp glare from Madden.

Rin frowned. "Kelevra."

"Relax," he shrugged as he turned them and headed back down the way he'd come, "you two usually go to target practice together."

That was true. Since last year he and Brennon were the most interested in spending time in the shooting range, working on their aim. Daylen and Calder were less invested, claiming they had until senior year to get good at shooting. Neither knew what position they wanted to take either, which made their slacking off not seem as big of a deal. They may end up just doing desk work for the rest of their lives for all they knew.

Rin thought that was a foolish take, personally, but he wasn't in charge of his friends' choices, and he and Brennon had been fine going on their own. Still, this obviously hadn't been the plan, and he was worried things were heading in a dangerous direction.

The building housing several separate shooting ranges was next door, so it didn't take them long to reach it. Then they were escorted up to the top level usually reserved for the seniors. The cadet manning the front desk merely bowed at Kelevra as they passed and that was all, ignoring the colors both Rin and Brennon wore that signaled they were sophomores.

The upper level was similar to the lower, except with smaller sections to make private sessions easier. The main area was a long and wide space with sleek flooring and high ceilings. The section to the right held a variety of blasters, some more advanced than others, many Rin hadn't yet gotten the chance to try himself. Each weapon was secured behind a plastic casing, accessed by scanning their emblem-slate to the panel at the side of each.

To the left, the space had been set with holographic targets and a computer system that would keep score and monitor statistics. The area to the far end was open, with a long table separating the target space.

Kelevra and Madden left them in the center of the room to go and retrieve standard-issue blasters, coming back in a few moments with one in each hand. They handed them off, and then motioned over to the open space, taking positions at the table so they were all together.

"These are real," Brennon noted, eyeing the weapon in his hand. The gun was only slightly heavier than the fakes they'd been training with.

"Of course they are," Madden said, pressing on the computer connected to the table to get the targets ready. Across from them, four lit up and a jingle played overhead. "They've been altered so there's no kill setting, however, only stun and injure."

"Meaning you shouldn't aim it at anyone in jest," Kelevra added, checking his as he spoke. "You could end up seriously injuring someone." He glanced over at Brennon. "One wrong move, and there goes a person's eye."

Brennon bristled.

Without warning, Madden adjusted his stance and aimed at the target before him, letting off a flurry of shots in rapid succession. The target lit up in neon red wherever it was hit, the spots remaining there so they could still see them after the fact. As soon as he'd emptied the chamber, the bells above chimed again signaling he was out, and then a scoreboard set in the wall directly over the target started processing numbers.

Madden cursed and Kelevra chuckled when the numbers settled.

"You're slow today," Kel pointed out. "I bet you my flower is better."

"Don't bring me into this," Rin hissed. Considering he was going to be stuck with Madden forever—if this betrothal really went through—the last thing he needed was to rub the guy the wrong way. They didn't need to be friends, especially since he wasn't even sure he wanted to be friends with anyone Kelevra knew, but it'd be best if they could avoid stepping on each other's toes.

Everyone knew Royal Madden Odell came from a high-standing family and therefore had a lot to prove. He also had a lot of pride and was competitive, though the rumor was he at least wasn't petty and didn't bother holding grudges. Mostly because he tended to get even as soon as possible, instead of letting things linger. He and Kelevra were a lot alike in that regard.

They both had an act first think later approach to life, something they could afford considering their backgrounds. Imperials and Royals all over the universe got away with things regular people couldn't due to their station, connections, and wealth.

Rin supposed marrying into the Imperial family of Vitality would come with certain perks, and though a better person probably would find that distasteful, he couldn't bring himself to. On his home world, his family was also prestigious and wealthy, though he'd rarely if ever been able to benefit from that in the same ways. His father wouldn't have let them, since he'd been so strict about their purpose from the start.

The twins had been born to continue the Varun line, nothing more, nothing less. It was cold even by Tiberan standards, honestly, but Rin had long since made peace with the fact he would never know parental love or caring.

"Your Consort placed third," Madden scoffed, crossing his arms and propping a hip against the edge of the counter. "Doubtful."

Well...a little competition never hurt anybody.

Rin checked his blaster and then aimed, opting to shoot the same way Madden had, quickly with little pause between each pull of the trigger. He barely paid attention to the spots lighting up on the four-ring target some thirty feet away until he was finished and the bell chimed for the third time.

Madden wasn't a bad shot by any means. He'd hit mostly the inner and second circles.

All eight of Rin's shots had landed in the center, with three of them overlapping.

Kelevra pulled the lollipop stick out of Rin's mouth, chucking it into an empty bin off to the side, and grinned.

Meanwhile, his friend had narrowed his eyes and was taking Rin in as if seeing him for the first time. "I should have figured after seeing you fight. Just how many secrets do you have, Varun?"

"I like to think of them as hidden talents," Rin said.

"What were you on Tibera?" Madden asked.

"A student." He smiled brightly, ignoring the way Kelevra snorted at his obviously over-the-top display of friendliness. "My father raised us for specific roles. The oldest was given extra tutoring and after-school classes to boost his academics, while the youngest was enrolled in military academy summer programs."

"From what age?" Kelevra frowned.

"Since we were five."

"They allow children to enroll in these camps?" Madden sounded just as surprised as everyone else around him appeared.

Rin shrugged. "It's pretty common where I'm from. They don't, like, put a real blaster in our hand on day one or anything like that. But they train us in hand-to-hand combat and teach us the proper way to shoot and hold various weapons."

"And you were the best at shooting?" Brennon guessed.

"I was the top in every category." It wasn't a lie, but Rin hoped none of them asked him to prove it.

"Aren't you oddly perfect for the role of Consort," Madden drawled. "We were all afraid we'd have to look after you as well, but it's nice seeing that won't be the case."

Rin wasn't ready to dive into all of that, so he turned to Kelevra. "What about you?"

"What about me?"

"Let's see what you've got, Imperial Prince."

"Teasing me will get you everywhere." Kelevra winked, and then he extended his arm toward the target, only, he didn't bother turning to watch where he was shooting. Instead, his gaze locked onto Brennon, making eye contact and holding unflinchingly as he fired all eight rounds.

Rin was scowling by the time he was finished, but Madden let out a low whistle.

"Nice," Madden praised, and it was enough to pique Rin's curiosity enough to glance over.

All of Kelevra's shots had made it in the center bullseye.

"The Devils of Vitality always hit their mark," Kel stated, though he was still starting Brennon down, and his true meaning wasn't lost on any of them.

"Don't threaten my friends," Rin said. He kept his tone even, knowing better than to make it seem like he was siding against Kelevra in front of others. A part of him also understood that the Imperial Prince was holding himself back by only taking things this far.

Sure enough, Kel grunted. "He's lucky I haven't already blown out both of his kneecaps for doing what he did."

"We've talked about it," Rin said, easing closer so he could position himself more firmly between him and Brennon. "He's apologized and admitted he was just drunk. It's not going to happen again. Besides, I'm the one it happened to. I forgive him, that's what matters here."

"Is it?"

"Kelevra." Rin waited until the Imperial Prince finally tore his gaze away and looked at him. "Seriously. If anything like that ever happens again I'll—"

"You'll let me kill him?" The challenging glint in his eyes shown bright in the florescent lighting.

"No," Rin stated, but before Kel could get mad, added, "I'll kill him myself. No one takes advantage of me. Period."

Brennon made a strangled sound but smartly didn't intervene in the conversation.

The corner of Kelevra's mouth tipped up slightly and he gave an almost imperceptible nod. "Noted, Consort. Just keep in mind, I let this pass because you'd be angry otherwise. That's the only reason. I'm not the forgiving type."

Rin couldn't forget that detail if he tried.

Chapter 30:

"Why do you bother with these every single day?" Rin asked, frustration ringing in his voice as he tugged on the thin white strings, tying the pale yellow corset Kelevra had selected for the day.

The Imperial was standing in front of him, facing the full-body mirror attached to the closet door, and whenever Rin met his gaze in the glass it was to find him watching with a massive shit-eating grin on his devilish face.

"Stop looking at me like that," he grumbled, pulling a little harder than necessary on the next strings before tying the whole thing off at the bottom.

"I can't help it," Kelevra replied. "My Consort is helping me get dressed in the morning. Surely that's something I should be allowed to find enjoyable. Even if you complained throughout the whole process."

"Seriously," Rin blew out a breath and stepped back, indicating he was done, "why go through this every day?"

"I like them," he shrugged and spun around to face him, "so it's not a waste of effort to me. Sort of like how you like *me* so trying to make this work by offering to help with my clothes and moving in here wasn't a waste of your efforts."

Rin glanced away.

"You're blushing," Kel pointed out. "Doesn't that mean yes?"

"Yes means yes," Rin corrected, only to have Kelevra advance a foot closer.

"Are you saying yes then, Consort?"

"You haven't asked me anything," he said. "Stop it. You've been summoned by your sister, remember? We don't have time for this."

"There's always time to fuck you."

"Not after making me struggle to do up those ties for fifteen minutes." Rin found Kel's clothing much more complicated than the simple t-shirt and cargo pants he was required to wear by the Academy. "I'm not wearing one of those. Don't even bother trying to make me."

"It takes a certain type of personality to pull these off," Kelevra said. "You're a little too rough around the edges. You'd dirty them up." He captured and shook Rin's chin lightly before laughing and heading toward the door. "Lyra didn't say what she wanted, are you sure you don't want to come? It's a good opportunity to see the Little Palace."

As the Heir Imperial and next in line for the throne, Lyra lived in the Little Palace—which was basically just a fancy mansion on the east side of the capital city. Kelevra had once lived there as well but had moved out as soon as he'd entered the Academy.

"Some other time." Rin had no interest in meeting with Lyra and potentially getting cornered again. He still hadn't figured out a way to deal with the Royal doctor situation, and was mostly just grateful Kel had yet to bring it up again since that day. "Do you think she's discovered something about Nila's murderer?"

Kelevra shook his head. "Unlikely. Madden says whoever did it covered their tracks too well. Even my Retinue is struggling to find anything. Whoever shot at me, they were smart about it."

Rin didn't like that. It made him uncomfortable not knowing what was up or what to expect. Whether or not he should be looking over his shoulders. "Let me take a look."

"You want to investigate? Don't take this the wrong way, Flower, but you're a sophomore. If my guys couldn't do it, what makes you so confident you'll fare better?"

"What makes you so certain I won't?" he countered.

Kelevra watched him for a moment and then lifted his multi-slate, sending off a message. A second later when Rin's dinged he motioned to it. "That's all they've gathered. Instead of focusing on who might be out for me—since that list is much longer—Zane concentrated on collecting data on Nila and any potential enemies she may have had. They couldn't find anything, but you're welcome to try."

"Thanks." Rin was already moving to the bed to perch on the edge and comb through the files.

"Flower."

"Hmm?"

"Consort."

At the firm tone, Rin glanced up. "What?"

"Aren't you going to thank me properly?" Kelevra asked.

"You realize you're entirely too needy for your own good right?" Despite that, Rin found himself rising and walking over. He stopped in front of the Imperial Prince and instead of giving him a peck on the cheek like he assumed the guy expected, he leaned forward and sealed their mouths together.

His tongue licked at the seam of Kel's lips and then dove inside when he parted them, tangling with his in a small bid for dominance that didn't last nearly as long as either of them clearly wished.

Far too quickly, Rin was pulling away, sighing in mild disappointment. He waved toward the open door at Kelevra's back. "You're going to be late."

"This is all so very domestic," Kel chuckled. "Who would have guessed I'd be into this sort of thing?"

"Ditto." Rin hated to admit it, but it was kind of nice. Having someone to come home to, to ask about his day. To care if he'd eaten or had enough water to drink. It was different, but nowhere near as stifling as he'd feared in the beginning when he'd first moved in.

"I'll call you when I'm on my way back," Kelevra told him, and then with a wink he spun on his heels and finally disappeared into the hall.

Rin listened to his retreating footsteps and then sighed, heading to the bed to go over the notes Zane and Madden had collected.

There really wasn't much. They'd conducted a few interviews with her friends and family and had opened an investigation into her disappearance initially. It'd been released finally a few days ago that she was dead, but since the body had never been recovered, there wasn't anything to go off of there either. They had Kelevra and Rin's statements that she'd been strangled and that was about it.

According to her parents, she'd acted normal leading up to that day, with nothing strange standing out. Her friends had said the same. There'd been no suspicious people in her life, and even a search through her multi-slate had backed that. She'd had conversations with her best friend and her boyfriend earlier that day and nothing else. No strange emails or messages from unknown numbers either.

The only odd thing was no one had heard her mention anything about going camping. Her mom had thought she was on campus studying at the library, and her best friend had been under the impression she was at the movies with her boyfriend. The boyfriend had nothing and merely stated they hadn't discussed their daily plans. Since they both attended the art academy and were fairly busy working on their final projects, everyone Zane spoke to mentioned this was fairly normal for them. They weren't the clingy sort of couple and could go a couple of days here and there without communicating.

Since there'd been an official death announcement, the police had tried to take over, but Kelevra had blocked them. The shot against him had to be kept hush-hush to avoid leaking into the media, so he hadn't wanted them involved.

An art major randomly decides to go camping in the middle of the forest near the Academy campus and ends up murdered. It was all types of weird. It would have made sense if she was actually a part of the mock case, but they knew now she hadn't been.

Though, it was a little strange that Rin knew all of the fake victims as well as Nila…Over the summer, he'd gotten to know a bunch of the students who went to Guest Fine Arts at the bars and a few parties Calder had held at his parents' place, but that didn't mean Rin knew the majority of the campus population.

There was a link to Nila's Imagine account, and Rin absently clicked on it and began scrolling. It'd taken him an hour to comb through the information collected just to discover Kel had been right and there really was nothing useful. They'd reached a dead end.

A particular photo caught his attention suddenly and Rin backtracked, frowning. The picture was of Nila with a group of friends at one of the bars downtown, Fireworks. It was on the ritzier side and was always packed, so Rin tended to pass on invites to go there. In the background of this particular photo, however, just over Nila's left shoulder, he could be seen in his Academy uniform with a beer in hand, laughing at something a person out of view of the camera had said.

Only, that wasn't Rin.

It took him longer than it should have to place the night in question, but he recalled once over two months ago when his brother had asked for them to swap and he'd gone along with it. Rin had been over being dragged all over town by his friends and had spent the night catching up on comics and sleep in Sila's apartment. They'd done it a few times that summer, switched when one or both of them were too burned out to follow through on prior commitments with their different friend groups.

Rin sat up straighter and switched over to the search section, typing in Arlet's name. He wasn't even entirely sure what he was doing, but he scanned through her account until he hit photos posted over the summer, stopping when he found another photo of himself.

Sila, dressed as Rin, had his arm draped over Arlet's shoulders, the two of them leaning over a round table, beaming at whoever was behind the camera.

That explained why she'd been overly flirtatious with him at Kelevra's pool party.

He switched over to one of the other fake victims from the mock case. Same thing. There were pictures of her with other cadets, sure, but there was one of just her and who she thought was Rin but was really Sila.

By the time he'd searched the other and found even more damning evidence, Rin was seeing red. A hypothesis was forming in his brain and he hated everything about it. He was already storming out of the penthouse and hopping into a cab before he realized what he was planning, mind reeling.

When he stepped back, his assumptions were weak at best, but knowing his brother the way that he did…

Banks had told them a member of their class had been assigned the role of killer. Rin hadn't seen any messages himself, so had assumed it wasn't him, but…He'd failed to recall he wasn't the only person who had access to his Academy email account.

He didn't even bother calling to check if his brother was home, storming up the stairs to the third floor and using his emblem-slate to unlock the door with the side panel. It shut behind him and he came to a stop just within the kitchen area, eyes landing on his brother who was standing by the bay window on the other side of the room.

The apartment was small, with two bedrooms, a single bathroom, and an open area that acted as the living and dining rooms, as well as the kitchen.

"What's up?" His brother turned from the window, eyeing him closely.

"I was going over the case files for the assignment and looking over what the Retinue managed to dig up on Nali's murder," Rin said. Now that he was here, he was less certain, but if there was even a remote possibility his theory was correct, he needed to know about it immediately.

"Ah." His brother gave nothing away, which in turn gave everything away if one knew what they were looking for where he was concerned.

Shit.

"Tell me it isn't you." Rin was overreacting. He did that sometimes—a lot. He did that a lot. This was just one of those occasions. That was all. There was no way—

"We don't lie to each other," his brother said matter-of-factly. "It's a rule."

Rin swore. "Are you serious? How could you keep this from me?"

He stepped away from the window, moving closer to the couch where Rin met him, tilting his head. "You're upset. It's not that big of a deal."

"Of course it is. What if I'd made a mistake because you didn't feel the need to read me into the situation?"

"It's not like I would have missed and hit you instead," his brother drawled.

Rin went cold. "What?"

"Oh." His brother stared back at him blankly for a long, drawn-out moment. "I thought you were talking about the incident in the forest. You mentioned Nila so I just assumed you'd figured it out."

If he'd stopped to consider things beforehand, Rin most likely would have, as it were, he'd jumped to conclusions and raced over here without giving himself the chance to. Maybe even subconsciously. Because this…

"I wasn't going to kill him," his brother said then. "Everything was under control. We just needed to shake him up a bit. Scare him the way he's been scaring you lately. Or, well," he gave him a once over, "he had been before. You're looking a lot better."

"Shut up." Rin gripped his hair and forced himself to inhale slowly and exhale even slower. He couldn't lose his cool.

"You meant the case though, right?" he didn't listen and kept going. "We were given the role of the killer and I assumed keeping that information from you would ensure we'd win. That's why I did it. At the beginning of the semester when we got the notice, you weren't involved with your Imperial, so winning was still important. I should have told you afterward, but I was honestly having fun setting up the crime scenes—by the way, all of those girls believe I was you when we did that. So if one of them thanks you for helping apply the stage makeup, you'll know what they mean."

"You shot at the Imperial Prince!" Rin couldn't believe he was wasting time talking about something as obsolete as a school assignment.

"Yes, I did also shoot at your Imperial Prince," his brother admitted. "He made you sad."

"I deal with my own emotions," Rin growled. "Remember? We discussed this!"

"But it wasn't a rule," he said.

Rin cursed.

"It's okay. The wound healed within a day. They heal fast here, just like back home. The bullet barely grazed his skin."

His brother was an epic shot, he'd had to be for the both of them to keep up the appearance as Rin. If he'd intended to murder Kelevra that day in the forest, he would have, and the two of them would be having an entirely different conversation right now. Most likely behind bars.

Just before their public executions.

"You got to see what he's really like in an emergency too," his brother continued. "He turned on you. If that's his base instinct, I rescind the encouragement I gave previously. Even if you have looked happier these past weeks since."

"If you look at it from his perspective, he had every reason to suspect me." Rin didn't mention how pissed he'd been after the fact though.

"I won't stand by if someone threatens us."

"*You're* threatening us!" Rin shoved him. "What if this gets out, hmm? What then?"

"How would it?" He didn't sound the least bit concerned. "I was careful."

"Why Nila? You promised you wouldn't harm innocent people when we came to this planet. That was one of the rules."

"Have you heard about what happens at the docks, brother?"

Rin frowned. "Yeah, the racing."

His gaze grew frigid. "Some people don't go there for the races."

"Don't." He held up a hand. Rin had enough going on without adding whatever other criminal activity he'd gotten himself involved in. "Don't tell me. Just answer this. Did you have a good reason?"

"She deserved it."

Rin blew out a breath. "All right." He snorted derisively at himself. "We're both so fucked up. Here I am, outright trusting you when you say you murdered someone, and there you are, running around shooting blasters at Imperials."

"He made you sad."

"Stop saying that!" Rin groaned and dropped back against the edge of the table. "New rule."

"You don't—"

"Yes," he stopped him with a steely look, "I do."

His brother considered it and then nodded once. "Then I get one as well."

Rin waved at him in the affirmative.

"Okay. What's the rule?"

"You never attack Kelevra again. I don't care about your reasoning. I don't care if you decide he deserves it. If he does something you don't like, you come to me about it. Leave him alone."

"Are you afraid I was sloppy? That this will get back to us after all?"

"He's got his entire Retinue searching for you."

"They won't find me."

"Confirm you understand the new rule, brother."

"What if he kills you?"

"He won't."

"What if he ends things with you then?"

Rin hesitated, not liking the way his gut twisted at those words.

"You're less convinced about that," his brother caught on. "Normal people are unpredictable. They're fickle and constantly changing their minds about everything. Your Imperial? He isn't normal. He's mercurial and selfish. Once he's bored of you, he'll toss you aside and your feelings will be hurt. You won't want to protect him then."

"Brother."

"Rules can change," he shrugged. "That's all I'm saying."

Rin nibbled on the inside of his cheek, hating that this was now swirling around in his head, but needing to ask anyway. "Do you think he will? Really?"

"Grow bored with you?" He hummed. "It's possible. Who can tell."

"Would you?"

"If I was truly obsessed with you the way he claims?" His brother smirked. "No."

This was stupid and not at all why he'd come rushing all the way over here. He'd planned on yelling at him for keeping a secret—he'd never imagined he'd end up worried about Kelevra in the process. Rin rubbed at his jaw and then sharpened his tone. "Confirm you understand the new rule. Sound it out for me."

His brother rolled his eyes. "I won't shoot a blaster at the Imperial Prince again. Even if he deserves it."

"You—"

The door swung open, cutting Rin off, and his eyes went wide when his father stood on the other side. His reaction only doubled when he realized Lyra and Kelevra were both with him.

His brother cocked his head, face enigmatic, and reminded Rin, "The doors here are paper-thin."

No…

One look at Kelevra's enraged expression confirmed the worst.

They'd heard.

"How much of that did you catch?" his brother was the one to ask, running a hand sheepishly through his hair. He made sure to apply the correct amount of nervousness into his voice, a show for their father more so than anyone else. His shoulders slumped slightly, playing the part. As the oldest, he was expected to show the most respect, the most regret. He was softer and more technical, which was why he'd been sent to the university instead of the Academy like his more outgoing brother.

Looking at him, no one would be able to guess he was the type of person who could even consider harming another person, let alone aim a gun at them. Standing there, dressed in the Vail University uniform, his brother slipped into the role of the Sila Varun their father was familiar with, with ease.

"You fired a weapon at the Imperial Prince of Vitality?" Crate was beat red, the vein in his forehead visible. He was doing his damnedest to maintain that Tiberan composure, his voice coming out clipped and steady despite the way his gaze conveyed how badly he wanted to skin them alive. "Do you have any idea what you've done? Where did you even get a blaster?"

"Is that all you heard?" His brother turned to him. "There's that, I suppose."

Lyra stepped into the apartment, her heels clicking against the cheap linoleum flooring. In her gold dress and matching heels, she sparkled far too brightly to fit in amongst the secondhand furniture and living space of two college-age guys. "Attacking an Imperial is an offense that results in death."

Rin looked to Kelevra, but Kel didn't say anything to his sister. It was hard to tell what he was thinking aside from anger.

"Your father came to collect your brother," Lyra said to Rin then. "When he arrived, I made it clear the Imperial family wouldn't get involved with your personal affairs. We came here to ask how Sila felt about leaving. But after this, he's no longer welcome on Vitality."

Rin straightened and stepped forward, still looking to Kelevra, but before he could get a word out, his brother moved closer and grabbed onto his arm.

He shook his head curtly. "You can't rely on him. Remember his reaction in the forest. We only have each other."

Kel had made his stance on betrayal perfectly clear. Knowing his brother was the one who shot him? He wouldn't forgive that. The truth of it was standing right there, watching silently as his sister and their father gazed at them with fury and disappointment.

Rin could understand where he was coming from if he stopped to think about it, he knew he could. But why should he? Why should he go that extra mile when Kel was unwilling to do the same? He knew how important his brother was to him, yet he was just going to allow his sister to off world him? Just like that?

It wasn't fair of Rin to expect anything less. If he were a better person, a kinder person, he knew he wouldn't. But he wasn't.

Maybe his brother was right after all.

Maybe they only had each other.

Maybe he really would only ever be part of one *us*, and it wouldn't be with the Imperial Prince standing across from him.

Why did that cut so deep? Since when had he started to hope for more? He'd convinced himself he was settling because that's what was best, but now…Now he was forced to acknowledge that it was possible he'd grown attached to Kelevra in more ways than he'd thought.

Somewhere between the rough bouts of explosive sex and tenderly spoken words when they slept curled into each other's sides at night…Rin had developed feelings for him. Rin liked him, flaws and all.

Only, if the Imperial Prince felt the same, he wasn't thinking about that now. No matter how long Rin stared at him, he never once met his gaze. Amidst all of this, he was choosing to ignore Rin.

Choice, in the face of an emergency.

He could have laughed.

Or cried.

"I am grateful for your mercy," Crate said, bowing low to Lyra. "If you'll still have him, I would accept leaving Rin in your care."

Lyra seemed torn but ended up nodding. "Yes, of course. The betrothal announcement has already been made, and though we only caught the tail end of the conversation, it's apparent Rin wasn't aware of his brother's part in things."

"Thank you, Heir Imperial." Crate bowed again. "I will depart with Sila immediately. We can be off-world within the hour."

"I'll give you one hour," Lyra agreed. "That is all."

Silently, Rin begged Kelevra to look at him. That's all he needed. Acknowledgment. Proof that Kel really did see him and it hadn't all been pretty bullshit to lure him in. The hypocrisy wasn't lost on him, but he needed it anyway.

For a tense moment, no one spoke.

And Kelevra didn't so much as glance in his general direction.

He wasn't even going to give Rin the chance for the two of them to speak or discuss things. He didn't have any questions about why, or how. Despite having promised he would ensure his brother stayed, he was going to stand there and quietly allow his sister and their fucking father to have their way.

The worst part?

Rin didn't even feel angry about it.

How could he, when it was his own damn fault for leaning into the fairytale in the first place. For arrogantly thinking something like this would never happen. That he wouldn't have to one day choose sides between two clashing personalities.

His brother and the Imperial Prince were too alike and yet polar opposites all at the same time. But the biggest difference between them was that his brother would do anything and everything in his power to protect Rin.

Kelevra Diar was not an *us*. He was a singular being, who thought only of his own comfort and desires. And while Rin certainly couldn't fault him for that, he couldn't forgive it either. Not when it came to something like this.

"Pack your bags, Sila," their father stated, the smugness not making it to his tone. He was too controlled for that. But it was in his eyes. Just a slight glimmer, only recognizable because Rin had seen it so many times growing up.

He thought he won. He'd made the two-week journey from their home planet to force his son to go with him, and now that he had the Imperial backing, he thought he'd beaten them.

Not. Going. To. Happen.

Years of carefully planned switches and rules and masks and chains, and in one swift move, he was going to tear them all apart. It was something the two of them should have discussed beforehand, but there was no time for that, and frankly, if his brother could make a bold decision like shooting at the Imperial Prince, then Rin could sure as hell make this one.

"Now, Sila," their father said.

Rin headed to the dining room table and snatched the pack from the surface, the Vail University crest pin flashing in the overhead lights as he started walking about the room, shoving clothing items and small knickknacks he'd purchased over the course of the past year and a half into it.

His brother was the only one who didn't seem confused.

"What do you think you're doing?" Crate asked.

"You said to pack," he replied, continuing to collect things, only partially seeing what they were as they were lifted and stuffed into the black backpack. That unsettling feeling was growing within him, his skin starting to feel too itchy and tight. If he didn't keep moving he'd lose it, and given his current state, he couldn't even properly guess which way he'd go, fight or flight.

He hoped for the first if it came down to it. At least then he could go out with some dignity.

"Don't be difficult," their father snapped.

"I'm not." He left the spare uniform hanging over the side of the couch alone, seeing as how he wouldn't be needing it on Tibera.

"Only Sila Varun will be allowed to leave," Lyra said, her cool voice nothing like the kind and open one from that day they'd met.

"Of course, Heir Imperial." He kept packing.

"Rin Varun!" Crate's composure cracked.

His brother slid his gaze to him. "Yes, Father?"

If a pin had dropped then, it would have sounded like an explosion.

Chapter 31:

A part of him wanted to storm across the room and put his fist into Sila's face, but knowing he was Rin's brother, and how upset that would make him, was the only thing holding Kelevra back.

He wasn't usually caught by surprise, but hearing it'd been Sila who'd taken a shot at him? That had stolen his ability to speak, so he'd stood back and allowed the others to discuss it, trying to curb the insatiable desire to attack first and worry about the consequences after. When his sister suggested banishing him as punishment, Kelevra held his tongue.

Aside from it angering Rin for a bit, he could see no beneficial reason to allow Sila to stay. If he'd fired a blaster at Kel, it could only have been because he thought he was doing his brother a favor. Then there was that comment about how he couldn't be trusted. Sila didn't want the two of them to be together. He'd become an obstacle between Kelevra and Rin. That was unacceptable.

He'd been so focused on planning all the ways he could make it up to Rin later, once they'd both cooled down, when Sila looked their father dead in the eye and responded to the wrong name.

Kelevra felt his mind malfunction, a flash of anxiety sweeping through him—which was odd since that was typically something he couldn't experience.

"You never could tell us apart," Rin spoke then and it was like watching a switch flickering on in both him and his brother, their demeanors shifting almost instantly. He dropped the bag at his feet and cocked out a hip.

Meanwhile, his brother stiffened to his full height, the nervous expression he'd been wearing—fake—dropping away, replaced by an eerily calm expression.

Kelevra had seen them like this before, Rin, angry and bitter, that perpetual scowl twisting his features. Sila was almost robotic in contrast but with a looseness to him. One was like ice, the other water. They were as he'd come to know them.

It became glaringly obvious their father could not say the same.

"It helped he never tried," Sila replied.

"Yes," Rin agreed. "That's true. Thanks for that I suppose. Certainly made our lives easier."

"It's the only good thing you've ever done, in fact."

"What is going on here?" Crate stumbled over his words. "Enough playing around. You aren't children anymore, do you really think this stunt—"

"He thinks we're lying," Sila said, the corner of his mouth tipping up in a way that was neither warm nor filled with humor.

"Flower," Kelevra didn't know what to follow that up with, freezing when Rin turned to meet his gaze.

"My name is Sila Varun," he said stiffly. "Giving nicknames to your fiancé's twin brother is unbecoming and genuinely frowned upon, Imperial Prince."

"He's no fiancé of mine," his brother—the imposter—chimed in. He looked to Lyra. "I will be contesting this betrothal, Heir Imperial. Although, I think we can all agree breaking things amicably is for the best all around."

"Stop this at once!" Crate huffed.

"Would you like to run a test?" Rin—because no matter what they said, Kelevra knew who *his* Rin was and he refused to call him any other name but—suggested without skipping a beat. The corner of his mouth turned up viciously, in complete juxtaposition to his twin. There was so much untethered emotion and rage there it was impossible to miss. "We know you've programmed your multi-slate to act as a blood tester."

"Pretentious," Sila chuckled, the sound just as empty as his expression. "How many years has it been since you've held an active role at Varun Hospital, Father?"

"Six," Rin supplied. Then he held out his hand. "Here. Prick my finger if you're so sure. Let's see which of us knows who we are best, shall we?"

"Am I to believe," Lyra interrupted the family moment, "that the two of you have switched places? When?"

"On and off since we were eight," Sila said. "It stopped for a while when we came here, but old habits die hard, so they say."

"And my brother fell for—"

Kelevra pointed at his flower before she could finish. "That one. That one's mine."

"Sila Varun isn't the name listed on the decree, I'm afraid," Sila—the imposter bastard who apparently was really named Rin—made a sound as though he felt bad for him.

That day in the bathroom when Rin had found out about the betrothal, he'd said some strange things that Kelevra just hadn't understood as odd at the time. Now it made sense. It also explained why he'd been so desperate to break the engagement despite how his body craved Kel's touch.

"That one is mine," Kel stated firmly. He held Rin's gaze.

"This one is a liar unfit for the Imperial family," he dared to say. "And as you've heard, I also happen to be on my way off planet."

The Imposter turned to his brother. "Forget this. The plan has moved up, that's all."

Rin frowned. "What do you mean?"

"I have a way. I've been working toward it ever since you caught the eye of an Imperial Prince. Great job."

"I already apologized," Rin sneered, that temper leaking through despite the situation and the audience.

"Don't worry, big brother," some of the blank mask slipped when he looked at Rin, "I've got us. Everything is in order. I just need to grab something and then we can be on the first ship off planet."

"Neither of you is going anywhere until we properly sort this out," Crate said, freezing up when the twins both turned his way in an almost eerie fashion.

Kelevra vaguely wondered what they looked like to their father, a man used to seeing them poised. Fake. His perfect sons, and yet one was empty and the other was seething with so much pent-up emotion it looked like he'd explode any minute now. While Kel was used to them being their true selves around him, he could imagine the shock Crate must be experiencing.

"Do you remember when I broke your award from that medical conference and you locked me out for the night during a storm?" Rin asked.

"Of course," Crate clipped out.

Sila held up his hand. "That was me."

"What about when I almost drowned Bo Brung?" Rin said.

Crate set a glare on Sila, but Sila merely lifted a second hand in the universal gesture of surrender or innocence.

"That *was* actually me." Rin shook his head at their father. "You never knew the difference. You don't know the difference now. Take a good look. Can't you see it?"

"Should we give him a computer eye," Sila suggested, his gaze lighting up with something manic, "like your Imperial Prince?"

Rin scowled. "Don't call him that."

Sila rested his elbow on Rin's shoulder. "We could take them, depending on how many protective detail the Heir Imperial brought along with her. Father is always too confident to bother with his. I bet he left them at the loading bay. And the prince…" He shrugged when he met Kel's gaze briefly. "His Retinue are baubles. He wouldn't have brought them here for this. He didn't even contact you to give you fair warning."

Those words must have hit home because Rin lifted his emblem-slate to check.

"Told you," Sila said when Rin obviously didn't find any missed messages.

Kelevra had intended to call, but he'd wanted to get here first and ensure nothing happened to his annoying brother. He'd actually meant well…This was why considering other people's wishes was a waste of effort.

"You're discussing treason," Lyra snapped and Sila lifted a single brow.

"We're discussing freedom, actually, Heir Imperial. If you'd be so kind as to grant it willingly, no harm has to come to anyone. If you insist on standing by our father…Well. We'll do what we must to get by you," the Imposter said.

"We'll leave immediately," Rin promised her, clearly trying to make her see reason. His tone was slightly warmer than the one he used with Crate, his eyes pleading. "We can be off Vitality in that hour you gave, and we swear not to return."

"I have enough funding to secure us safe passage," Sila reassured. "It'll take me ten minutes at most to collect my belonging from the Vail University campus."

Rin's lips pursed, and it was obvious to Kelevra he knew exactly what his brother was referring to and he did not approve, but he wasn't going to argue with him over that now.

It truly hit him then that these two could read each other better than anyone. That they could *be* each other. That they'd been doing it for long enough their own father couldn't tell the difference and was confused seeing them act this way. And they'd done it on Vitality as well?

The Imposter had said as much. They'd been running around the planet, switching identities like clothing…and *no one* had taken notice?

They were brilliant.

And terrifying.

Kelevra fucking loved it.

They'd never pulled that stunt on him because his eye would have detected the physical differences neither of them could control, like how Rin's body heat tended to flare with his concealed emotions, while Sila burned low with little change.

The person he'd been with this entire time had been his flower, without a shadow of a doubt. Whether he'd lied about his identity to the rest of the world or not, he'd never tried to lie to Kel. Sure, that was most likely because he'd known he couldn't get away with it, but it was still the truth.

"You aren't going anywhere," Kelevra found himself saying, anger and animosity swirling through his gut. His hands clenched into fists and he slipped them into his pockets, doing his damnedest not to give in and cross the room, grab his flower by the scruff of the neck, and toss him to the ground. His inner devil was screaming that he fuck him here and now, for all the occupants in the room to see so they would know who belonged to him.

So his flower would remember that fact as well.

"I told you before." Finally, Rin looked at him, and the matching anger and betrayal in his mismatched eyes momentarily threw Kelevra for a loop, because what the hell did he have to be angry about? "We go everywhere together."

"If you'd like to try to separate us," Sila stepped forward, and Rin didn't so much as attempt to hold him back, "you're more than welcome to."

"No blood on the carpet," Rin said blandly. "We need that deposit."

"We don't," he disagreed. "I've got us covered financially. We're set, brother. We don't need them. Any of them."

"If you attack an Heir Imperial," Rin added, "we'll never make it off this damn planet."

"I won't," Sila promised. "She's the only one here who understands. Don't you?"

Rin clicked his tongue. "Don't be rude."

"Apologies. I meant, don't you, Heir Imperial?"

The fact that his flower was scolding his brother for rudeness even at a time like this was almost enough to have Kelevra laughing. Because it was just so very him. Lyra had been kind to Rin, and therefore he'd return that so long as she didn't change her tune on him first.

"I don't know how you managed to remain oblivious their entire lives, General Varun," Kelevra said, watching the twins closely. "The two of them are so obviously different it seems more ridiculous to not see it."

"Ah," Sila smirked. "Have you decided to be interesting after all? At the final hour?"

"This isn't the final anything," Kelevra corrected. "You aren't going anywhere with what's mine, Imposter."

He chuckled. "Technically, I'm not the imposter you've always claimed, Imperial Prince. My name is Rin Varun, and I am a sophomore at the Academy. The man who made friends with Daylen, Calder, and Brennon last year was me. The man who attended classes with them and ate with them and hung out on the weekends with them, all me. You're the one who had my name added to the betrothal announcement. You're the one who told the entire planet you want me. There is no fault here for anyone but you. You tried to take that which you did not understand and you failed. The. End. The decree was already made, and as per your insanely restrictive laws, you're only allowed to announce one Royal Consort in your lifetime. Sounds pretty final."

Kelevra took a threatening step closer, ignoring the way his sister tensed.

"Thinking you can change the law?" Sila asked. "I don't think so. Unlike some, I've paid attention. Your sisters might spoil you rotten, but there are still lines. They never let you get away with breaking tradition. It would cause too much trouble with the high council, isn't that right?" he directed this last part to Lyra, but didn't wait for her response. "Our father is like that too. Appearance is what matters, and no one wants to bother fighting a tedious battle when it can be avoided. They won't let you change the name on that decree, no matter how much you beg or plead or threaten."

"I would never threaten my own family," Kelevra stated. "Which is why I'm done playing games with you."

Rin bristled, but Sila merely cocked his head, catching on much more quickly than his brother.

"Interesting," Sila mused.

"Neither of you are going anywhere."

"You aren't marrying my brother," Rin growled.

"Of course not. I'm marrying Rin Varun and you, Flower, are the only Rin Varun I acknowledge. Here's the thing," he took another step closer, watching as the twins held their ground, "I don't have to change the decree. All I have to do is swap the DNA samples provided by the two of you to the Academy and Vail."

"Kelevra," Lyra said. "Think things through. Don't make any rash decisions."

"I'm not being impulsive, sister," he reassured. "I know exactly what I want." He stopped only a couple of feet away and held Rin's gaze. "Did you think you could escape if you had a different name? Is this what you've been hiding from me?"

He'd known there was something, and maybe he should have guessed what it was but...The twins had always come off as distinct opposites to him, so he'd never even imagined they might switch places and fool others. Judging by how pale Crate was, clearly he wasn't the only one shocked, though for different reasons.

Rin stubbornly kept his mouth shut, eyeing him suspiciously.

Which admittedly irked Kelevra, since he wasn't the one here who'd kept a major secret and lied. "You're the one who wanted trust, remember? Hypocritical of you, wouldn't you say? If for that alone, you owe me. Which means you're going to be good and agree to my demands. Isn't that right, Flower? I swore I'd never let you go. I meant it then, I mean it now."

"He can't make us do anything we don't want," Sila leaned in and said to Rin.

"That's where you're wrong," Kelevra stated. He didn't want to have to make them, however. He didn't want to risk getting into a confrontation with his flower's brother. This wedge between them because of his father and this secret was already uncomfortable enough as it was.

"What," Rin licked his lips, hesitating, "...What are your demands?"

"You'll both agree to swapping your samples and taking on the names attached to them permanently. You," he pointed to the Imposter, "will be Sila Varun from here until the end of time. And you," then to his flower, "will be Rin. *My* Rin. I don't," he held up a hand when Sila opened his mouth, "care what you do in your free time. You can't fool me anyway. But we need this to be official on paper and I absolutely refuse to refer to my flower by the same *Sila*."

"Even though that was the name I was given at birth?" Rin asked.

"You aren't attached to it," Kel pointed out. "If you were, the two of you wouldn't have switched for such long periods. And you wouldn't be such a damn good shot."

They must have done it back then to help keep up the rouse as well, since their father had always intended for the youngest to join the Academy, and yet his flower was the oldest and so good with a blaster.

"Why should we agree to that?" Rin wasn't convinced. He always made things difficult.

"Because if you're my Royal Consort then I made you other promises that night as well. You stay, he stays. Neither of you will be leaving, that can be by choice, or—"

"I'm curious—" Sila began, only to have Rin cut him off like that time at Friction.

"No, you aren't."

"I guess I'm not."

There was little doubt in Kelevra's mind that Sila had been about to suggest they fight just to see which of them would be victorious.

"This is absurd," Crate announced. "Heir Imperial, forgive my family for causing this trouble. I'll be taking them both and removing them from your presence at once. They will pay for their deception and—"

Kel turned, his positioning making it clear he was standing with the twins. It was risky, giving them his back, especially since one had admitted to shooting at him in the past, but if Rin needed him to make a clear stance in his favor, he'd do it, risk and all. "General Varun, your presence seems to have upset my Royal Consort. As such, I am obligated to ask you to leave. Alone. You see, your sons are part of the Imperial family of Vitality now and we don't turn on our own family. Do we, sister?"

She held his gaze for a weighted moment before finally sighing. "No, no we do not. Unfortunately, General, it seems you've come all this way for nothing."

"You can't be serious?" He turned to her. "Heir Imperial, they're young, the boys and your brother. It's our duty as their elders to make the right decisions on their behalf. Surely you don't want liars anywhere near your bloodline."

"Tiberans can't procreate with Vitals," Sila drawled in mock innocence. "Remember, you told us that yourself, father."

"You even went so far as to say that was one major reason you were allowing us to come here," Rin added. "Because it meant there was no chance of either of us getting anyone pregnant and sullying the family name."

Lyra's eyes narrowed. "I see."

"They're lying, Heir Imperial," Crate reassured.

She merely turned to Kel for confirmation.

He shook his head. "He's the one lying."

"My decision stands," Lyra announced. "It seems the two are under the protection of my brother, and if he's claimed them, there's nothing I can do. They'll be staying here, on Vitality, and that is final."

"You can't do that! This is kidnapping! I'll tell the Empress of Tibera you're holding hostages! This could mean war," Crate snapped.

"I'll call her personally and explain the situation," Lyra said. "If you'd like to still try your side of things once you finally arrive home in two weeks, that's your prerogative, General. But no matter what you claim, it's very clear that both Sila and Rin Varun would prefer to stay here than go anywhere with you. Is that correct, boys?"

"Yes," the twins said in unison.

"Well," Lyra held out her hands primly, "there you have it. The guards in the hall will escort you back to your landing bay, General. I'll ensure you have a seat on the next ship off planet."

"You can't do this!"

"We're adults," Rin told his father. "Recognized as such both in this galaxy and the Crystal Sea. Father, legally there's nothing you can do to keep us."

"If he keeps being difficult," Sila suggested. "We could always handle him."

"We are not murdering our father." He pinched the bridge of his nose in frustration.

Kelevra noticed the moment it finally clicked for Crate. His gaze pinged back and forth between his two sons and it was as though he was looking at strangers.

"Giving you two life was the biggest mistake I have ever made," Crate said.

"Unless you want one of us to take yours," Rin stated, "you'll be on your way now, Father."

"Goodbye," Sila added. "You'll forgive us for never speaking to you again."

For a moment, everyone went quiet, the twins staring their father down.

Then Crate moved, pulling a blaster free from a hidden holster beneath his shirt. His arm swung up and he aimed at Sila, but before he could get a clear shot, Rin shot forward.

Kelevra tried to stop him, his hand catching air as Rin moved at a speed faster than he was aware he was capable of going. He'd read that Tiberans were light on their feet after he'd discovered that's where Rin was from, and he'd witnessed that firsthand when they'd been running through the forest, but it still caught him off guard seeing it now.

Rin latched onto his father's wrist, the blaster going off. A bullet zipped through the air, shooting into the side of a dresser, splinters of wood flying. The sound of bone snapping came shortly after, and then Crate was dropping to his knees, screaming.

The blaster was snatched from his useless hold, his wrist now broken, and Rin lifted it, muzzle pointed directly at Crate's forehead.

Kel reached him, settling a hand lightly on Rin's arm. "It's okay, Flower. It's okay now, you don't need this."

"If he's gone, it'll all be over," Rin whispered darkly.

"That's the anger talking, sweetheart. You aren't Sila, you aren't cold-blooded. This will haunt you forever if you go through with it."

He pursed his lips, tilting his head slightly to the side so he could send a sideways glance toward Kel. "Not Sila, huh?"

Right. Damn it.

"Be Rin," he urged, settling his other hand at his narrow back. He traced circles there with his thumb. "Be my Rin."

His frown deepened as he considered, and then his arm lowered a fraction.

It was enough distraction for Kelevra to take the gun from his hand. He dipped it and aimed lower, firing off a single shot into Crate's right thigh before anyone could see it coming.

Crate screamed as blood instantly began to pool from the wound.

Rin's eyes went wide, but Kel kept tracing those circles, knowing it was important he maintain their connection with all of this ensuing chaos around them.

"Guards!" Lyra called when Crate's face turned beet red.

"Don't touch me!" He pulled his arms free from the Imperial Guards' hold when two stepped forward to remove him from the room, neither of them bothering to be mindful of his injury even though they saw it and had heard the shot.

A bloody trail was left in his wake, the sounds of his screaming echoing down the hall as he was forcefully removed.

"Was that necessary?" Lyra asked, pinching the bridge of her nose. "Now I'll have to explain to the Empress of Tibera why her star general has a hole in his leg."

"Just tell her the truth," Kelevra suggested, handing the weapon over to her as he spoke. "Say he tried to take one of our citizens against their will, and then he had the gall to draw a blaster on them."

If he'd had his way, he would have offed him just now, but since Crate was still Rin's father he'd reined it in. Still, that hadn't meant he didn't deserve to be punished. If it was up to Kel, he'd show Crate far worse.

"I'll ensure he finds himself off the planet," Lyra told them. "But the two of you," she motioned between Kel and Rin, "owe me. Big time."

"Of course, sister." He grinned at her.

"Thank you, Heir Imperial." Rin bowed his head, then forced his brother to do the same. If he was mad at Kelevra for shooting his father, he wasn't showing it.

Which meant he wasn't.

There was that, at least.

She exited the room, the door to the apartment closing behind her.

Kelevra held his hand out for his flower and waited.

"Don't," Sila said, even though Rin hadn't made any moves to take the offering.

"I'm not going to hurt my own Consort," Kelevra growled. His patience was gone. He just wanted to go home where he could feel secure in knowing Rin was locked up in their penthouse without anywhere else to run to. Then they could work through this together like a couple. He certainly wasn't going to lower himself to having that personal and private discussion here, in a shitty college student's apartment, with the Imposter hovering like a mother hen.

"If he's injured, I won't be firing a warning shot next time," Sila told him darkly.

"Enough." Rin put himself between them. "I have to go with him. He and I have a lot to discuss."

Sila didn't seem convinced.

"I'm forgiving that stunt in the forest," Kelevra said. "Only because it'd be a hassle otherwise. The only reason I haven't put you in the ground for shooting at me is because it would hurt my flower."

"I said enough," Rin growled. He grabbed his hand and dragged Kel toward the exit.

"Call me," Sila stated, and got a hand wave in agreement. "Or answer when I call you. I mean it."

As soon as they were out in the hall, Rin released him, and though he was tempted to capture his hand once more, Kelevra allowed him to pull away, keeping a close eye on him as he briskly walked ahead, leading the way out of the building toward the front where Kel's car was parked on the side of the road.

"Get in, Consort," Kel ordered when Rin hesitated, pushing at his narrow back to propel him forward. He had the door open and Rin slipped into the passenger seat in no time. Then he rounded the car, took a deep breath, and got in.

"Home," he said as soon as he was pulling out onto the street. "We'll talk once we're home."

For once, Rin didn't argue.

Chapter 32:

The first time they'd done it, they'd been eight. Rin—the real Rin—had pushed Stax Hyuk off a cliff to see how far down the drop was and had felt no remorse after the fact when she'd ended up with a broken arm. She'd tried to tell their parents the truth, but by then, Sila had already stepped forward and swapped their clothes. He'd taken on the role of his younger brother, easily emoting the way one should in a situation like that.

He'd cried and pleaded and apologized until tears were glistening in his eyes, and since emotions that strong weren't typically shown amongst anyone not family, it'd made the Hyuk's uncomfortable enough to question their own daughter. In the end, they'd believed him that it'd been an accident and told their daughter she was merely misremembering due to shock.

The second time, Sila had wanted to learn how to shoot a blaster, something Rin wasn't all that interested in. The younger twin felt killing a person that way was uneventful. He'd much rather get up close and personal and be able to watch the life drain from their eyes. They'd been ten then.

Practically their entire lives they'd been switching places, fooling those around them. Sometimes it was to help keep them hidden, so no one would be able to guess that the older twin felt too much and the younger twin didn't feel enough, but other times it was for the fun of it. To get out of doing something one didn't want to do but the other was interested in. The personalities had come easily enough, though were carefully crafted and built upon over time, so it would be easier for them to slip into the right role whenever they needed to.

Sila became known as the quiet and studious older brother, and Rin the outgoing, always up for an adventure younger brother. They fit into their father's molds for them, one to become a chief of medicine, the other destined for a seat on the council. It'd made sense.

Until they'd been able to escape Tibera. Here, on Vitality, they were supposed to be able to let most of that go. They'd started in their proper places, and all of last year they'd kept to those roles. Sila had been Sila and Rin had been Rin. Then Sila had made a discovery and had asked for Rin's help one last time and…Well. Things had quickly returned to how they'd been shortly after that. They'd switched around all summer, easily getting away with it.

It'd been a little disheartening honestly, at least for him—for the real Sila. He hadn't made many friends his freshman year, happy to coast through unnoticed for once in his life, but even those few hadn't been able to tell him from his brother. And when this year had begun and his brother still hadn't solved the issue he'd asked of him, they'd agreed to keep playing each other.

Neither of them had said out loud they'd realized they preferred it, that they preferred being in the other's shoes, but it was apparent that was the case. That was why neither had forced switching back. When his brother had asked him to a few weeks ago, he'd even been a bit nervous he'd wanted his name back permanently—more so since they'd been in the thick of this situation with Kelevra.

A part of him had wanted to be Rin Varun so badly, even if he couldn't admit it.

But now here they were.

He was quiet the entire drive to the penthouse, giving both himself and Kelevra time to cool down and collect their thoughts. On the one hand, part of him did think this could have been a mistake after all. Kel wasn't exactly known for his understanding, and he'd made it clear after the thing with Brennon that he didn't forgive either. But on the other...

Maybe he was a fool, but he really just wanted it to be real. For once, Rin wanted to be Rin and no one else. He wanted to have a home and a place, somewhere he didn't constantly feel the need to run or hide from. Someone that made him want to stay in the same identity instead of switching it around with his brother the way other siblings shared clothing.

He followed Kelevra from the parking garage to the elevator and then across the roof to the side entrance. Neither of them spoke as they moved up the stairs and down the hall to the bedroom, though he ended up hesitating in the doorway.

Kelevra went straight for the end table and Rin knew without having to see what he was getting from there.

"Kel…"

"We can't solve all our problems through sex," Kelevra said, straightening and turning back to face him. "You said that. You said a lot of things if you recall, some of them more hypocritical than others. Despite what I did for you and your brother back there, make no mistake, Flower, I'm pissed right now."

"I know." He didn't bother adding the Imperial Prince had a right to be. Rin understood that. "I lied. I didn't mean to but…"

"Were you ever going to tell me the truth?"

He dropped his gaze.

"This is how this is going to play out, Consort." Kelevra held out his palm. "Same game as our first night together, only with a twist. Either you take the black pill, or I take the white one. If I do that, we're going to have sex after all, but it won't be gentle or sweet, and afterward, there's a good chance we'll both hate each other. I stand by my claim to you. I won't let you go. You're mine. So choose. Either you be absolutely honest and you put your trust in me, or we fuck and resent one another for the rest of our very long lives."

Rin's heart was pounding in his chest.

"This is it," Kelevra said. "This is the actual fight or flight scenario. Decide."

His biggest secret had already been revealed, so it shouldn't be so daunting to think about popping that truth pill into his mouth. It shouldn't be more terrifying to imagine being honest than it was imagining being thrown to the ground and brutally fucked in anger, but it was.

Still, there was too much at stake here for Rin to give in to fear, and in many ways, he owed Kel an explanation.

Rin took the black pill and brought it up to his mouth, but Kelevra grabbed him by the wrist.

"Wait," the Imperial Prince demanded, and at Rin's frown, added, "I don't need you to take that to know whether or not you're lying to me."

"I know." This was a test. Rin wanted to pass. He swallowed the pill before Kel could stop him again.

Kelevra watched him closely. "You didn't have to do that."

"You told me to choose. I chose."

"Yes, but—"

"You just wanted to see if I would choose you," Rin cut him off with a nod. "I know."

"Then why—"

"Because if we're going to get through this, any doubts you may have need to be quelled. And I think I need this too. I need to know I can trust you with everything I've got." Brennon may have kissed him at the bar that night, but there was no doubt in Rin's mind if it'd been his brother there in his stead, the same thing would have happened.

Brennon would have kissed his brother and been none the wiser.

A lot of that was their own fault. They'd created these personas and had stuck to them, even once they'd come to this planet, so he couldn't really fault his friends for not noticing. But that didn't mean he didn't still yearn for acceptance and belonging, the same as everyone else.

"It feels hot in here." Rin fanned himself and then allowed Kelevra to move him so he was seated on the edge of the bed.

"That's the pill," Kelevra said. He ran a hand through his curly hair. "Your mouth might start to feel dry as well, and everything is going to get a little hazy. It'll help you feel less focused and then you'll answer all of my questions without thought. Are you okay?"

"Yes." The room was spinning a bit, and Rin dropped back so he was lying on the bed gazing up at the ceiling. His reflection showed down at him, his cheeks bright red, his golden hair messy. He looked either close to tears or about to physically break something, and for some reason, he found that infinitely funny.

"What is it, Flower?" Kelevra sat down next to him.

He pointed up. "Sila."

"You're going by Rin now, remember?"

"Oh." He dropped his arm.

"Does that bother you?" Kelevra tipped his head and Rin shook his. "Not even a little?"

"I have no attachments to either name." He never had. "It's just a name. You saw it yourself. It doesn't mean anything. It doesn't mean anyone can see me through it." His father never had. "We even had a tell in the beginning. If we were in the same room and one of our names was called, more often than not, we'd both look up. People probably assumed it was because the other was curious who was calling their brother, but it was actually because sometimes we'd forget for a split second which role we were playing that day."

"Roles?" Kelevra planted an arm onto the bed on the other side, so he was leaning over him. "Is that what you two call them?"

"There's Sila Varun and there's Rin Varun," he said. "There's him and there's me and there's us."

"Us."

"Yes." He pulled his eyes off the mirror and stared at Kelevra instead. "The pill is working, isn't it?" There was a light feeling to his body, almost like he was floating, but different since he could feel the plush mattress and the silky comforter beneath him. "Is this all you wanted to know?"

"Is there anything else you want to tell me?" Kel asked.

He tried to think it over, but his thoughts felt like a jumbled mess, and before long they were tumbling out of him like an untethered stream of consciousness. "You know I'm an overthinker? It's exhausting. I hate it. But I have to be careful. If I slipped up and someone discovered what we were doing, we'd be in serious trouble. That's why we wanted to come here and live our own lives."

"You were at Vail last year."

"I was. We decided to try it out. Being ourselves. It was nice getting to enjoy the quiet, and I didn't have to make too many friends, which meant my emotions weren't always going haywire and I didn't have to monitor my expressions so much. But then—" He stopped abruptly, frowning.

"Then what, Flower?" Kelevra prompted.

"You're going to be mad."

"That ship has sailed, sweetheart."

"No, like, murderous mad."

"Consort."

"You know you do that a lot? You call me by something specific to get across a specific point. Flower when you're being possessive. Consort when you're reminding me of my place. Cadet when you want me to fall in line. Sweetheart…well. That one is pretty self-explanatory, isn't it?"

"Do you not like it?" Kel asked.

"Of course I like it," he said. "No one calls my brother any of those things. Those names are mine. Just mine. It's nice having something all mine. Don't tell him though. I don't want to hurt his feelings. He has some. It seems like he doesn't, but he does."

"Why am I going to be mad, Cadet?"

Rin made a face. "There. Like that. I asked my brother to switch places at the start of the summer. I felt like I was being followed. Someone was stalking me and I was worried if I dealt with it on my own my temper would get in the way and I'd do something rash."

"Someone was stalking you?" Kelevra's brow furrowed.

Rin dropped a hand over his to keep him from pulling away when it was clear he was about to. "Don't. There's nothing for you to do. My brother is handling it."

"Like hell."

"Seriously. It's his problem now. It's the rule. I don't get involved in his problems unless he asks and vice versa."

Kel's eyes narrowed. "What about how he shot at me in the forest? Doesn't that count as him getting involved? And what are these rules?"

"The rules were made a long time ago, though I did add one today so he'd never shoot at you again. You're welcome. They're simple really. We don't kill or harm innocent people. We don't tell anyone the truth about who we are. We respect the other's choices. Blah blah blah. There are a lot. I don't want to list them all. You get the point."

Kelevra still looked like he wanted to call up his Retinue and demand they go searching for Rin's potential stalker.

Rin moved faster than either of them could process, shoving Kel down and straddling his hips. He laughed as he planted his hands on his chest to keep him down, fingers splayed out over the small silver threading that made rose patterns in the pale yellow corset vest he'd helped with this morning.

"You're so flashy," he murmured. "I love it."

"You're constantly complaining about it," Kelevra stated.

"Only so you don't catch on." He traced the boning on the side. "I still don't want to wear one myself, but they look so good on you. I try not to say because your ego is already the size of a moon, but it's true. I thought you were pretty from the beginning. Aren't most deadly things?"

"Consort. We're still fighting."

"Are we?" He hummed. "I don't have a right to be mad at you, and I suppose you're allowed to be angry. I'm sorry I tricked you. I didn't mean it. You came onto me. All of these things are true."

"You *were* angry with me though," Kelevra pointed out. "Why?"

Rin's brow furrowed and his hands stilled. "Even knowing how important my brother is to me, you were just standing there. You were going to let them take him."

"According to your brother, that was never going to actually happen."

"Of course not," he agreed. "There were four guards in the hallway, your sister would have stood aside, and our father isn't young anymore. The only one who stood a chance at stopping us from escaping was you."

"Would you have fought me?"

Rin thought it over. "I'm not sure."

"You would have."

"If you continued to stand there like a statue when I needed a real partner?" he snapped. "Yeah. Probably would have."

Kelevra lifted a hand and gently trailed the tips of his fingers down the length of Rin's throat. "Don't be mad, sweetheart. Didn't I stand with you the second I realized? Didn't I ensure you got exactly what you wanted in the end?"

"It took you long enough."

"Were you worried?"

"That you were going to abandon me?" Rin asked. "Yeah."

"I was worried about the same thing," Kel admitted. "Do you plan to? Your brother said he had money. The two of you could sneak away—"

He snorted. "Like I don't know you've already ordered one of your Retinue to add our names to the No Fly list." Rin had seen Kel try to sneakily do it on their way up in the elevator. "We couldn't run now even if we wanted to."

"Are you angry?"

"No."

"Why not?"

Rin grinned. "I like that you want to keep me. It's nice being wanted. It's nice knowing it's *me* that you want." His gaze took in the corset again. "You're so flashy."

"This pill is more annoying than I anticipated," Kelevra said. "You sound like you're drunk."

Rin was only partially listening, trailing his hand down, down, over his hip to—He yelped when Kel rolled them, pinning him to the bed with his wrists up by his head.

"We aren't doing that right now," Kelevra told him. "Sex can't solve everything, remember?"

"I think I lied then too," he said, only to have Kel click his tongue. "Come on. I want to. You want to." To help drive that point home, he lifted his hips, grinding up against the impressive bulge already forming in the Imperial Prince's pants. "See?"

"We're talking."

"We can manage to do both at the same time."

"This is serious." Kelevra searched his gaze. "Did your father ever hurt you?"

"We got sick a few times when he locked us out of the house at night," Rin admitted. "And he'd raise his hand now and again, but nothing major. It wasn't about that for him. He wanted control. He and I are very similar in that respect."

"Except you want to give control up, don't you remember, Flower?"

"Only sometimes," he corrected. "Only with you."

Kelevra paused. "Do you even like me?"

"There are times I want to drown you in the nearest body of water," he said honestly. "But I've liked you since you first lured me up here and made me take that pill. It was…fun. I liked being forced. Why do you think I didn't try to fight you off?"

"You didn't want to risk getting your brother and you thrown into prison," he guessed dryly.

"That too." Rin snorted. "But no. It was deeper than that. Yes, you're the Imperial Prince and I had to be more cautious. I couldn't just hit you like I did Brennon last week."

"I'm still mad about that too, Flower."

"It didn't mean anything, and his breath was awful."

The corner of Kel's mouth twitched. "Was it?"

"The worst. Even if you and I hadn't been together, I would have pushed him away. I've never wanted him like that."

"Like what?"

"Like how I want you."

Kelevra settled himself more firmly over him. "Tell me you'll become Rin Varun for real. On paper."

"I already said I would. My brother will do the same. He likes being Sila. He just won't admit it."

"Why do you think that?"

"Because I know him." The two of them had always known each other. That's probably what kept them from going crazy. "We never had a mother, and our father was never interested in forming any sort of bond with us. For the most part, we had only each other to rely on. Then you came along…I hated you that day in the locker room. When I found out about the betrothal? I hated you so much that day."

"The decree said Rin Varun," Kelevra easily understood what he meant. "You were worried I'd trap your brother or discover your deception."

"It was supposed to be one night, what we did here. Then you were meant to get bored and forget all about me."

"That was never going to happen, Flower. I was far too invested in you from the start."

"I wasn't Rin," he said tentatively at first, the pill allowing him to do this when he would have been far too embarrassed to otherwise, "and so the decree felt like a mockery. Here was a person willing to pull me out of my father's control, me and my brother, who was gorgeous and great in the sack, and he wanted me. But he thought I was someone else. For once, our switching places seemed like it was going to be the end of us. If you found out and your temper took hold, what then?"

"You didn't protest because you didn't want a future with me," Kelevra sounded awed by that notion.

"I'd never considered having a future with anyone until you," he said. "You're egotistical and possessive, and you drive me mad, but you backed off in the library when you realized I was legitimately uncomfortable. And you didn't hurt me our first night together even though you could have. Maybe I'm crazy for being happy about the bare minimum, maybe not. I *could* see a future with you though, and that was the problem."

Rin tugged on his right wrist and after a moment, Kelevra released him. He brought his hand to the side of his face, tracing the line of his jaw with the tips of his fingers. "You made me want to be Rin Varun. I'd never cared about the name before, but this past month…These last few weeks especially…"

"You are Rin Varun," Kelevra reassured. "I'll make it so, Flower. And if you want to quit the Academy—"

"I don't."

"You said you enjoyed studying at Vail."

"Sure, but I like it at the Academy even more. It's more my style when you think about it. I get to burn off energy sparing and training. My brother was always better suited for the University lifestyle, originally we even considered coming here having already switched, but our planet sent over our medical files and our DNA samples were included. Ultimately, we decided to try and see how it went. Be ourselves. Part of me thinks that's why he's been drawing things out with the stalker for this long. He didn't want to switch back either."

"If you two are so close, why couldn't you have simply said as much?" Kelevra asked.

"Even when you're close to someone, you still have vulnerabilities." Besides, before he even could, this whole mess with the Imperial Prince had begun, and they'd sort of been stuck in their roles from there anyway. "Are you still angry I lied?"

"Yes and no," Kel told him. "I should be furious with you. My pride should be wounded and I should have had both you and your brother shipped off-world immediately. That's what Lyra expected, that's for sure."

"But you didn't."

"No."

"Because?"

"Isn't it obvious?" Kelevra licked at Rin's palm, laughing when he made a sound of disgust. "I love you, Flower. It's my fault you didn't know already." He paused then, "How do you feel about me?"

"I like you a lot," he said. "But I don't know if it's love yet. Is that...all right?"

"Considering all we've been through?" Kelevra smiled at him, though it was impossible to miss the hint of sadness in his hazel eyes. "Of course. So long as you think you can love me."

"I do."

"Then for you, I can be patient." Kel lowered and captured Rin's mouth in a rare soft and slow kiss. "For you," he brushed a strand of hair off Rin's forehead, "I can be forgiving."

Rin wasn't sure why, but a tear slipped past his defenses and rolled down his cheek then. He sniffled and made a sound of annoyance. "Damn it."

"Will you marry me," Kelevra asked, waiting for him to meet his gaze, "Rin Varun?"

He sucked in a breath, his mind swirling and his heart thumping wildly in his chest. "Yes. Yes, I will."

Because he was Rin, well and truly now, and he could make that choice for himself.

Epilogue:
Two Months Later

"All done." Ome, the Royal doctor, removed the device he'd just used to take a blood sample from Rin's finger and then stepped off to the side to go over the data on his tablet.

They were in the living room at the penthouse, with Rin and his brother seated on the couch. The doctor had arrived twenty or so minutes ago and gone over everything with them before pulling out his tools to begin taking samples.

Kelevra stood by the mini bar, ever vigilant, tensing slightly whenever the doctor stepped up to Rin—almost as though he'd forgotten he was the one who'd ordered all of these tests to happen in the first place.

Rin shook his hand, waiting for the slight sting to dissipate, and then leaned forward. "That's it?"

"We've collected all the necessary data to confirm your identities," Ome glanced between him and his brother. "We'll of course need to run a full health examination on you before the wedding, just so everything is up to date, but you'll need to come to the hospital for that."

"Does that mean I can go?" His brother stood without waiting for an answer, rolling down the sleeves of his Vail uniform. "There's one last mock crime scene I need to set up."

They'd all agreed to allow him to continue playing the part where that was concerned since he'd been doing it all semester already. With only a week left before their three-week break, not a single cadet had come close to catching him in the act, even with him lingering around the scene for a few minutes afterward, as was required of him.

At this rate, Rin would win, and he didn't even have to do anything in order to. As soon as he'd discovered he was the killer, there'd been no reason for him to work on the case. He'd kept up appearances with his friends, going to the crime scenes with them if he happened to be there when they got the alerts, but otherwise always made excuses as to why Calder and Brennon hadn't seen him actively working on it.

Usually, those excuses involved Kel. The second Rin mentioned the bedroom his friends tended to change the subject fast.

He felt a little badly toward them, since he was cheating and all, but since he'd been assigned the role of a criminal, he'd convinced himself he was merely leaning heavily into the part.

"Who's the victim this time?" Kelevra asked absently.

"Cindy Hin."

The Imperial Prince lifted his multi-slate and clicked a few buttons, eyes narrowing slightly a moment later. "And which one of you met with Cindy at the bar this summer?"

"He's on Imagine." The corner of his brother's mouth turned up, a wicked glint entering his eyes.

Rin groaned and dropped back against the couch, covering his face with the back of his hand.

"That so?" Kelevra drawled, even though neither of them had verbally answered his question. Then there was a pause before he said, "You should be on your way, Sila. Wouldn't want to keep Cindy waiting."

Rin got to his feet, but almost as though he'd been anticipating that much, Kel was on him in a flash, planting a hand on his shoulder and shoving him back down with one hard move.

"I was talking to Sila, Flower," Kelevra chided, bending down so they were at eye level. "Remind me, what's your name again?"

"Sorry for interrupting, your majesty," Ome said, and as soon as he had Kel's attention, he waved the tablet. "The data has been officially submitted. From here on out, that," he pointed to Rin, "is Rin Varun, and that," then to his brother, "is Sila Varun. As requested, I've ensured any past medical files have been wiped from the systems."

"Perfect," Kelevra straightened but kept his hand firmly on Rin's shoulder. "We'll make an appointment with you soon for my Consort's physical. That will be all for today."

"Of course." Ome bowed low and then returned the gesture to Rin before exiting.

His brother—Sila—stretched his arms and then nodded. "I'll call you later."

"He'll be busy," Kel stated. The two shared a look and then Sila gave one last nod and followed after the doctor without so much as another glance Rin's way.

"Traitor!" Rin called after him, rolling his eyes when he heard his brother chuckle a second before the door to the penthouse shut behind him.

Their relationship hadn't changed, even after they'd agreed to permanently swap their birth names. The only contact they'd had from their father had been one final attempt when he'd returned to Tibera, but after a conversation between the Emperor of Vitality and the Tiberan Empress, all communication had stopped.

He'd once felt trapped in his own skin, but now…Rin glanced up at Kelevra to find the Imperial Prince already closely watching him.

"Can we at least take this up to the bedroom?" he asked.

Kel grunted. "Know exactly what's coming, do you, sweetheart?"

"I remember the photo I took with Cindy," he admitted. "I'm guessing that's what has you in a mood."

"I'm not in a mood."

Rin lifted a brow. "You're not jealous, even a little?"

If their roles had been reversed, he certainly would be. Cindy was a pretty Junior at Guest who Rin had been introduced to at one of Calder's parties. She'd been funny and kind, more introverted than some of the others he'd met, so he'd spent more time hanging out with her that night. They'd ended up getting a little tipsy and a friend of hers had posted a photo of the two of them, Cindy's head on his shoulder, a smile on his lips.

"That depends," Kelevra said. "Does she know what you taste like, Flower?"

He tapped at Kel's wrist until the guy finally moved his hand, allowing him to rise to his feet. Then Rin stepped in closer. "Three minutes after that picture was taken, Calder threw up on his mom's new carpet and the party came to a screeching halt."

"And after the party?"

Rin shook his head. "I never saw her again. Well," he tipped his chin, "I guess I might see her later, if I end up checking out the crime scene."

Kelevra's arm wrapped around his waist and pulled him in. "You'll be too busy sinking down onto my cock, I'm afraid."

"That so?" He brushed his lips against the curve of Kel's ear. "I think we should head upstairs."

"I *think* you should stop thinking."

"You going to make me, Imperial Prince?"

Kelevra kissed him the whole way out of the living room and up the stairs, the two of them tripping over one another and stumbling more than once. He swore when he slipped and his shoulder connected with the wall, but Rin pulled him away and dragged him up the final steps laughing.

Somehow, they made it into the bedroom and onto the bed in one piece, Rin tumbling back onto the mattress with Kel following quickly after. He opened his mouth for the Imperial Prince, their tongues tangling, his hips already lifting to grind against the hard bulge in Kelevra's pants.

A second later, the Imperial Prince froze, and Rin laughed again.

"What," Kel pulled back slightly to stare down at him, "do you think you're doing, Flower?"

Rin kept his eyes up at the reflection above them, carefully working the switchblade he'd just pulled out against the black strings of the blue and charcoal-colored corset Kel was wearing. He moved the knife higher, cutting through his second string, smile broadening at the satisfying popping sound as it gave.

"Removing your corset vest," he said, slicing through another.

The material loosened around Kel's shoulders but he didn't move to stop him. "Should I tell you how much this particular suit is worth?"

"And ruin the mood?" Rin pulled his gaze off the mirror just long enough to wink at him. "Better not."

"How long have you had that knife on you?" Kelevra asked

"Always," Rin said. "I carry it all the time. It's the same one I pulled on you at Friction. You remember?"

"I remember fucking you on the bench, and up against the lockers," Kelevra tipped his head, eyeing him, "and I know exactly what you're doing."

"Our past sexcapades are hot," he confirmed Kel's suspicions. "Thinking about them always puts me in the mood." He finished with the strings and then reached up, grabbing onto the top of the silky material where it rested in the center of Kelevra's chest.

The corset vest came away easily, and Kel switched his weight to either arm to help Rin remove it. He only cringed a little when the now ruined garment was tossed carelessly to the side toward the window, but then Rin's gaze was tracing the contours of his abs and his hand was following suit and it became apparent Kelevra forgot all about his suit.

"You want me to forgive you for that photo of you and Cindy, Consort?" Kelevra asked, lifting himself to help Rin tug his pants down his hips.

"The one taken before you and I even knew one another?" Rin met his gaze and then smirked. "No."

Kelevra chuckled. "There's my filthy flower."

Rin tugged his t-shirt over his head while Kel got to work on his pants, both of them already hard and achy by the time they were finally naked, sprawled out on the silk sheets. He dragged his fingernails down Kelevra's back when the man captured his mouth in another scorching kiss and then rolled them so he was straddling the Imperial, their lips still pressed together.

Reaching back blindly, he found Kelevra's cock, groaning into his mouth when he came into contact with that solid heat. Then he shifted back, lined him up, and eased down, taking him slow and deep until he was fully seated on him. The stretch and the burn had him gritting his teeth, but any hint of discomfort left quickly, replaced by the familiar electric need that spurred him into undulating his hips.

"Filthier than expected," Kelevra said, reaching up to rest his hands on Rin's thighs, spreading him wider, causing him to sink back down all the way. "Did you prep yourself before the doctor arrived, Flower? Stretched yourself nice and good for me?"

Rin nodded. "I was hoping to go a round before he got here, but you were too busy talking with Madden on the phone."

"I was supposed to be punishing you," Kelevra's gaze trailed down his torso appreciatively, "but I guess I should be making it up to you instead."

He nipped at his lips. "Why not both?"

Kel switched their positions just as quickly as Rin had earlier, but wasted no time, thrusting into him hard enough to make him cry out. "Do you have any idea how hot that is? Thinking about you in here, your fingers stretching your ass for me?" He growled and pumped in faster. "Remind me to punch Madden next time I see him for making me miss it."

Rin wrapped his arms and legs around him and dug his nails into his shoulders, just enough to break skin the way he knew Kelevra liked. The Imperial Prince's movements were rough, but he tried to match his pace as he fucked into him.

"Relax," he said, sucking a sharp breath at one particularly brutal punch of that thick cock before continuing. "You can catch the next show. We've got our whole lives, after all."

Kelevra groaned and reached for his dick, pumping him in the same frenzied motions as his hips. "Come for me, Flower," he ordered. "Rin. Come for me."

He'd been rushed earlier and hadn't been able to get off before the doctor's arrival, so Rin's body was already primed and ready for the orgasm that ripped through him. He tossed his head back and moaned as he came, Kelevra's cockhead battering against his prostate all through it.

"Kel," he forced himself to make eye contact, even as his orgasm continued to zip through him. He'd been planning on saying it for a while, but the right moment had never appeared and he'd been too self-conscious to spit it out randomly. Now, with his mind practically mush and his body slipping into oversensitivity, the words tumbled out of him as if of their own accord. "I love you."

Kelevra sucked in a breath and then hit his own peak, thrusting in deep and holding himself there, bathing his insides with waves of warmth as he came. He settled over him, his cock still twitching inside of Rin, and peppered his face with soft kisses and quick laps of his tongue against his chin and the curves of his jaw.

"Say it again," he demanded, shifting his hips to keep himself buried, nipping at his cheek when that had Rin crying out instead of giving him what he wanted. "Tell me, Consort."

"I love you." It was wild and crazy, but then again, so were they.

Kel rewarded him with another domineering kiss, one that had both of them ready for a second round within moments. Before either of them was aware of what was happening, Kelevra was fucking him again.

"I love you, too," the Imperial Prince said, resting his forehead against his as he slowed down the pace. Usually he had to wait until Rin was asleep and then wake him like this in order to get him to do things gently and slowly, but when it became apparent he wasn't going to be urged to quicken, he grinned. "I love you, Flower."

"You won't get bored of me?" He was only saying it to be difficult, those fears having left him a while back.

But Kelevra took the comment seriously, moving to run his fingers through his golden hair tenderly as he continued to stroke into his body slow and deep. "Never," he promised. "How could anyone ever grow tired of you, Rin Varun?"

"In that case." He grabbed Kel's head and bit down on his bottom lip, drawing blood. "Come for your consort, Devil of Vitality."

They both plunged over the edge a second time, their orgasms just as intense as the first, and he watched his reflection in the mirror above them, took in his flushed cheeks and how tightly he was wrapped around Kelevra, clinging to him as they came in their bed. In their home. On their planet.

Rin Varun stared up at his reflection.

And he smiled.

These Silent Stars

Chani Lynn Feener has wanted to be a writer since the age of ten during fifth grade story time. She majored in Creative Writing at Johnson State College in Vermont. To pay her bills, she has worked many odd jobs, including, but not limited to, telemarketing, order picking in a warehouse, and filling ink cartridges. When she isn't writing, she's binging TV shows, drawing, or frequenting zoos/aquariums. Chani is also the author of teen paranormal series, *The Underworld Saga*, originally written under the penname Tempest C. Avery. She currently resides in Connecticut, but lives on Goodreads.com.

Chani Lynn Feener can be found on Goodreads.com, as well as on Twitter and Instagram @TempestChani.

For more information on upcoming and past works, please visit her website: HOME | ChaniLynnFeener (wixsite.com).

Printed in Great Britain
by Amazon